PRAISE FOR *THE R...*  *'A*
AR...

"Read-in-one-sitting . . . Banash masterfully interweaves guilt, love, remorse, and yearning with a bit of playfulness, creating a tale that is multifaceted in its content and spirit."

—*Booklist*

"Banash's sublime new stunner immerses us in an intoxicating female friendship between two young singers, each striving for pop stardom, until one of them suspiciously dies, later leading a *Rolling Stone* journalist to dig out the truth no one seems to want uncovered. A psychological why-done-it about the glittering allure and tragic cost of fame, and the heady bliss of bonding, all set against an unforgettable soundtrack of love and deception."

—Caroline Leavitt, *New York Times* bestselling author of *With or Without You* and *Pictures of You*

"Gritty, propulsive, and complex. Banash paints a vivid picture of two young women navigating their way through the dark side of the music industry and the journalist who uncovers their shocking truth years later. I found myself completely transported into Banash's world of glittering stages, bright city lights, and deeply nuanced, compelling characters. *The Rise and Fall of Ava Arcana* is an addictive read that will leave you wanting more."

—Julia Spiro, author of *Full* and *Someone Else's Secret*

"I devoured this suspenseful and perceptive read about the price of fame, the dangerously blurred boundary between envy and admiration, and the tantalizing pull of those who recognize your potential and your desires. Urgently narrated in dual timelines, *The Rise and Fall of Ava Arcana* introduces us to three unforgettable women: the passionate, dogged Kayla; the dreamy, yearning Ava; the irrepressible, brazen Lexi. I'll be thinking about them for a long time."

—Caitlin Barasch, author of *A Novel Obsession*

"*The Rise and Fall of Ava Arcana* is one of the sexiest novels I've ever read. While it is a thriller, a mystery, and an excavation into the backstabbing glamour of the music industry, Jennifer Banash is also first and foremost an absolute master of sensual details and whip-smart dialogue, making her female protagonists leap off the page in an electrical storm. This novel is one part propulsive beach read, one part feminist deep dive into the ways women ferociously love, impulsively betray, and ultimately redeem each other. And did I mention that it's hot?"

—Gina Frangello, author of *Blow Your House Down* and
A Life in Men

"I binged this twisty mystery thriller that probes the darker side of fame and female friendships. *The Rise and Fall of Ava Arcana* is as addictive as any Netflix series."

—Liska Jacobs, author of *The Pink Hotel*

"This dark, sexy novel combines the rocker-chick moxie of *Daisy Jones & the Six* with the psychological-thriller plot twists of *Social Creature*. Banash's clear, lush prose makes *The Rise and Fall of Ava Arcana* a gripping read."

—Kate Christensen, author of *The Last Cruise* and *The Great Man*

The Essential Elizabeth Stone

ALSO BY JENNIFER BANASH

The Rise and Fall of Ava Arcana

The Essential Elizabeth Stone

a novel

Jennifer Banash

LAKE UNION
PUBLISHING

Published by Lake Union Publishing, Seattle

www.apub.com

Amazon, the Amazon logo, and Lake Union Publishing are trademarks of Amazon.com, Inc., or its affiliates.

ISBN-13: 9781662505430 (paperback)
ISBN-13: 9781662505447 (digital)

Cover design by Caroline Teagle Johnson
Cover image: © jakkapan21 / Getty; © Cara Dolan / Stocksy; © Olga Moreira / Stocksy

Printed in the United States of America

For mothers and daughters everywhere

Prologue
ELIZABETH

1986

Elizabeth Stone tied the sash of her apron in a neat bow as she walked out the kitchen door of the farmhouse, the facade nearly obscured by a trellis of climbing roses in sugared peach and ivory, a stretch of coastline appearing just beyond the picket fence. Reporters filled the cobblestone courtyard, talking and laughing while nibbling at fried squash blossoms, golden and delicately puffed, and buttery periwinkles still tasting of the sea. Loaves of New England brown bread rested on the long wooden tables, and a collection of antique pitchers, each holding a tangle of wildflowers, were placed sparingly across the top. Rings of driftwood, each cradling snowy linen napkins, were set before each china plate, the surface filmed and iridescent. She didn't need to turn one over in her hands to know they were Spode, so unmistakable was the quality.

Harold approached, taking her hand in his own and squeezing it reassuringly, looking over with an encouraging smile. His full head of salt-and-pepper hair shone in the light, and his suit of cream-colored linen was one of the many he'd had tailored at a small shop on Madison Avenue. "You know what to do," he whispered gently, the low timbre of his voice barely audible over the buzz of the courtyard. "Just be yourself."

She nodded, her lips stretching into a smile, one unadorned by lipstick, just a swipe of clear gloss that glistened in the late-afternoon sunlight—golden hour, her mother had always called it. The white cotton shift she wore set off the beginnings of her summer tan, and a curtain of butterscotch hair grazed her shoulders in a neat line. Just below her wide blue eyes, a spray of freckles dotted her nose and cheeks like the faintest dusting of nutmeg on a peach tart.

Be yourself. But who was that exactly?

A patch of lavender filled the afternoon air with its calming medicinal scent, and the round, linen-draped table placed strategically beside it held neatly stacked copies of the book that had occupied her every waking moment for the past year—*Entertaining with Elizabeth Stone.* A mound of promotional flyers sat beside it, the pages lifting slightly in the wind. Elizabeth walked to the edge of the courtyard, her eyes scanning the grass, and bent down to pick up a large, mottled rock in shades of blue and gray. She walked back over to the table, placing the rock directly on top of the unruly paper, then stood back, eyeing her work. Not only did it solve the problem, it also gave the tableau the perfect touch, finishing the tablescape like a carefully placed signature.

When she and Harold had first discussed the launch, he'd suggested La Côte Basque or Tavern on the Green, laying out pros and cons, turning them over with the same methodical consideration with which he approached every major decision. But Elizabeth had always been ruled by instinct, that little voice inside her head and the accompanying dip in her gut that let her know when she'd gone off track. And that little voice knew immediately that Harold's ideas for the launch, whether he realized it or not, weren't even in the vicinity.

"Neither," she interrupted, gently. "Harold, they need to see it all in action. To see me in action. This isn't just a book of recipes—it's a lifestyle. That's what we're selling. But the cost"—she frowned apologetically—"will be considerable. We're setting the stage. It has to be perfect."

And in the consumption-obsessed landscape of the early 1980s, it was lifestyle that the masses coveted—the asiago, the sun-dried tomatoes, the pine nuts for making homemade pesto in the hefty marble mortar and pestle that was never put away because it was bought to be seen, sitting there on the counter, which was more than the sum of its very expensive, imported parts.

"Say no more," Harold said brusquely, reaching over and brushing a strand of pale hair from her face. "I trust your vision. And that's what this is about, bringing that vision to life."

She'd found and rented the house herself, a fairy-tale cottage tucked in a quiet hamlet out on the shores of Long Island, a few doors down from the former home of Truman Capote. As legend had it, Capote had once lugged an enormous tin of Beluga caviar from Manhattan out to his country house for an impromptu garden party, then promptly walked across the road to purchase freshly dug Yukon Golds at the neighboring potato farm as an accompaniment. The literary pedigree gave the party an extra something, Elizabeth knew, a sheen of vintage glamour. She could almost imagine Capote's ghost wandering the grounds in his trademark pair of heavy black glasses, tipping his hat at passersby, imparting his blessing.

The media darlings were just beginning to arrive, and Elizabeth made her way through the courtyard and into the house. In the kitchen, the vast butcher-block island was covered in platters of crisp fried chicken (the secret was cornflakes), oysters on the half shell resting on a bed of coarse salt, a dish of lemon and diced shallot mignonette placed nearby. There were bowls of vinegary potato salad, an enormous tray of bright-red lobsters, and ears of corn rubbed with the garlic-and-rosemary butter she'd mixed herself. Raspberry tartlets waited patiently for a drizzle of balsamic reduction, and a cake stand topped with fresh rhubarb shortcakes sat on the marble counter, a bowl of heavy cream beside it, already whipped into soft peaks. She watched in horror as one of the caterers Harold had hired, a young blonde of no more than eighteen, grabbed the bowl and began attacking the cream with a whisk, as if she wanted to beat it into submission.

Without a word, Elizabeth walked over and plucked the bowl from the young girl's hands, placing it in the ancient but serviceable fridge, exhaling in relief as she shut the door. She'd been training for this moment for what felt like her entire life—and she wasn't about to blow it over a bowl of cream that some clueless teenager had unknowingly solidified into butter. Until now, it had all been a series of finely tuned dress rehearsals, but tonight was the real thing. Tonight, she would finally move into the spotlight.

There was no room for error, and she knew that this night, and the book she had spent months writing, would make her name, would make all the evenings she'd spent working straight through till dawn worth it, testing the recipes over and over, every pot and pan she owned strewn across the kitchen counters. As she stepped forward into the throng of reporters, she could still hear Eunice's voice in her head, the slight shakiness in it that reminded her of Katharine Hepburn, the grit and smoke of old money.

We eat with our eyes first, Billie.

A young reporter stepped toward her, smiling brightly. She was in her late twenties with dark, curly hair that was beginning to frizz in the humidity, surrounding her heart-shaped face like a cumulus cloud. "I'd love to hear a bit of your backstory," she asked, holding a pad and pen. "Get at the woman behind the recipes, so to speak."

"I grew up on the Maine coast, in Bar Harbor," Elizabeth began, taking a deep breath, "the daughter of a homemaker. My mother cooked delicious meals, arranged flowers, sewed, and entertained—but in a way that made the everyday seem magical. Each August, when the wild blueberries were ripe, she'd top them with homemade lavender syrup and whipped cream, dotting each mound with a few tiny purple buds. I've always longed to recreate that feeling for a mass audience, so that everyone might experience the same kind of effortless alchemy. But of course," she went on, the line she'd practiced in the mirror for months sliding off her tongue, "the real magic isn't a book of recipes, or even me—it's you. Your families, your stories. I'm just here to inspire."

The reporter scribbled a few notes on her pad, the pen scratching against the paper. Elizabeth was aware that she was sweating, her linen dress damp beneath the arms. That wouldn't do at all. She looked over at Harold for reassurance, but he was engaged in what looked like a heated conversation with an editor from Condé Nast.

"That doesn't really answer my question, though."

She looked back distractedly at the reporter, who was now peering at her with interest. "I'm sorry?"

"I asked about you," the reporter said pointedly, punctuating the air with her pen. "I'm familiar with your bio—it's right on the book jacket. I'm looking for something a little more . . . personal." She smiled again, exposing rows of white teeth, the incisors slightly pointed.

"So tell me: Who is Elizabeth Stone?"

Chapter One

JULES

Juliet Stone had always dreaded November.

April was said to be the cruelest month, but November, with its endless parade of gray skies, the cold drizzle that chilled her down to the very bone, had always been the ultimate letdown. How could it help but disappoint after the explosion of red-gold leaves each October, the colors so bright and pure that they made her chest ache with longing, the air redolent with the smoke of bonfires, even amid the grime and bustle of Manhattan?

Jules arranged the Japanese tea set, adjusting the teapot, the cerulean glaze shining in the overhead light, so that it sat on the polished wooden surface at a slight angle. The plate of mini tarts sat at the center of the table, yellow custard glistening seductively in each round shell, a bowl of crimson berries waiting patiently in a shaft of sunlight. She'd ventured out early that morning in search of simpler fare, a few croissants that might remind Mark of their days honeymooning in the South of France. But when she'd passed the window of the small Japanese tearoom on Canal Street, she'd impulsively stepped inside, unable to resist the pastries gleaming like jewels, citrine and ruby, in the clear light of the sparse interior.

"Perfect," she muttered, cringing inwardly the moment the word left her lips. It was exactly the kind of thing her mother would say; her mother, whose entire life had been spent in the pursuit of nothing less. Jules looked around the kitchen of their Chelsea apartment. When they'd first moved in, Elizabeth had the Carrara marble countertops trimmed back to make way for the extra-wide range that Wolf had gifted her for a cookbook shoot. Behind the stainless-steel expanse of the stove ran a backsplash of Fireclay tile, each hand-painted with a subtle ochre wave. (An Instagram ad that had run for what felt like months showed the tile being first painted, then installed in her kitchen.) The soap was Aēsop, the candles Diptyque, the pots Great Jones, the crystal Riedel. Copper pendant lights dangled from the exposed beams above the kitchen island like works of art, more sculpture than mere illumination. Everything had been chosen and approved with the careful nod of Elizabeth's head, the decisive motion that had ruled the first thirty-six years of her daughter's life.

"Why not get a place that we can actually afford?" Mark had whispered, the first time Elizabeth had taken them to view the unit, pulling Jules into the hallway while her mother chatted gaily with the broker. "Someplace we can really make our own? Something a little . . . simpler, maybe?"

Jules bit her lip, wishing she could flee, just to avoid the awkwardness of what she knew would inevitably follow. The money—Elizabeth's money, to be exact—the vast fortune that would one day be her own, stood between them, a boulder perched precariously on the edge of a cliff. The trust Elizabeth had established for Jules when she was born, coupled with her mother's endless generosity, meant she never had to worry about affording her daily Starbucks runs—or expensive Manhattan apartments.

"Sure," Jules heard herself say quietly, knowing even as the words fell from her lips that doing so would absolutely kill her mother. "We can do that. We're a team, right?"

A look of relief washed over her husband's face, and he leaned forward and kissed her quickly on the lips. "Right," he replied.

They walked back inside just in time to see Elizabeth shaking hands with the broker. Jules's heart sank at the sight. "Welcome home, kids!" Elizabeth said as she turned to greet them, her face stretched in a triumphant smile, the same one that regularly lit up TV screens across the country. "I'll have my banker call you with the details," she said offhandedly to the agent before walking toward them.

"Elizabeth," Mark began hesitantly, his expression reflecting the uneasiness Jules knew he felt inside. "We can't possibly. It's way too generous. In a few years, I'll be able to—"

"Nonsense!" her mother said brightly, as if the matter had already been decided. "I'm thrilled to do it. In fact, I already have sponsors lined up! The renovation won't cost a dime. Now, Julie, I was thinking we could put an island over here, and maybe knock down that adjoining wall," she said, as she moved around the room like a woman possessed, her energy so infectious that the Realtor began nodding frantically in approval. Jules just stood there, helpless, while her husband stared at her as if she had suddenly morphed into someone unrecognizable. *Say something,* her mind screamed, but instead Jules watched herself, as if from above, as she stood there and did nothing. The resulting book, *Elizabeth Stone Beginnings,* had sold well over a million copies in its first printing, and prominently featured the renovation of their apartment, before going on to chronicle the revamping of first homes of couples across the country.

Now, years later, standing in that same space Elizabeth had not only paid for but curated so carefully, Jules could almost see the flicker of her mother's ghost as it moved around the room, stopping to fill a silver vase with lilies, pausing to nestle her face in the blossoms, her eyes closing as she drank in the heady perfume. Her transparent form draped in a linen shift, her elegant feet housed in the ballet flats she'd always loved. But this, Jules knew, was impossible. Elizabeth Stone was resting (*rotting*—she could not help but think it) peacefully in a cemetery in

Westchester, six feet underground, where she could no longer bend things—and people—to her formidable will.

Including her only daughter.

"What's all this?"

Jules blinked rapidly, her eyes the same guileless blue as her mother's, and turned to face her husband, dressed for another day at his office on Wall Street in a white button-down and a pair of gray flannel trousers, his blondish hair brushed back cleanly, beard neatly trimmed.

"Good morning to you, too," she said with a smile as she walked over, twining her arms around his neck. He folded her against him as if she were always meant to fit there, her stomach dipping as his lips found her own. It was still there, that pull that ran between them, tight as an electrical wire and just as likely to spark unexpectedly.

She'd felt it from the moment they'd met in the fall of their senior year at Cornell, autumn leaves falling in a shower of gold, echoing the sunny tones in his hair. There had been no shortage of boyfriends over the years: prep school boys in tortoiseshell glasses, boys who rode motorcycles, boys who taught Jules to shoot pool in smoky bars, boys who made Elizabeth roll her eyes in exasperation.

For God's sake, Juliet, are you trying to give me an aneurysm?

But there had been no one like Mark, who had loved her fiercely and unreservedly right from the start. Even her mother, who'd taken a shine to approximately none of her daughter's former suitors, approved of Mark almost immediately. "He's so *good* for you, Julie!" Elizabeth proclaimed excitedly on that warm summer day when Jules had introduced them, flitting around the living room in a caftan the shade of linden blossoms, stopping to straighten a magazine on the coffee table until it sat at a faultless angle.

"As always, your mother and I are in perfect agreement," Harold chimed in from the kitchen, his afternoon coffee ritual in full swing, steaming kettle in hand as he bent over a Chemex, carefully moistening the grounds. Juliet had simply nodded, looking out past the french doors framing an exuberance of wildflowers in the garden.

Spring had always been her mother's favorite season—*I just love the* possibility *of it!*—and it was hard to imagine that she would never see another, never watch the buds just beginning to green on the rough branches in Central Park. Elizabeth had slipped quietly from the world in the heat of August, a season her mother had always loathed, the air-conditioning in her bedroom on full blast, the walls painted a soft, clear ivory. The apple trees lining the drive of her sprawling stone house would burst into full bloom without her next spring.

Jules didn't think she could bear it.

"You know I'm a sucker for pastry," Mark said, as he gently extricated himself and ambled over to the kitchen table, hungrily eyeing the tarts, "but don't you have that meeting this morning?"

She sighed in response, her stomach curdling in dread. The minute she'd informed Margaret, her father's cousin and interim CEO of Elizabeth Stone Enterprises, that she'd finally be coming in to address the entire staff, Jules had promptly forgotten all about it, which wasn't like her in the slightest. Like it or not, she had inherited her mother's attention to detail, and generally prided herself on being more of a walking to-do list than a human being. But ever since Elizabeth's death three months earlier, Jules had found herself struggling to remember even the smallest of commitments. Particularly this one, which she wished she could escape entirely.

"We have time," Jules said as she took one of the tarts, placing it on a white china plate and handing it to her husband, who immediately raised the pastry to his lips and took a bite, groaning with pleasure.

Mark was a creature of habit, much like Jules herself, who felt best when her world was meticulously ordered. She knew without even asking that her husband had been up since 6:00 a.m., reading the *Wall Street Journal* on his phone while running a brisk four miles on the treadmill before heading into the office. Still, there had been moments of spontaneity in the early days of their courtship, long weekends in the Hudson Valley, summers spent strolling Montauk, the sand sparkling with shards of beach glass, the edges worn smooth by sand and time.

Trips to the Greek islands, Páros in the early fall, honey and feta on her tongue, the retsina they drank surprisingly bitter.

"Are you ready?" he asked, reaching across the table for one of the cups of green tea she'd poured, its earthy flavor complementing the rich sweets. "I know it's a lot," he said, raising the cup to his lips.

A lot didn't even begin to cover it. Her father, Harold, had died five years earlier, and now, in the wake of her mother's death, Juliet was the sole heir to the entire fortune Elizabeth had amassed over the last thirty years. Elizabeth Stone Enterprises was a multimillion-dollar business, one that everyone involved believed Jules was ill equipped to run.

"The brand, the books—she left you an empire," Mark said quietly, placing the cup down on the table. "Sooner or later, you're going to have to deal with it."

Empire. The word conjured up dynasties, succession, and the divine right of kings. Or queens, as it were. Her mother's eye for detail and penchant for storytelling, tales that often included her own perfect family, had made Elizabeth into a domestic goddess on par with Julia, Ina, and Martha. There were whole shelves of cookbooks, but also a cooking show, a monthly newsletter, and a blockbuster biopic starring Charlize Theron as Jules's own mother. Sometimes while channel surfing late at night, Jules would catch a glimpse of the actress in one of her mother's straw hats, walking around a set that so closely resembled Jules's childhood home it made her dizzy to even look at the screen for more than a few seconds. It was nothing that Jules had ever coveted—or even asked for.

"You'll be great today," Mark said as he leaned over to kiss her once again before heading for the door and stepping outside.

She nodded, then turned away as the door shut, the key turning in the lock. She walked back to the table, her gaze resting on the white apron on a brass hook by the stove, her name embroidered in red thread on the front pocket, a gift from her mother the Christmas she had turned thirty. The tears came all at once, bubbling up from that torn place inside her, and she reached for a teacup, her hand brushing against the porcelain harder than she'd intended. The amber liquid splashed over the table, the remaining sweets drowned and useless.

∼

By the time Jules made it to the Midtown office, her stomach was roiling as if she were at sea. Just being in proximity to the place where she'd spent much of her childhood coloring in the conference room, rolling out her own sticky mound of biscuit dough in the test kitchen, was enough to bring the threat of hot tears to her eyes. She hadn't been inside the building once since her mother's death, and she braced herself, as if going to battle, before pushing through the revolving doors. It was hard enough to maintain a sense of equilibrium in her own home. But here, surrounded by the familiar sounds of her childhood, the echo of heels clicking in the marble lobby, the swift elevator ride to the fourteenth floor, it felt all but impossible.

As she entered, Jules kept her eyes fixed on the middle distance, largely so she wouldn't have to stop and make obligatory small talk—or answer any questions. And as she moved through the reception area, a chorus of whispers hissed at her back. *Only been a few months . . . surprised she's here at all.* Jules concentrated on staring straight ahead as she walked down the corridor, her face impassive, until she arrived at the door of her mother's office. She stood there for a moment, reaching out one hand to touch the brass plaque hanging on the wall, tracing the letters with her fingertips.

E. STONE, CEO.

As she opened the door, she almost expected to see Elizabeth sitting behind the desk, the wooden surface piled with photo proofs and paperwork, her mother's scuffed loafers kicked into a corner. *My angel,* she'd say, her eyes brightening. Her mother had always waxed poetic where her daughter was concerned, even though Jules had never felt anywhere close to angelic. And as soon as she made it inside the office, Elizabeth would look her over from head to toe, her mother's eyes greedily drinking Jules in, her long, elegant fingers reaching out to smooth down the curls that grew from the top of her head in concentric spirals. "No idea *where* you got this unruly mop," she'd say lovingly, only halting her course to pluck a few invisible specks of lint from the front of Jules's sweater.

The office was just as Elizabeth had left it, as if time itself had stopped along with her mother's heartbeat. Dust motes drifted lazily through the air like specks of gold dust in the light streaming through the half-open blinds. The desk was cluttered with all she had left unfinished: splayed-open cookbooks and fabric swatches, stacks of unopened invitations, the cream-colored envelopes heavy and thick.

A silvery-gray pashmina, one of her mother's favorites, was draped on the chair behind her desk. As if in a trance, Jules walked over and picked it up, bringing the soft cashmere to her face and inhaling deeply, breathing in the faint scent of L'Air du Temps, its sweet top notes of peach and neroli conjuring her mother's spirit in a way that the contents of the room, the scattered remnants of a life cut short, could never hope to. Jules raised her head from the shawl, holding it to her chest like a newborn, as a soft knock sounded on the door before it creaked open.

Margaret stared at her apologetically from behind thick tortoise-shell frames, her carroty hair pulled back in a bun. She wore a navy shirtdress, the ballet flats on her feet a dull burnished gold. *Just like Mom,* Jules thought, attempting what she hoped was a reassuring smile. Margaret and Elizabeth had always shared the same taste in clothing, in food—in just about everything. *Thick as thieves, those two,* her father had always said with a chuckle.

"They're ready," Margaret said quietly. "Are you?" She sized Jules up through the lenses of her glasses, her hazel eyes magnified. Something about Margaret always made Jules feel as though she were falling short, as if her clothes were on inside out. Jules couldn't bear that kind of scrutiny from anyone other than her mother. It was bad enough when Elizabeth had subjected her to it. From anyone else, it felt completely intolerable.

"No," Jules replied, dropping her mother's shawl on the desk and walking to the door. "But when has that ever stopped me?" Her voice was brittle and strange, almost unrecognizable as she followed Margaret out of the room, closing the door behind them.

Elizabeth Stone Enterprises was a small company, and there were no more than forty employees clustered around the long table when Jules entered the boardroom and stepped to the front. "My mother may be gone," she said, her voice wavering, "but we are going to make sure the work that was the linchpin of her entire career will live on as her legacy." There were a few nods, but mostly everyone looked tired and apprehensive. Jules took a deep breath and continued, though all she wanted was to hide beneath the table and never come out. Words like "innovation," "leadership," and "determination" fell from her lips, but the room seemed distant and unreachable, as if she were trying to communicate through a thick pane of glass. "And as we move Elizabeth Stone Enterprises into the future," she finished, trying to sound both encouraging and authoritative, "I plan to lead by her example."

There was a weak round of applause, and Jules felt her cheeks flush with embarrassment. Not once had she ever commanded a room, and while it didn't feel as awful as she'd expected, attempting to fit into her mother's impossibly narrow size six shoes wasn't exactly comfortable, either.

After everyone slowly left the room, Margaret stayed behind, closing the door as the last employee filed out. She turned to face Jules, walking over to the table where Jules still stood. "There are some things we should discuss," she said, her tone light, but with an undercurrent that suggested an agenda below the surface. "When your mother died, we lost the face of this company, and the fact of the matter is that our demographic isn't getting any younger. Your mother's passing took us all . . . a bit by surprise." Margaret looked away, her voice faltering. "She hid her diagnosis for way too long, Jules. We weren't prepared to lose her."

"When would we ever have been?" Jules said before she could stop herself. She felt like an open wound, all exposed nerves and sinewy tendons. That scorching day last August came rushing back, the cold dish of rice pudding in her hands, her mother's blank expression as she turned her face away from the spoon, that marked refusal.

I followed your recipe exactly, she'd said in as coaxing a tone as she could muster. *There's just a little cinnamon.* Her mother's eyes were ringed with ashy circles, the fine bones in her face too prominent, too sharp. The cancer had consumed her from the inside out, a ravenous monster whose cellular rampage Elizabeth had hidden for as long as she could. From everyone.

Even her own daughter.

"I knew just about as much as anyone else," Jules muttered, unable to keep the bitterness from her voice. "Which is to say, practically nothing. Until it was way too late."

"That's why we have to act quickly." Margaret sighed, pulling out a chair and sitting down. "Every day that passes, the company falls deeper into stasis and debt. We need to figure out where we fit in the current landscape."

Jules exhaled, aware of the sweat beneath her arms, wet and telling, a feeling she doubted her mother had experienced even once in her lifetime. *Don't let them fuck it all up,* Elizabeth had whispered in her ear the day before she'd stopped breathing, motioning weakly for Jules to bend down. Her mother never swore, and Jules's eyes widened at the harshness in her voice. An unfamiliar smell clung to Elizabeth's skin, overripe, like a bowl of rotting fruit.

"My mother wasn't big on change," Jules said, sitting down across from Margaret. "I could barely get her to embrace Instagram, and even that was a constant struggle. She would die all over again if you got a bunch of twenty-year-olds to do coordinated dances on TikTok wearing one of her signature hats."

"Don't be ridiculous." Margaret snorted. "But there is something I wanted to discuss with you while you're here. Something rather pressing. We've received an offer from Target. And it's big."

"Target?" Jules asked, the word leaving her lips as if in slow motion. "Did my mother know about this?"

"Not in full, no . . ." Margaret said slowly. "We'd discussed the possibility of it before she passed. But she didn't live to see it come to fruition."

"What exactly are we talking about?"

"A line of branded products," Margaret said smoothly. "High quality but low cost. They've made up some prototypes, and I think they're very much in line with the Elizabeth Stone brand. Your mother was a fan of accessibility. That's partially what made her famous, her belief that the way she lived should be within everyone's reach—that we create our own magic."

Look, Julie. Jules could hear her mother's voice in her ear, as clear as if she were suddenly standing right behind her. She was four years old again, her thumb pushed into her mouth in a flood of safety. Elizabeth held up a flower crown she'd woven from the yellow blossoms in the garden, the ends tied with silk ribbons in shades of pistachio and rose, her blue eyes so clear that it could break your heart. *I crown you Princess Juliet,* she said as she placed the flowers atop Jules's head.

Jules stood, blinking back the tears that had sprung up once again and turning her back on Margaret. *Breathe,* she told herself sternly, as she forced air into her lungs. Jules closed her eyes. Ever since her mother died, it felt as if the mere thought of touch alone, no matter how benign, might shatter her into a million pieces.

There was a rustling sound as Margaret came up behind her, placing one hand on Jules's shoulder. Jules wiped her eyes with her fingertips, taking a step forward before turning to face her again. "One other thing," Margaret said slowly, apologetically. "Sydelle called this morning. She'd like to set up a lunch meeting."

"Why?" Jules asked in surprise, and Margaret just shrugged her slim shoulders, her face impassive. The last time Jules had seen her mother's editor was at Elizabeth's funeral. She'd taken both of Jules's hands in her own, tears streaking her face, the sight at odds with her carefully coiffed silver bob. *I knew her before you were even born,* she said, her words tinged with surprise, as if that information were as mystifying and unexplainable as the fact of Elizabeth's body lying motionless in a mahogany coffin. The scent of lilies was suddenly overpowering, and Jules felt her body sway slightly in the closeness of the room, sweat beading her upper lip.

"There's something she wants to discuss with you; I'll let her fill you in on all the details."

Jules hadn't heard of any new books in the works in the months since Elizabeth's death and couldn't imagine what Sydelle could possibly want with her, but she just nodded numbly, as she had with all requests that had been thrown her way since her mother's passing.

"What about Thanksgiving?" Margaret asked tentatively, and Jules blinked in the harsh light of the corridor, as if emerging from the depths of sleep. "Are you sure you're up to hosting?"

"It's a family tradition." Jules shrugged, smiling tightly while pushing her curls back from her face with one hand, securing them with a black tie she wore around one wrist.

"I'm aware of that," Margaret said dryly. Her hazel eyes behind the thick frames were etched at the corners, the thin skin spiderwebbed with the passing of time. Sometimes Jules wondered whether those lines were the only real cracks in Margaret's steely surface, the sole marker of her human frailty. "I can make the calls, Jules, let everyone know you're not quite up to it yet."

"Don't be silly." Jules let out a short laugh. "I mean, what could possibly go wrong? Besides," she continued, walking toward the door and placing one hand on the knob, "Thanksgiving was her favorite holiday. She'd spin in her grave if I canceled."

The turkey, the flowers, the table settings. Her mother's famous cranberry sauce, redolent of orange peel and clove. The lobster bisque that always preceded the main course. The cheese board: Boursin, Comté, ash-dusted goat. Fig jam, her father's favorite. The silver bowl filled with toasted walnuts and hazelnuts. But this time, Jules would have to do it all alone, without her mother to guide the way.

When Jules turned to look back, Margaret had one hand on her hip, her expression vaguely annoyed. "OK, but we still haven't discuss—"

"I need more time," Jules said, cutting her off.

"We need to give them an answer by next week. I'm not sure you understand the—"

"They want the deal?" Jules snapped, unable to keep the irritation from her voice. "They'll wait." She turned, ready to make her escape.

She stepped out into the narrow hallway, the walls lined with framed magazine covers: Elizabeth in the walled garden of her Westchester estate, her arms filled with freesia; at the farmers' market, a ripe tomato cupped between her hands. Elizabeth standing at the shore, her white linen dress blowing in the wind; holding Jules in her arms, a blanket swaddled around her small, fragile body.

"Let's have a baby," Mark had taken to murmuring into the crook of her neck over the past few weeks, and Jules had frozen at the thought each time, turning over in bed and curling in on herself, drawing her knees up to her chest, as if in protection. All these years, her day had begun with the insistent ringing of the phone, her mother's voice in her ear, her questions and ideas rushing like water from a broken dam. *Is the chapter on sauces derivative? Tell me the absolute truth! What about the black dress for the James Beard Awards, the one with the beadwork?* There was no time, not enough space, it seemed, to even consider anyone else, much less a tiny person with demands of its own. And now that Elizabeth was gone, the idea felt unthinkable. How could Jules walk that road of motherhood, stumbling along heedlessly without her own mother to guide her?

As she walked down the hall toward the bank of elevators, her mother gazed down at her with every step she took. Her eyes, perfectly framed by dark brows, following her daughter's every move.

Chapter Two

As she walked through the front door of Gramercy Tavern, Jules felt the ever-present knot in her stomach relax slightly, a kind of unwinding that took her off guard and made her feel slightly dizzy, as if she'd had one glass of wine too many. The restaurant was decorated for the impending holidays with pine garlands and twinkle lights, but its oak-lined interior and low lighting always seemed festive and welcoming, no matter the season.

Even though the restaurant had built its reputation on its impeccable cuisine, the tavern, far less stuffy than its celebrated formal dining room, had made its name on how effortlessly it bridged the gap between high- and low-end dining. You could get grilled arctic char or duck liver mousse if you wanted it, but the lunch crowd was generally there for one reason and one reason only: the tavern's signature burger. Her mother had loved sitting at the bar, a burger and a seafood tower placed between them to share, along with a pair of extra-dry Grey Goose martinis. She would turn to Jules, her cheeks flushed from the warmth of the room and the alcohol coursing through her bloodstream.

Tell me everything, she'd say, squeezing Jules's hands in her own. *Don't leave out a single detail.*

Jules had always complied, talking slowly, shyly at first before the liquor loosened her tongue. But Elizabeth rarely offered anything substantial in return. Nothing particularly personal, anyway. Her mother's confessions mostly revolved around work, which was all that seemed to dominate her thoughts, especially as she grew older. And after the diagnosis, she'd become almost monomaniacal in her focus, working late into the evenings and insisting that Margaret do the same. At the time, Jules hadn't understood her mother's need to push things into overdrive twenty-four hours a day. But now she did.

The biggest mistake we make, her mother had muttered near the end, *is thinking we have time.*

This was her first visit to the tavern since her mother's death, and as she walked past the host, who was busily arguing with a group of red-faced tourists, she wondered whether every street corner of the concrete city would hold her mother's ghost now, whether every inch of the place she'd loved for as long as she could remember would now be forever haunted.

She scanned the room for Sydelle's bob, a glimpse of abalone in a sea of black-and-gray flannel, and walked toward the table at the back of the room, a smile pasted on her lips. Would she ever smile from a place of real happiness again? The only emotions she seemed to experience these days were numbness and a deep, bottomless grief that felt as if she'd managed to tumble headfirst down a well, the stones slippery beneath her hands, resisting any kind of traction.

"Jules." Sydelle stood as she approached, leaning forward so Jules might kiss her cheek. She leaned in, and as she did so, a familiar scent engulfed her: jasmine and musk, the pulse of white roses tinged with morning dew. Joy by Jean Patou, a perfume Elizabeth had worn as well, mostly for special occasions. The scent, and the flood of memories that accompanied it, made the room swim dangerously.

"It's nice to see you," Jules managed to get out as she sat down at the table.

Sydelle smoothed the front of her simple black dress, a chain of thick gold links gleaming at her throat, and sat back down, her dark eyes missing nothing. Not the nervous smile on Jules's lips, or the plaid woolen poncho she wore, the collar dotted with moth bites, the tight black jeans Elizabeth had always hated, or the clunky leather boots on her feet, her hair a spiraled blonde mop. Although Sydelle was in her early sixties, she possessed the kind of exuberance that made her seem far younger. It was Sydelle who'd gotten Kay Thompson herself to sign Jules's beloved copy of *Eloise at the Plaza*, hand delivering it to her at her eighth birthday party with an armful of silver Mylar balloons in one hand, a box of delicate petits fours in the shape of butterflies in the other. Elizabeth, always loyal to a fault, had steadfastly refused to work with any other editor, routinely turning down seven-figure deals at rival publishing houses just to stay with Sydelle. Jules shifted uncomfortably in her chair, looking over at the third empty seat placed between them.

A seat her mother should have occupied.

"I was surprised to hear from you," Jules said, pushing the heavy maroon menu to the side. "I haven't seen you since . . ." Her voice trailed off. She couldn't bring herself to say the words.

"It was a lovely service," Sydelle said, breaking into her thoughts and picking up a glass of iced tea, taking a long swallow. "I'm certain she would have been pleased."

Jules nodded, wishing she could erase the entire memory of that awful day, how she'd stolen away to a cramped bathroom on the second floor of the funeral home, a wad of paper towels shoved in her mouth to stifle her sobs. Her stomach churned with nausea, and suddenly, the idea of eating seemed inconceivable. Grotesque, even.

"Should we get a seafood tower?" Sydelle said brightly, glancing down at the menu. "Your mother loved them so."

"No," Jules said abruptly, the word ricocheting across the table like a bullet. "I mean, I'm really not that hungry," she said more softly.

"Just a little nosh then." Sydelle nodded, waving a hand in the air to beckon a server, who materialized almost instantaneously, bending his head to conspire. The room was warm and noisy, and Jules realized she was sweating. Everyone was too close, too tight, and the smells of grilling meat and the plates of hamburgers ringed with piles of the duck-fat potato chips the tavern was famous for now seemed obscene in their excess. To distract herself, Jules unfurled the white napkin placed on the center of her plate, smoothing it over her knees. That small action, as routine as it was, calmed her. The whole world might have been turned upside down, but at least there was still the civility of everyday life, the rituals of the table, a language that still made sense.

"Now," Sydelle said briskly, as soon as the server had departed, "we can get down to business. I know it's only been a few months, and I know you must be overwhelmed, but since your mother's passing, her fans have not only been completely bereft, which was to be expected, but absolutely *clamoring* for more content."

"She left a completed draft of the next book, didn't she?" Jules asked, picking up the glass of ice water and swallowing hard.

"She did," Sydelle replied. "And we're expediting the production schedule as quickly as we can to meet demand. Look, I'm going to cut right to the chase here. How would you feel about writing your mother's definitive biography? We're thinking of calling it *The Essential Elizabeth Stone*."

There was a burst of laughter at a neighboring table, and Jules flinched, her pulse racing inexplicably. Ever since her mother had died, the city Jules had once loved with every fiber of her being seemed oppressive, noisy, and worst of all, indifferent. How could people still laugh in the face of loss? How did they go on as their world crumbled around them, the ground tilting like a broken carnival ride?

"I've never written anything in my life," she said, looking back over at Sydelle. "I could barely finish term papers in college, much less write a whole book."

"Well, you wouldn't be solely responsible for the text," Sydelle said quickly, her dark eyes glimmering the way they always did when she had a new idea. "We're envisioning a kind of hybrid structure where you'd work alongside a seasoned writer."

"A ghostwriter?"

Before Sydelle could answer, the server rematerialized, holding a heavy silver tray. There was a platter of oysters on a bed of rock salt, a Caesar salad, a basket of herb-studded focaccia, and a plate of radishes and butter, a dish Jules knew for a fact wasn't on the menu but had always been made especially for her mother. At the sight of the cluster of crimson vegetables, the yellow orb of butter in a small ceramic dish, Jules felt her throat constrict.

"Maybe I should've ordered the burger, too," Sydelle fretted as she surveyed the table, which was now full to bursting.

Please don't let her order any more food, Jules prayed silently as Sydelle reached across the table and slid an oyster into her mouth, tilting her head back, her eyes shutting in momentary bliss. "Spectacular as always," she said with a sigh as she wiped her lips with a napkin. "Where were we?"

"I asked if you'd be hiring a ghostwriter."

"No. Not exactly. More of a collaborator. Have you heard of Noah Sharpe?"

"The guy who wrote *Decimation*?"

"The very same."

In 2012, Sharpe's first novel, a brutal examination of the breakup of a marriage and the subsequent mental breakdown of a Wall Street tycoon, had been an overnight success, making him the darling of the literary world. There was the glowing review in the Sunday *New York Times* that lauded Sharpe's literary promise. His good looks, along with the black-and-gray tattoos covering his arms, cemented his reputation in publishing as the bad boy du jour, and his eyes, sleepy and languid in their magnification, had only fueled his rapid ascent to stardom.

The publishing world had waited breathlessly for his sophomore effort. But with each year that passed, first two, then four, Sharpe's readership dwindled. Gone were the profiles in prominent magazines and literary journals, and then came the lawsuit, a media circus splashed across Page Six as his publisher sued him for the return of their multimillion-dollar advance.

"But why would he be interested in *this*?" Jules wondered aloud. "Does he have a secret affinity for clam rolls and flower arrangements?"

Sydelle smiled, her eyes drifting behind Jules's head.

"Why don't you ask him yourself?" she said archly. "He just walked in."

Chapter Three

Noah Sharpe strode toward them, the cover of Joy Division's *Unknown Pleasures* album silk-screened across the front of the black T-shirt he wore, the silver hardware on his leather jacket catching the light. His jeans were faded, his hair an unruly ebony, and behind the heavy frames he wore, his eyes were the olive green of a faded army jacket, his jaw covered in at least two weeks' worth of dark stubble. Elizabeth, Jules knew, would've hated Noah on sight. She would never have chosen him as the writer of her website copy, much less anything as important as her definitive biography.

Sydelle jumped up to greet him, and there was a round of air-kissing while Jules sat there uncomfortably until Noah disengaged himself and took the empty chair in between them. "Noah Sharpe," he said, holding out a hand for Jules to shake, his voice deeper than she'd imagined. His lips turned up in a slight grin that felt uncomfortably close to a smirk, and his eyes slid away from her before they'd even broken contact.

"I was just telling Juliet about the project," Sydelle said, sitting back down and immediately selecting a piece of focaccia, dipping it in a dish of bright-green oil. "Eat, you two!" She laughed, gesturing at the table groaning with food.

Noah reached over, plucking an oyster from the dish and sliding it expertly down his throat before turning to Jules. "Want one?" he asked, raising an eyebrow, as if it were a challenge.

"I'm not very hungry." Jules shrugged with a tight smile.

"Huh," Noah said, looking at her curiously. "Hard to believe Elizabeth Stone's daughter isn't a foodie, but I guess I've seen stranger things."

"When exactly. . ." Jules said slowly, "did I say I wasn't?"

"Didn't have to," he retorted, grabbing another oyster, and using it to point at the pristine china before her, oyster liquor spattering the tablecloth like drops of rain. "That empty plate speaks for itself."

"Guess you didn't do your research," she replied, unable to keep the edge from her voice. "Which is kind of strange for a writer, isn't it?"

"I remember Juliet scarfing down a plate of sweetbreads at La Côte Basque at, what? You must've been six or seven," Sydelle mused, trying to defuse the tension that had arisen without warning.

"I was nine," Jules said, unable to keep the knife's edge from her voice.

"Let's start over," Sydelle said firmly, dabbing her rose-colored lips on her napkin. "Jules, this is Noah Sharpe. Noah is interested in collaborating with you on your mother's biography."

"Why?" Juliet asked.

"Why . . . am I interested?" Noah said slowly, as if the question itself were absurd.

"Yes. Why would you be interested in chronicling the life and work of, as you put it, 'a foodie'?" There was a moment of silence as they looked at one another, neither of them willing to back down.

"I'm sure you remember Noah's novel *Decimation*," Sydelle said smoothly, shifting into elevator-pitch mode. "In the years since, he's carved out quite a successful career as a ghostwriter of celebrity memoirs. He's written a number of books for clients of mine—people that he and I are both legally bound to not mention in close proximity to his name. This would be a little different, however; on this project, he's hoping for cover credit."

"Why is that?" Jules asked, turning to look at Noah, her mother's voice suddenly in her ear, the slight edge that meant she was displeased.

He's no Michael Ruhlman, she pointed out. *Why, he's not even in the same league.* And by *league,* Jules knew her mother meant someone who was part of the same small world she inhabited. Someone who knew food intimately, who planned dinner as he finished breakfast, saving restaurant reviews like talismans.

"Well"—Noah chuckled softly—"I'm not getting any younger, so I figure it's time to finally redeem my good name in arts and letters. But I must confess; I'm wildly curious about your mother's origin story," he said, leaning his elbows on the table. "How was Elizabeth Stone created? What was the genus behind it all? For instance, what do you know about your mother's early childhood?"

"Just what she told me over the years." Jules shrugged. "That she grew up in Bar Harbor, that her own mother was known for her parties and events. That even a casual weekday dinner at home might be infused with an element of . . . magic. Candied violets on tea cakes. Flavors that wouldn't appear to go well together, but somehow did. A kind of whimsy," Jules finished, her cheeks flushing. "My mother worshipped her. I think one of her biggest regrets in life was that my grandmother died before I was born. That I never got to meet her."

"What about your other relatives on your mother's side?"

"All gone," Jules said, her voice tight, as if a python had made its way around her throat, slowly constricting its coils. "And my mother was an only child."

Noah nodded. "We'll need to rely on people who knew her when she was young—and your father's side of the family. If you decide to work with me, that is. Maybe we got off on the wrong foot," he said, his tone sincere now, "but I'll be honest: I really want this gig. Your mother's a cultural icon. I'd like to try and do her story justice, if I can."

"Was," Jules pointed out, a glimmer of pain sparking in her chest, the word itself as heavy as iron.

Noah just looked at her quizzically. The room was dense and close, and Jules felt a trickle of sweat beneath the poncho she wore, inching its way slowly down her side.

"She *was* a cultural icon," Jules said flatly.

"Of course," Noah replied, relief crossing the planes of his face, if only in understanding.

"I'll need to think about it," Jules said haltingly. "I may not have the bandwidth for this. My mother died without any real warning, and she left behind more work than I know what to do with. I'm a bit . . . overwhelmed."

"Of *course* you are," Sydelle said, reaching across the table and placing her hand atop Jules's own. "How could you not be? And by no means do I need an answer today. No one expects you to immediately commit. Think about it carefully and take your time. But not *too* much time, Jules. We need to strike while the iron is hot."

Right. While my mother is still economically viable, Jules thought, pulling her hand away.

"Now I see where you're going in that overactive brain of yours, Juliet." Sydelle chuckled. "You know as well as I do that publishing is all about timing, and interest in your mother's life and career is at its zenith right now. Yes, of course this is about money. But as your mother's editor for nearly forty years, it is important to me personally to do all I can to preserve her legacy, to leave a record of the extraordinary work she accomplished in her lifetime—a life that was cut far too short."

"I want to help you tell that story, if you'll allow me the opportunity." Noah leaned forward, gazing at her plainly. "And I mean *all* of it, from the grit of the early days catering private parties for peanuts to million-dollar book and movie deals and the glamour of the red carpet," he said quietly. "I think I'm the right guy for the job. I may not know the path your mother walked as intimately as you, but I do know what it's like to be an overnight success, and the pitfalls and problems that go along with it. Also, I love to eat." Noah smiled. "Which is probably essential to this job."

"That it is," Jules said grudgingly as she stood up, the prospect filling her with the sort of dread she had only ever associated with being unprepared for a test, the questions on the page swimming before her eyes, a sea of incomprehensible gibberish. She grabbed her bag from the back of the chair and slung it across her body. All these years in New York City and Jules still couldn't understand how some women strode through the streets, a handbag carelessly dangling from one shoulder, though she often wondered what it was like to be that fearless, so assured of your safety, the unflinching belief you could walk through the world unscathed.

"No dessert?" Sydelle asked, her face falling slightly.

"Not today"—Jules smiled—"but you two go ahead without me. If I know one thing about my mother, it's that she firmly believed if you were going to skip dessert, you might as well not eat at all." She smiled, turning to walk away, but she'd made it no more than a step or two when she heard Noah's voice at her back.

"What if it's different?" he asked, and she turned around, halting in her tracks.

"Excuse me?"

"Different than what you expect. Working on the book. What if it allows you to put it to rest? All of it."

"How so?"

"Maybe it's a way of saying goodbye," Noah said simply, the silver hardware on his motorcycle jacket glinting in the light. "Maybe it would help to think of it in those terms."

Jules glanced over at the bar, where a woman sat on a stool at the end, golden hair just brushing her collarbone, her head thrown back as she laughed, open-mouthed, her entire being radiating joy. *She should still be here,* Jules thought, a sudden fury overtaking her. *She should be sitting at that bar, drinking a martini and boring me with her latest thoughts on ceviche.* She blinked away the tears rapidly filling her eyes, and turned back toward Noah, who stared up at her curiously, as if she were a puzzle he couldn't quite figure out.

"I'll consider it," Jules said gently with a dip of her chin, and before he could say anything else, she turned and walked out of the restaurant.

Chapter Four

Jules hung over the bathroom sink, splashing cold water on her face with splayed fingers, raising her head to meet her own eyes in the bathroom mirror, the blue orbs bloodshot, circled in darkness. Thanksgiving had come and gone, the weekend passing in a blur of cooking and cleaning that had left her spent in a way she hadn't felt since her mother's funeral, as if something inside her had been violently wrung out until she was stripped bare, a bone picked clean by scavengers.

Even though she'd pulled out her mother's recipes days in advance, penning grocery lists and following instructions to the letter, the mashed potatoes somehow came out gluey, the turkey so horrifically dry that gravy couldn't even compensate for the rubbery meat (*don't think about the hard lumps in the gravy, either*), the cranberry sauce too tart, stinging her mouth like needles. Even the cheese plate had rebelled, the ash-dusted goat steadfastly refusing to come to room temperature.

At least the long dining table had looked acceptable, draped with a cream linen tablecloth, a souvenir from Elizabeth's last trip to France, vases of marigolds placed in a line down the center, her mother's gold flatware shimmering in the candlelight. She had done her best, dutifully placing bowls of roasted nuts and dried fruit throughout the living and dining room, dried apricots and walnuts still encased in their hard, brittle shells. But Jules knew that no matter how artfully she arranged the flowers or how carefully the white linen napkins were folded, she could never compete with Elizabeth's easy elegance, her mother's bouquets of chrysanthemums and asters, or the large, circular wreath of autumnal foliage she made herself every year, her hands twisting the russet leaves effortlessly around the wire frame. "Another masterpiece," her father would always say, shaking his head in awe as he leaned in for a kiss.

"No one ever eats these stupid walnuts," Jules had grumbled a few years ago, clanging the bowls down on end tables resentfully while Elizabeth looked on, a bemused smile on her lips.

"It's not about whether anyone eats them, Juliet," she said, her voice gently chiding. "It's about how it makes people feel. Maybe one day you'll understand that."

Jules understood now, too late, it seemed, that even if she devoted the remainder of her life to the pursuit, she'd never possess even a tenth of her mother's innate ability to fashion entire worlds with the touch of her hand, the ordinary day suddenly gilded. Elizabeth had always demurred when asked her secret, insisting that her recipes weren't spells or incantations, but merely suggestions. They were the spark, she had always claimed, not the resulting fire. But Elizabeth was wrong. And now that she was gone, everything seemed dull, colorless beyond recognition. How could Thanksgiving have hoped to be any different?

But once Margaret had swooped in, her arms laden with chafing dishes, thyme-and-sage-scented steam wafting from the platters as she uncovered them, there was an audible sigh of relief. Which only made Jules feel worse. Elizabeth's presence was everywhere she turned, the weight of her mother's disapproval like a heavy coat she couldn't shrug off as she welcomed the first guests inside, her black sweater dress dotted with stains she knew would never wash out. When everyone had finally left, Jules had peeled off the dress in the kitchen and stood there in her bra and panties, gooseflesh breaking out on her arms and legs, her biceps flexing as she used all her strength to ball the fabric up in one hand, shoving it to the bottom of the trash.

But there was no time to brood over the mess she'd made of Elizabeth's favorite holiday. On Monday morning, Jules found herself heading to the subway to take the train uptown to the one place she dreaded more than a family gathering these days: her mother's office. The train was packed with commuters, but Jules had always found the crush of bodies comforting, the teeming mass of humanity that pushed and jostled unrelentingly, the stench of urine at the subway entrance giving way to the heat of the airless platform, the metal rails on the tracks a kind of warning. Jules held on to the silver pole, her body swaying lightly as the train rocketed through one station after the next.

No matter how famous she'd become, Elizabeth had always taken the train, had absolutely insisted on it. *It keeps you connected to the real world,* she'd said, pulling the brim of her hat down low over her eyes. She never admitted it, but Jules suspected the real reason her mother loved the subway was for the anonymity it offered. Underground, her mother was just another commuter, swiping the same MetroCard as everyone else, walking up the same endless flights of stairs to reach the expanse of open air. As she moved through the belly of the city unseen, those small moments of invisibility offered a respite, a place where she didn't have to be Elizabeth Stone, lifestyle maven and homemaker extraordinaire, but was just another woman navigating the winding corridors of her life. And almost as if she'd cast a kind of reverse glamour over the crowds lining the platforms, she was rarely, if ever, recognized.

I can turn it on and off, her mother had told her once with a smile, gazing in the mirror almost lovingly at her reflection. *When I want to be invisible, I just pull it all back inside.* Jules, who was only six years old at the time, had stared at her mother in confusion as Elizabeth's expression slowly dimmed, the light in her eyes gradually fading until the spark was all but snuffed out, and with it, a pang of fear bloomed in Jules's stomach. Suddenly, her mother looked plain, unremarkable, her face blank and unrecognizable as a stranger's, and in that moment, Elizabeth became a foreign entity, no one Jules knew at all. Her mother had just laughed at her stunned expression, breaking the spell, reaching out and smoothing the blonde curls behind her daughter's ears.

It's just a trick, baby, she whispered, pulling Jules toward her. *I'll always be your mommy . . .*

The doors slid open at Times Square with a bang that startled Jules back into the moment, and she followed the crowd out of the train and through the station, pulling deep breaths of stale air into her lungs to calm her wildly beating heart. By the time she'd fought her way through the crowds and walked the six blocks to the office, she felt almost calm again, the chai latte she'd picked up at a nearby Starbucks warming her hands and imparting a sense of normalcy. It was just like any other day, and she was just another woman heading to work . . . except for the fact that she was expected to take over the day-to-day operations of one of the biggest companies in the Northeast. *I'm not my mother,* Jules thought as she waited for the ping of the elevator that would whisk her up to the hushed quiet of the conference room. *I can't even cook a turkey properly, much less fill her insanely expensive Ferragamo loafers.*

You could always give up, her inner critic reminded her, its voice a singsong lilt.

"Shut up," Jules muttered under her breath as the elevator arrived with a ping, the metal doors opening wide before they swallowed her whole.

~

"I think what they've managed to do in so short a time is remarkable," Peter Cobb said as he stared at Jules across the boardroom table piled with fabric samples in shades of cream, tan, and beige, the neutrals her mother had always preferred. There were a few outliers too, swatches in deep ocher and a luscious chocolate brown that Jules knew Elizabeth would have rejected on sight, though Jules herself loved their rich hues.

Too intense, her mother would've sniffed, pushing them to the side. Jules picked up one of the samples, letting the fabric move through her hands like water. The weave was a bit too loose, the telltale sign of low thread count, something Jules knew her mother would never tolerate, even from a mass-market retailer like Target. Elizabeth had always wanted everything she touched to be the best version of itself possible, the most finely realized, and she had worked tirelessly to make sure that her name was synonymous with absolute quality.

Margaret, seated next to Peter, cleared her throat, but softly, as if she were almost afraid to elicit a response. She wore a pumpkin wrap dress that matched her gingered hair, and her tortoiseshell frames dwarfed her face, perpetually sliding down her nose in a way Jules knew had driven her mother batshit. One Christmas she'd given Margaret a delicate pearl chain from Tiffany so she could hang her glasses around her neck when she wasn't wearing them, a gift that was promptly buried beneath the stacks of proofs and photo spreads littering Margaret's desk.

"I think they're a good first start," Jules said, aware that they were waiting expectantly for her reaction.

"They're the final prototype," Peter said bluntly. "There isn't time for revision."

"What's the rush?" she asked, dropping the samples back on the table.

Peter sat back in his chair and crossed one leg over the other. Tall and lean, even in his early sixties, his once-dark hair now silvered at the temples, he radiated the vitality of a man half his age, a frenetic charge that seemed to raise the tenor of the room. Today, as always, he wore an impeccably cut gray suit, a linen shirt like the cool glow of the moon.

"We know your mother was always reluctant to lend her name to anything at all, to license or sell products affiliated with the Elizabeth Stone brand," he began firmly. "But frankly, we don't have a lot of other options at this point. We need to make revenue, and we're running out of time. If nothing changes, we've got a few months, six tops, before we go under completely."

Jules felt a frisson of shock echo through her. Six months? It felt impossible.

"Elizabeth is gone," Margaret said softly, and Jules recoiled visibly from the words, felt them like a sudden, sharp sting. "The new cookbooks are gone too, the cooking show. In the eighties you could make a ton of money off cookbooks, but now? All we have is her back catalog—we can't keep recycling old material. And these days, everyone gets their recipes online, anyway. As I mentioned last week, we need to find some lucrative way to move forward. Something that makes sense."

"What exactly are we talking about?" Jules asked. "Bed linens? Dish towels? A few decorative items?"

"A full line of products," Peter answered. "All bearing the Elizabeth Stone moniker. Everything from linens to furnishings—all with the unmistakable quality and attention to detail her brand is known for."

"This is huge, Jules," Margaret said. "Elizabeth Stone cookware was selling like mad for a while there in 2020, when everyone and their mother was suddenly nursing a sourdough starter. Unfortunately, that moment is long over. But now, your mother's line could be in every Target store across the country. They've promised prime placement in stores in all major metro areas, and huge displays."

"But can a chain like Target really deliver the kind of quality Elizabeth made her name on? You know as well as I do that my mother detested anything even vaguely mass market. These samples are passable," Jules said, reaching out and fingering the material once more, "but I think you both know that she would never approve them as is. Not in a million years."

"It's true that your mother had extremely high standards," Margaret interjected before Peter could respond. "Standards that we did our best to honor for many years but that weren't always . . . realistic. Now we need you to do what she couldn't, to make decisions that will actively benefit the financial health of this company."

"You want me to sell her out," Jules said, her voice rising, her ears hot, as if they'd been singed with a lit match. "Not even six months after her death? Is that what you're asking, Margaret?"

Margaret's eyes flashed once in anger, and she looked away for a moment to compose herself.

"I'm asking you to be *practical*, Juliet," she said simply when she met Jules's gaze again. "Do you think that I, of all people, would sell your mother out just to make a buck?" All at once, a memory arose in

Jules's mind, Margaret and Elizabeth two Christmases ago, glasses of hay-colored wine in their hands, laughing uproariously as her mother stirred an enormous stockpot of lobster bisque, reaching over to tip Margaret's wineglass into the pot. *Margaret is family,* her mother had always said, her tone making it clear that she was not to be argued with. *She knows what's best for the company, and her instincts are impeccable. Now that your father is gone, she's the person I trust most in this world—in business and in life.*

Not me, Jules had retorted silently. *Never me.*

"But consider the alternative," Margaret went on, her tone softening. "If we do nothing, the company folds, and her name and all she accomplished will disappear from the public eye. It will slip away little by little, until her legacy is erased completely. Do you think she would want that? After how hard she worked to make this company a success?"

"Of course not," Jules replied instantly, because it was true. Her mother had fought hard throughout the years to stay relevant without reinventing herself completely. It took hard work and discipline, not to mention a certain amount of ingenuity.

"There may be other options," Peter began cryptically. "But they would require you to take an active role in ways I'm not sure you're comfortable with. For instance, you might consider taking over the cooking show. The Food Network has expressed interest in exploring that angle."

"Cooking my mother's *recipes?*" she blurted out incredulously.

"We've batted around a few different scenarios," Peter said, folding his hands in front of him as if in church. "We can talk about it when you're ready. But again, time is of the essence."

"There's a lot to consider," Jules said as she stood up abruptly. It seemed that she was always walking out of rooms lately, cutting conversations short, dodging things she didn't want to deal with.

"Take the samples home for the night," Peter urged, gesturing at the table. "Really get a feel for them. Margaret has already emailed you the proposal and the mission statement from corporate. I think that if you really read it, you'll see that they have the best intentions."

Jules nodded as she scooped up the piles of cloth from the table and turned and headed toward the door.

"I'll walk out with you," Margaret said quickly, getting up and following Jules. *Just as she did with my mother,* Jules thought as she stepped out into the corridor. When had she ever seen one of them in the office without the other? There was the dizzying feeling that she had become her mother suddenly, that if she reached up, there would be a straw hat perched inexplicably atop her head.

As soon as Margaret exited the conference room, Jules began walking down the hall at a clip. That old feeling had taken over, the one that told her she had to run, to get away so she could pretend that everything was fine, that she wasn't walking through Elizabeth's old stomping grounds daily, and that most of all, her mother was still alive. Somehow, on a busy city street or a plane, the past was intact. And in that space, Elizabeth Stone stood unaltered by the ravages of time and disease.

"Jules, wait," Margaret called from behind, her voice breathless and sounding enough like Elizabeth's to make Jules stop in her tracks. She turned to face her, and the pain on Margaret's face took her aback. It was raw, naked. The same kind of pain that Juliet pushed away every day—every hour, it seemed. Until nightfall, when, as she lay beside her sleeping husband in the dark, his breath coming slow and easy as a mantra, she finally let herself cry.

"You know, I loved her too," Margaret said as a UPS deliveryman pushed past them, his arms filled with packages. "It may be her name on the door, but this company has always been my baby. You need to trust that I won't let her reputation be sullied in any way. But we need to act, Jules, before it's too late. We're running out of time."

Jules nodded, aware that the samples were still balled up in her hands. Without thinking, she shoved the mass of fabric down in her tote, out of sight. "I know," she said. "I just can't help but think she would've despised all this. Rejected it on principle."

"Your mother was brilliant," Margaret said with a sigh, turning to smile reassuringly at an intern as she passed by, young and blonde, a black ribbon holding her silken tresses away from her heart-shaped face. Just the kind of girl her mother always hired, handpicked by Margaret in Elizabeth's absence, no doubt. "But—and it pains me to say this—she didn't always make the right decisions. She was often rigid in her thinking, too myopic, and she sometimes got stuck on minute details."

Jules felt herself bristle. "That rigidity, as you call it, made her a star. She was a visionary, Margaret. Everyone knows that."

"That she was." Margaret sighed as they reached the bank of elevators. "But the best visionaries consider other perspectives, too. They let people in. She wasn't the greatest at that, Jules. Not in business, and not in her personal life, either."

"What do you mean?" Jules asked. Margaret opened her mouth, but just as she began to speak, Jules's phone buzzed loudly from the depths of her bag. When she retrieved it, the number on the screen was one she didn't recognize. "Spam," she muttered, ready to shove it back inside her tote when something inside her told her to answer, a feeling she couldn't explain. When her mother had died, Jules's cell had droned on the bedside table over and over in the early-morning hours, her stomach churning as she turned over and faced the wall. In that one awful moment, she knew that her mother was gone, that there was nothing she could do to bring her back. She just wanted a few more minutes of normalcy, where she didn't know the truth.

Before her life changed forever.

"Sorry," she mouthed at Margaret as she answered.

"Jules? It's Noah Sharpe." His voice seemed lower on the phone than she remembered, as if he'd just rolled out of bed. "I hope it's OK that I'm calling. I got your number from Sydelle."

"Yeah, it's fine," Jules said confusedly, turning away from Margaret and running a hand through her hair, her fingers catching on her curls. God, she needed a haircut.

"Do you have time to meet up this afternoon?"

"Meet today? With you? Look, Noah, I already said I'll think about it, and I will, but—"

"I'm downtown. I can meet you wherever."

"Today is impossible. I'm sure whatever it is can wait."

There was a beat of silence, the sound of wind rushing past before he spoke again.

"Actually, I don't think it can."

"Why is that?" Jules asked distractedly, turning around as the elevator arrived with a ping.

"It's about your mother."

Chapter Five

The café she'd chosen was on Mulberry Street, once a vibrant Italian neighborhood that had spanned countless streets on the Lower East Side, now reduced to half a block of bakeries, the cookies laced with a whisper of anise, the crunch of pine nuts, butcher shops where sausages hung from the rafters, the mozzarella hand pulled. Instead of the old-school red-sauce joints that had once graced every corner, the neighborhood had been infiltrated over the years by twee coffee shops, and a seemingly endless influx of dim sum parlors.

As she pushed open the door, her breath hung in the air, and she was glad she'd thrown on her favorite black wool coat when she'd left the apartment that morning. She'd fallen in love with its minimalist design on a trip to Tokyo two winters ago, the way the yards of cashmere fell softly to her boot tops. Elizabeth, however, had felt otherwise. *It's too big!* she'd lament, each time Jules wore it. *You're so tall and slim, Juliet— it positively swallows you!* Then the head shaking would commence, her lips pursed in dismay, as if the garment itself had caused her physical pain. Jules would roll her eyes and change the subject, compliment her mother's new hat or the latest episode of her cooking show. Only then would Elizabeth's eyes brighten, the coat seemingly forgotten . . . until next time. Strangely, Jules found herself missing that well-worn routine now.

Maybe because she knew she would never hear it again.

Noah sat at a table in the back, drumming his fingers on the table, lost in thought. But as she approached, his eyes snapped into focus behind his glasses, and he smiled, standing to greet her. He wore a tan sweater and a pair of dark jeans, the stubble on his jaw approaching beard status, his leather jacket strewn carelessly across the table, marking his territory.

"Thanks for coming," he said, reaching out to take her hand in his. His fingers were warm against the iciness of her own, and she withdrew sharply, pulling out the adjacent chair and sitting down quickly. There was something about Noah that got under her skin. A certainty that teetered on the edge of entitlement.

"What's this all about?" she asked, shrugging off her coat, exposing the gray cardigan beneath, a sweater that had once belonged to her mother.

"Do you want a coffee?" Noah asked, taking a hesitant step toward the counter. "Tea, maybe?"

"I'm fine," Jules said tersely.

Noah strolled back over to his chair and sat down, pulling his jacket from the tabletop and tossing it on the empty chair beside him.

"What's this about?" she repeated.

"You get right to the point, huh?" He smiled, pushing up his sleeves and exposing his forearms, thick with dark hair, a tattoo in black and gray of an anatomical heart, thin steel needles piercing the muscle.

Jules just stared at him, unable to disguise her annoyance. Off the top of her head, she could think of about fifty things she should've been doing at that moment instead of wasting time with Noah Sharpe.

"If this is an attempt to get me to make up my mind about the book, you're wasting your time—and mine," she pointed out. "I haven't decided anything yet."

"That's not why I asked you here," Noah said quickly.

"On the phone, you mentioned something about my mother?"

Noah exhaled, sitting back in his chair as if he'd been suddenly deflated. "Nothing about what you told me checks out," he said, quietly. "Not one thing."

"What do you mean?" Jules asked, feeling her heart quicken. Ever since the funeral, the smallest, most insignificant thing could get her adrenaline pumping like a startled animal's: the sound of a bus backfiring, the way the doors clanged shut on the train, the clatter of a dropped pan in the sink. But this didn't seem small. Or insignificant. Whatever Noah was about to say felt as if it might have the power to change the course of her life forever.

"There *is* no Elizabeth Stone," Noah went on, a grenade tossed casually onto the table. "Not from Bar Harbor, anyway."

Jules opened her mouth in silent protest, then closed it. The espresso machine let out a cloud of steam, and the smell of coffee beans, so rich and comforting moments before, now made her stomach twist with nausea. "I don't understand," she managed to get out, as she felt her stomach wrench once, violently. Her face felt hot, her cheeks glowing like coals in a woodstove, Noah's face blurring in and out of focus. She blinked and looked away, willing her heart to slow. "That's impossible."

"She just doesn't exist." Noah peered at her from behind his glasses, his face implacable, as if this were a series of facts to him, nothing more, instead of her life unraveling right before his eyes. "Your mother isn't who she claimed to be."

"Of course she is," Jules went on, her words stumbling against one another, her pitch rising even as she tried to stay calm. "Was." The words hitched in her throat, and she looked around the room helplessly, as if trying to wake from a nightmare. *She's my mother. My mother . . .* The words reverberated in her brain, as though repeating them endlessly could somehow make sense of it all.

"What do you really know about her?" Noah asked, leaning forward so his elbows rested on the table.

"Everything," she sputtered, suddenly indignant, and even through the haze of anger and disbelief, she knew it was easier to be angry with

Noah than Elizabeth, that the heated space she was currently occupying was far less dangerous territory.

"Are you sure about that?" Noah asked, unable to keep the tinge of skepticism from his voice. "Because none of this—and I mean not a single thing—checks out."

"I'm her daughter," she snapped. "I would know, wouldn't I?"

Noah just stared at her, his silence filling in the blanks without him speaking a word.

It was true, wasn't it? She knew the long road of Elizabeth's history as if it were her own. Her mother had built an empire on the back of that origin story, told it over and over throughout the years until Jules herself could repeat it verbatim. But if there was any real validity to what Noah was saying—and she could barely wrap her head around that possibility—then it was clear that the facts Jules had spent her entire life believing in were nothing more than an elaborate fiction.

"Once I realized there was something amiss here, I haven't been able to stop thinking about it. I've done some digging, and I'm telling you, her story just doesn't make sense. For starters, there's no record of an Elizabeth Stone growing up in Bar Harbor—or anywhere on Mount Desert Island. Not that I can find, at least. Birth announcements, yearbooks, white pages, police blotters—nothing."

"Police blotters?" she interrupted.

"You'd be surprised where people show up, especially when they're young," Noah said with a half laugh. "But even if your mother was squeaky clean, she'd be *somewhere*. People just don't fall off the face of the earth. But it's weirder than that. It's like she never existed."

Jules sat there in silence, her mind swimming with thoughts she couldn't control, thoughts that wouldn't slow down long enough for her to sift through the detritus of her memory. *Mom,* she thought as she took a deep breath, her eyes fluttering closed for a moment before opening once more. "But . . ." she began when she could speak again, the bell over the door ringing sharply as a man walked in, bringing a gust of cold air with him, and Jules shivered once, hard. "My mother's been profiled exhaustively since before I was even born," she pointed out. "How come no one else has ever suggested . . . she somehow doesn't exist?"

"Because no one ever looked all that hard," Noah said simply. "She told a story—a good one at that—and she had the style and skill to back it up. You know," he said with a conspiratorial smile, "food media isn't known for asking a lot of tough questions in the first place. It's not exactly hard-nosed journalism, Jules. If your mother wasn't who she said she was, no one probably cared all that much—they were invested in the myth that grew up around her. That's what sells books."

"But why?" she asked, forcing herself to remain at least outwardly calm. "Why would she lie? It doesn't make any sense."

Noah took a swig of his coffee. "I've been wondering that myself," he said, placing his mug back down on the table gingerly, as if the sound might scare her off.

Jules felt her eyes fill with tears, even as pangs of anger gnawed her belly. If she wasn't careful, Jules knew that kind of rage could eat her alive. Her mind spun back to those final days before her mother's death, how one morning near the end, Elizabeth had awoken in the early light, her face turned toward the chair in which Jules slept. When Jules opened her eyes, her mother was looking right at her, a curious expression on her face, a kind of wistfulness. *I hope you don't hate me someday,* she said softly, her blue eyes no longer cornflower but faded now, already looking past Jules and out the window and far away, the one place Jules knew she couldn't follow.

It all came back in a dizzying rush, as if she'd been suddenly ambushed by everything she'd failed to notice over the years, the things she hadn't wanted to see. The absence of family snapshots or photo albums. *I'm not particularly nostalgic,* her mother had always said with a dismissive wave of her hand. But there were pictures, weren't there? Clusters of framed photos in her mother's house, the place where Jules had grown up, her own eyes staring back at her from the fireplace mantel, the end tables in the living room.

Elizabeth was only nostalgic, it seemed, when it came to her own daughter.

"What are you thinking?" Noah asked, his voice shattering the memory. Jules reached up and touched her cheeks, her hands coming away wet.

"I'm not sure," she muttered, grabbing a balled-up napkin from the table, a napkin Noah had probably used to blow his nose, and dabbing at her eyes with the rough paper. "I'm not really sure of anything right now."

"I can imagine," he nodded, draining the last of his coffee. "But setting the book aside—although I'll admit, as intrigued as I was before this discovery, now I'm downright fascinated. I mean, don't you want to know who your mother really was?"

I do know, that little voice in her head piped up defiantly. But it sounded weaker than before, less sure. "I have to think about all of this," she muttered. "I—"

"Look," he began again, his voice softer now. "Whatever you decide, I'll accept. It's not like I really have a choice. But this is bigger than a book, Jules. It's your life."

∼

When she arrived home thirty minutes later, the apartment was quiet and still. She could never quite get used to how darkness came swift as a thief in the winter, the sunlight disappearing from the sky as if a switch had been thrown, streetlamps glowing warmly in the cold. As she walked in the front door, Colbie, the ginger calico they'd adopted years ago, slunk into the dim hallway to greet her, meowing plaintively.

"Yes, yes," she mumbled as she switched on lights and made her way to the kitchen, Colbie following in her footsteps. She tipped some dry food into the cat's dish, which she attacked at once, chewing noisily and pushing her bowl around the kitchen floor. But other than that, the apartment was quiet, the air heavy with that deadened quality that told her she was alone.

There was nothing in that space that failed to remind her of Elizabeth: the muted gray walls that surrounded her, the paint her mother had mixed by hand to ensure the perfect hue; the carefully selected antiques, pieces Jules had always despised but couldn't bring herself to complain about; her mother's books lined up on the bookshelf in chronological order. There were so many things she thought she knew about her mother, details as solid as her own last name. But now, as she looked around her carefully curated apartment, everything seemed tinged with omissions and half truths.

You never really know anyone, her mother had said offhandedly once, as they worked side by side in her greenhouse, Jules's hair frizzing in the humidity as she watched her mother's long, pale hands place a bulb carefully into a pot, patting the soil down gently with her fingers. *Not completely.*

Her mind flashed back to every birthday party, every graduation, the talks they'd shared that had lasted deep into the night, the plates of cookies, gingersnap and chocolate chip, shared over episodes of *Gilmore Girls*. In all these years, she'd never once thought of her mother as anything but an open book.

Until now.

There was the sudden music of keys in the hall, then the front door opening, Mark's voice filling the silence that threatened to engulf her. He strode into the kitchen, arms laden with paper bags, a wine bottle tucked under one arm. His bright hair was tousled, his cheeks pink, and her heart leaped at the sight of him. For that one moment, he could have been the boy of her youth, striding across the quad to meet her.

"What's all this?" she asked, as he placed the bags and bottle down on the marble island, the familiar scent of fried dumplings filling the room.

"Chinese," he said, shrugging off his coat and throwing it over one of the stools. "I figured you wouldn't want to cook."

"You figured right," Jules said as she opened one of the bags, removing a tray of dumplings and several white containers. "Garlic shrimp?" she asked, holding one up.

"You know it." Mark laughed as he rummaged through the cabinets and retrieved a pair of wineglasses. The same ones Elizabeth had given them for their last anniversary, Baccarat crystal, and Jules had to look away, a lump forming in her throat, sticky as a ball of rice.

"You get any crab rangoon?" she asked as she opened the other bag, pawing through it distractedly.

"What do you take me for?" He scoffed as he pulled a corkscrew from the kitchen drawer, removing the cork from the neck of the bottle with a few practiced movements. He poured her a glass of white burgundy, sliding it across the island toward her. When she wrapped her hands around the glass, she could feel that the wine was already chilled. Mark was good about remembering small details, making sure to grab a cold bottle from the case instead of just pulling one off the shelf.

"How'd it go today?" he asked after she'd taken the first swallow, turning to remove two plates from the cabinet. Using one of the plastic forks tucked into the take-out bag, he began piling the plates with white rice, then covering it with the heavily sauced shrimp, the pungent scent of garlic filling the room.

"It was . . ." she began, setting her glass back down on the counter, "not great. Like I said this morning, everyone thinks I'm completely unqualified." She popped the lid off the tray of dumplings, placing one on her plate, and burning her fingers in the process.

"That's crazy," he said, the fork in his hand hovering over the plate as he looked at her in disbelief. "Who better to lead than you? You knew Elizabeth better than anyone, what she wanted for the company."

Jules sighed, the smell of the food suddenly overpowering, as if the dumplings had been fried in rancid oil. "Not," she said, pushing away her plate, "as it turns out."

"What do you mean?"

"I met with Sydelle last week," she began, pausing to take a sip of wine, hoping it might dislodge the words from her throat, "right before Thanksgiving. She wanted to discuss a book proposal."

"A cookbook?" Mark asked, spearing a dumpling with his fork, popping it into his mouth, and chewing thoughtfully.

"No," Jules said, holding the wineglass between her hands, as if to warm them. "A biography of my mother's life and work. She brought a ghostwriter with her. Noah Sharpe."

"Interesting," Mark said. "Is that something you'd even want to do?"

"Sydelle seems to think it's a good idea." Jules shrugged. "Apparently Elizabeth's audience is clamoring for more content. Now that she's . . ."

Dead. Your mother is dead.

The nausea she'd felt in the coffee shop with Noah returned with a swiftness that made her knees buckle, and she gripped the island with one hand, afraid of what could happen if she let go. She concentrated on her breathing, the air moving in and out of her lungs, air that Elizabeth no longer had access to, her chest still and rigid in the wooden box that held her, under mounds of loamy, blackened earth.

There was a sudden clatter as Mark dropped his fork on his plate, and then he was at her side, taking her in his arms in that familiar way that made her feel as if all were suddenly right in the world. But this time it wasn't enough, this time the wound in her heart seemed to expand, even as he held her, his body the same haven it had always been.

He smelled like Mark, of fried dough and ginger, the heat of his skin. But despite the familiar weight of him, Jules felt as if she'd been let loose in the sea, the shore a blurry, indeterminate shape far in the distance. A small cry escaped her lips, and she sank to her knees, so cold that she wondered if she would ever be warm again.

~

Later, in bed, her husband's lanky frame wrapped around her, the room suffused in the soft glow of a bedside lamp, the words finally came. She could have been discussing the weather, or the stock market, so little did she feel anything at all now, her insides stopped dead as a bell jar. When she'd finished, Mark was quiet for a moment, and then sat up. She turned to look at him, his face half in shadow.

"Jesus, Jules," he said, exhaling heavily as he rubbed one hand over his beard. His eyes, the same denim blue she'd loved for so long, looked as stunned as Jules had felt in that coffee shop with Noah, listening to her world unravel. "You know you have to go, right?"

"Go where," she answered woodenly. All at once, exhaustion crept over her, and all she wanted was to close her eyes and fall into the dark void of sleep, a place with no secrets, where no one could reach her. Not Mark. Not Noah.

Not even her mother.

"*Maine,*" Mark said, as if she were impossibly dense. "If he's right, this is huge, Jules. You have to find out if it's true."

"It's not," she said, her voice wavering, despite the inertia of her limbs, her heart. "It can't be."

"Why?"

"You knew my mother. Can you imagine her doing something like this? Hiding her real identity for all of these years?"

"I think," Mark said slowly, "it's probably more common than you think."

Jules was silent, but inside she felt the same anger mixed with the uncertainty and fear. The same nagging sensation she'd felt in the coffee shop with Noah, that horrid little voice inside her head, muttering along unchecked, one that couldn't help but wonder, *What if he's right? What if she lied all these years?*

"Maybe Noah is just bad at his job," she said irritably as she turned away, her cheeks flushed, as if with fever.

"You really think he'd suggest some wild-goose chase if he wasn't sure?" Mark asked. "If he didn't look under every rock imaginable first? C'mon, Jules. The guy wants this gig, right? It doesn't make sense."

"I know," she said quietly. "But I still can't believe it."

Mark lay down beside her again, pulling her close. "Why?" he asked, his breath warm in her ear.

Because she's my mother. Because mothers don't hide their identities from their children. Because I was her daughter. Because she wouldn't have left without telling me why.

Because she's gone now, and I can't ask.

"Because if he's right," Jules began, the words catching in her throat like jagged bits of glass, "then my entire life has been a lie."

The starkness of those words reverberated in the quiet of the room, words that had the power to change everything she'd once believed in, to alter her whole life, making it shadowy, unrecognizable. There was the sound of traffic outside, the familiar cacophony of the city, as soothing as a glass of hot milk, the sudden honking of a horn, impatient, restless, punctuating the silence, and before Mark could say another word, she turned over so that she could lay her head on his chest, his heartbeat reverberating against her cheek, rhythmic as a drum.

Chapter Six
BILLIE

There was nothing like a Maine summer. Not that Billie had anything to compare it to, but that was hardly the point. Even at twenty-one, she knew there was no need to travel the world to prove that the months of June through August were, in a word, magic. The trees were lush and green, the wind rustling gently through the leaves whispering their elusive secrets. The ocean sparkled sky blue near the shore, turning the deepest indigo farther out, smooth, gray rocks hugging the shoreline as if they'd been placed there for the sole purpose of stretching out with a book and a sandwich. Maybe that was why the population nearly tripled by July each year. *Vacationland,* they called it. But to Billie, it was just Winter Harbor, the tiny corner of the world she loved most—and the place she couldn't wait to escape.

Graduation had come and gone three years ago, but she could still hear the slight lisp of Maggie McCann, the class valedictorian, congratulating the class of 1977 as if it were yesterday. The absence of projects, homework, and college applications had left her feeling numb and adrift, searching for anything to fill the void stretching endlessly before her. She'd worked diligently through all four years of high school, her head bent over a stack of books, her hair, the indiscriminate brown of pencil shavings, falling over her face. There were weekends volunteering at the rest home just outside town, cleaning bedpans and reading to the residents, who looked at her through clouded, myopic eyes. There were SATs, and acceptance letters, racing to the mailbox each day, pulling out the thick envelopes awaiting her with a triumphant grin.

And it had all led to nothing.

There's been an issue. At work.

The words had stopped Billie's heart cold. It was late spring of her senior year, which meant it was still chilly and damp in Maine, the sodden ground beginning to awaken after its long slumber. The small blue house at the end of the dead-end road was quiet, but for the ticking clock on the kitchen wall, and the sky outside the kitchen window was as clouded and hazy as her thoughts.

"What do you mean?" she asked tentatively, afraid to know the truth.

"They've cut my hours," her mother said, shaking her head as if she herself couldn't believe it quite yet. "To part-time." She sighed, sitting down at the kitchen table, still wearing the blue smock she donned each morning, *Lambert's Grocery* stitched across the pocket in white thread. "I just don't see how I can make school happen right now. Money is just too tight. And without your father . . ." Her words trailed off, and she looked down at the top of the kitchen table as if she couldn't bear to meet her daughter's gaze.

Billie remembered visiting her father's office at the insurance agency when she was just a little girl, her legs stretched out before her on the bright-green carpet, the color of newly mown grass. At last year's company Christmas party, her father had rested his head on the table at the end of the night, empty glasses surrounding him, the room filling with nervous whispers. By New Year's, he was gone. His side of the closet empty but for a few lone hangers.

"What about financial aid?" she asked, unable to keep the desperation from her voice. There would be no dorm room at Penn State, she knew, no pink-and-beige pillows lined up in a neat row on her bed. It was as if a golden door had closed, the key slipping from her outstretched fingers.

"It isn't enough, Elizabeth. Not nearly."

Billie felt her mouth go suddenly dry, the desperation rising in her throat. Her mother never used her given name unless things were serious. She'd been Billie almost since the day she was born, a nickname her father had bestowed upon her the very first day she arrived home from the hospital wrapped in a blanket her mother had knitted, the wool a blushing apricot, the same delicate hue as Billie's plump cheeks. *Why not Betty?* her mother had asked. *Or even Lizzie?* But her father wouldn't hear of it. Despite her mother's protestations, the name had stuck, and she'd been Billie ever since.

Her mother stood up and walked to the fridge, opened it, and peered inside before closing it again. She leaned against the door, then glanced away, as if she couldn't bear to look at her daughter. Even in her midforties, people still considered Billie's mother beautiful with her thick caramel mane, gray strands shimmering like tinsel, her eyes a clear, unmuddied blue. But now, she looked as if she'd aged a decade overnight, the lines on her forehead as sharp as paper cuts.

"You can go next year. We can defer your enrollment," she said with a shrug, as if everything Billie had worked so hard for weren't disintegrating right before her eyes.

~

She woke in darkness, the scent of roast chicken sliding under her nose, her stomach rumbling loudly in response. She was always exhausted after a shift at the Lobster Pound, her wrists aching from the heavy trays she carried back and forth from the tables to the kitchen, her hair trapping the thick scent of fried food, leaving an oily residue. She sat up, her limbs heavy and slow, a drugged feeling that always overtook her whenever she napped during the day, blinking until the room came into focus.

She made her way to the door, then down the stairs, the scent intensifying as she moved through the hall and into the kitchen, where her mother stood at the counter, a wooden spoon in her hand, sautéing a pan of garlic and onions. The image was so much a part of her childhood that for a moment it was as if time itself had stopped—the scene was that familiar, and always the same. Her mother wore a soft yellow T-shirt, a white apron tied around the waist of her sweatpants, her hair twisted in a neat bun. As Billie approached, she turned and smiled, the creases around her eyes deepening.

"Hey, sleepyhead. Want to help with dinner? I've got a chicken in the oven," she said, opening the oven door to reveal the bird, golden brown, the juices spitting in the pan. "I'm just making a quick stuffing."

Billie shrugged, walking over to the cutting board, where freshly washed stalks of celery and peeled carrots lay like naked soldiers. She picked up the chef's knife on the counter and began chopping the vegetables for the mirepoix, just the way her mother had taught her, tiny, rectangular shapes that would match the onions already sizzling in the pan.

Her mother's cooking was honest and simple. Not the kind that garnered accolades outside of family, save the occasional neighbor raving about one of her mother's summer pies, but no less memorable for that. It was the way she held a leek or parsnip up to the light, letting it hover there before slicing it into translucent ribbons, the way she turned up her nose at the wilted, anemic bundles of asparagus that appeared in the produce section in the winter months.

The garage was stuffed with the antiques her mother had collected over the years, lugging them home in a borrowed truck and stripping off coats of old latex paint, coaxing the wood back to its former glory. The living room couch strewn with the blankets and throws she'd crocheted by hand, some made from cashmere in shades of beige and pale pink, the wool weightless as a cloud.

Billie watched her mother deftly scoop up the pile of vegetables from the cutting board, toss them into the pot with a hiss and stir the contents with a wooden spoon, then walk to the fridge, removing a bottle of white wine and pouring a dribble over the vegetables, a cloud of steam obscuring her expression. Grace Abbot was kind, her demeanor gentle, but she was also forged from impenetrable steel. When she'd fallen on icy pavement in March, dislocating her right shoulder, she'd driven herself to the ferry one-handed, then to the hospital in Bar Harbor, where she sat stone faced in the emergency room as the hours ticked by. When they finally took her back to the triage room, she'd stared at the doctor uncomprehendingly when he mentioned the twilight sedation necessary to reset the joint.

"Just put it back in already," she said coolly. "I've waited long enough."

"Mrs. Abbot," he explained patiently. "It will be extremely painful. You'll require sedation."

"It's *Ms.*," her mother replied matter-of-factly. "And I won't. Just do it."

The doctor just shook his head as a nurse began winding a bedsheet around her mother's wrist. When he finally pulled her arm roughly down, popping the joint back into place, there was an audible crack, but her mother had barely flinched.

"Why don't you tear up the bread?" her mother asked now, placing a hand on Billie's arm and directing her toward the loaf waiting on the counter. Billie grabbed at it, happy to have something inanimate to take out her anger on. She began pulling the bread apart, breaking it into small pieces and tossing them in the baking dish. Her mother added a splash of chicken stock to the simmering vegetables, then poured the mixture over the stuffing. She opened the oven with one hand, sliding the pan onto the bottom rack before closing it again.

Her mother turned toward her, leaning against the warmth of the stove. She reached up and unfastened her hair, and it tumbled down, hitting the tops of her shoulders. Unlike the other mothers in her town, hell would probably freeze over before Grace ever cut her hair shorter than shoulder length. Though she wore it up most often, it was, Billie knew, her sole vanity.

"You're never home these days," her mother said lightly, as she pulled a set of plates from the hutch and began to set the table.

"I'm trying to save everything I can. Somehow, it's never enough. Not for tuition. Or books, even." She swallowed hard, her stomach rumbling again.

"You'll go next year," Grace said decisively. "All that matters is that you *go.*"

There it was. The same refrain Billie had heard every year since graduation, the same myth, the same hope, the same empty promise. But one year had turned into two, then three, time slipping from her grasp, her days filled with one job after another, work stacked like poker chips, hoping for a winning hand.

"I don't know if I believe that anymore," she said, grabbing an apple from the fruit bowl on the counter, turning it over between her hands. "Maybe it's time to accept the fact that I might never go. To college, I mean." She searched the skin for defects before placing it gently back in the bowl. "I have to stop living like this is temporary."

"What do you have in mind?" her mother asked, pulling a pair of water glasses from the cabinet over the stove.

"I don't know." Billie shrugged. "I always thought I'd figure that out at school."

"You're as good a cook as I am," her mother proclaimed, setting the glasses down on the table with a clink. "Maybe better. Start there."

"You want me to be a housewife?" she asked, her voice tinged with disbelief, hating herself the minute the words left her lips. "Mom, it's the eighties now!"

Her mother stopped where she was, her spine stiffening.

"Is that," she began, looking at Billie coolly, that look she'd seen only a handful of times in her life, the look that told her that her mother was not only wildly disappointed, but wounded to her core, "what you think I am?"

"That's not what I meant. You know that I—"

Her mother put up a hand like a traffic cop, cutting Billie off before she could say another word. "Go wash your hands for dinner," she said sharply, turning to pull the chicken from the oven, the meaty scent filling the room, hinting at the depth of its flavor, the skin golden and crackling.

Billie walked down the hall to the bathroom, shut the door, and turned on the faucet, watching as the water ran endlessly down the drain in noisy circles. She looked up at her own reflection, her blue, almond-shaped eyes, the dark spray of freckles across her nose that she was forever trying to lighten with lemon juice but that stayed stubbornly present. Her mother had lost her chance to live an extraordinary life. It had drifted away from her like a lone feather floating along the breeze, and whether it had happened by fate or chance didn't really matter now. As she stood there, willing her life to change, Billie was more determined than ever to not make the same mistake.

Billie Abbot was going to be somebody.

Anyone but herself.

Chapter Seven

"They think they're better than everyone," Nate fumed, kicking the rocks lining the long drive leading up to his house with the toe of his dirty white sneaker, the path strewn with crushed oyster shells that glowed opaquely in the twilight. "Like they run the damn town."

"Well, don't they?" Billie asked, bored already even though the conversation had just begun.

"They're summer people," he scoffed. "They're only here two months out of the year."

Like most things in her life, Nate was almost good enough. With his unruly lock of dark hair falling over his forehead, those brooding eyes the color of dark chocolate, but just a little too narrow, too closely spaced, his shoulders a touch too wide and broad, it all added up to something just north of handsome. But in a town like Winter Harbor, Nate was a god. *You're so lucky,* the girls had breathed in her ear whenever Nate sauntered across the football field at practice. Nate was almost cute enough, nice enough. But enough for what? For whom? A simpler girl, one with far less ambition.

Not her, that was certain.

But long after Nate's varsity six-pack was softened by beer bought without the need of a fake ID, they were somehow still together. When she'd first mentioned that she was taking a year off (the truth felt too humiliating to utter aloud, even to Nate, who had barely managed to make it through senior year), he'd let out a whoop, picking her up off her feet and spinning her around in his arms. *It'll be perfect,* Nate had whispered in her ear, and with those words, she felt the sky close in around her.

Now I get to keep you, he said triumphantly, and with those words, the tinge of smugness in his intonation, she felt a wave of panic rise in her throat, and she smiled weakly in response. For Billie, it was like being voted into a club she had no desire to join.

For the last few years, like many of the kids she'd grown up with in Winter Harbor, she'd cobbled together something resembling a livelihood, juggling what felt at times like a dozen different jobs (for a few breakneck weeks each July and August) and at other times, namely deep winter, like nothing at all. Winter Harbor might have been a small town, but it had no shortage of gigs, stints, projects, and opportunities that paid a few bucks an hour—everything, it seemed, but an actual career. She'd done anything she could to make a buck in the years since she'd worn a cap and gown, short of digging clams. Instead, she waited tables, served coffee, shelved books, scooped ice cream, and pulled weeds.

But in early June, the summer of 1978, Nate struck gold, landing a job working as a driver at an estate in Bar Harbor for the season, steering the Archibalds' silver Rolls-Royce around town with one hand, picking up dry cleaning, and ferrying Eunice Archibald to an impressive number of lunches and garden parties. If he was lucky, the gig might even stretch into late summer—if the Archibalds stuck around long enough this year.

If they didn't, Nate planned to join his dad's roofing company, taking as many gigs as they could before the winter storms hit, the snow and ice making the act of standing on rooftops scattered with half-rotted shingles as precarious and unstable as their coupling. But somehow, when she sank into his narrow twin bed, his arms pulling her close, his lean body pressed against her own, solid as the oaks outside his window, none of that seemed to matter.

Especially now that she was stuck in Winter Harbor. Back when she believed her days in Maine were numbered, she'd been almost sad at the prospect of leaving. There were things she loved about the town, the old library with its smell of cedarwood and old books with their yellowing pages, a fireplace on the second floor that was always lit in the winter months; the tree-lined streets; the weathered salt antique capes lining the roads leading to the shore; and the harbor itself, the water steel-gray in the winter, achingly blue in summer.

But now, after three years of monotony, she dreaded opening her eyes to face the endless repetition of each day, the sun hitting the walls of her room like an assault. She didn't know how much longer she could stand it, the hours passing one after the next on an endless loop, her feet traversing the same well-worn path until she longed to throw her head back and scream into the wind.

She splashed water on her face as if in a trance and brushed her hair, a shoulder-length, nondescript brown, more mouse than chocolate, before walking the half mile to the ice cream stand where she'd managed to cobble together a few shifts a week. By the evening, her fingers were numb and frozen from scooping Rocky Road and Blueberry Crumble for the flocks of tourists who stampeded their way through town each summer. From that moment on, Billie despised ice cream, its icy sweetness a cloying reminder of her own helplessness.

She watched the cars as they pulled in and out of the lot, memorizing license plates as if they were a spell that could release her from purgatory: New York, Rhode Island, Vermont, Florida, California. Places she'd seen only in movies. She furrowed her forehead, brooding the way she always did when she fell into a funk she couldn't snap out of. Nate didn't know how good he had it. The Archibalds' estate was a new kingdom he entered daily, a passport to a world of satin dressing gowns, of yachts tethered out in the harbor, the sails unfurling in the breeze, ready to disembark on a whim for exotic ports of call. A place of possibility, where freedom was secured daily with stacks of crisp hundred-dollar bills.

"Are we going?" he asked, jamming his hands in his pockets and tilting his head to the side, that sly smile on his lips that usually made her clothes slide from her bones piece by piece. But at that moment, sex was the furthest thing from her mind. Her skin prickled slowly, inch by inch, as a flash of inspiration came over her, a spark she hadn't felt even once since her whole world had come crashing down. There was the sense of unshakable clarity, a tingling in her brain, her nerve endings sparking all at once.

"Forget about the bonfire for one second," she said impatiently as she plucked an elastic band from one wrist, pulling her hair back into a ponytail. "Do you think you could get me an interview? At the Archibalds' place? I can't believe you're getting paid five bucks an hour to drive a Rolls around the island, and I'm getting Popeye arms scooping ice cream for barely more than two."

"I guess so." Nate frowned, taking a step toward her, pulling her close to him so that her head rested on his shoulder. "But why would you want to do that?"

"Because," she said, pushing him away sharply and taking a step back, "I need to make some decent *money* for once." The anger had appeared suddenly, as if let out of prison, and she stood there burning, her whole body on fire. But somehow it felt right, as if after weeks of cold, dead slumber she were finally alive again. She thought of the way her father had waited every Friday afternoon for her mother to deposit her check into his waiting hand. How he would drink it all away before Monday had even arrived. How she'd had to stand by and watch as her friends packed their trunks and headed off to college, waving goodbye on the dock of the ferry, leaving her behind.

"For what?" he asked, the challenge in his voice ringing in the breeze that lifted her hair from the back of her neck, the air cooling rapidly as dusk fell. "Look, Billie, as soon as I have enough saved up, we can get a place of our own. Get married, maybe."

She felt her breath halt in her lungs at the thought. She wasn't sure what might be worse, marrying Nate or spending the rest of her life stuck in Winter Harbor. All she knew was that she didn't want to find out.

"Unless," he said, his eyes narrowing, "you think you're too good for this place." He went on, "Too good for me, maybe?" There was a glint of fear in his eyes, buried deep. The worry that he wasn't enough, not for her. Not for himself, either. That maybe he never would be.

"Not a chance," she said sweetly, swallowing the hard ball of her anger, dense as a lump of cartilage, as she moved closer to him, twining her arms around his neck. His irritation clung to him like static, but as their lips touched, she felt his limbs loosening as their kiss deepened and he drew her closer, his arms tightening around her waist.

Got him, she thought as she pulled gently away, a smile dancing at the corners of her lips.

"Damn, Billie," he said softly, almost as if he were surprised. "Look, if it's so important to you, I'll see what I can do," he added, shrugging as he walked around to the driver's side of his blue Ford pickup, a hand-me-down from his dad. "But I'm not promising anything."

Her smile grew wider as she opened the passenger-side door and jumped in, a feeling of relief sliding over her. Something had clicked into place, and she felt lighter already. The key swiftly turning, the tumblers moving fluidly, gracefully, as the door unlocked. She was always more grounded, more productive when she had a plan, something to bend to her will.

As they drove down the gravel road, bone-colored dust enveloping the car in a dense cloud, Billie could feel the apathy of the last few years sliding away, her driftlessness disappearing into the night air like a genie stuffed precariously back into its bottle.

~

The Archibalds' formal living room was like nothing she had ever seen, even though she'd taken the ferry across the narrow swath of water to attend the parties at the homes of the summer kids, families that swelled the population of Bar Harbor by a third each June. There had been fleets of cars, cavernous living rooms, yachts paneled with mahogany, gleaming with brass. But nothing could have prepared her for the sheer grandeur of the Archibalds' estate.

She rode her old red Schwinn down the long, gracefully curving drive and parked it in the bushes beside a silver Rolls-Royce, stopping to gaze up at the sprawling stone exterior. It was as if she'd stepped into a fairy tale, the ocean shimmering just beyond the stately gardens, the trees laden with early peaches, the hard green nubs of apples. The flower beds lining the circular drive were impeccably manicured, the hydrangea bushes, blue tinged with violet, appeared airbrushed, so perfect were the petals. Even the tangle of blush and crimson climbing roses stretching across the walls of the garden seemed to tiptoe carefully over the rough stone, resisting their own tendency to bolt.

Most magical of all was the stone fountain placed directly across from the front door. Bright sprays of water surrounded a mermaid, her hair long, falling in gentle coils, her tail carved with intricate scales. She gazed at Billie beatifically through the fine mist, rainbows shattering on stark white gravel, a whorled seashell resting between her two outstretched hands.

In the Archibalds' formal living room, Billie sat on a chair covered in yards of blush fabric, the overwhelming flounces of chintz reminiscent of a small bed. A Persian rug in shades of rose and ocher unfurled over the polished wooden floorboards, the crystal chandelier overhead sparkling gaily in the light streaming through the long french doors. The ceiling, impossibly high and painted a surprising, dusky blue, was the color of the robin's eggs tucked in the rafters of her own house in springtime, eggs that languished in nests fashioned from rough sticks and bits of paper, life fluttering inside each thin, pearlescent shell. Just from looking around at the room she waited in, or even the house itself, full of antiques polished with beeswax to a dull gleam, it was clear that Eunice Archibald abhorred disorder of any kind.

She wiped her palms distractedly on her jeans, wishing she'd thought to wear a skirt. The afternoon was uncharacteristically humid for Maine. Even in summer, temperatures generally stayed mild before turning downright chilly each evening. But today the air was sweltering, the humidity like a noose tightening, and Billie reached up, pushing her lank hair back from her shoulders as a woman entered the room, her mouth set in a tight, closed-lipped smile, her short, salt-and-pepper hair cropped close to her head in a pixie cut, like Audrey Hepburn's older sister.

Her slightly hooded eyes sized Billie up as if she were a tomato plucked from the estate's extensive gardens, in search of flaws that might render it unpalatable. She wore a pair of black cotton trousers and a black-and-white-striped boatneck top, the pallid square of an apron tied neatly around her waist, a pair of black ballet flats on her feet.

"I'm Adeline," she said as she approached, holding out a hand. "The house manager. You must be Billie."

Billie stumbled to her feet, taking the woman's hand in her own. The house manager's grip was firm, her hand cool and dry against Billie's own damp palm, and she recoiled in embarrassment, her cheeks flushing as she sat back down.

"You were referred by . . ." Adeline began, sitting on the couch directly across from Billie.

"Nate Proctor," Billie said quickly. "He mentioned the Archibalds might need summer help?"

Adeline stared at her thoughtfully. "Have you ever worked on an estate?"

"Well . . ." Billie began, hating how weak her voice sounded. She heard her mother's voice in her ear, a low hiss. *Sit up straight. Stop acting like you're lucky to be there.* When she'd told her mother that morning where she was headed, she'd folded her arms over her chest, leaning against the kitchen counter, her mug of Earl Grey steaming on the granite, untouched.

"Don't let them walk all over you," she said quietly, but firmly. Billie had just rolled her eyes, drinking the glass of orange juice her mother had poured for her in one long swallow. But now, sitting there amid all that opulence, Billie was starting to see how it might be possible to bend to that kind of will, to acquiesce so fluidly and gracefully that you might not even know you were doing it at all.

"I work at the Frozen Cone most afternoons. And the Lobster Pound on weekends."

Adeline was quiet for a moment, and for the first time, Billie noticed that although the estate was bustling with staff, the butler who had greeted her at the door, the chef in the kitchen, the maids she'd passed in the hallway, and the Archibalds themselves, the house itself was so still that it seemed almost uninhabited. She could hear birds twittering in the garden outside the long windows, the chaotic whir of a lawn mower from somewhere on the property. But unlike her own house, there was no yelling from room to room, no doors opening and closing, no sound of toilets flushing. She supposed that was what real money bought you, that silence.

"The position available is for the downstairs maid," Adeline said, breaking the quiet. "You would be in my charge, reporting to me directly."

"What would that . . . entail?" Billie asked, swallowing hard.

"You'd assist me in ensuring that the day-to-day operations of the house run smoothly. Help with any parties or events, and even work in the kitchen if need be. Marcus, our chef, is very particular, so I suggest you stay out of his way, unless expressly told otherwise." She nodded once sharply, as if to herself, then abruptly stood. Billie grabbed her worn black backpack from the floor by her chair, scrambling to her feet.

"Follow me," Adelaide said, turning and walking quickly out of the room. Billie took long strides to keep up, thankful for once for her height, the length of her legs, two things that had made her the butt of every joke in elementary school. *Giant,* they had screamed at her on the playground. *Beanpole.* She followed behind, as they walked out of the sitting room and down a long hallway, gilt-framed paintings of ships adorning the walls, the water a froth of indigo and turquoise.

The kitchen was empty but for racks of copper pans that hung from the ceiling, the windows overlooking a large herb and vegetable garden, the lush greenery punctuated by scarlet fruit. The counters were white marble, as was the cook's island that dominated the space. There was the ghost of bacon in the air, a quiche cooling on the stovetop. A pair of berry tarts rested on the marble counter, raspberries and blueberries glistening beneath a sugared glaze.

Adeline opened a drawer tucked discreetly beneath the island, pulling out a checkbook and a pen. It was then that she looked up, holding Billie's eyes with her own. Could she see it? Billie wondered. The hunger deep inside her, the unrelenting need to escape the only life she'd ever known?

Adeline nodded almost imperceptibly, then lowered her eyes as she flipped open the checkbook cover and began to write, the room quiet but for the sound of pen on paper. She pulled the check from the leather-bound book with a flourish, cutting the air as she held it out. "The salary is one hundred dollars a week," she said firmly. "I hope that's acceptable because the Archibalds don't negotiate. Here is a week's pay in advance—if you think the Frozen Cone can spare you, that is." Her thin lips twitched with a smile.

"That will be fine," Billie said quickly, too stunned to say more. In that moment, relief washed over her, and for the very first time in her young life, she felt the certainty that money could buy, the peace it might offer. She could save up for college, maybe buy some new clothes. Standing in the Archibalds' pristine kitchen, she was more aware than ever that her jeans were at least two inches too short, hovering at her ankles. She could pass it off as deliberate in the summer months, but every time she looked down, she knew the truth.

As she took the slip of paper, her fingers brushed against Adeline's. The woman's eyes widened, and she pulled back as if she had been scalded. Without a word she turned abruptly and strode out of the room, Billie quickly following as they walked down the long hall once again.

"You'll start tomorrow," Adeline commanded, without stopping or turning around, and soon they had reached the massive oak front door, which opened soundlessly under Adeline's hands, the scent of summer drifting in, roses and freshly cut grass hovering on sea air. Billie stepped outside, a lawn mower whirring in the distance, and as she turned to face Adeline, a shaft of sunlight cut between them, sharp as a blade. The door closed and Billie was alone on the doorstep, her future hovering so close she could almost reach out and touch it.

Chapter Eight

The garden, strung with fairy lights, was Cinderella's kingdom, the clock striking eight, hours to go until midnight. The silver tray of canapés she held between her hands was lined with small bites of seared sea scallops and crimson roe, the shellfish bathed in butter and sautéed till golden, and though her stomach rumbled in protest, she didn't dare sneak even a morsel. Billie plucked at the collar of the short-sleeved blouse she wore, sweating beneath the demure high neck, the sleeves puffed as mooncakes.

When she'd stepped out onto her front porch earlier that night in the required staff uniform—the white blouse and a pair of black pants—she'd felt hopelessly overdressed. But here, among the gowns that trailed the floor in flashes of sequins and gold, satin the color of the midnight sky, a trail of sparkling jet beads, she faded into the background immediately, like a pencil drawing being slowly erased on a stark white page. That sleight of hand, Billie supposed, as she watched the guests swirl around the garden, white teeth and scarlet manicures flaring in the light, was probably the entire point.

It was the first party of the season, Bar Harbor's elite all awaiting the same impeccable experience, the same seamless luxury, as in years prior. "It is imperative," Adeline had told them as the help had lined up as if it were a military drill, "that there are no mistakes. The Archibalds do not tolerate errors of any kind." And by *the Archibalds*, Billie knew she was referring to Eunice, who, even after working at the house for the past week, she had yet to meet. Admiral Archibald had passed by once or twice, humming to himself as he strolled past her and into the kitchen, squat and gray-haired, with a sizable paunch. She could hear him rummaging in the fridge for one of the platters of hard-boiled eggs and slices of aged cheddar that were kept in readiness for him. "Protein!" he would call out jovially. "That's the ticket!"

She'd heard Eunice's unmistakable nasal voice echoing through the halls of the enormous house, but when she peeked her head out, the corridors were always empty, and only her perfume still hung in the air, the laconic stupor of hot milk, exotic spices that called to mind silken tents and sweets fashioned from candied almonds. Turkish delight. Rose petals steeped in sugared cream.

It was the scent of crisp bills. Of limitlessness.

Of freedom.

In the past week, Billie had polished furniture and swept until the muscles in her forearms stood out like cords beneath her skin. When she arrived home each night, she fell into bed exhausted, and no matter how much she bathed, the scent of beeswax and lemon clung to the tips of her fingers. But despite her hard work, the results never seemed to be enough to satisfy Adeline, who watched her ministrations with the keen eyes of a hawk. "Do it right, Billie," she said on more than one occasion, taking the tin of polish from her hands, the soft rag, and wiping an armoire in clear, deliberate circles. "Or don't do it at all."

She spent her days trailing after Adeline, shadowing her as if she were a stray dog, watching as she nimbly folded a white linen napkin into the shape of a swan, placing it on the gleaming cherrywood of the Archibalds' dining room table. The few times they'd walked through the kitchen, Marcus, an impossibly tall, thin presence who towered over the other cooks, would nod tersely whenever they made eye contact. *You do not belong here,* his eyes seemed to inform her without his deigning to speak a single word.

"Remember to stay out of his way," Adeline muttered one unseasonably warm June morning as they passed through the stifling kitchen on the way to the back gardens. "Unless he says otherwise." The ovens were on full blast, the yeasty scent of freshly baked bread filling the humid air, and Billie reached up, surreptitiously wiping the sweat from her brow with the palm of one hand as she followed her out the back door, a clipboard tucked under one arm. Adeline moved in long strides over the grounds, toward the burly crew of landscapers Eunice had hired to "spruce up" the gardens. Looking around, Billie could hardly imagine how anything might be improved upon at all, the profusion of roses and peonies, their shy, drooping heads the color of a maiden's blush, the winding path of crushed oyster shells leading down to the greenhouse, the strip of azure sea just beyond.

Suddenly, there was a rustling, an intake of breath, and the buzz of conversation came to an abrupt halt as Eunice Archibald entered the garden clad in a long white gown, as if the moon itself had been harnessed and spun into satin, the material so artfully draped that it seemed an extension of her spare frame, wasp-waisted in the center and flowing out like the undulating sea to pool at her feet. In her early forties, Eunice Archibald seemed invincible, at the very height of her sexual power. A force emanated from her, a kind of magnetism that caused the guests to turn toward her, as if welcoming the sun. Billie watched, open-mouthed, as Eunice swept through the crowd, shaking hands and air-kissing soft, powdered cheeks, the breath catching in her throat as she realized that not only was Eunice moving in her direction, she was headed right for her.

Up close Eunice Archibald was even more dazzling. Diamonds dropped from her earlobes, long sprays just grazing her bare shoulders. Her skin was flawless and unlined, the color of milk, a bluish tint lurking just below the surface, offsetting her carefully drawn scarlet lips, her glossy blonde hair pulled back in a neat chignon resting at the nape of her long neck. She took Billie in coolly with a practiced gaze, and under that scrutiny, Billie felt her hands begin to shake, the tray of canapés she held wobbling dangerously.

"We need more champagne glasses," Eunice said, staring at her pointedly, taking in the blouse she wore, almost threadbare at the collar, her gaze moving lower to catalog the cheap black pants, the scuffed black shoes on her feet.

"I'll get them," Billie said, swallowing hard before turning and heading for the kitchen, glad for any excuse to escape Eunice's penetrating gaze. She navigated the garden path, careful not to trip (that would be a disaster, she knew), and opened the back door, which led directly into the kitchen. Cooks stood around the stove, and the counters were full of food: oysters on the half shell surrounded by lemon wedges, thinly sliced prosciutto wrapped around balls of cantaloupe, platters of meticulously arranged water crackers fanned out in a circle surrounding wedges of brie and triple cremes, silver dishes of green olives, red eyes glistening in their glossy, oiled skins.

Marcus stood at the island, rolling out pastry into sheets so thin they were almost translucent. He wore a pristine white chef's hat, and when he looked up, his dark eyes, though sunken, took her in factually, cataloging her as if she were just another ingredient to work with. He was clean shaven, the bones of his face prominent and sharp. His hands were dotted with age spots, and the dusting of hair under his chef's cap was pure white.

"Yes?" he barked. "What do you need?"

"Champagne glasses," she said apologetically.

"The *coupes* are over there," he muttered, pointing with his knife to a stack of boxes on the floor, then turning his attention back to the shallots.

Coupes, Billie repeated to herself as she walked over and grabbed a box of them. She liked the way the word sounded on her lips, how wide the mouths of the glasses were, the crystal sparkling like a rare gem.

Just as she was about to walk back out the door, there was a cry, then a sharp clatter. Billie turned round to see one of the cooks standing at the stove, a look of horror on his face as he brought one hand up to his mouth. The room went silent, everything came to a halt, the other cooks frozen in their tracks, as if a magic wand had been waved. A baking sheet that had once held mini butterscotch soufflés, each tucked into its own ramekin, was strewn across the tile floor. Miraculously, none of the dishes had broken, but the soufflés inside had sunk disastrously, as if they'd been rendered suddenly lifeless.

The offending cook stood there, his face ashen, his eyes fixed on the floor. "I can make more," he said quietly. "I'm sorry, chef."

Marcus strode over, his lips set in a thin line. "There isn't time," he snapped. "Pick all this up." The boy just stared at him, as if paralyzed by fear. "NOW!" Marcus yelled, and the room sprang into action. Billie stood there, still gripping the box of coupes in her arms. Without thinking, she set the box down on the floor and strode over to the mess, picking up the ramekins one by one and placing them deliberately on the marble island. Before anyone could stop her and working entirely on instinct, she grabbed a spoon and, taking one of the dishes between her hands, began stirring the deflated soufflé. On top of tumbling to the ground, the soufflés had been plucked from the hot oven too soon, and the cake hadn't set enough, the centers still liquefied.

"Is there any whipped cream?" she called out, and seconds later, a metal bowl appeared at her side. Billie spooned the white clouds into the ramekin, stirring the cream vigorously until the color lightened to pale beige. She was lost in her own thoughts, moving from one dish to the next, when a hand on her shoulder snapped her back into the present. She looked up to find Marcus peering at her intently, his bushy white eyebrows raised.

"What exactly," he began, "do you think you're doing?"

"Do you have any raspberries? Fresh mint leaves?" she said quickly, her brain still on autopilot. "You can just say it's a summer pudding."

There was a long silence, and the room was still. Billie was aware of the cooks and caterers hovering nearby, how the servers who had entered the kitchen in the middle of the catastrophe now waited silently in the doorway. Her hands were still wrapped around a ramekin, the whipped cream still stood in soft peaks in the silver bowl, but now the full weight of what she had done crashed down on her shoulders, her cheeks flushing hot with blood. They would fire her, she knew. She had trespassed unforgivably, breached the boundaries of decorum and upset what she now realized was a delicate balance. She felt it in her bones, that misstep, like a stumble on rough pavement.

"I'm sorry," she said quietly, releasing the ramekin and taking a step back, her hands now empty. She looked down at her feet, at the low-heeled pair of black pumps she wore. Anything to avoid seeing the judgment of the servers, the look of dismay on the chef's face. He released his grip from her shoulder, and she sighed, wondering if there was any way she could head for the back door without making eye contact with anyone.

But before she could take even one step, Marcus's voice rang out, sharp and authoritative, and she looked up in surprise. "You heard her! Bring what she needs!"

The room exploded once again in a bustle of activity, as if a switch had been thrown, and a basket of raspberries was plunked down in front of her alongside a pile of freshly washed mint leaves. She turned back to the ramekins still waiting on the counter and began carefully garnishing the makeshift puddings with careful sprays of fruit and herbs, her hands moving quickly, as if someone might snatch it all away at any moment.

"And who has taken over my kitchen?" Marcus asked, and for the first time, she noticed the hint of an accent in his voice, buried beneath the gruffness of his voice and all but lost over the years.

"I'm Billie," she said as she placed a berry atop the final dish. "Billie Abbot."

"Would you like to work in this kitchen? Three mornings a week, perhaps?"

Billie's hands froze in midair.

"I . . . I need to check with Adeline," she stammered as Marcus reached over and began arranging the puddings on a silver tray.

"I will speak to Adeline," Marcus grunted in a way that might have been laughter, or as close as he ever got to it. She felt her lips twitch at the corners, then stretch tentatively into a smile. The sweat beneath her arms and the dots of perspiration on her forehead felt good and cleansing, the heat from the stove radiating like a sauna.

But then, there was a prickling along her spine, her arms turning to gooseflesh as she turned to see a flash of silver satin in the doorway, briefly, briefly. So quick that she could almost convince herself she had imagined it. She turned back around, hoisting in one hand a canister of powdered sugar that Marcus had placed at her elbow and sprinkling it liberally over the tops of the puddings. As the sugar landed like freshly fallen snow, she replayed Eunice's disdainful glare in her mind, a look that let her know without a doubt that she didn't belong at this vast estate any more than she belonged in Winter Harbor.

But someday I will, she told herself firmly as she finished dusting the last of the puddings, hastily wiping her hands on the front of her pants and leaving a trail of stark white on the thin black cotton.

Chapter Nine

"Aprons are in there," Marcus commanded, pointing at the long closet off to the side of the kitchen, near the back door. Billie walked over and opened it, grabbing the starched white cloth from a row of hooks inside. She tied it around her waist before walking back over, standing tentatively behind him. She'd been up since 5:00 a.m., tapping one foot rhythmically against the table leg, drinking cup after cup of black coffee long before her mother entered the kitchen in her pink robe, still yawning, her hair tousled from sleep.

"Good god, Billie, stop that banging!" her mother snapped, putting the kettle on for her usual mug of Earl Grey. Her mother could hardly be described as a morning person, and judging by her tone, today was clearly no exception. Sometimes Billie would wander downstairs at 3:00 a.m., her throat parched, half-bleary from the labyrinth of her dreams, to find Grace sitting at the kitchen table, a bowl of bread dough rising quietly in a ceramic bowl glazed the blank blue of a midsummer sky. Her mother loved the pin-dropping silence of the middle of the night, how that stillness performed its own elaborate sorcery, lengthening time until every passing hour felt like three. In the light of day, the click of the gas jet on the stove was reassuring, a sound that had always meant home and safety to Billie, but despite that fact, she still couldn't seem to relax.

"They're just people," her mother grumbled, shaking her head as she retrieved the container of half-and-half from the depths of the icebox. "At least in the kitchen you might actually learn something useful."

But now that she was standing in the Archibalds' kitchen, early-morning sunlight splashing over the terrazzo floors as she awaited instructions, Billie couldn't help wondering whether she was up to the challenge. Practically speaking, she knew just enough to get her in trouble, and the few tricks she'd picked up from her mother over the years hardly made her a culinary prodigy. She shifted her weight nervously from one foot to the other, waiting for the axe to fall.

"*Beside* me," Marcus barked, taking her by the shoulders and moving her so that she stood next to him at the counter. "Never behind or you will be in my way. And I do not like *anyone* in my way."

Billie swallowed hard, surreptitiously wiping damp palms on the front of her apron, watching as he walked over to the refrigerator, opened the door, and rummaged around inside, grabbing a large glass bottle of heavy cream before turning to look at her pointedly. "You know how to make crème anglaise?" he asked, putting the bottle down in front of her in a way that let her know this wasn't a mere request, but a challenge.

"I do," she said, her relief palpable. Her mother had shown her last summer in a tart phase, spending her weekends obsessively perfecting her crust and fiddling incessantly with the oven temperature while Billie handled the fillings. Without asking permission, she reached up, plucking a gleaming copper saucepan from the rack overhead, turning it over in her hands.

"Then get to work," he said, pointing over at the stove, a silver-and-black restaurant-style range with six burners. The height and heft of it frightened her, and she took a deep breath, steeling herself, as if entering into battle. She'd only ever used the old GE range in their kitchen at home, the back burner fussy, lighting only half the time. *Does it use gas? Does it have temperature control dials and an oven? Then you can handle it,* her mother said in her ear, and without missing a beat, Billie put the pan on the front burner, filling it with rich cream that coated the bottom of the saucepan luxuriously, the grassy scent filling her senses.

~

That first week in the kitchen flew by in a blur. She chopped endless piles of vegetables, her hands red and raw as beef carpaccio from running them under a stream of hot water, her knuckles slivered with cuts that made tears spring to her eyes whenever she squeezed the tough skin of a lemon or added a sprinkling of coarse sea salt to a dish, her fingertips redolent of the onions she diced, the garlic cloves she coaxed from their skins.

She sautéed and browned butter until her hands moved automatically and her past and future were distant memories. She thought of nothing beyond what she might do after the golden cubes of butter were added, the sauce thickened, the water boiled. Each night when she collapsed into bed, the minute her head hit the pillow, she sank into deep, dreamless sleep, as if she'd been born to it.

In a way, it was a relief.

After only a few days working alongside Marcus, they fell into a kind of rhythm, a dance, one that felt nearly effortless. She seemed to know what he needed seconds before he might turn and ask, and she knew how to stay quiet, working in the silence he not only preferred but demanded. It was reverent, as if the kitchen and the gardens stretching behind were their own chapel. Not built of stone and glass, but of herbs and the crisp heads of lettuce Billie learned to pull from the garden beds in the early morning, dew still clinging to the tight, verdant leaves.

The kitchen staff erupted into whispers when she walked past, snickering under their breath, so quick was their demotion upon her arrival. But despite those small, daily annoyances, there was a feeling of rightness, of belonging in that space that seemed to exist for her alone. Each time she pulled a tray of plump cinnamon rolls from the oven, setting them on cooling racks for the Archibalds' midmorning tea, or glazed a peach tart, the apricot jam thinned out with hot water the way Marcus had shown her, Billie felt a sense of lightness steal over her, a peace she'd experienced nowhere else. Her mother's tutelage had been the spark, the inspiration. But the precision and level of detail she was expected to master in the Archibalds' enormous kitchen were in another league entirely. The crust of the tart was flecked with nutmeg, the caviar at dinner accompanied by silver bowls of sour cream, florid green chives she snipped from the herb garden with kitchen scissors, eggs she plucked from the henhouse, brushing off the errant feathers stuck to the warm brown shells before they were hard-boiled and chopped.

The Archibalds did things differently, Billie noticed. They were one of the only wealthy families in the vicinity who insisted that their gardens remain free of pesticides, that the food they consumed sprang from the island's rocky, temperamental soil as much as possible. "Each spring, she brings in enough compost to start her own farm," Marcus explained. "They have adopted the French way, eating with the seasons and from the land."

"Is that where you're from?" she asked, unable to stanch her curiosity.

Marcus snorted, shooting her a look of disdain. "I am Belgian," he said. "But I have lived here since the war."

"What do they do . . . in New York?" Billie asked quietly, unable to imagine mounds of rich, dark soil delivered in piles to the wraparound terraces of the Archibalds' penthouse apartment.

"They travel much of the year, and are hardly there," Marcus said with a shrug of his bony shoulders. As much as he cooked and baked throughout the course of a day, Billie had never seen him ingest even the smallest morsel. He seemed to be nourished by the warm, fragrant air of the kitchen itself.

In contrast, Billie fell to the staff meal she helped assemble at 1:00 p.m. each day as if she'd been starved for weeks. The food wasn't fancy: huge salads with watercress, endive, and lettuce still warm from the rays of the sun. Lamb chops grilled with sprigs of rosemary. Angel hair pasta flecked with lemon and studded with finely minced garlic. But it was alive in a way Billie had never experienced before. The long bunches of onions she brunoised for stews and sauces still had dirt clinging to their stems. The tomatoes she plucked from their fragrant, herbal vines seemed to pulse in her hands, richly red and flooded with tiny seeds. When she cut bunches of basil from the prolific patch near the garden gate, she couldn't help bringing the green leaves to her nose and drinking in their aroma, as if it were rich perfume.

"Colin has graduated from Yale, like his father before him," Marcus muttered as he stuffed potatoes whipped with butter, cream, and Gruyère back into their jackets. "Presently, he is up to God knows what in Europe somewhere. I shudder to think of it." His words dripped with distaste.

"Who's Colin?" Billie asked absentmindedly as she passed Marcus the bowl of fresh parsley she'd just finished chopping.

"The sole heir to the Archibald name, of course. Everything rides on him. Though I doubt he's up to the challenge." Marcus let out a small laugh, opening the oven door and sliding the tray of soon-to-be twice-baked potatoes inside. "He'll show up here eventually. He always does."

She nodded, wiping down the wooden cutting board with a wet cloth. It made no difference to her. Ever since she'd started working for the Archibalds, she'd seen Nate less and less, which had proved less difficult than she'd anticipated, considering they worked in the same house. But Nate was often in town, driving the admiral to the yacht club or Eunice to one of her many clubs and lunches, so they were rarely, if ever, in the same location at even remotely the same time.

There was a series of quick, light steps in the hall, the sound coming closer, advancing toward the kitchen, and Marcus stood a bit straighter, his back stiffening in anticipation as Eunice Archibald entered the room dressed in tennis whites, a gold bracelet shining on one bare wrist. Her pale skin was flushed from the sun, the top of her patrician nose pinkened. Her blonde hair was pulled into a low ponytail, the slope of her forehead both intelligent and unlined. Even dressed casually, her spine was straight as a broomstick. Her perfume hovered in the air, salt spray and Sicilian lemons, and Billie found herself transfixed, unable to look away.

"So," Eunice said after a long moment, her steely gaze fixed on Billie's face. "You're the girl who saved my party from certain disaster."

Billie swallowed hard, nodding once, quickly, in agreement.

"Adeline tells me your name is Elizabeth," Eunice went on, trailing her fingertips along the marble island.

"It's Billie, actually."

Eunice looked at her in surprise. "I have always hated the practice of abbreviating one's name. In fact, I firmly believe it does one no good whatsoever to make herself smaller in any way. The world will make one small enough, in due time. Don't you agree?"

"I guess I've never really thought about it," Billie said, aware that all eyes in the kitchen were upon her. That the rest of the cooks had stopped in their tracks and were listening intently.

There was a long moment where Eunice just looked at her, a hint of questioning in her gaze, and in that moment, Billie wondered what, if anything, might cause Eunice's blood pressure to rise. She could not imagine her angry, or in the throes of passion, twisting beneath the admiral the way Billie often did in Nate's bed, her body moving in a rhythm she didn't have to think about, one that was as natural as the migration of the birds south every fall, in search of balmier climates. She could barely imagine the woman standing before her breaking a sweat on the tennis court. Even standing there, fresh from the game, Eunice didn't tolerate anything as plebeian as perspiration. Instead, she glistened, the creases in her skirt perfectly placed, as if it had just been ironed moments before.

"I was wondering if you might join me for tea at the Claremont this afternoon? I like to meet with all of my staff personally, just to get acquainted."

Billie's head spun. She thought of the petits fours she baked each morning, covering the small cakes in thick slices of pink and white fondant. The finger sandwiches she arranged so carefully on the sil-ver tea stand: cucumber and watercress, salmon and cream cheese, the spread flecked with fresh chives. How would she know which fork to use? What on earth was she even wearing? She looked down at her navy cotton skirt, marred with flour handprints. Her mind raced with ques-tions, one more daunting than the next as Eunice stood there, waiting for an answer.

"Sure," she managed to squeak out, and Eunice dipped her chin, then turned her back and, without another word, walked out of the kitchen. As the sound of her steps receded, Billie finally exhaled. When she looked down at her hands, they were lightly trembling, not only from nervousness, but excitement, too. But there were distractions at hand, and so she busied herself with preparations for the midday meal: searing the flank steak, grilling the long, green stalks of asparagus that would accompany the potatoes.

As Marcus pulled the tray from the oven, Billie's gaze drifted out over the back window to where Eunice stood in the garden, her back to the house, the profusion of blossoms and greenery framing her silhou-ette as if she'd been planted there herself, overshadowing the foliage and dominating it completely.

Chapter Ten
JULES

Maine in the early winter was frigid and wet, the mud sticking to Jules's boots as they trudged through the rental car lot at the Bangor airport. The flight had been smooth, and she'd spent the duration of it staring into the empty sky while Noah took notes on his laptop beside her, the sound of his fingers tapping the keys bringing her to the precipice of sleep. Every time she thought about her mother, Jules felt her eyelids grow heavy, the exhaustion of the last few months clinging to her like a stubborn child.

Aside from a weekend trip to Ogunquit with her father when she was six years old, Jules had never spent any real time in Maine. Her mother had always preferred the beaches of Cape Cod and Martha's Vineyard. *Maine is far too rocky,* she'd say disdainfully. *The Cape is so much more civilized, Julie.* Over the years, and despite her roots, Elizabeth had somehow managed to avoid the state altogether.

Maybe that should've been her first clue.

$\sim$

Jules had stood in the kitchen the following morning, after Mark had left for work, the scent of coffee beans hovering in the air, Elizabeth's old cashmere robe wrapped around her like good French butter. Her mother's things were still where she had left them that August morning she had slipped away, her aprons still on brass hooks on the kitchen wall, her straw hats neatly stacked by the back door, her garden dead and withered now, the ground beginning to freeze. But Jules knew the myriad possessions Elizabeth had left behind, her silver hand mirror, the memorabilia and magazine cover stories packed neatly in boxes in the attic, her mother's clothes hanging in the closet, arranged by color and season as if they were waiting for her to return home—those paltry things couldn't even begin to tell her who Elizabeth really was.

Before she could think too much about it or change her mind, she grabbed her phone, scrolling through her contacts until she found Noah's name. She moved quickly, scared she might not send a text at all if she waited even one second longer.

I'm in.

His response was almost immediate.

You don't want a few days to think about it?

Jules had never been the type to laboriously ponder her choices until they became fuzzy and indistinct, losing all meaning. But over the past few years, she'd grown meek, hesitant, smaller. More unsure, a quality that Elizabeth's death had only amplified. It was hard to believe she was still the same woman who'd once booked flights to Zurich or Milan on a whim, throwing a few articles of clothing in a duffel bag, arriving at the airport with only moments to spare.

She could do this. She could do hard things. Maybe, like so much of her personality, the things she'd hidden away over the years, stuffed inside the cavern of memory until they were the faintest of glimmers, she'd forgotten that about herself.

She was her mother's daughter, after all.

~

The Maine sky was the color of concrete, a light drizzle pelting their backs as they climbed into the rental car, a black SUV with four-wheel drive, which the attendant explained was "crucial" at this time of year. The road to Bar Harbor was dotted with late snow, resting in patches on the side of the road, the trees bare as sylphs, bending in the wind as if to entice them. Jules shivered, reaching over to blast the heat.

"I was surprised to get your text," Noah said. "I thought you'd need at least a week to think it over. Actually"—he laughed—"I thought I'd probably never hear from you again."

"I considered it."

"What? Never contacting me again?"

"Yep."

"Was it my wit, my charm, or my impeccable journalistic skills that made you change your mind?"

Jules fought back a smile as she rummaged in the folds of her coat for her phone.

"None of the above," she said as she opened her text messages, replying to her last thread with Mark. **Made it**, she wrote before shoving her phone back into her pocket, where it buzzed in response almost immediately.

Love you, he'd written when she'd retrieved it once again, a sentiment she hearted in return before tucking it away.

"Ouch." Noah chuckled, turning onto the highway. "But seriously, why did you? I'm curious."

"You're curious about a lot, aren't you?"

"Comes with the territory."

"I thought about what you said," Jules began, glancing over at him. Noah was dressed for the cold in a heavy navy sweater and black wool coat, jeans stuffed into boots. His dark hair looked freshly trimmed, and unlike their first meeting, he was clean shaven. It made him look younger somehow, more like the man whose photo she'd seen in Page

Six years ago, grinning into the lens as if the world of fame and privilege he found himself inhabiting were an inside joke to which only he knew the punch line.

"I say a lot of things. What are you referring to in particular?"

"That I should know who my mother really was."

"You seemed pretty sure of that already," Noah said as he flipped on the radio.

"If I were, I wouldn't be here," Jules replied, reaching up to rub her eyes, her mother's face appearing out of the darkness like an X-ray, outlined in brilliant pulses of light. Jules sighed, then opened her eyes again, leaning forward and turning up the volume, the car filling with the mournful plucking of guitar strings.

Noah stayed quiet, his eyes focused on the road, every mile marker bringing them closer to the truth.

~

Bar Harbor was storybook cute, its main street lined with shops, most shuttered for winter, the buildings painted in a rainbow of coral pinks and vibrant blues that echoed the harbor that surrounded them. There were stores selling homemade fudge and chocolates; ice cream stands; storefronts cluttered with souvenirs, T-shirts, and tote bags; antique shops, their windows stuffed with old rocking chairs and intricate quilts, the cotton faded to the barest suggestion of color, like a whisper in a dark room.

With the tourists all but gone, the streets were deserted, and as they parked on a side street and exited the car, Jules clutched the wrinkled snapshot in her hand, one of the only photos she had of her mother as a young girl. In the photograph, Elizabeth stared into the camera, smiling broadly, her hair a muted brown, so different from the sleek golden tresses that had propelled her to stardom. Hair that had fallen out almost immediately as soon as the chemotherapy began, strands of it clumped on the marble floor of her shower like the nests perched outside her kitchen windows.

In the first few stores they entered, the owners looked at them blankly as soon as Noah made it clear that they weren't shopping. "I was hoping I could ask you a quick question, actually," he began. "I'm looking for someone who grew up here, and I was wondering if you might recognize her," he'd add, then hold out the picture.

"Don't know her," one man said gruffly before turning his back on them and disappearing behind the counter and into the back before they could ask any more questions. At the candy shop, the air rich and sweet with the scent of melting chocolate, the long cases filled with dense blocks of fudge in every flavor, the cashier glanced quickly at the photo, then shook her head.

"I just moved here a few months ago," she said apologetically. "I'm sorry."

In a faded turquoise storefront, T-shirts hung from racks, waving in the wind out front, and inside, there were snow globes tucked onto the counters, crystals balls surrounding the hulls of ships, the white pillars of a lighthouse. The elderly shopkeeper peered at the photo through the thickest pair of bifocals Jules had ever seen. Her white hair was cut into a neat bob, and she pushed an errant strand behind one ear as she took the photograph in her hands, studying it closely. "I wish I could help," she finally said, her voice shaky, tinged with regret.

"You really don't know her?" Noah pressed, as she placed the photo back on the glass counter. "She lived here a long time ago, in the 1970s."

The old woman shook her head, and when she looked up, her dark eyes were cloudy and myopic. "I'm sorry," she repeated. "My memory isn't what it used to be, but even so, I don't recognize her." The door to the shop opened again, and a young couple entered, two small boys trailing behind them, immediately letting out a screech as they ran toward the small selection of toys in the back.

As soon as they'd left the shop, the wind coming off the water cut through her coat as if it were made of paper, gusting around them, and

Jules turned to Noah in frustration. "Maybe you're wrong," she muttered as they stood in front, bells chiming at their back. "Maybe this is a waste of time."

"If you really believed that," Noah said as they began to make their way down the street, stopping on the sidewalk in front of her, his breath puffing white smoke in the cold air, "you wouldn't have come."

Jules stared at him, hating the fact that he was right, racking her brain for a smart reply and coming up empty. "I'm hungry," she finally blurted out, which was true, but wasn't at all what she wanted to tell him. What she wanted to say was, *You don't know anything about my mother.* But even though they hadn't uncovered a single clue yet, she also knew, albeit grudgingly, that she was impatient, and he was right. Her empty stomach growled noisily in protest—the last thing she'd eaten was a small pack of peanuts on the plane.

"I think there's a place down the street," Noah said, cupping his hands in front of his face and blowing into them for warmth.

～

Jake's Diner was as old-school as it got, with its red leather booths and chrome-dipped stools lining the counter. Jules's heart leaped at the sight of the sugared doughnuts stacked under a glass dome, the carousel of thickly frosted cakes and latticed fruit pies spinning lazily near the front counter. Everything in the place was slightly worse for wear, from the chipped Formica tables to the scuffed, yellowing linoleum on the floor, the doughy scent of pancakes, and the smoky sizzle of bacon hanging in the air. The place was nearly empty, but for two lone customers silently eating the lunch special: a roast beef sandwich au jus flanked by a mound of mashed potatoes. It was the kind of food her mother had unexpectedly loved.

Home cooking is honest, she'd always said. *Unafraid to show its hand.*

The waitress, a woman who looked to be in her sixties, her short hair dyed a flaming red, approached them slowly, coffeepot in hand.

Without asking, she filled the porcelain cups before them with a tight-lipped smile, then slapped down two menus before walking off. Chilled to the bone, Jules was glad for the warmth of the coffee, if only to wrap her hands around, the steam rising from the inky liquid. She reached for the metal pitcher of cream, pouring it into her mug until the color lightened to a creamy beige.

"This is going to be harder than I thought," she said, as Noah shrugged off his coat.

"Did you honestly think we were going to just waltz into town and figure it all out in the first five minutes?" Noah laughed, grabbing his mug and bringing it to his lips.

"Maybe she wasn't from Bar Harbor at all," Jules pointed out, dodging the question. "Or even New England. Did you ever think of that?"

"That's what we're here to find out," Noah said, removing his glasses and rubbing his eyes distractedly. "We'll keep asking questions, and if the photo doesn't pan out, I'll check out city hall, really dig into the archives—and there are a few spots your mom mentioned in interviews that I want to check out to see if details track. If they do, we'll at least know she spent significant time here, whether she was born and raised in Bar Harbor or not. We may not get to it all in this trip, but we'll get there. The beginning is always the hardest part."

His eyes, she noticed, were tired looking and bloodshot. The rush to the airport, the plane ride, the long drive from Bangor had taken their toll. Without the armor of his glasses, his face looked softer, more exposed. She knew almost nothing, she realized, about him at all. "Did you always want to be a writer?" she asked impulsively.

"God, no." Noah laughed, running a hand through his hair, leaning back against the booth. "When I was a kid, I wanted to be a firefighter. Then an explorer." He laughed again, picking up his mug and holding it aloft. "Which would've been pretty hard to pull off in Chippewa Falls. But in high school, I got involved in the school paper, and went on to major in journalism at Northwestern. And the minute I got my diploma, I headed for New York." He paused for a swallow of coffee.

"I'd seen all the movies. Read the profiles in the *New Yorker*. Why be on the metro desk at the *Milwaukee Journal Sentinel* when I could be rubbing tweed-patched elbows with Mailer and Rushdie?"

"Well, if those were your options." Jules raised an eyebrow.

"Believe it or not, I really thought they were." Noah smiled. "I ended up sharing a two-bedroom apartment in Hell's Kitchen with four other writers," he said, shaking his head as if in disbelief. "I was a total cliché, sitting in dive bars and coffeehouses, scribbling down every thought that raced through my brain. I wanted it more than I'd ever wanted anything: the front-page review in the *New York Times*, the book parties at KGB Bar, readings at the 92nd Street Y."

"I guess you got what you wanted, right?"

Noah just looked at her, his green eyes tinged with sadness. "Not entirely," he said after a long moment. "Not exactly."

"How so?"

"Well, I'm definitely more comfortable now than I was back then," Noah said lightly, putting the mug back down on the table. "At least financially. I have Sydelle to thank for that."

"Ghostwriting pays well, then?"

"I have no complaints," Noah replied. "It's easy work in the sense that the books pretty much write themselves. I conduct a series of interviews, pick and choose the best stories, and write it all down." He shrugged. "But what about you?" He picked up the menu in front of him, glancing at the first page.

"Me?" Jules answered blankly.

"I mean," Noah said, looking up, "you're the sole heir to your mother's legacy. But is that really what you want to do? Be Elizabeth?"

Her mother's photo was still gripped tightly in one hand, and Jules uncurled her fingers, placing the wrinkled snapshot on the table. Elizabeth's soft, unlined face smiled up at her, and the hope in those blue eyes, a kind of wistful naivete, made her chest ache. She thought back to afternoons in the darkroom at Cornell, agitating a print in its bath of developer with a gentle rocking of her wrist, the image shimmering into focus. She could've stayed in that room for days, only the gleam of the red bulb to sustain her, her hands working so surely, as if their skill were not merely practiced but innate. That one small room, she realized now—too late—was the one place in the world where she did not, even once, doubt herself.

You're so gifted, Julie, Elizabeth had marveled when Jules laid out her senior portfolio on her mother's dining room table, a series of underwater self-portraits, the ripples marking the soft planes of her face, as if she'd aged suddenly overnight. *I have the most marvelous idea!* she'd exclaimed, grabbing Jules's arm and squeezing it firmly in her excitement. *You must do the photos for the new book!*

Jules thought of the email she'd sent to a gallery downtown, and the enthusiastic reply waiting in her inbox, offering her an internship. *We need you desperately,* her mother went on, and her voice quieted as she leaned closer, her eyes searching Jules's own.

I need you.

And with those words, Jules felt herself weaken, the last remnants of her resolve sliding away as Elizabeth's hand grasped on more tightly, until Jules finally nodded, her mother's face relaxing into a smile.

"You ready to order?" the waitress asked, snapping Jules out of her reverie, and she looked up, startled, before glancing down at the menu, ravenous now. She wanted it all: a cheeseburger deluxe and a pile of crispy golden fries. The lobster club with potato chips, a dill pickle on the side. A wedge of French silk pie, a cloud of whipped cream on top.

"Ham-and-cheese omelet, hash browns, and rye toast," Noah said decisively, handing over his menu.

The waitress accepted it with a terse nod, sticking the glossy plastic under one arm and turning to Jules. "You?" she asked, her lips the same vibrant red as her hair, her lipstick slightly smudged at one corner.

"A cheeseburger, please," she said, flustered. "Medium rare. Fries, too."

The waitress nodded once again, looking down at the table, her gaze resting on the photograph. She bent closer, peering at the image as if committing it to memory. "Well, I'll be damned," she said softly, her lips pursing to let out a low whistle.

Jules couldn't speak, suddenly; just when it mattered most, she was paralyzed, her lips refusing to move.

"You know her?" Noah asked, glancing over at Jules.

"She worked over at the Archibalds' place," the waitress said, reaching over and picking up the photograph to get a better look. "Long time ago," she muttered under her breath, shaking her head as if in disdain, dropping the photo back on the table.

"The Archibalds?" Noah echoed as he reached into his pocket for his cell, opening the notes app, his brow furrowed as he pecked at the screen.

The waitress grunted. "Summer people."

"Do they still live here?" Noah asked, looking up from his phone.

"Eunice does, last I heard. The admiral passed some time ago."

"Where is it?" Jules heard herself say. "The house, I mean."

The waitress looked warily at Jules, then at Noah, before reaching one hand into the front pocket of the apron she wore, retrieving a pen. She pulled a white paper napkin from the dispenser in the booth next to them, placing it on the table.

"You'll need a map."

Chapter Eleven

The house sat at the end of a dead-end road, a slice of the silver sea visible through the bare branches. When Jules rolled the window down to get a better look, the air smelled of brine and woodsmoke, the sharpness of pine needles. The heavy iron gates, rusted in patches, were slightly ajar, and Noah got out, pushing them open so they could drive onto the estate. There was no intercom, as was typical in modern properties of such scale. Unless the gate was locked, anyone could walk right in.

Which suited Jules just fine.

When she stepped out of the car, Jules was greeted by the mournful cry of seagulls overhead, and the rustle of the wind made her chest ache with loneliness. The melancholy was palpable. It made her nostalgic for something she couldn't quite name, as if the land itself were a harbinger of loss. The house sat silent, mournful as a funeral, the dark windows shuttered like sightless eyes, the stone facade elongating as they drove up the long circular drive. The grounds were deserted, and one lone silver car sat in the driveway, an older-model Rolls-Royce, the paint gleaming like it had just been driven off the lot.

There was a fountain in the center of the circular drive, directly across from the front door, the figure of a young maiden in the center, her hair cascading down her back. Her eyes were downcast and heavy lidded, her lower half covered in scales. It was the same mermaid her mother had described so many times, a conch shell held between two outstretched hands.

"This fountain," Jules muttered, aware that Noah was standing beside her, looking at her curiously. "I know it."

"You've been here before?" Noah asked, shoving his hands into the front pockets of his coat, shifting his weight from one foot to the other.

"I've never seen this place in my life," Jules said, walking slowly around the perimeter of the fountain. "She told me about it."

"Your mother did?" Noah asked, coming around to peer at the fountain more closely. The bottom was dry, filled with leaves and bits of sharp, pointed sticks that had fallen from the trees in the wind. But it was laid with mosaic tile, blue as the deepest stretches of water in the bay. A Grecian blue, her mother had always called it, recalling the white, sun-washed roofs of Santorini, the cloudless sky of Ithaca.

They walked up to the doorstep and stood there waiting, as if for a sign. "Here goes nothing," Noah finally said as he reached out, pressing the tarnished brass doorbell on the side of the vestibule, a bell that rang once, shrilly. There was a long pause where Jules strained to hear movement behind the wooden door, the clatter of footsteps that never arrived.

"Maybe she's not here," Jules said nervously, turning to look around. "They were summer people, right?"

"Maybe," Noah said, walking away from the front door and into the garden, his curiosity getting the better of him. It was clear to Jules, even from the short time they'd known one another, that they were an odd pair. Noah wasn't much of a rule follower, while Jules, it seemed, hardly ever stepped out of the box, one she had largely created herself. Trespassing onto private property was the most adventurous thing she had done in years. A move, Jules knew, that would have caused her mother to have an apoplexy.

When you were little, you were fearless, her mother used to recall, shaking her head and grinning as if the memory amused her. *I thought you'd be the absolute death of me.* But where had that little girl gone? Jules wondered as she followed Noah. "Hang on," she called out, her feet stumbling on gravel, like walking through quicksand, but Noah ignored her and kept moving, first around the side of the house and then into the backyard.

The gardens stretched as far as the eye could see in rows of raised beds, plots that were wildly overgrown. There was the remnant of what appeared to be a neglected hedge maze, and a rusting greenhouse in the distance. Even in its neglected state, it was clear this garden had once been someone's pride and joy. But now, it served only as a painful reminder of days gone by, a fading memory of what once had been. Despite this, it wasn't hard to imagine the candlelight shining gaily in the windows, the flower beds surrounding the house in full, flagrant bloom. If Jules squinted, she could almost see the fairy lights that surely would've been strung in the branches of trees, the sprays of roses climbing across the stone walls, the lilac bush perfuming the night air with its soft, fleeting scent.

Noah walked briskly down the garden path, skirting the edge of the property, a steep slope that dropped off toward the sea, Jules still moving briskly to catch up, when he stopped short.

"What is it?" Jules called as she came up to meet him. And then she saw her. A figure standing at the top of the ridge, surveying the ocean beyond as it frothed and swelled. She stood there as if the sea itself were her domain, much like the house and grounds themselves, as if it had been placed there merely to do her bidding. She was clad in a pair of beige wool trousers, the cut impeccable, a mink coat hanging from her slim shoulders. Her white hair was cut bluntly along her jawline, her posture straight and practiced, as if an invisible stack of books were balanced atop her head. A pair of Ferragamo loafers graced her small feet, the same style Elizabeth had always favored, the leather as burnished as deeply roasted chestnuts. Jules couldn't help but smile at the sight of them, her lips curving into a grin, one that faded slowly as the woman turned to face them, her gaze both shrewd and imperious. Her disdain was immediate and palpable, the air shifting around them in quiet disruption. As the woman glared at her, Jules was startlingly aware that she could have been looking at her own mother, if only Elizabeth had lived twenty-five more years.

"What are you doing on my property?" There was a slight waver in her voice, hoarse with old money, the consonants sharply clipped. Beneath the coat she wore an ivory cardigan, a gold watch on one slender wrist, the links fine and delicate as a spider's web.

"So sorry to intrude," Noah began, stepping forward, "but we're looking for someone, a girl who may have worked here a long time ago."

"There is a thing called a *telephone*," the woman said dryly. "Marvelous invention." She stared at Jules, daring her to speak.

"You're Eunice Archibald?" Jules asked, holding her gaze.

"So I've been told," Eunice said, as she stepped forward, brushing past in a heavy cloud of gardenia, beginning the slow trek back toward the house. "Not that it's any of your business."

Jules looked at Noah helplessly, the moment they had hoped for slipping through their fingers with every step that Eunice took back to the house. As she moved, Jules noticed the way Eunice's gait was interrupted by a small limp with every halting step she took, much like Elizabeth's own walk as she grew close to the end. In the weeks before her death, she had relied on a cane, a polished column of wood topped by a brass phoenix, its wings spread in triumph. Elizabeth had found it in an antique shop in Darien back when her legs were lean and strong, well before she needed help of any kind. Had the purchase been a premonition? Some kind of foreshadowing? Jules didn't know the answer. All she did know was that if she didn't act now, she might never learn the truth about her mother at all.

"Wait," Jules called out, walking quickly over to Eunice, who looked up at her in surprise. "Please," Jules said, pulling the photograph from her pocket and holding it out so that it was directly in Eunice's line of vision. "Do you recognize her?"

There was a long moment where Eunice simply stared at the photograph. Jules could hear the ragged sound of the old woman's breath as she inhaled sharply, as if startled. The wind gusted hard, blowing the pale strands of her hair back so that her face was fully exposed, deeply lined around the eyes and mouth, but her cheekbones still high and elegant. She brought one hand to her throat, her fingers splayed along her collarbone, and she looked over at Jules, her eyes devoid of emotion, one clouded with cataracts, the other clear as the morning sun.

"That depends," she finally said, "on who's asking."

"Her daughter," Jules said, her voice barely above a whisper. "Her daughter is asking."

The world seemed to stop while Jules waited for a response, the garden blurring at the edges in a kaleidoscope of deadened green, the crash of the sea receding into the distance, Noah's figure a dark shape on the periphery, as she waited for what felt like an eternity.

Eunice nodded tersely, taking a deep breath in as if to steel herself for what was to come, and reached out, her birdlike fingers taking Jules firmly by the elbow, an anchor, rooting her to the earth once again. When she spoke, there was the faintest hint of a smile on her lips, her voice tremulous but her gaze unwavering.

"I think you'd better come inside," she said.

Chapter Twelve

As they stepped through the french doors and into the living room, Jules's mouth fell open in amazement. The room was a time capsule, stubbornly clinging to the past, the once-opulent furnishings long faded but still possessing a quiet elegance. It was all just as her mother had described, albeit a bit worse for wear, the long, rose-colored sofa now sun bleached, the gold-tasseled pillows almost threadbare. But the gilt-framed photographs atop the marble mantel still shone, logs of white birch blazed away merrily in the hearth, the silk curtains still flawless. It was all there, right down to the fountain beside the front door, the same one her mother claimed had graced the courtyard of her childhood home.

Noah sat down on the sofa, pulling his phone from his pocket and switching on the voice recorder. The coffee table held a silver tray arranged with a squat sugar bowl, a milk pitcher, and a cup and saucer, a border of pale-purple violets around the porcelain rim, so finely painted that Jules could see the striations in each emerald leaf. In the center of the table was a silver vase of peonies and peach roses, their petals soft as Elizabeth's powdered cheeks, cold as granite the sweltering day in August when Jules had leaned over the coffin and kissed them for the last time.

"Out of season." Eunice harrumphed, pulling her mink from her shoulders and sitting down carefully in a silk-upholstered winged-back chair in the palest of green, more pistachio than watercress. "I have them flown in every week. An extravagance, I know. Highly impractical. Still, one must have one's small pleasures—especially at my age."

"That fountain out front," Jules said as she slowly traversed the perimeter of the room, taking in the silver snuffboxes tucked away on every end table, the Persian rug beneath her heels, the three-tiered chandelier above, rows of crystals dripping like icicles, the ceiling painted a clear blue. "The mermaid," she said, turning to face Eunice.

"The Nereid?" Eunice nodded approvingly. "She's at her best in the summer months, wouldn't you agree? Without water, she seems quite . . . discontented."

"My mother described that fountain in detail . . ." Jules stammered, unable to make sense of it in her mind. "She said it belonged to . . . the house she grew up in." She glanced around the room as she spoke, and everywhere she looked, there was something else her mother had claimed as her own: the pewter statue of a rearing stallion on an end table, the Tiffany lamps filling the room with a soft glow, the stack of straw hats piled on a chaise near the french doors. Jules brought her hand to her mouth, as if to stifle the emotions running through her, a swell building offshore.

Noah looked over at Eunice sharply, and for the first time, Jules saw the old woman's gaze fall upon the phone placed prominently on the coffee table in front of him.

"Well, in many ways, this *was* her home," Eunice said, her tone matter-of-fact. "And she certainly did grow up here—in more ways than one."

"I don't understand," Jules managed to say, her thoughts awash in confusion. The stories Elizabeth had passed down, the house her mother had lived in as a child, those quaint streets of Bar Harbor, were an integral part of Jules's own childhood, her mother's early memories entwined inextricably with her own—stories that apparently were crafted with more fiction that fact. It occurred to Jules as she stood there in that opulent house, a place that Elizabeth had described so exhaustively, so intimately, that she had believed wholeheartedly in a history that had never existed. Her entire origin story was nothing more than an empty kingdom.

A land of make believe.

"Young man," Eunice called out, pointing one finger at Noah, a diamond cocktail ring sparkling in the light, the stone so large that it might have been gauche on anyone else. But much like the rest of her attire, on Eunice, the ring was effortlessly elegant. "Are you recording me on that godawful contraption?"

Noah looked blankly down at his cell, then back at Eunice. "Just for accuracy," he said quickly, apologetically. "I can turn it off if you like."

"Please do," Eunice said crisply, and Jules watched as Noah fumbled with his phone, pressing a few buttons before sliding it back in his pocket, then holding up his hands to show they were empty, his palms exposed, as if in an arrest. "Do you know how to boil water?" Eunice asked, pointing at the tea set in front of her. "This has gone quite cold." She turned to Jules, smiling apologetically. "I'm afraid I let the help go months ago."

Noah stood, awkwardly making his way over to the coffee table and picking up the tray, the dishes clanking ominously. "The kitchen is through there," Eunice commanded, pointing at the grand foyer behind her. "And do be careful," she said under her breath as Noah walked off. "I bought those dishes in 1959 in Paris," she went on, staring at Jules. But it was clear that although they sat in the same room, Eunice was somewhere far away, slipping in and out of a world all her own. "The admiral said they were extravagant, but of course I insisted."

Eunice's voice trailed off, and the room was quiet but for the sound of logs crackling in the hearth. As she looked around the room, a painting on the far wall caught Jules's eye, the image pulling her across the room as if by gravity, until she stood right in front of it.

A dancer in a tutu, bisque white, stood on one pale-pink pointe slipper as if ready to take flight, the satin ribbons winding up her faintly muscled calves, the scene bathed in a radiant nimbus of light. The scene was hauntingly familiar, one Jules had heard described to her more times over the years than she could count. *It was nearly priceless,* her mother had said reverently. *I wish you could have seen it, Julie.* There was a rustle of movement, the sound of slow steps, and then Eunice appeared beside her, a contented smile on her lips.

"This was . . . she told me it was my grandmother's," Jules whispered, her eyes filling with tears. "My mother described it exactly. She said it was donated to a museum before I was born."

"The Degas is one painting I never could bear to part with," Eunice said, her voice catching. "These days I can barely see her from across the room, but it is a comfort to know she's watching over me." Eunice nodded to herself, reaching out to pat Jules's arm absentmindedly. Jules felt her knees grow weak, and a rush of heat ran through her body, as if the room were suddenly aflame. Were they still discussing the dancer in the painting? Or something much more pointed? Jules wondered, turning to face the old woman.

"Who are you, exactly?" Jules asked, and before she could think better of it, she went on. "I mean, who were you to my mother?"

Eunice sighed, walking slowly over to her chair again, easing herself back down carefully. "I suppose I've been trying to answer your first question for as long as I can remember." She laughed softly to herself. "The second"—she looked up at Jules, her one clear eye surveying Jules carefully—"is much easier. I suppose I was Elizabeth's mentor once, though at the time it felt a great deal more than that." A faint smile played along the edges of her lips. "One makes certain choices in life, offers a leg up when one can. But I digress. In many ways, Elizabeth was the daughter I'd never had. One boy, you see, despite so much trying. It all works out for the best—or so I've been told. Still, one has one's doubts from time to time . . ." Her voice trailed off; her vision clouded with the past.

"Were you aware," Jules began slowly, "that my mother essentially co-opted your life? Your house? Your garden? That she wove them into her own narrative as if they were hers alone?"

Eunice looked over sharply, her eyes snapping back into focus. "I considered it an honor," she began, a steely edge to her voice, "that Billie was so inspired by her time here."

"Billie?" Jules repeated, looking at her in confusion. "My mother's name was Elizabeth."

"She was Billie when she came, Elizabeth when she left." Eunice chuckled softly. "I can still see her the day she stormed out of here, that determined look on her face, how her eyes swept each corner of the garden as if trying to commit it to memory. As if she could ever forget."

"You knew?" Jules stared at the old woman incredulously. "All this time you knew she made this place, your life, part of her own story, her *narrative*—and you never said anything?"

"What was there to say?" Eunice said as she shrugged her thin shoulders. "My dear, it's quite clear that you have no idea who your mother really was."

There it was. The same assertion Noah had made less than forty-eight hours ago, the very one that made Jules's blood rise, her cheeks flushing in immediate protest. The same sentiment that made her so angry when Noah had voiced it, and the very same thought that had echoed through her brain every night since, staring into the darkness and finding nothing. But suddenly, Jules wasn't interested in arguing. For the first time since Noah had imploded her well-ordered life, she wanted to listen. If she didn't have the slightest clue who her mother really was, then dammit, she wanted to learn. To finally know the truth. Wasn't that why she was in Maine, creeping around a stranger's garden with a man she hardly knew, freezing her ass off on the cusp of winter?

At that moment, Noah returned with the tea, placing the tray back down on the coffee table. "What did I miss?" he asked, looking at Jules, then Eunice, before sitting on the sofa. Jules ignored him. There was no way she was going to come all this way to watch Eunice drink tea and rattle on about the past. Not unless those ramblings included Elizabeth.

"Tell me, then," Jules said, walking over to the sofa and sitting down beside Noah. "Tell me about my mother."

Eunice reached across the table, pouring herself a cup of tea, the rising steam filling the room with the herbaceous scents of chamomile and lavender. "I can still see her now for the first time, balancing that tray, her head held high . . . but her hands shaking. It was like looking in a mirror," Eunice began, settling back in her chair, holding the cup and saucer gently between her hands, "so strongly did I see myself in her. Determination, I suppose you might call it. Certainly grit. But she couldn't see those things in herself. Not then." She paused, bringing the cup to her lips and swallowing. "Not yet. But I knew from the beginning, you see, that she had what it took. She just needed a firm hand."

"And you gave it to her?" Noah asked.

"I wonder if you can imagine the thrill of it," Eunice said thoughtfully as the fire snapped and popped, punctuating her sentences. "Seeing a young person come into her own. Bearing witness to that kind of transformation. It is a potent thing indeed, being on the precipice of one's power." Her thoughts drifted away again, somewhere far in the past, where the rooms were still gilded, where time itself had stopped, where they could not follow her. "There was, of course, that unpleasantness with Colin . . ." She frowned, wrinkling her nose in distaste. "But that is another story entirely."

"Who's Colin?" Noah asked, turning to look quizzically at Jules.

"My son," Eunice said with a sigh. "But as I said, it's a long story. One for another time perhaps." She turned to stare into the fire, the logs burning to embers, her profile still finely etched, and for a moment the years fell away, and Jules could see Eunice as she had once been, radiant with youth, her skin supple and unlined, her eyes sparking with danger. And then, like a parlor trick, the illusion vanished, and an old woman sat before them once more, turning to look Jules in the eye, the passage of time plain on her face.

"I have time," Jules said quickly, trying not to appear overeager. *Colin.* The name was unfamiliar, but something about it rang softly true, like a mournful melody carrying through the trees. "I've got all the time in the world."

There was a long silence, marred by only the howl of the wind, the waves lapping against the rocks, as Eunice leaned slowly forward, grimacing as if even that small movement caused her pain. "Very well," she said, placing the cup and saucer back on the table with a discernible clink.

"Let us begin."

Chapter Thirteen
BILLIE

The Claremont, a collection of stark white buildings set back from the sea, was like no hotel Billie had ever seen. Turrets like egg whites whipped to firm peaks rising toward the sky, the rolling green lawns, the garden restaurant lined with cherry and apple trees, the pale lavender petals falling like a benediction in the spring. The clapboard bungalows surrounding the hotel were decorated with sumptuous carpets and twinkling chandeliers of blown glass, flown in, Eunice informed her, all the way from Murano, Italy.

"Near Venice," Eunice said knowingly, lighting a slim cigarette and leaning back against the buttery leather seats of the Rolls-Royce. Nate winked one blue eye at Billie in the rearview mirror, a chauffeur's cap perched jauntily on his head. The interior smelled of vanilla and ash, of cigars and powerful men, and of Eunice's perfume, a fleeting trail of hyacinth and rain-splattered lilac. It was the scent of summers spent abroad. Of Tuscan hill towns and bills paid in full. The more time she spent at the Archibalds', the more Billie understood that money, while it might not buy happiness, could certainly buy freedom. And freedom, it seemed, might be the most valuable commodity of all.

But that concept was still as foreign as the table settings of heavy silver, the centerpiece of rosebuds and baby's breath in front of her, the servers who strolled the courtyard in their starched, white linen jackets. The sky was cerulean, ultramarine, cloudless, and Eunice sat beside her at the round table, watching her thoughtfully. Their placement at the center of the courtyard felt deliberate, the adjoining tables filled with women wearing large straw hats and ropes of ivory pearls. There were fingernails painted cerise, strawberry, claret. The bleached flags of tennis skirts, diamonds sparkling on thin wrists. And there was Eunice, her simple black sheath offsetting her summer tan, her hair pulled back in a french twist, pearl studs gleaming in her ears.

Billie folded the starched, cloth square of the napkin over her knees, mostly to cover the skirt she wore, once a deep blue, but now nearly gray from so many washings, and busied herself studying the menu, thick as a phone book. Some things were familiar. But not the Coquilles Saint-Jacques. Not the moules meunière. Not the tisane of rose hips and lavender. There were no fewer than three separate forks beside the empty plate in front of her, and she looked up at Eunice blankly, forcing herself to smile.

"You are quite the open book." Eunice laughed softly.

Billie felt her cheeks flush in protest, the shame of being so easily unmasked. "What do you mean?" she asked.

But Eunice just smiled and motioned over the waiter with a wave of her hand. "Tea for two," she said. "And a pot of Lapsang souchong." The waiter nodded, bowing slightly and retrieving the menus on the table in a series of deft movements so smooth they were nearly undetectable. "It's an acquired taste, but I think you'll like it," she said as soon as the waiter was out of earshot. "This particular blend is from the Fujian province of China, I believe."

"Why are we here exactly," Billie blurted out.

Eunice sat back, surveying her calmly, as though weighing a decision. "I feel it is essential to have some measure of trust in the people one chooses to surround oneself with. Wouldn't you agree?"

"Did you bring Nate here, too?" Billie asked impetuously.

"Don't be ridiculous." Eunice sniffed, her eyes drifting out over the crowded courtyard, the noise of chatter, the delicate music of silverware surrounding them. "I brought you. Perhaps you should ask why. That might be a better use of your time. And mine, for that matter."

Just then a waiter approached, pushing a small trolley holding a three-tiered stand piled with scones, tea sandwiches, and a plate of macarons in sky blue, pale lavender. He placed the stand in the center of the table, where it was quickly joined by a teapot, two cups and saucers, a pattern of blueberries, plumply indigo, circling the perimeter.

"Will there be anything else, madam?" the waiter said, turning to address Eunice.

"No, Charles, that will be all," Eunice replied with a smile, and her teeth, small and even as seed pearls, glowed against her tanned skin. She picked up the teapot and began pouring the dark brew into both cups, steam rising from the surface.

"So why?" Billie asked, taking the bait. "Why did you bring me here?"

Eunice laughed softly, placing the teapot back on the table and picking up her cup and saucer, her fingers wrapped around the delicate handle. "I suppose I see something of myself in you, Elizabeth. Perhaps it's as simple as that."

"It's Billie," she said, eyeing the scones on the top tier, studded with currants, shiny with a sugared glaze.

"I find Elizabeth much more refined," Eunice replied matter-of-factly, plucking a scone from the tray and dropping it on Billie's plate. "If it's good enough for the queen of England, it should be tolerable for you, I should think."

But Billie didn't respond. When she touched the scone in front of her, it was warm, redolent of citrus, and when she sliced the pastry open with her knife, the center was still hot, the cake dense and moist.

"Clotted cream? Jam?" Eunice asked, nodding at the small, circular dishes on the tray that held both. *Clotted cream,* Billie murmured to herself, fascinated by its thick, pillowy consistency. "You might think of it as a cross between whipped cream and butter," Eunice explained, pointing with one long, manicured finger.

Billie spread a thin layer of the cream on one half of her scone, then covered it with a dollop of jam, bloodred and flecked with dark seeds. The first mouthful made her close her eyes, the sounds of the courtyard falling away. The warm pastry, along with the tartness of the jam, tasting of ripe, sun-warmed berries and cool cream, made her wonder if she'd ever consumed anything as delicious in her entire life, so strongly did the moment embed itself in her consciousness. When she finally opened her eyes, blinking stunned-wondrous in the light, everything had changed.

Eunice watched her, nodding approvingly, and when Billie took her first mouthful of tea, bitter and black, with a smoky aftertaste that lingered like perfume, she could not help but smile with pleasure. All her senses seemed heightened, the warm breeze caressing her bare arms and legs, the sun hitting the top of her head, transforming her with its heady rays, the air alive with possibility.

"What is it," Eunice asked after a long moment, "that you *really* want?"

Billie looked around at the courtyard, the beautifully composed plates against the stark white cloths, the scarlet lobsters, the dainty leaves of watercress, the clay pots of lavender waving in the breeze.

"This," Billie said quietly, meeting Eunice's unwavering gaze. "I want this."

Eunice nodded slowly, a smile gracing the corners of her lips, and in that one movement, Billie knew that she was understood, completely and implicitly. Eunice's stare exposed everything, searching down to Billie's bones, into her very cells, seeing her with a kind of crystalline clarity, a depth that even Nate looked right past.

"I can help you," Eunice said, as a plump bee flitted lazily around the flower arrangement, its wings fluttering as it dipped and swooped close to the rim of her water glass, flirting with danger, and Billie felt her own smile building slowly, her lips stretching, pulling away from her teeth before breaking into a wide grin.

Chapter Fourteen

Billie kept a careful watch on the capellini as it bubbled in a large stock-pot, quickly fishing out a strand to make sure it was cooked al dente, the way Marcus had taught her. She planned on reserving a cup of the water for a lemon-cream sauce, tossing in a handful of arugula at the end for a sharp, peppery bite. There was a layer cake with thick swirls of cream cheese frosting, a ring of tiny wild strawberries placed along the top, and silver bowls of roasted nuts, twists of candied ginger she'd prepared the day before, the ends dipped in dark chocolate. Freshly boiled lobsters lay prone on the cutting board, ready to be dismantled, folded into homemade mayonnaise, spiced with paprika and dotted with chives.

Three weeks had passed since her lunch with Eunice, weeks she'd spent mastering the maddeningly elusive alchemy of the baguette, first overproofing the dough, then underbaking it entirely so that the center was the texture of library paste, while Marcus looked on in dismay, his face as scarlet as the gazpacho she'd blended that day for lunch. She'd dug new potatoes from the garden until her hands were chafed and raw, picked zucchini and harvested bunches of herbs, arranged endless bundles of flowers, an old straw hat shielding her face from the midday sun. But aside from exchanging a nod as they passed in the corridors, nothing had really changed—much to Billie's chagrin. Until the morning Eunice strode into the kitchen, a stricken look on her face, her pallor ashy beneath the coppery sheen of her tan.

"Elizabeth, Marcus is out sick," she said in a hushed tone. Even so, the other cooks looked up curiously at the intrusion. "The timing is *most* inconvenient. I need you to take over."

"Me?" Billie said in surprise. "You want me to—"

"To take his place," Eunice said, cutting her off impatiently. "I expect you know how important today is. It is the first family meal we've had all summer."

Billie nodded, listening for the strains of guitar solos drifting down from Colin's room on the third floor, but there was only silence, unlike yesterday afternoon, when he'd first arrived, opening the front door with a bang that made Billie jump at the cutting board, nicking her finger on the side of the blade. She'd ventured out into the hall, a dish towel wrapped around her hand as a boy entered, tall and lanky, throwing a dusty backpack into the foyer, a flagrant display of careless disorder that would normally leave Eunice sputtering with rage but that somehow elicited no reaction whatsoever when she walked quickly into the hall, her placid expression vanishing in an instant as she broke into a grin, opening her arms in welcome.

Billie was transfixed, knowing she should retreat to the kitchen, but unable to take even a single step. She watched the boy lean into his mother's embrace, and as he hugged her to him, their eyes met over Eunice's shoulder. Billie drew in a sharp breath, and there it was, the same drunk whirl of feeling as leaning over a vase of peonies, or the fresh tomato sauce bubbling on the stove, the astringent scent of basil filling her nose, a kind of homecoming. His eyes were luminous as sea glass, his hair, just hitting his collarbone, streaked with gold, his skin tanned from days spent traipsing around Sicily, the white T-shirt and pair of faded jeans he wore clinging to his frame as if they'd been tailored to his measurements alone.

She knew what would come next as if she'd already lived it, knew everything that would happen between them, knew he was a planet as radiant as the sun, one she was fated to orbit, knew what it would be like to touch him before they even once shook hands, how his fingers would tighten around her own. It was the most dangerous minute of her life, and as she stood there, her blood staining the towel in fat, red droplets, she wondered, before they had ever spoken even one word to each other, if the small flap of skin that now gaped open was a foreshadowing of things to come.

"Get to work then," Eunice said briskly, snapping Billie back into the present and striding out of the kitchen. "I'm counting on you," she tossed over her shoulder as she exited. Billie exhaled once, heavily, and then turned back toward the pots on the stove, the other cooks staring at her expectantly.

"You heard her," Billie said, her voice like the sharpened blade of her knife. And with those words, the cooks sprang into action, the kitchen humming with a quiet music, the noise of production, of life itself. And as she diced piles of herbs for garnish, she was humming under her breath almost without even realizing she was doing so at all. She knew in the kitchen, surrounded by the textures and scents of the strange, intoxicating kingdom of the Archibalds' estate, that even if the lunch was somehow ruined beyond repair, the sauces separated, the tart crust gummy and tasteless, for this one moment, she'd never been happier.

~

"A revelation, my dear," the admiral called out as she arrived to collect the dishes and ready the table for the dessert course, the taper candles filling the dining room with the honeyed scent of beeswax. Her cheeks flushed with this unexpected praise, and she lowered her gaze, in part to keep herself from glancing over at Colin, who was seated next to Eunice. The admiral, placed at the head of the table, lorded over the scene contentedly as he refilled his glass from a bottle of Château Margaux he'd brought up from the cellar.

But as hard as she tried to focus on the task at hand, stacking plates and glassware, her eyes inevitably drifted over in Colin's direction.

His hair was pulled back in a ponytail, and he wore a starched white dress shirt, pulling at the collar distractedly, as if wanting to break free. Instead of the ripped jeans he'd arrived in the day before, he was now dressed in a pair of tan chinos, his feet covered not in dirty sneakers but chestnut loafers, the leather buffed to a soft shine. When their eyes met, she felt herself draw back, flustered, and instantly looked away. *He's your boss's son!* her inner critic yelled, the voice that sounded curiously like her mother's, as she stacked the dirty dishes on the sideboard.

And what about Nate? You already have *a boyfriend.*

But the moment she'd laid eyes on Colin in that foyer, Nate had become a distant memory. She could feel him growing smaller and more insignificant with every passing moment, as if he'd been reduced to a speck in the rearview mirror of her life. She knew that instead of watching Nate clown around with his buddies in a parking lot downtown that evening, she'd be in bed, thinking about Colin's tanned skin, the way his biceps strained against his white cotton shirt, imagining what he might do to her.

Imagining what she might do back.

She busied herself clearing the remainder of the dishes, waiting to roll out the antique trolley that was used for tea service, but when she reached Colin's seat, she stopped dead. His plate of pasta, the dish she had worked on so laboriously, testing the sauce again and again to make sure it was citrus-flecked, silky perfection, was practically untouched, as if he'd taken one or two bites and given up entirely.

"Is there something wrong?" she asked, reaching down to retrieve the plate so she could scrutinize it more closely. The pasta was beginning to congeal, the arugula she had folded in at the last moment strewn on the side of the plate, as if plucked out by the hands of a picky toddler. At that moment, any attraction she'd felt evaporated into the warm summer air, as if it had been a mirage, water glimmering in the distance, her thirst slaked by only a mouthful of sand.

"It was fine," he said neutrally, and Billie felt the heat inside her begin to rise at his indifference. It was the worst word in the English language: *fine*. Her life in Winter Harbor was *fine*. Her job at the Frozen Cone was *fine*. Nate as a boyfriend was *fine*. *Fine* was average. *Fine* was unremarkable.

Fine was everything she never wanted to be.

"It's the jet lag," Eunice said knowingly, nodding to herself before settling back in her chair and crossing one leg over the other, her napkin a perfect white square across her lap.

"No, it isn't," Billie replied, her tone like a whip, and Eunice's eyes widened. "Tell me," she began again, turning to Colin, holding the plate out in front of her and giving it a firm shake for emphasis. "What didn't you like about it?"

In the silence that ensued, they locked eyes. Billie could hear the clock ticking away on the marble mantel, the cooing of birds in the trees out front. The admiral looked up from his wineglass, bemused. Everything felt magnified, as if the entire room had grown larger around them. But it was too late to turn back now. She had said it, and now he would answer.

"It's just that . . ." he finally replied, his voice as cool as the dew that hung on the petals of the roses every morning, the impossible spectacle of them as they sprawled across the stone walls of the garden in a symphony of pinks and whites. "In Italy, they use fresh pasta. I guess I kind of got used to it."

Eunice reached over to swat Colin lightly on the shoulder, her mouth falling open in shock. "Don't be *ridiculous*," she said, aghast. "Please excuse my son's manners—or the complete lack of them. The dish was superb. Why, it reminded me of that marvelous trip we took to Capri right before you were born," she said, nodding at Colin and turning to face the admiral, who grunted in agreement while pouring himself another glass of wine. "That little pensione where we had that divine pasta course with the grilled octopus and lemons."

Colin looked away, down at the blank space where his plate had been, and Billie just stood there as Eunice continued chattering away, awkwardness descending with every passing minute. "I'll just clear this away," she said woodenly, turning her back on the scene and walking quickly out of the room. In the kitchen, she tossed the contents of Colin's untouched plate in the trash, the lid closing with a bang, then stood at the counter, her hands shaking. *How dare he,* she thought as the other cooks moved around her in a tuneless dance. She moved to the sink and began the dishes, making the water as hot as she could stand it, wishing she could evaporate in the steam that fogged the kitchen window, the garden a waterlogged miasma of green.

There was the guttural sound of a throat clearing, a polite *ahem,* and she whirled around, her heart racing, hands still covered in bubbles, to see Eunice standing there in the silk day dress she'd worn to lunch, a rose blush, her gilded hair in a neat chignon. "Don't pay any attention," she said evenly, "to my son." There was a glint of amusement in her eyes as she spoke, a light chiding. "Or to men in general, I daresay. You know full well that dish was impeccable." She went on, her shoulders moving in the tiniest of shrugs, "You know it implicitly. What should it matter what he thinks? It has nothing to do with you in the slightest."

"Doesn't it?" Billie muttered, wiping her wet, soapy hands on the front of her apron. Eunice's eyes narrowed slightly, and Billie rushed on before Eunice could reply. "He barely even tasted it."

"And why would that matter to you?" Eunice replied, arching one fine, thin brow.

"Because it does!" Billie exclaimed hotly, tears springing to her eyes. "Because if a meal isn't a complete success, then it's a failure. It's as simple as that."

Until that one moment, Billie hadn't realized how the kitchen had become her whole world, how much it had come to mean to her. But standing there, uttering those words, she could no longer deny it. Whatever she was doing in that space, the alchemy of a soufflé, a well-laid table, it was a part of her future, as inarguable as the cells that made up her DNA.

Eunice nodded once, briskly. As usual, it was difficult to tell whether she was speaking to Billie directly or merely entertaining herself with her own thoughts. "You can waste your life," she said smoothly, as her gaze floated out the window and into the garden, away from the tears that threatened to fall at any moment, "holding yourself to impossible standards and worrying about what everyone else thinks. Or," Eunice continued, looking back over at Billie sharply, her eyes hard now, unwavering, "you can listen to your own voice instead. The choice, as with everything in life, is entirely yours."

Eunice smiled, her lips pressed together tightly, and walked toward the door, the other cooks averting their eyes, as if it were somehow dangerous to look right at her. Billie stood there, her jeans splotched with uneven patches of damp in the narrow shape of her own splayed fingers. She knew her hair was hanging lankly around her face in the heat, the fabric beneath the arms of her cotton blouse wet and clammy. She didn't want to let Eunice down, that fact was as irrefutable as the marble cutting board sitting beside her. But if what Eunice said was true, then the only opinion that really mattered was her own.

"It will be most interesting," Eunice mused, turning around to face Billie one last time, "to see what choices you make." She turned her back, her spine a symmetrical row of bones clearly visible beneath the silk dress she wore, and like an apparition, a phantom whose translucent form floated along the vast corridors of the house when darkness fell each night, left as quickly as she'd arrived.

Chapter Fifteen

Billie turned the handle of the pasta machine, beads of sweat dotting her brow as she fed another golden sheet through the rollers, her fingers cramping as she worked. She'd found it the previous afternoon, tucked away on the top shelf of the pantry, and before she could second-guess herself, she'd pulled it down, placing it on the counter. It sat there squatly, daring her with its small steel heft. When she'd returned home that night, she'd barely slept, ransacking her mother's cookbook collection until she came across a sauce-splattered tome by Marcella Hazan, propping the book open with one hand and studying it like a psalm until the sky cracked open with light.

"What in the world has gotten into you?" her mother asked when she wandered into the kitchen that morning, already dressed for work, staring incredulously at Billie, who was still hunched over the pages. "Since when do you read *cookbooks*?"

"Since now," Billie muttered, licking a finger and turning the page. "I thought this was what you wanted. You should be thrilled." She chuckled, looking up at her mother, whose eyes flickered with irritation, like a light bulb sputtering in a dark room.

"I wanted you to learn it for yourself," she said, an edge to her voice. "Not to impress a bunch of stuck-up swells."

"I *am* learning for myself," Billie said evenly.

"You sure about that?" her mother asked, one hand on her hip. "What are you *wearing*?" she exclaimed, pointing at the simple navy shirtdress, the pair of cream-colored loafers on Billie's feet, gold buckles shining in the overhead light. "Exactly who," her mother went on, "are you trying to impress over there?" Billie looked down at herself, flustered and indignant, knowing that anything she might say in protest or defense was meaningless. Her mother had already made up her mind, and nothing short of a miracle would sway her.

The previous morning, Billie had been immersed in the tedious task of polishing the Archibalds' sizable collection of flatware, pulling one piece at a time from a velvet-lined box and rubbing it carefully with a soft cloth, when Adeline had entered, looking at her intently. "Mrs. Archibald would like a word," she said quietly, and Billie's heart jumped in her chest. She nodded, wiping her hands on a clean rag, and followed Adeline up to the third floor. It was the first time Billie had ever been invited past the ground floor, and her pulse quickened with every step. Adeline stopped in front of a door at the end of the hall, knocked once, briskly, then opened it, revealing a suite of rooms papered in a dainty floral print of cream and mauve, the linens on the king-size bed a froth of ivory-colored lace, a satin canopy draped over the top.

"In here," a voice called out, and she followed Adeline over to the closet in the adjoining room, double doors thrown wide. Inside, there were day dresses, ball gowns, rows of trousers lined up on wooden hangers: wool, silk, cotton. Sequins and satin, marabou feathers, and intricate beading. Rows and rows of shoes, elegant pumps, kitten heels, and loafers in every hue imaginable. An entire wall of handbags, tiny clutches patterned in jet beads, satchels in tender calfskin, and so many wide-brimmed straw hats that Billie immediately lost count.

"Ah, there you are," Eunice said while hanging a black satin gown on a padded hanger. "I was doing some spring cleaning, and I thought you might want first crack at these," she said, pointing at a neatly folded pile of clothing placed on the thick carpet.

"It's summer," Billie said before she could stop herself, looking around the room, the chandelier hanging from the ceiling, the creamy white walls.

"So it is," Eunice said distractedly as she gathered up the pile from the floor, placing it in a large shopping bag, the words Bonwit Teller stamped across the front. "I think these might fit you as well." She held out a pair of loafers, the smell of leather both fierce and feral, and Billie turned them over in her hands, the shoes seemingly unworn, the bottoms smooth, void of scuffs.

When she slipped them on her feet later that evening, standing before the full-length mirror in her room at home, she held out one foot, then the other, standing back to get a better look at herself. In the glass, she was transformed. It was the magic slipper incarnate, the ball gown dripping with crystals, a glittering tiara in her hair. But now, as she sat in the tiny kitchen she'd known her entire life, the place where she'd taken her first steps, her tiny feet pattering across the worn wooden floors, Billie watched her mother's features twist in contempt as the clock struck twelve, her newfound finery turning to rags and ashes.

"They're just using you," her mother went on, plucking her keys from the blue enamel bowl on the counter, the sound as jangled as Billie's own thoughts. "I wish you could see that for yourself."

The words stung, the blade dipping in and out with precision, and Billie's eyes widened, as if she'd been startled awake. "Is it the cookbook that's really bothering you?" she said, closing the book with a hard slap. "The clothes? Or maybe you think you're the only one qualified to teach me anything."

The minute she said it, Billie wished more than anything that she could stuff the words back in her mouth like a hunk of bread and swallow them whole. Her mother's face fell all at once, the ice of her gaze melting, her eyes filled with a sadness so deep it knocked the air from Billie's lungs and made her want to flee. But before she could so much as stand, her mother walked across the floor in three long strides, the back door banging behind her. The sudden stillness rang in Billie's ears as the house settled around her, and she sat there feeling more alone than ever, her heart helpless.

In the Archibalds' kitchen, Billie halted her determined cranking, as much to rest as to survey her handiwork. The first sheets of pasta she'd attempted had unfurled from the mouth of the silver machine in various degrees of thickness, almost translucent at the edges, far thicker toward the middle. She'd arrived hours before she was due at work that day, mixing batches of dough in the early-morning light until her hands were sore, glad that Marcus was still confined to bed and couldn't roll his eyes at her ineptitude.

She wiped her damp hands on her apron, then began turning the handle again, making sure to apply the same steady pressure as the dough made its way through the rollers, pulling it off in one sheet at the end and placing it on the floured countertop. She stood back, admiring her handiwork before quickly slicing the dough into thin strips and covering them with a damp towel. She moved to the stove, lighting the flame beneath the copper pan she favored, tapping in a knob of butter and a drizzle of olive oil. While the water boiled, she tossed the asparagus spears she'd already blanched into the sizzling pan, adding in a handful of fresh green peas and thin slices of fennel, along with a squeeze of lemon, using a set of silver tongs to pluck the noodles from the bubbling froth, dropping them into the skillet.

Just as she slid the pasta onto a plate, there was the sound of approaching footsteps, and she raised her head as Colin walked in, wearing the same ripped jeans he'd had on the day he first arrived home, and a black T-shirt, white wings stretching across his chest, the logo of the band Aerosmith. His hair was damp and loose, and he moved toward her, his hands jammed in his pockets, a sheepish smile on his lips.

"I'm sorry," he began, clearing his throat, a guttural sound that hinted at nervousness, "for what happened at lunch yesterday. My mother insisted that I come and apologize."

"Do you always do what your mother tells you?"

"Hardly." Colin laughed. "But in this case, she was right. I was kind of an asshole."

Billie wanted to smile, but instead she pushed the steaming plate in his direction, then plucked a fork from the kitchen drawer, setting it beside the plate and banging the drawer closed with one hip.

"What's this?" he asked, looking down at the plate, picking up the fork she'd given him, but gingerly, as though it were laced with arsenic.

"Fresh pasta, obviously. Thought you were some kind of expert?" she said with a bright smile, relishing his discomfort. *Tit for tat,* her mother would've said.

"For me?" he asked in surprise. "And what did I do to deserve this?"

"You pissed me off," she retorted, taking a step back and crossing her arms over her chest. "Try it."

It was a command, not a request, but still he hesitated before twirling the spaghetti around the fork. He brought a neat bite to his lips, chewing thoughtfully, then wiping his mouth on the back of his hand. He stared at her, then looked back down at the plate in wonderment. "Wow," he said quietly. "You made this for *me?*"

"I made it to prove that I could," she said. "You happened to walk in when it was ready."

"And if I'd come ten minutes later?"

"You'd be out of luck," she said, grabbing another fork from the drawer and twirling the pasta around it. She brought the fork to her mouth, strands dangling messily, closing her eyes as the flavors enveloped her. The lemon and fennel melded seamlessly on her tongue, the sauce a gloss of olive oil and a slick of butter, but still somehow weightless, as if infused with sunlight. She opened her eyes to find Colin staring at her, his eyes blinking lazily.

"I wasn't wrong," he said with a grin. He pushed his hair from his face with one hand, exposing a dimple in his left cheek, and for the first time she wondered if she made him feel as ungrounded as she did in his presence, a dizzying free fall that made her want to run away as much as rush toward him. She longed to dispense with pleasantries and pull him to her, her mouth finding his own. She wondered how he would taste, wanted to inhale the scent of his skin, sea-salt soap, and rosemary shampoo.

He's off-limits, she told herself. *Stop it.*

But she knew it was too late. It had been too late from that first moment he'd walked through the front door. He was a cliff she was compelled to drive over, rushing up to meet the edge of the world. All she could do was delay the inevitable. Which might, at the very least, buy her time to think.

"Why don't I take you out on the boat this afternoon?" he asked, his fingers drumming against the counter to an invisible melody. "Let me make it up to you."

By *boat*, she knew he meant the thirty-foot yacht docked in the harbor, *The Eliza*, named for the admiral's long-dead mother, as rumor had it. And in that moment, the attraction she'd felt for him only moments before promptly faded away, leaching out of her like a curl of woodsmoke, her heart the burned-out remnants of a bonfire, charred sticks, and inky soot. Her mother's words came rushing back, filling her thoughts like a knife piercing the cloudy heights of a soufflé.

Stuck-up swells.

They're just using you.

"You mean your father's boat," she muttered, picking up the plate and walking over to the trash, scraping the china clean with a few sharp motions of her wrist. "You think it's as easy as that?"

"As easy as what?"

"I'm not for sale," she said quietly, placing the plate in the sink and turning around to glance despairingly at the clock on the wall. The rest of the kitchen staff would arrive soon, and she was already behind on lunch prep. There were fillets of cod to grill; basil, pine nuts, and parmesan to turn into a pesto; the salad to assemble; tender Georgia peaches to slice; and goat cheese to crumble. She didn't have time for this. She barely had time to breathe.

"I never said you were," he replied, blanching noticeably, as if she had struck him. "It's a beautiful day, and I thought you might enjoy it. Sorry if I offended you . . . again," he said as he turned his back and shuffled toward the door.

Billie felt her bravado turn to belladonna as her breath caught in her throat. *Wait!* she wanted to yell out. *Don't go!* But she couldn't make herself say the words. Her pride somehow always managed to get in the way, putting a steel barricade between herself and what she really wanted. Until, in the aftermath of it all, she would convince herself that she'd never wanted any of it in the first place.

But just as he was about to leave, Colin stopped suddenly, then strode back into the kitchen until he stood in front of her, so close that she could feel the heat coming off his skin, see the thin slice of a scar along his chin, a crescent moon. "You sure," he asked, his voice a low rumble, "you won't change your mind?"

Billie felt her lips twitch, once, then again, and despite herself, a laugh overtook her, shaking itself loose from her chest. "You really don't handle rejection well, do you," she said in mock disapproval, but smiling, nonetheless.

"Is that what's happening?" Colin mused. "As far as I can tell, you haven't decided anything one way or the other."

There was a sudden rustle at the back door as the staff began to arrive, filing in one by one, hanging their jackets on the hooks and looking over at her quizzically. "OK, fine," she muttered quickly, anything to get him to leave. "I'm off at three," she said as she walked over to the fridge, pulling out the cod wrapped in brown paper and laying it on the counter. "I'll meet you at the harbor."

She didn't wait to see his reaction, couldn't bear his smug grin. Instead, she busied herself unwrapping the fish as he left the kitchen, focusing her attention on the white fillets blushed with pink, lighting the flame beneath the pan with the sharp strike of a match.

Chapter Sixteen

He was the sea that curled and swelled in the distance, beyond the rocks decorating the shore like rough jewelry, the gulls soaring restlessly overhead. Before he'd ever touched her, she had known, and the first time he'd reached out a hand, standing on the dock and sweeping her hair from her eyes with careful fingers, she knew beyond a single doubt that they belonged to one another in a final, resounding way she would never find with anyone else.

When she'd rolled up on her bike that afternoon, the sun still warm and high in the sky by the time she arrived at the harbor, the boat stood at the end of a long dock, huge and majestic, *The Eliza* scrolled across the hull in a gentle script, the chrome gleaming as if it had been polished moments before her arrival. He was barefoot, in a pair of cutoff shorts and the same T-shirt he'd worn earlier, his grip on her hand sure and steady as he helped her aboard, that sense of certainty flooding her being, as if she'd drawn his face from memory throughout the course of her life without knowing it, the contours familiar and sure.

The weeks passed in a blur of hot sun and cool nights, his sweater wrapped around her shoulders, Irish wool, the softest cashmere. Makeshift picnics on the beach he led her to blindfolded, a stretch of deserted white sand underfoot instead of rocks and gravel. Oysters he shucked with a pocketknife by the shore, their flesh still quivering as he placed them on her tongue, the taste of the sea briny with salt. Tiny wild strawberries they found in the woods beneath tender green leaves, and fat scarlet tomatoes from the garden, leaves of basil as big as her palm.

From the very beginning, she wanted to tell him the secrets of her heart. How, in the kitchen, it was as if she'd become some grand conductor, baton poised as the music rose and shifted, the flavors as varied and dense as the notes themselves, singing on her palate as the ripest plum, the tart citrus rinds she peeled so carefully. He spoke of Italy, of Spain, the cured meats he'd tasted in small shops, the gelato melting in a puddle of sweetness on the tongue, vanilla bean and stracciatella. How he'd thought so many times of tossing his mother's letters as they'd arrived, refusing the money waiting at the bank and disappearing into the olive groves, sweet chestnut and Mediterranean cyprus, his life of privilege receding like a bad dream.

"But if you had," she pointed out, as his lips drank from her own as if she were a flower, the butterfly hovering over the bloom, "you never would've met me." Her only answer a kiss as he pulled her to him, the woods around them disappearing in a burst of sunlight, the trees hiding them from view with their jewel-studded leaves.

"Try this," he said, and she opened her mouth without protest, again and again, in anticipation of what he might place inside. A crumble of aged goat cheese, his own fingers, wet with wine. She could not help but close her eyes, the bees circling them drunkenly, as if intoxicated in their wake. Their bed was the moss underfoot, the soft carpet of it, as palely green as lichen, and when he entered her for the first time, she cried out, startled by the rightness of it, the unmistakable feeling of a key turning smoothly in a locked door.

He had unleashed the innermost part of her, that place she had shown no one, the secret heart of her being, the uncharted landscape she'd allowed no one to touch until that moment. And in the clearing, the light illuminating the ends of her hair, the air infused with the scent of the pine needles, the damp earthiness of the ground they'd lain on, she knew as she stood there, as naked as the day she was born, that there was no going back.

She'd ended things with Nate the day after the first sail, broken it off cleanly, her words leaving him little hope she'd change her mind. Still, she saw in his eyes that he didn't believe her, not fully, that with the delusion of youth, he thought she'd be back. But he couldn't know, didn't know, what lay in the remote corners of her mind, the depths of her soul that Colin had touched so effortlessly, and God help her, she'd let him in, let him in all the way, as if she'd never had any defenses at all.

"I'm yours," Nate had always said, fiercely, defiantly, as he wrapped her around him at night in his truck, the windows steamed. "Mind, body, and soul."

But it was Colin who owned Billie's heart, capturing it with a single kiss.

"What is it," she asked him a few weeks later, as they sat on the bow of the boat, staring out into the sea, the boat drifting gently as the sun dipped lower in the sky, the clouds tinged with orange and gold, "that you really want?"

"I don't know," he said simply, turning to take her face in between both of his hands so that she was looking right into his eyes. "Not exactly. But I know I want this." He picked up her hand and brought it to his lips, closing his eyes as if the musky perfume of her skin made him swoon. She felt her heart pattering in response as she pulled him toward her. It wasn't everything. Not yet. But it was only a matter of time.

Of that, she was sure.

Chapter Seventeen

JULES

When they'd left Eunice, a blanket tucked around her knees, staring pensively into the fire, they'd headed straight to the first bar they passed, the kind of place Jules hadn't been since her college days. Sawdust on the floor and baskets of stale popcorn on the scarred wood of the bar, the jukebox blasting Skynyrd and Zeppelin. Noah ordered two beers, and they settled in at a rickety table in the back, the top sticky with spilled liquor. Jules had finished half of her beer before they spoke a single word, the silence between them almost companionable now, the story she'd just heard still careening through her brain, her thoughts spinning dizzily.

"No doubt this isn't the right time to bring it up," Noah said after a few moments, taking a long swallow before continuing. "But we need to see if there's anyone else left. Your grandmother is long gone, but there could be a cousin or two. Someone Eunice didn't know about."

"My mother was an only child," Jules mused, staring into the glass, foam still hovering on the surface. She hated beer. The smell of it, like a fermented frat house, damp carpeting underfoot. The stink of red SOLO cups and regrettable choices. "So was her own mother."

"Respectfully, Jules," Noah began, pushing his glass to the side and leaning his elbows on the table, "we can't be sure anything Elizabeth ever told you was true."

"If she'd had people, Eunice would've known," Jules pointed out. "We asked, remember?"

All gone, Eunice had said repeatedly, shaking her head, her voice wavering. *Like ice cream!* She'd giggled triumphantly as Noah and Jules exchanged worried glances.

"Eunice isn't exactly playing with a full deck." Noah snorted, one corner of his lips curved in a half smirk, drumming his fingertips on the table in time with the crash of the music.

"Can you stop that?" she snapped, rubbing her eyes, gritty with exhaustion. "It's highly annoying." Her head ached. She'd been awake for what seemed like forever. It felt like days, not hours, had passed since the flight earlier that morning. All she wanted was a bed, a glass of water on the bedside table. The silence of motels, heavy and distinct. The pillow a slab of marble beneath her head, cool and hard as a gravestone.

"Sorry," Noah said, halting his rapid-fire movements.

"I need to get back," Jules said, exhaling heavily—the company, Peter, the Target deal, all hanging above her head like the blade of a guillotine waiting to fall. She was returning to the city with no answers, none but the story Eunice had let loose in disjointed fragments. She needed weeks in Maine if they were to have any hope of unraveling fact from fiction, not a day. She needed everything to stop, to slow down. Most of all, she needed what she didn't have: her mother's arms to enfold her, Elizabeth's voice in her ear, steady and sure.

But her mother was gone, and now Jules was more alone than she had ever been. There was no comfort even in the memories of her childhood, now suspect, raising more questions than answers. The moments with her mother Jules had cherished for so many years, tainted now, each memory, every Christmas and birthday, the graduations and weddings, celebrations and happy smiles built on a foundation of lies and deceit.

This is how it will be from now on, she told herself. *So get used to it. You're on your own.*

~

The Bangor airport was almost deserted but for the few passengers milling around at their gate restlessly, their flight back to New York delayed, fog swirling outside the plate glass windows like smoke, wrapping itself around the building, hovering above the land like the residue of her dreams from the night before. When she'd arrived back at the motel that night, she'd felt disoriented, out of sorts. As she splashed cold water on her cheeks in the bathroom sink, the tile shining cruelly white, it was Elizabeth's heart-shaped face she saw when she looked up into the glass, her mother's blue eyes looking back at her, brimming with secrets. Was she still her mother's daughter, if so much had been so purposefully obscured, so many facts hidden from view?

It was hard to know for sure.

"Look," Jules said, shoving the open laptop resting on her knees at Noah. "I found forty-three different Grace Abbots on Whitepages last night. I pulled every one of them who is over seventy-five and lives within three hundred miles of Winter Harbor into a Google Doc— maybe one of them is actually my grandmother?"

Noah grabbed the computer, shaking his head in disbelief. "What did you do?" he groaned under his breath.

"I cross-referenced them by age and distance from Winter Harbor," she said smugly, pointing at the screen.

"You're never going to find anyone you're trying to look for like that, especially with a last name like Abbot." Noah shook his head disdainfully. "Lucky for us, the Hancock County Historical Society digitized the archives of the local paper, and our answer is there: a death notice for your grandmother ran in 1987," he said, sliding his phone toward her, an image with two paragraphs of bleeding type on the screen.

As she stared down at the screen, Jules felt the hope she'd clung to before this moment evaporate suddenly. Even though the idea that Grace was still alive after all these years had seemed impossible, she'd hung on to the faintest shred of hope (*denial*, her mother would've called it), that she would one day sit in her grandmother's sunny kitchen, her words making sense of all that had been hidden away for so long. But now, that possibility was gone forever. It was as if something had been stolen, its value revealed only when it was far too late. Her hands shook as she scanned the short announcement, nothing close to a full-on obituary, each small detail about her grandmother wildly new—she worked at a grocery store; she died after a short illness, outliving her estranged husband by only a few years. The last line made her shudder, a single tear crawling in a slow trail down her cheek: "She is survived by her daughter, Billie Abbot, of Winter Harbor."

Billie Abbot. A stranger.

"What about Colin?" Jules asked. The bar, Eunice, her frail hands and sudden bursts of startling clarity, the Archibald manor all receded from her thoughts as flight attendants began to cluster around the podium at the front of the gate, and she sighed in relief at the sudden activity, the story Eunice had told them haltingly, starting and stopping like a skipping record, still haunting her.

"There's nothing like first love," Eunice had said, her eyes dreamy and distant. "Nothing to compare to it at all. The thrill of it, that sudden newness—it colors one's whole life, you know." As Eunice rambled on, Jules couldn't help but think of Mark, their early days at school, how her heart had skipped frantically at the sight of him. Had it been the same for Elizabeth? It was hard to imagine her mother moved by anything but a carefully orchestrated tablescape. Even her relationship with Harold had always seemed so . . . sedate. So very orderly.

"I poked around looking for Colin too, and he's basically a black hole. Guy has no social media accounts, no presence on the internet whatsoever, which doesn't mean that he doesn't exist, just that I'll have to work harder to find him. Couple of dudes with the same name in Wyoming, Nebraska," Noah said distractedly, scrolling through his phone, "but ancient—like eighty-five. Not our man."

"He's our only chance," Jules said, as the flight attendant began to announce boarding. "I have to get back to my life, Noah. I've left so much up in the air." All at once she was out of breath, overcome by the enormity of it all, the same feeling she'd had at her mother's funeral, one thing piling endlessly on top of another ever since Elizabeth had died. A memory resurfaced as she gathered her things, preparing to board, her mother staring at her gravely, holding out a clipboard, a pen fastened to the top, the early-morning sun setting the ends of her hair aflame.

I made a list of things I might do better at, Elizabeth had said, as Jules took the clipboard from her hands. *With you,* she added pointedly. *Just check off the ones I can improve at.* The list was long and numbered, and Jules stared down at it in confusion. She was nine years old. What did she know of clipboards? Or grading her own mother on her parenting skills?

I was just a kid.

"I'll keep looking, Jules," Noah said reassuringly as he stood up, handing her back her laptop. She stared at it in confusion, as though it belonged to someone else entirely, so lost was she in her memories. "We've only just begun."

But that was exactly what worried her. What else would they find as they sifted through the detritus Elizabeth had left behind, winding their way through the maze of her deception? How many more lies would they uncover as they went along, Jules wondered. Maybe it was better to wash her hands, blackened with earth, to stop all the digging and let the dead rest.

Jules glanced impatiently at the boarding gate, open now, as the flight attendants scanned phones and welcomed passengers aboard. Elizabeth had always loved flying—and airports—for reasons Jules had never quite understood.

It's a liminal space, Julie, her mother had always said, her cheeks flushed with excitement, *where no rules apply. Just lean into it!* And

Elizabeth had lived by those words, prowling the aisles in the duty-free shop, stuffing her basket with piles of trinkets she'd never even end up removing from their bags, ordering an illicit glass of wine with her blood-rare cheeseburger in the early morning, dawn barely streaking the sky.

But Jules had always viewed airports as nothing more than enormous waiting rooms, a hectic and hellish infinity chamber, one where she might sit indefinitely, waiting for her number to be called. Where everything was out of her control. And that vagueness, the feeling of being trapped between two worlds, the very thing her mother had so adored, made Jules want to climb out of her own skin. But as they approached the gate, shuffling closer in line, Jules took a deep breath before handing her phone over to the agent and pasted a wide smile on her face, just as Elizabeth would've done.

~

When they landed at LaGuardia, the sky was dark, a light rain falling outside. Jules felt shattered, her entire body vibrating with exhaustion. As they stood in a line at the curb, waiting for a cab, Noah turned to her with an inquisitive look. He'd slept most of the flight, and his eyes were red and bloodshot. "I've been meaning to ask, but it's never felt like quite the right time," he said. "Have you gone through your mother's things yet? Her personal papers? Maybe there's something in there that might be helpful."

"I've been avoiding it, to tell you the truth." She groaned as a yellow cab pulled up, the engine idling at the curb. Noah grabbed her bag, handing it to the driver, who had gotten out and was standing at the trunk. "But you're probably right. I know she left a bunch of stuff up in the attic. I can have some boxes couriered over."

"Great," Noah said as the driver slammed the trunk shut, and Jules opened the door and got into the back seat. "Get some rest. I'll let you know what I find. If anything."

"Thanks," Jules said, as Noah shut the car door behind her. As the car sped off, leaving Noah at the curb, she stared at her own reflection in the dark window, the lights of the city shining in the distance as they moved closer to Manhattan, and home, the city she had lived in for the better part of twenty years. She thought of her mother's house in Tarrytown, standing silent and still, the windows darkened. The halls still faintly smelling of Elizabeth's perfume, her mother's copper pots hanging from the rack in the kitchen, buffed to a soft shine, waiting patiently for her return.

Sooner or later, Jules knew, she'd have to deal with it all, maybe even sell the house. But right now, she couldn't think about that, sifting through the shipwreck of her mother's life, folding her sweaters, wrapping her trinkets in Bubble Wrap, and placing them in boxes filled with crumpled newspaper, couldn't even begin to entertain the idea, or she'd go mad. *It's like burying her all over again,* she thought, as the car sped toward the lights of the city.

~

By the time she turned the key in her apartment door, it was after eight. All she wanted was a hot bath and the safety of her own bed, Mark's arms around her as she drifted off into sleep. When she walked in, he was in the living room, standing with his back to her, looking out the window, the phone pressed to one ear. He was wearing the same old pair of black sweats he habitually changed into after work, and a clean white T-shirt. If she touched him, she knew he would smell of laundry soap, of the coffee he'd drunk right before her arrival. When she placed her bag down on the floor, he turned around, smiling broadly at the sight of her. "OK," he said, walking toward her. "Hang on, she just walked in." No one ever called their landline except telemarketers, and Jules found herself immediately annoyed. Whatever it was could wait until she'd had a decent night's sleep.

"Peter," her husband mouthed, as she brought the phone to her ear.

"I've been trying to reach you for days," Peter snapped.

"I've been out of town," Jules said, shrugging off her coat and throwing it over the back of the couch, where it promptly slid to the floor. "What's up?"

"We're moving forward on the Target deal. We can't just put the future of this company on hold while you gallivant around."

"I wasn't gallivanting," Jules protested, knowing he was barely listening. "I was taking care—"

"It doesn't matter," he said, cutting her off. "We can't wait any longer for you to make up your mind. We're moving forward on this. With or without your blessing."

Jules began to pace, her thoughts as jumbled as her clothes stuffed into the carry-on she'd packed so carefully only a few days ago. "What about the TV show?" she asked, a note of panic in her voice.

"You didn't seem interested in pursuing that opportunity," Peter said coolly. "Have you reconsidered?"

Jules sighed. The thought of looking into the camera wearing Elizabeth's signature smile and introducing her mother's most beloved recipes filled her with dread. But she also knew Elizabeth would have never accepted a deal of this magnitude, had she been still alive and breathing, without every *T* firmly crossed, every sample reworked until she was completely satisfied. The cooking show, as excruciating of a prospect as it was, would at least buy her time. And time was the one luxury she didn't have right now.

"I'll do it," Jules said firmly before she could change her mind. "Let the network know."

Chapter Eighteen

The set of *Cooking with Elizabeth* was a perfect replica of her mother's Tarrytown kitchen, right down to the copper pots hanging overhead, the walls painted the same delicate shade of celadon, the white granite countertops shot through with the thinnest veins of rose-colored marble, imbuing the room with a quiet sparkle. Peter and Margaret stood at the craft table, chatting animatedly to the show's producers, their irritation momentarily assuaged by the glimmer of success, Jules stepping seamlessly into the role her mother had perfected.

It had been almost a week since she'd returned from Maine, the days passing in a whirlwind of meetings and plans, and as she stood there, willing herself to walk onto the set and begin, she couldn't shake the feeling that at any moment, Elizabeth might sweep into the room, smiling broadly, stopping to pour herself a coffee or nibble a doughnut, breaking the pastry into small bites and popping them in her mouth one by one.

Her mother's collection of aprons, bought on trips to Provence each summer, hung on a series of brass hooks, next to a sideboard piled with straw hats, Elizabeth's gardening shears protruding from a small wicker basket. Looking at that elaborate backdrop, a place that felt almost as familiar as her own home, she almost expected her mother to walk out at any moment and begin discussing the importance of a *truly* ripe avocado.

In the mid-'90s, when the show was first pitched to the network, the producers had tentatively broached the idea of shooting on location at Elizabeth's estate—an idea her mother had vetoed almost immediately. "Absolutely not," her mother said, as legend had it. "The last thing I need is some camera crew traipsing through my gardens and trampling my creeping phlox." The producers had grumbled endlessly about the extravagance of building the set according to Elizabeth's exact specifications, but when the show first aired in the spring of 1994, it was an immediate sensation, the ratings soaring far beyond anyone's initial expectations.

But I knew all along, Julie, her mother said years later, seated behind the desk in her office at Elizabeth Stone Enterprises, peering at the script for the latest episode and marking out dialogue she didn't care for with careful strokes of her red pen, reading glasses perched on the end of her nose. *I always know when I can't miss. Your father quite agreed with me.*

Harold had been gone for five years, his limp body sprawled on the hard, tiled floors of the bathroom of the Hotel Danieli in Venice, the stroke sudden and swift, and Jules missed his calm, gentle presence every day. It was Harold who'd attended her school plays, every soccer match when Elizabeth was traveling for a book signing, filming an episode on location in the Napa Valley or a Riad in Morocco. Harold who'd walked Jules down the aisle on her wedding day, his careful steps matching her own. He'd stood quietly at Elizabeth's side throughout her entire career, never missing an episode of *Cooking with Elizabeth*, and when Jules was small, instead of leaving her at home with a nanny, he'd often bring her to the set, giving her a bowl of green beans to snap, or a small dish of flour and water to mix together with a wooden spoon on the floor of her mother's dressing room.

She would sit cross-legged, singing quietly to herself and watching as the flour sucked up the liquid and became a paste. It was like magic, she thought, as her small hands moved in circles, or something like it. She liked to pretend it was the thick white icing Elizabeth used to frost her three-tiered cakes, a tangle of edible wildflowers adorning the top.

Even back then, Jules realized as she began to sweat from the hot lights in the room, she'd been playing her mother. Maybe it all had been leading up to this one instant, the moment she would step into those bright lights and turn to the camera as her mother did at the start of every episode, smiling warmly into the lens.

She felt her hands begin to tremble, the four cups of coffee she'd downed that morning buzzing through her veins as she smoothed down the front of her navy shirtdress, a garment Elizabeth's wardrobe stylist had insisted on, and something Jules would never be caught dead wearing in her real life. She would feel better, she knew, more at ease, if Mark were there to take her hand in his own, the warmth of his palm soothing the frayed fibers of her nerves. But that morning, as she'd stepped from the shower, he'd appeared in the doorway, a sheepish look on his face. *Work,* she heard him say, the rest of the words garbled, rushing quickly past like the water spinning down the drain. *Unavoidable,* he'd continued before taking her in his arms, pressing her wet skin to the length of his own as if in apology, her face buried in his neck.

As the makeup artist swiped a dusting of powder across her forehead and nose, Jules's phone pinged with a text, and she pulled it from the front pocket of her dress. It was Noah, only two words, but Jules felt her heart seize at the sight of them.

Got him, it said.

Who, Jules wrote back, her fingers tapping furiously.

Colin! Noah answered, and she could almost feel his impatience through the screen. He's in New Orleans. Changed his last name, so it took forever and a day to find him. So when are we leaving?

Work is nuts right now, she typed furiously. I don't know when I can break away. I'm filming my mother's show.

Her cooking show??? How did that happen?

She looked up to see Margaret at the front of the set, beckoning her closer.

I don't have time to explain, she wrote.

Ok, Noah answered after a few seconds. I get it. I'll be here when you're ready.

I'm sorry, Jules thought as three dots flashed, then disappeared. Lately, between Noah, the show, and the precarious state of the company, it seemed that no matter which direction she went, she was always letting someone down.

Most of all herself.

All at once, the set was too warm, too loud, and the bustle of the PAs as they straightened flower arrangements in window boxes, wiping down Elizabeth's heavy wooden cutting board, set Jules's nerves on edge. It was all too close, too much, the lights flashing in her eyes, her vision blurring around the edges. She tried to steady herself by taking a deep breath, and walked toward Margaret, who stood behind the large kitchen island wearing an encouraging smile, her eyes bright with excitement.

"You're going to be *great,*" Margaret said as a bell rang, signaling the start of filming. She smiled once, reassuringly, and then moved quickly out of frame. Jules turned toward the camera, knew from so many years watching her mother on set that she needed to look into not the lens directly, but the tiny red light just above. That way, her eye contact with the viewer wouldn't be overly jarring or intense. When she looked up, she could almost see her mother standing patiently in the corner near the double oven, clad in the same dress she was buried in, her face expressionless, her eyes sealed shut forever.

Jules felt her lips move, speaking the words she'd rehearsed so many times in the past week, standing in front of the mirror at home. She plucked a single egg from the ceramic bowl on the counter, the speckled brown shell at room temperature, just as Elizabeth had always preferred. But as she held it up in the air, the room began to tilt without warning, dimming around the edges, her heartbeat slowing to a crawl. Jules looked helplessly into the lens, her limbs glued into place, her legs heavy as firewood. But then her instincts took over and she bolted, running from the set as if her life depended on it.

She entered the bathroom, turning the lock and sitting down on the closed lid of the toilet, her breath ragged in her throat. She reached over to the sink, turning the faucet on full blast, the water drowning out the whispers on set. *You're a failure,* the voice in her head hissed above the sound of the rushing water. *Just a cheap stand-in,* the voice went on as Jules bent over, her head in her hands, the hair at her temples damp with perspiration.

There was a sharp rap on the door, and Jules lifted her head, reaching up to wipe her tears quickly away. "It's me," she heard Margaret say softly, as if from a far-off distance, and she reached out and unlocked the door, her fingers deadened and clumsy, to allow Margaret to step inside.

"I know," Jules muttered, grabbing a handful of toilet paper off the roll beside her and blowing her nose noisily into it as Margaret shut the door behind her. "I was terrible. You don't have to say it."

Margaret just looked at her, her tangerine hair curling around her face, the front held back with a thick black headband, her glasses mirroring the tortoiseshell glint of her eyes.

"On the contrary," she said, as Jules blew her nose again, probably smearing her makeup beyond repair in the process. "I had actual chills. I felt like I was watching your mother up there."

"What?" Jules replied, looking up in surprise, her hands filled with wadded-up tissue.

"The way you move, how you speak. I was beside myself. We all were."

"I find that hard to believe," she said slowly, in disbelief. "I froze up there. I couldn't do it."

"But you did do it," Margaret said evenly. "You *were* doing it. You just have to get up and do it again."

"You make it sound so easy," Jules muttered, standing up and throwing the tissue in the trash.

"Jules," Margaret said firmly, "you were born to do this. You just have to relax and get out of your own head." She came up behind her, placing a hand on Jules's shoulder and giving it a squeeze. "Take a few minutes and collect yourself," she said as she walked toward the door, "and then we'll try again."

The door closed behind her and Jules stood at the sink, gripping the porcelain with both hands, the water rushing into the basin. *Put your wrists under the tap.* She could almost hear her mother's voice in her ear, feel the weight of her presence. *The cold water will calm your nerves, Julie, bring down your adrenaline.*

She placed her wrists under the stream and held them there, a welcome shock. She shivered once, her shoulders wrenching violently. But before turning off the faucet, she reached one damp hand to the back of her neck, lifting her hair up and pressing her cold fingers against the skin, closing her eyes. Time seemed to halt entirely, and in those few seconds, Jules could almost believe she wasn't alone in the fluorescent light bouncing brightly off the tiles.

"What if I can't do it?" she said aloud. "What then?"

But what if you can? came the immediate answer. *After all, what choice do you really have?*

Her mother, as always, was right, Jules thought, as she took a deep breath before drying her hands on a paper towel, tossing it into the trash on the way out the door.

Chapter Nineteen

BILLIE

"The flowers should circle the top," Marcus said, reaching over to straighten the cake plate, round and made of milk glass, opaque and thick. Billie began arranging the mix of candied violets and nasturtiums along the border of thick white frosting, her brow set in concentration. There was a small pile of borage on the counter, the blue petals recalling patches of dense, secret woods, the iridescent wings of fairies. "But not as if one is trying too hard. You understand?"

Marcus looked at her shrewdly, his face lined and drawn. When he'd returned to the kitchen a week after falling ill, it had been clear that something was amiss, some essential spark lost. Despite his great height, his shoulders slumped with an air of defeat. His cooking was as exacting as ever, but had dimmed almost imperceptibly somehow, the flavors muted, as if a light had been all but snuffed out. "Arrange them neatly," he went on, fixing an errant smear of frosting along the sides of the cake with a metal spatula. "But not *too* neatly. It cannot be precious. There is nothing she detests more than artifice."

Billie nodded in agreement, as she arranged the last blossom and carefully covered the cake with a dome, blown glass that resembled spun sugar, so delicate that even one tap against the countertop would cause it to break into shards. She spent her days in pursuit of careless perfection, the plating of the midday meal the highest of arts, but one that was curiously undone, if executed correctly. There was a delicate balance, a tightrope she was learning to walk barefoot, with only her instinct to guide the way.

But her nights belonged to Colin.

Billie reached up, her fingers tracing along the side of her neck, the spot his lips had brushed against so gently the night before. When she thought of how he'd looked at her, his eyes searching her own in the dark of the harbor, she shivered, a secret thrill. Each evening, after dinner, she ducked out into the night, closing the front door on her mother's disapproving glare, the cicadas' song filling her ears as she ran across the lawn, hopping onto her bike and pedaling down to the harbor, where he waited on the dock, his speedboat bobbing in the waves, his hands filled with coarse rope.

The summer was moving fast, as if time itself had sped up inexorably, falling away like grains of sand between her fingers as they hurtled toward fall. She spent her days avoiding Colin's gaze at the table as she placed a plate in front of him. In the kitchen, braising lamb and shucking oysters, every footstep overhead made her pulse quicken. Each time he brushed by her in the downstairs hall, the pull between them so strong that it took all her willpower not to push him up against the wall beneath the family portraits, her mouth greedily seeking his own. She knew implicitly that whatever was between them could only exist away from prying eyes, away from questions neither of them could answer.

But it didn't matter. He was the sting of salt air against her flesh, the rust on the garden shed door, rough on her fingertips. He was jagged hunks of obsidian and pale chunks of moonstone, glowing in the dark. A devil's bargain. He was gravity itself, and she could no more give him up than she could alter her own destiny. Colors were brighter now, the world filled with an almost unbearable beauty. Each leaf in the trees overhead, the water swirling playfully around the rocks at the shore, even the barrens dotted with the birth of tiny berries, cornflower blue, felt as if they might break her heart. It was as though she'd gone through all her life on autopilot, but now she was suddenly alive, humming under her breath as she snipped chives in the garden. Each time she glanced in the mirror, she hardly recognized herself in her own happiness.

There was the sound of heels against the marble floors, and Eunice strode into the kitchen, her eyes sweeping the room. Billie grabbed a damp rag and began scrubbing at the daubs of frosting that had hardened and stuck like dollops of plaster on the marble countertop. In the past weeks, Eunice had begun a series of sporadic, impromptu lessons, first summoning her into the vast coat closet in the front hall to explain the difference between Irish wool and Scottish, thick scarves cradled in her hands, muted shades of green and gray. There was an afternoon at the china cabinet, watching as Eunice tilted a large platter until the sheen caught the light, opalescent, a rainbow slick of oil floating on water. There was silver that shone in its velvet-lined box, tablecloths fashioned from the finest handmade lace, the intricate stitching along the hem done by nuns at a convent in Avignon.

"You cannot fake quality," Eunice was fond of saying. "You cannot buy taste. Money does one absolutely no good without an inkling of what is really worth owning. Value is relative," she would murmur, holding an emerald bracelet up to the light, the stones glittering against her crimson nails, the tips neatly squared, "but quality is unmistakable. You must learn to recognize it."

"Marcus," Eunice began, "I was hoping you might spare Billie for a few hours? I need her assistance in town."

Less than thirty minutes later, Billie was nestled in the back of the car, Nate glancing in the rearview mirror as they pulled out of the drive, his eyes flicking over her in disgust. Ever since she'd ended it after that first night on the yacht, Colin's kiss branded on her lips like a tattoo, Nate had done his best to avoid her at work, even going so far as to head in the opposite direction whenever she appeared.

"Give me one good reason," he'd asked that stifling afternoon on her front porch, the same spot they'd stood so many times before, splintered wood beneath their feet, and she looked away, not wanting to see the hurt in his eyes, pain she knew she had inflicted with her words. But she also knew there was nothing she could say that would make him understand, no explanation she could offer but the truth: her heart belonged to someone else.

In town, Billie watched as Eunice entered one store after the next, the shopkeepers rushing to greet her the moment she walked through the door in a creamy trail of honeysuckle and jasmine, the scent so thick it could make one gasp. Billie watched transfixed as Eunice perused stacks of duvet covers, the linen in soft shades of cream and pewter. She weighed disks of bath soap in her palms, the surfaces flecked with buds of lavender and clary sage, and tried on dresses of smooth satin, silk peignoirs trimmed with yards of velvet ribbon.

"Look at the detail." She held up a bed shawl fashioned from delicate cream-colored lace. "This workmanship is so fine, so intricate. I can almost see my hand through it," she marveled.

"Who made it?" Billie asked, as Eunice handed her the shawl, as weightless as air between her hands.

"Labels don't matter. Only craftsmanship. Quality goods, made with care, will last forever. What is disposable is quite worthless." Eunice sniffed, bringing the shawl to the register. "Put it on my account," she commanded, and the saleswoman nodded, wrapping the garment in pink tissue paper, then sliding it into a shopping bag, the handles secured with ivory ribbon, bells tinkling behind them as she followed Eunice out the door.

～

When they returned late that afternoon, Billie lingered at the front gate, where she had left her bike early that morning, her eyes searching the windows of the manor, praying for movement, but the house was silent and still. Just as she was about to leave, the front door opened, and Colin stepped out, the fading sun gilding his hair, falling loosely to his collar. He held up a hand in greeting and began walking down the gravel drive. At his approach, she couldn't hold back the smile that appeared on her face, growing wider as he stopped in front of her. For a moment, they simply stood there, looking at one another, and in that moment, Billie thought she had never seen anything so beautiful in her life as the boy standing there in the dappled sunlight.

"Let's take a walk," he said, reaching out to take her hand, closing his fingers around her own. Before she could utter even one word, he had pulled her into the vast thicket of woods, a worn path underfoot where the grass had been flattened by pairs of shoes over the years, small divots in the ground she could feel with every step she took. The air inside the woods was a few degrees cooler than in the full sun, their bodies casting long shadows on the path strewn with pine needles, the wide arcs of the branches protecting them with sprawling, benevolent arms.

They came into a clearing, the ocean appearing suddenly, and she drew in her breath sharply, as she always did at the sight of it, the shore lined with rocks, hopping from one to the next, the late-afternoon sun warming her head and shoulders. They sat down on a flat stone, its surface worn smooth by the sea, Colin's arms encircling her, his chin resting on the top of her head.

There was the sound of water lapping against the shore, the mournful cries of the gulls. And then the thoughts came, streaming through her brain in a rush, thoughts she could not control or suppress. How many girls had there been? she wondered. Girls just like her, looking out at the vastness of the ocean, believing summer might last forever?

"In a few weeks, it'll turn cold," she said quietly, tilting her chin to glance up at the sky, the fading light streaking the clouds with violet and rose. "You'll leave."

"It seems like a hundred years from now," he said, his voice already far away, as if over a telephone wire.

"But it isn't," she said, and in that moment, a wave of sadness washed over her, so strong she had to fight the tears hovering at the corners of her eyes. *Keep it together,* she told herself, as she exhaled heavily.

You knew this was coming. You knew it all summer long. And it was true. He would leave at the end of the season, she knew, as all summer people did, returning to their lives, the months they'd spent together a distant memory, a blur of bonfires and woodsmoke swirling in the air. Her only consolation was that he would never know how much it would break her to watch him go.

"I can't imagine my life without you," he mumbled, his voice muffled as he buried his face in the warm hollow of her neck.

"I think you're going to have to." She pulled herself away, drawing her knees to her chest and wrapping her arms around them as if to protect herself. The words were like the burn from a cast-iron pan, the skin blistering on contact.

The wind coming off the water was beginning to cool, a chill suffusing the air, one that Billie knew intimately. It arrived at the end of every summer without warning, like a bothersome old friend popping up for a visit. Only the night before, she'd woken suddenly, the sky an inky black, the air coming through the open window cool enough to raise gooseflesh on her limbs, and she'd reached for the quilt at the end of her bed, drawing it up around her shoulders. Even half-awake she understood, the realization dawning on her as she slid uneasily back into sleep.

Summer was almost over.

"Listen to me," Colin said, a note of urgency in his voice. She could feel his agitation, a restless fluttering of wings, and she turned to face him, forcing herself to not look away. "I want to be with you," he said. "You know I do."

"What does that mean?" she asked, unable to keep the edge from her voice. "You're with me now. And that's all the time we have, isn't it?"

He took her face between his hands so that it was inches from his own. "Don't do that," he said softly. "Don't brush this off like it's nothing. You know it's not."

"But what does it matter," she protested, despising the pleading note in her own voice, a vulnerability she'd always run from, the soft contours of her heart exposed. "You're leaving."

There it was. The indisputable fact of it all. He would leave her behind, joining his father at his Manhattan law firm, sitting behind a desk, squirming uncomfortably in a three-piece suit, and all the while, she would sink further and further into memory, a story he'd tell at cocktail parties. A girl he had known one summer. Nothing more.

"What if I didn't," he said, releasing her and sitting back on his heels, the wind blowing the hair from his face.

"Didn't what?"

"Didn't go back to New York. What if I stayed here? With you."

"But you can't," she sputtered. "What about your—"

"I don't care about any of that," he said, reaching out and taking her hands in his own. "All I know is that I want to be with you."

"You can't be serious," she said, pulling away from his grasp. "You're leaving, Colin. You'll go to work for your father, and sooner or later, you'll marry some society girl and carry on the Archibald family name. You know it and so do I."

"Not if I don't go back."

She laughed then, a harsh gasp, a sudden pain in her chest, blooming there like a black flower.

"Listen to me," he said, pulling her toward him again, reaching up and brushing the hair from her forehead, his hands tender and sure. "I'm serious, Billie. I love you. I can't imagine being with anyone else."

"But what about your family? Do you really think they'll understand"—she gestured helplessly at the air between them—"this?" She thought of Eunice's face, blanched white as Colin's words fell like an anvil in the living room, the admiral's protestations. Most of which she knew were valid. *Climber,* he would call her. *Opportunist.*

Impostor.

"You think too much." Colin snorted, shaking his head as if she amused him. "I said I'll handle it, and I will. Now shut up and kiss me." He grinned, leaning down to press his lips against her own. She pulled him closer, her misgivings tumbling away like stones from her pockets. And when they broke apart, she knew from the look in his eyes, determined and resolute, that he'd meant every word.

Chapter Twenty

Billie stood before the bathroom mirror, pulling a brush languidly through her hair, a smile tugging at her lips. There was a lightness to her days now. As she rode the ferry each morning, she could not help but lean over the edge of the railing, pushing her face into the wind, the sea below mirroring the excitement in her blood. Each rose in the garden seemed clearly outlined now, as if the petals had been cut out carefully with a razor, then pieced back together, a collage of color and light.

"You can't think he's serious about you." Her mother's voice rang at her back, and Billie turned around, the brush still in her hand. "Not for one minute."

Grace stood in the doorway in a pair of old denim cutoffs and the blue Yankees shirt she wore when working in the garage on one of her projects, a shirt that had once belonged to Billie's father. The sight of the faded blue cotton wiped the smile from Billie's face, and she turned back to the mirror, securing her hair in a ponytail. She'd been careful to cover her tracks—or so she'd thought. But by the look on her mother's face, it was clear Grace hadn't bought even one of Billie's paltry excuses.

"I don't know what you mean," Billie said, turning on the faucet so the water gushed loudly into the sink, ending the discussion. But before she could even pick up her toothbrush, her mother was at her side, reaching over to turn the tap off again with a wrench of her wrist.

"You know *exactly* what I mean. Sneaking out of here every night? Did you honestly think I hadn't noticed?"

"I wasn't sneaking," Billie protested. "I just didn't say where I was headed is all."

"I'm not stupid," her mother said, moving her hands to her hips. "I haven't seen Nate around here in months."

Billie moved past her and over to the closet, grabbing a macramé tote from the hook on the back of the door, a bag Grace had made two summers ago after a class she'd taken at a yarn shop in Bar Harbor. Her mother was always doing things like that, picking up new talents, as though they were finely whorled shells she'd found along the shoreline. It was one of the things Billie loved most about her.

"So what," she mumbled. "You don't know everything."

"I know there's no way it's Nate that you're running out of here every night to meet. I know that," her mother said triumphantly. "What is wrong with you, Billie?" The exasperation was plain on her face. "I raised you to be smarter than this. He'll *leave*. That's what they do."

Billie whirled around, her face flushed as much from the closeness of the room in the summer heat as her own anger. "That's your story," she said, her words blunt as the hilt of a dagger. "Not mine. You don't know anything about us—Colin and me."

There was a silence, and then Grace sighed once, long and heavy, as if the weight of time rested on her shoulders. "I've lived enough, and I know enough," she said wearily, the fight gone from her now, "to see how things will end. This isn't some fairy tale you've wandered into, Billie. This is real life. He will leave at the end of the summer. Because that's what summer people do."

"You're wrong," Billie said, her anger a fiery trail moving up from her chest, setting her tongue alight.

"For your sake, I hope you're right." Her mother turned to face her, her clear blue eyes so like her own. "Because for boys like him, you're a distraction. A pretty new toy—one he'll tire of soon enough."

Billie's eyes flashed, and her lips parted, but instead of releasing the torrent of words she knew would drown them both, she turned her back on her mother, the room, walking to the door, slamming it behind her until the wood rattled in its frame.

~

In the Archibalds' kitchen, she arranged a vase of roses as Eunice had taught her, the morning's irritation hanging over her so that before she realized it, she nicked her finger on the small, sharp utility knife she was using to strip the thorns. One single drop of blood bloomed scarlet, marring the purity of the marble counter. The crystal vase Eunice preferred for the bouquets on the entry hall table was currently cradling a bright cluster of sunflowers, so she headed out into the main hall, opening the utility closet in search of a replacement.

But just as she opened the door, a rumble of voices floated down the corridor from the admiral's study, and she crept slowly down the hall, the vase forgotten now, the voices growing louder still, until she hovered directly outside the half-open door. *Leave now,* she told herself. Nothing good ever came of eavesdropping, she knew, but something told her not to walk away.

"Preposterous," she heard the admiral say in disgust. "Completely out of the question."

"You need to listen to me," Colin replied urgently, and she could hear the defiance behind his words. Standing there, just inches away, she knew he was pacing the perimeter of the room, raking his hands through his hair. "She's special, Dad. Unlike any girl I've ever met. I'm not going to lose her."

Billie stood with her back against the wall and closed her eyes, a wave of disappointment buckling her knees so that she almost sank to the carpet. It was almost as if she knew what would come next, before the admiral had uttered even one word in response. The clock on the hall table, an ornate piece that she had always hated, chimed ten times in a row, and when the air was still, the admiral spoke again, his tone subdued now.

"That's your choice," he said bluntly. "But don't expect me to fund it."

Billie opened her eyes as her heart sank through the polished floorboards. She could hear a desk drawer open and close, a match being struck, and she knew the admiral had lit one of his cigars, one brown end placed between his lips. The smell of tobacco filled the air, cloyingly sweet, and her stomach turned sharply.

"So if I marry her, that's it then? I'm cut off?"

"If you want to make bad choices, son, you'll do it on your own dime," the admiral replied offhandedly, as though it warranted no further discussion. She knew without even looking that he was leaning back in his chair, his expression hidden by plumes of smoke that curled around him, shielding him from view.

"Can we just talk about this?" Colin pleaded, and Billie closed her eyes again at the desperation in his voice. "If you just got to know her, I'm sure you'd—"

"Enough!" the admiral yelled, slamming one fist on the desktop, and Billie flinched, her eyes snapping open. "This discussion is finished. Am I making myself clear?"

"Yes," Colin whispered, and with that one word, Billie felt her heart splinter, cracking in two, and before she could hear any more, she ran down the hall to the kitchen, pushed open the back door, and bolted out into the garden, the grass beneath her feet still wet with dew, dampening her bare ankles.

"Wait," a voice behind her yelled, but she kept moving. "Billie, wait!" Colin yelled again, and Billie spun around, her hands balled into fists, her face streaked with tears.

"What do you want?" she asked, her chest so tight she felt as if she might stop breathing.

"I'm sorry you had to hear that," Colin said quietly, shoving his hands into the pockets of his cargo pants. Standing there, with his hair falling softly to his collarbone, the sunlight tingeing the ends with gold, he was the most beautiful thing she'd ever seen in her life. *It's always this way,* she thought as his eyes searched her face, pleading for understanding, *right before you lose someone forever.*

"I'm sorry too," she said hotly, reaching up and wiping the wetness from her face with one hand. "Sorry we ever met."

"Don't be like that," he said, taking a step forward.

"Don't touch me," she snapped, pulling sharply away. "You don't get to ever touch me again."

"It's not what you think, Billie," he shouted, removing his hands from his pockets, and throwing them in the air. "You don't understand the kind of pressure I'm under."

"So explain," she said, crossing her arms over her chest. The back of the T-shirt she wore was damp with sweat, her shoes felt too tight, and all she wanted was to be home in her room, where she could cry in peace, a pillow muffling her sobs.

Colin just stared at her, their entire summer reflected in his eyes, the droning of the boat as it cut through the waves, the taste of his skin, salt and woodsmoke, how he'd stacked the logs one on top of another, scouring the beach just to keep her warm. The way the firelight cast a tangerine glow around their bodies, naked and wet from the sea. And she knew then, as she had in the hall, as he'd accepted defeat, that no matter what explanation he might give, it was over. Completely and irrevocably finished.

"You didn't fight for me," she said, her voice a harsh whisper.

"I know." He stared down at his shoes, as if he were too ashamed to look her in the face, ashamed of his own weakness, his passivity, his dependence on the luxuries he'd taken for granted all his life. It came to her with a sudden clarity, what she'd tried so hard to ignore all along, the red flags he'd waved like roses. The story would always end the same way. She would forever be a girl standing in a garden, surrounded by indescribable beauty, heartbroken and alone.

"Are you ready to give up everything for me?" she asked brazenly, already knowing the answer as she stepped forward and reached out, tapping him squarely on the shoulder. The hard smack of her hand against his flesh felt strangely satisfying, and as she stood there looking at him, it took all her willpower not to do it again.

He considered the grass, refusing to look her in the face, and she felt her lips curling in disgust, self-righteousness coating her tongue, thick as molasses. "You don't understand," he mumbled.

"Sure I do," Billie said, as she pushed past him, her steps brisk and purposeful as she moved hurriedly through the garden, despite the fact that all she wanted at that very moment was to take it all in for the last time, to linger among the carefully pruned vegetable beds, the explosion of poppies against the stone walls, their petals mirroring the spilled blood of her heart. As she approached the back door, too soon, she knew with a sinking finality that she would never step foot in that house again.

~

The light came and went. The moon rose in the sky and disappeared again, replaced by the heat of the new day. The shadows crept across the walls of her room like thieves, the globe of the sun rising each morning like an unwanted gift. Days passed, one blending into the next until somehow it had been weeks, and Billie still lay in bed, the same pair of old shorts and a T-shirt sticking to her flesh, the curtains at the open windows unmoving in the August heat. Each time she closed her eyes, she saw Colin's face framed by the wall of green, his eyes downcast, refusing to look at her.

When she'd arrived home that terrible afternoon, the front door insurmountably heavy as she closed it behind her, Billie had leaned her weight against the hard, wooden surface, her tears coming faster now, unchecked. "What is it?" her mother said as she entered the hall, reaching out reflexively to feel Billie's forehead, her palm cool as water.

"You were right," she finally said, noting the concern on her mother's face, the way her forehead creased with worry.

"Right about what?"

"Don't make me say it," Billie replied as she broke into a bout of fresh sobs, her shoulders shaking with pain.

"Oh, honey," she said quietly, pulling Billie against her so that her head rested on her mother's shoulder, the scent of wood polish mixed with the chemical haze of paint stripper cutting through the grief that threatened to annihilate her. Her mother patted her back, her hands moving in a rhythmic circle, just as she had done so often when Billie was small. "Oh, honey, I'm sorry," she murmured, and something about those words stanched the flow of Billie's tears, igniting the spark of her anger once more.

"Are you happy now?" Billie said as she pulled away, her voice tinged with bitterness.

"About what?" her mother answered, the confusion in her expression giving way to dismay. "Oh, Billie, no. That isn't how I—"

"Just leave me alone," Billie muttered, pushing past her mother, her feet carrying her up the carpeted stairs, the same ones she'd climbed daily for the past twenty-one years of her life. And as the days passed, one after another, her room became the eye of the storm, the hallway outside her bedroom door lined with plates of untouched food. Sourdough toast drenched in butter, carefully cut into triangles placed alongside a pair of soft-boiled eggs. Chicken soup left to congeal in the bowl. A salad of crisp lettuce from the garden, a ripe tomato, a dish of her mother's homemade ranch dressing on the side.

"Dammit, Billie, you have to eat!" Grace shouted in exasperation through the door, but Billie just turned over, burying her face in the quilt. There was no reason to get up. No reason to even move.

Until the doorbell rang, the sound insistent as it was unwanted, and Billie groaned, placing the pillow over her face to drown out the noise, her hair lank and greasy against the sheets. There was the sound of voices in the front hall, first hushed, then insistent, and she pushed the pillow from her face and sat up.

Resting, she heard her mother say, her voice tight. *Nerve just showing up here . . .*

And then there were footsteps on the stairs, the last step creaking noisily, the way it had for Billie's entire childhood. There was a knock at the door, two sharp raps, military in their precision, and the bedroom door swung open. Eunice Archibald stood in the doorway in a beige sheath dress, her hair pulled back in a chignon, her lips a vivid slash of carmine, ropes of pearls circling her throat.

"May I come in?" she asked politely, stepping inside and shutting the door behind her before Billie could reply.

"You already are," Billie said flatly, drawing her knees to her chest, as if to hide behind them altogether.

Eunice stood there, clasping her red leather handbag in front of her, her eyes surveying the room, the posters on the pale-blue walls, the antique writing desk her mother had refinished pushed into one corner. "Your house is quite charming," she marveled as she took a few steps in, stopping at the foot of the bed.

"What are you doing here?" Billie asked, irritated now, and done with pleasantries.

"May I?" Eunice said lightly, pointing at the end of the bed, covered by an afghan Billie's grandmother had crocheted so long ago.

"I don't care." Billie shrugged, looking away, and Eunice lowered herself gingerly, as if the bed might sink to the ground beneath her weight.

"I've brought your last check," Eunice said, crossing one slim leg over the other while opening her purse, pulling out a long, white envelope. "I assume from your prolonged absence that you're quitting."

"You assume correctly," Billie said, all too aware of the clothes strewn across the floor, the plates of food outside the door, moldering in the summer heat, the smell of her body, rank as a bowl of onions left in the sun. How long had it been since she'd showered, she wondered as Eunice looked at her as if she were as unpredictable as an experiment, waiting for what she might do next. She held the envelope out in the air, and Billie took it, the heavy paper smooth and cool in her hands.

"My son is nowhere near good enough for you."

Billie raised her head sharply to find Eunice surveying her thoughtfully, her eyes glittering in her angular face.

"You knew?"

"My dear." Eunice laughed softly. "Of course."

This was a woman who was incapable of ignoring even the most minuscule imperfection in her world, who would take offense if the sitting room rug lay off center by a quarter of an inch. Who might proclaim the bread overbaked with only a casual glance. Yes, of course she had known.

"But that fact notwithstanding," Eunice went on, "what I am telling you is quite true."

"Right," Billie scoffed, looking down and picking at a loose thread on the edge of the sheet, wishing she could disappear. "Isn't it the other way around?"

"My husband is a buffoon," Eunice scoffed. "He wouldn't know a good thing if he tripped over it. Besides," she went on with a shrug of her shoulders, "what were you going to do—work in my kitchen forever? My dear, you have bigger fish to fry, as the saying goes."

Billie swallowed hard. That was exactly what she had hoped for, though she would prefer to be drawn and quartered than ever admit it now. She would take over for Marcus when he retired, she'd imagined, running the kitchen in the summer season and traveling with Colin in the fall and spring. They would see the stone streets of Paris, maybe even the cherry blossoms in Kyoto, pale pink petals strewn in the tangle of her hair. It all seemed ridiculous now, a life meant for another girl.

One who didn't exist.

"You will see," Eunice said as she stood abruptly, hanging her purse over one slim wrist, "when you open it, that I've included a bit extra. I hope you will take it in the spirit in which it is offered."

"A payoff?" Billie asked incredulously, looking up to meet Eunice's eyes, holding them with her own.

"Don't be daft," Eunice snapped, her impatience rising to the surface like cream at the top of a bottle of milk. "You need a new start.

Away from this place you so love and despise in equal measure. You will do important things in this world, Elizabeth. I am sure of it. But you cannot do them here."

"Can't or won't?"

"They are one and the same." Eunice smiled. "As I think you well know."

There were so many things Billie wanted to say, so many questions she needed to ask, but she knew none of them would be any use. What was done was done. No words would change any of it now.

"I've taught you what I could. Not much, I know, but you'll make it into something, I'm certain. Something worthwhile."

"How do you know?" Billie asked, blinking back her tears.

"Because I see myself in you, I suppose. And that is how I know that one setback isn't going to break you. Men will come and go. But what you create in this world, what you *accomplish*, no matter how small, that, my dear, is forever."

When Eunice left, she did so silently, the door barely making a sound as it shut, leaving Billie alone in the sanctuary of her room once again, the sun beating urgently against the shingles of the house. *Go now*, it seemed to be saying. *Before it's too late.* Twelve hours later she was on a Greyhound bus, a note left on the kitchen table, the paper torn from her mother's battered copy of *The Joy of Cooking*, Billie's script covering the instructions for Baked Alaska in a tight scrawl of black ink.

> Mom,
> I love you, but if I don't go now, I never will.
> I'll write soon. Don't worry.
> Love,
> Billie

She stared out the grimy window and watched the land roll by, the convenience stores blurring before her eyes, the highway unfurling like a length of ribbon, her gaze hard and determined. New York would be different. It had to be. And there, in that mythic, shimmering city, she would become someone else entirely, the girl she once was disappearing, as if into a dense fog.

Elizabeth Abbot wasn't a bad name. It had a certain cachet, Eunice had once mentioned offhandedly as she poured an amber stream of tea into a china cup. But, for all its charms, Billie knew that to cling to that particular moniker would allow the past to come knocking, demanding entry into her perfectly ordered world. She would never again, she knew, be reduced to the girl in that bedroom, wondering how she would wake each morning, opening her eyes to a new day, her heart torn at the seams. Would never again be that girl in the garden, the kind of girl men like the admiral could discount so easily, hot, angry tears burning her cheeks like water hissing in a cast-iron skillet.

Abbot would not do.

She would miss the rocky coast of Maine, the hard, unyielding nature of the place, a land that did not suffer fools gladly, that did not bend to one's will. She would create a fortress, impenetrable as that coastline itself, her heart hardened as the ice coating the rocks that lined the shore each winter, the water turning from periwinkle to gray.

Granite, she thought, as the bus sped down the highway, taking her farther away with every bright-green mile marker. *Rock.*

Stone.

Chapter Twenty-One
JULES

She threw her coat over a bench in the front hall, the wood oiled and sleek, the familiar scent of the house tugging at her memories, the calm of lavender and the richness of beeswax, that smell that meant she was home. It was as if at any moment, Elizabeth might appear in the hall, wooden spoon in hand, her arms outstretched in welcome. Jules couldn't step even one foot into her mother's house without the past rushing back, clawing at her with desperate fingers. The Limoges vase perched on the stone mantel, her mother's Burberry trench hanging in the hall closet, the cluster of framed photographs on the hall table. All of it seemed to serve little purpose but to bring Elizabeth back from the dead.

But although it was early morning, the day was overcast, the sky tinged with soot, the house suffused with a distinct chill, one that seemed to intensify with every gust of wind. Jules shivered, turning the heat up on the thermostat, knowing even as she did so that she'd need to build a fire in the hearth just to get the house to a reasonable temperature. Built from stone in the 1800s, the house was always drafty, no matter how much insulation her mother had blown into its gaping cracks and crevices.

She moved into the living room, flipping on the lights with a sigh, and sank into the sofa, drawing her feet up beneath her. What she had expected to find there, in the place her mother had so adored, she didn't know. *It's my peace, Julie,* her mother had always said. *The only peace I've ever known.* Sitting in her mother's house, where she'd spent so much of her life, both soothed and wounded Jules in equal measure, like tonguing a rough scrape on the roof of her mouth, an irritant and a salve.

"We need to sell it," Mark had begun repeating lately, as if dismantling her mother's life, and her own childhood, were that simple.

"Sell the house?" she'd wondered aloud, as if the idea were unfathomable. "My mother adored that house. She'd never sell it."

"Your mother's gone, Jules," Mark would gently remind her, and each time she would shake her head and walk from the room in a daze, as if she could put off the idea entirely by simply avoiding it.

There was so much she needed to do, to sort through, an entire life to unpack and catalog, so many boxes in her mother's temperature-controlled storage space in the garage, her bedroom closet full of shoes and handbags, lined up in meticulous rows. But each time Jules walked through the portal of the front door, exhaustion overtook her, her limbs weighted and heavy. She found her eyes closing drowsily as she leaned back against the plump velvet pillows, the jasmine of Elizabeth's perfume rising from the cabled throw folded neatly beside her on the couch.

A sudden rap at the front door jolted her from sleep, and she sat up, wiping her mouth with the back of one hand as she stumbled to her feet. Her hair was a mess, she knew, as she walked to the front door, but she reached up anyway, trying to smooth her ropy curls with anxious fingers. The gray sweatshirt she'd borrowed from Mark hung loosely to her thighs, covering her black leggings. She was losing weight. The leggings, almost too snug a month before, now bagged loosely at her waist and ankles.

When she wrestled the door open, Margaret stood on the threshold, smiling awkwardly, a beige wool coat tied firmly at the waist. She blinked at Jules from behind her thick frames, waiting to be invited in.

"What are you doing here?" Jules wondered aloud, her voice rough from sleep.

"I called the apartment," Margaret said, never one for patience as she pushed past Jules and into the house, untying the sash on her coat and shrugging it off. "But Mark said you were here."

"You could have tried my cell," Jules pointed out as Margaret opened the hall closet, hanging her coat neatly inside. Beneath it she wore a plain black sweaterdress that hung shapelessly on her thin frame. Her mass of gingered hair was, as always, tied back from the stark bones of her face.

"I did," Margaret said, closing the closet door. "Several times. Chilly in here," she remarked, shivering delicately as she followed Jules into the living room.

"I was going to build a fire," Jules said weakly, looking over at the stone mantel, the charred, desiccated bits of logs, piles of gray ashes in the hearth reminiscent of a funeral pyre, and she looked away, a sour taste in her mouth. "But I must've fallen asleep."

"It's understandable," Margaret said, sitting down in the armchair adjacent to the fireplace. "Grief is exhausting. Not to mention everything else."

Jules nodded, moving over to the fireplace. She bent down, grabbing a handful of kindling from a woven basket, stacking it neatly in the hearth, and placing two birch logs on top, the way her mother had shown her. When she lit the small scraps of kindling, there was always a moment of deep satisfaction as she watched it catch fire, the blaze moving through the twigs and bits of paper and into the wood until the logs burned merrily.

"You still haven't told me why you're here," she said, as she stood up and walked back over to the sofa, sinking into the cushions once more and staring into the flames, marveling at their intricate dance, how they moved from pale orange to violet at the edges, the bright, intermittent sparks a shower of confetti.

"As you know, the reboot aired last week," Margaret said, crossing one leg over the other.

Jules couldn't bring herself to watch it, the TV remaining dark and silent, devoid of life, no matter how many times Mark had suggested inviting a crowd over to toast the show with flutes of champagne. "It's a new era, Jules," he'd reminded her (as if she needed reminding). "We should celebrate."

But what were they celebrating exactly, Jules wondered. The fact that her mother was dead and in the ground, where she could no longer protest the changes that would've turned her whole world askew? Or the fact that Jules was trying desperately to replace her? A party felt almost ghoulish, as if they were tap-dancing on Elizabeth's grave.

"The reviews for the first two episodes, as I'm sure you know, have been extremely positive," Margaret went on. "But the ratings . . . are another story."

"What do you mean?"

"They were pretty negligible, Jules, even with all the advertising dollars the network sank into promos. They aren't happy. They've decided to cut their losses and cancel the show."

"After only a few episodes?" Jules said, unable to hide her surprise.

"It's an established series," Margaret went on, her voice patient and slow, as if Jules were a toddler again. "The dip in ratings isn't a good sign, from their perspective."

"But I only just took over. Don't they want to give it a few more episodes? See if it picks up steam?"

Margaret just shook her head. "Unfortunately not. We need to move on to plan B. Which is why I'm here."

"The Target deal," Jules said, her voice flat and resigned. She had done her best Elizabeth Stone impersonation, smiling so widely into the lens that she feared her face would crack, and it had all led to nothing. It seemed as if all doors in her life were shutting, one after the next in a long line. *When God closes one window, he opens another,* her mother was fond of saying when things didn't go her way. But God, it seemed to Jules, wasn't interested in opening windows or doors, just barricading them shut with steel bars.

"There's more," Margaret said, and Jules could hear the reluctance in her voice, see it in her face in the way she lowered her eyes briefly, almost in apology before looking up again. "As you know, we were really hoping the show would give us a bump in the online store . . . but that hasn't happened, either."

No sales. No money. Jules didn't need to ask for more explanation. It was as simple as the fact that Elizabeth was gone. The sense of defeat was a million hornet stings, and her skin prickled with shame. "OK, then," she said, exhaling heavily. "I guess there's no choice now. Let Target know. Assuming they're still interested."

I tried, Mom, she thought, looking away from Margaret and out the bank of long windows framing the garden, the trees black and devoid of leaves, the grass withering in the freezing air.

I'm sorry.

"I'm glad you see things from our perspective," Margaret said smoothly as she stood up. "We've really exhausted all other options. This is our last shot at keeping the doors open."

"It's really that bad?" Jules murmured, unable to believe it completely.

"I wouldn't be here if it weren't. I take no pleasure in this, Jules. None at all. You think I don't know how your mother would've felt about all this? Of course I do. But I also know she was a fighter, that if push came to shove, she'd never let the business tank just to prove a point. She wasn't stupid. And this company was her baby. Her pride and joy."

Juliet felt herself flinch at those words, words that somehow rang truer than they ever had before. "Maybe that was the problem," she muttered, biting her bottom lip, the pain a welcome distraction from the chaotic thoughts in her brain.

"That isn't what I meant, Jules," Margaret said softly as she walked toward the front hall. "And you know it."

When the front door closed, Jules lay back against the cushions, drawing the blanket, still bearing traces of her mother's Joy perfume, up to her chin. *Mom, if you're here, give me a sign,* she pleaded silently, staring up at the ceiling. *Tell me what to do.*

But there were only the muffled groans of the house settling around her, creaking like the old woman Elizabeth had never lived to become. Jules's eyes slipped shut, and the room slid away in a rush of darkness.

$\sim$

When she arrived home that afternoon, after fighting traffic as the line of cars crept back toward the city, Jules sighed as she turned the key in the front door. As usual, she'd gotten nothing accomplished. Maybe Mark was right, she thought as she walked into the kitchen. Maybe they should just hire someone to deal with it all, clean the house out and prepare it to be sold. The expense would be considerable, but so was the toll doing it all herself was taking on her.

There was a sudden thump, the sound resonating from the back of the apartment, and Jules made her way down the long hall. It was too early for Mark to be home, and a sudden fear gnawed at the pit of her stomach. *It's probably just Colbie,* she thought as she reached the closed door of their bedroom. *Mark probably locked her in by accident,* she thought with relief as she swung the door open. But the room was empty, their bed neatly made, just as she had left it that morning.

There was another thump, the sound clearly emanating from Mark's office this time, unmistakable now, and she walked down the hall, standing in front of the door, which was slightly ajar, gathering her courage before pushing it open. Late sunlight shone through the blinds, casting deep shadows on the floor, the white walls, and the desk that Mark sat behind, his skin glowing against the black leather chair. A woman perched on top of him, her back to Jules, a river of blonde hair cascading down her back, her muscles rippling as she moved against him.

"Oh," Jules said reflexively, her hand still on the doorknob as if it had been momentarily frozen in place. Just then the woman looked over one shoulder, gazing at Jules with one blue eye, her brow raised imperiously. It was Lauren, she realized, the shock reverberating through her, the intern. A sophomore at NYU, all of nineteen years old, if that. Margaret had hired her back in August, choosing her from the legions of diligent, hardworking girls, their hair fine as silk, shiny as a plate glass window. But why she was in Jules's house, straddling her husband across his desk, her clothes in a pile on the floor, was anyone's guess.

"Jules," Mark said, his face draining of color as he pushed Lauren off him hurriedly, reaching for a shirt to cover himself. "It's . . . it's not what it looks like."

The simplest explanation, her mother had always said, *is usually the truth.*

Jules stared at her husband, at the bottle of wine open on the desk, the rare vintage she'd bought for their last anniversary, the one they'd forgotten to drink, promising to save it for next year, as Lauren grabbed at the scraps of black fabric, knocking one foot into one of the crystal goblets Elizabeth had gifted them last Christmas, the glass shattering, wine spreading across the concrete in a sea of red.

Without a word, she closed the door behind her, her limbs moving as if she were on autopilot, the shock taking over, numbing her like a shot of novocaine. As she moved through the apartment, the floorboards she traversed were the same ones she'd walked over for the last ten years, creaking with her footsteps, the paintings on the walls the same bright abstracts she'd passed a hundred times as she moved from room to room.

But now, her life was unrecognizable.

By the time Mark caught up with her, a towel wrapped around his waist, Jules had one foot out the door. "Wait," he yelled, as she moved into the hallway, following her as she pressed the elevator button, praying it would arrive quickly.

"What?" she said, turning around to face him. "What could you possibly have to say?"

"I thought you were staying at your mother's," he said, standing beside her, looking anxiously down the hall, and with those words, Jules felt herself balloon with rage, as if the anger inside her had become a living force, pushing through the numbness that threatened to engulf her completely. "I'm sorry," Mark said, reaching down to adjust the towel, pulling it tightly against his waist.

"You're sorry," Jules said slowly. "Sorry that you got caught, maybe. Not that you fucked an intern."

"Listen, Jules," Mark began, his face flushed red, his tone indignant. "Ever since Elizabeth . . ." His words trailed off, his face contorted in frustration. "You've been completely checked out. You're hardly home anymore, and even when you *are* here, it's like I don't exist. How do you think that makes me feel?"

"My mother died, Mark," she said through gritted teeth. "I'm sorry it's been such an inconvenience."

"That's not what I meant, and you know it!" he yelled, his voice punctuated by the ping of the elevator, the metal doors opening.

Jules stared at her husband as if she'd never seen him before in her life. His lower lip pushed out like a grumpy baby's, there was a sheen of sweat on his forehead, and in that one instant all she had felt for him over the years they'd been together left her body in a swift, dizzying rush. She reached out, pushing the button that would take her to the lobby, the street below, toward the safety of noise and traffic. And when the metal doors closed, Jules leaned against the wall, her rage smothering the tears she forbade to fall.

Outside, she walked aimlessly, the light darkening in the sky, the streetlights switching on above her, shop windows aglow, the temperature dipping as the night closed in. She stopped in a Starbucks for the warmth, as well as the sense of normalcy it provided, ordering a matcha latte under fluorescent lights, then taking a seat in the back near a group of teenage girls laughing animatedly, their faces so clean and full of promise. Had she ever been so young? It seemed hard to remember it now. She pulled her cell from her pocket and dialed Noah's number, holding the phone to her ear.

"I'm ready," she said quickly when he answered. "To go to New Orleans."

"Well, hello to you, too." He chuckled, and in the silence, before either of them spoke again, she heard a muffled voice in the background. Was it the TV, she wondered, a podcast? Or maybe a woman.

"I'm interrupting," she said quickly, her cheeks suddenly hot.

"It's not a problem," he replied evenly. "When do you want to go?"

"As soon as possible," she said, wrapping her hands around the cup, the matcha still steaming hot. "Tonight, if you're available."

"O . . . K," he said slowly, as if he were trying to ascertain whether she was serious. "It's short notice, but I can probably make it work. But what about the show? Did you talk this over with your husband?"

"Fuck my husband," she said, her anger igniting again as she remembered the girl's long back, how she'd moved sinuously, and Mark's panic-stricken face when he saw Jules standing there.

"Fair enough," Noah said after a long pause. "I'll start packing."

Chapter Twenty-Two

ELIZABETH

New York was tall skyscrapers and the blaring of horns, neon in cobalt and scarlet, the glittering lights of Times Square blinking in time with her beating heart. The city was a refuge, a place where she could be whoever she desired, where she was free to want the unfathomable. It was the hustle, rushing madly from one job to the next, always late, hanging from a subway strap, her palms damp with sweat, the frenetic pulse of the city like a song she couldn't shake.

It was humid subway platforms and the glow of newsstands hung with glossy magazines, the scent of newspaper ink in the air, the radio blaring from a parked car, children dancing in streams of water arcing from a fire hydrant. It was a cheap glass of red wine, and the wail of a saxophone in dusky jazz clubs in Greenwich Village. It was bagels and bialys, pasteles on the Lower East Side, and pan-fried dumplings on Mott Street. Cannoli in Little Italy, the crisp shells breaking like ice under her teeth, powdered sugar coating her tongue. On her days off, she wanted nothing more than to wander the streets in the fading summer heat, the hum of air conditioners from passing windows mixing with the tinkling melody of the ice cream trucks parked on every corner. She would duck into a dimly lit dim sum parlor, pointing to dishes on the menu she could not read.

She'd landed a job with Midnight Caterers, after circling the ad in the classifieds section of the *Village Voice* the very first day she'd arrived, using the last of her change on the pay phone. "You're hired," a raspy female voice said when she explained why she was calling, and that night she was at her first gig, a black-tie event at the Waldorf Astoria, passing trays of canapés and flutes of champagne to Manhattan's elite. That first month, she'd lived at the Constance, a hotel for women on West Forty-Fourth Street, sharing a bath down a long hallway with the four other girls on her floor, secretaries mostly, in sensible pumps, who kept to themselves, refusing to return her smiles when they passed each other in the hall.

At one-fifty a week, the hotel was a bargain, but even working four or five nights a week, at the end of each month, she was down to her last dollar. She needed a better job, her own apartment, a place where she could paint the kitchen a sunny yellow, climb out on the metal fire escape with a mug of tea. But the way things were going, it would take forever before she'd saved enough. No matter how many hours she worked, or how she tried to cut back on her spending, mostly subsisting on the leftovers at work and the cans of tuna fish she stacked on the dressing table in her room, her wallet was always empty.

Her life back in Maine felt as if it had been a dream, one she couldn't help but long for each night as she lay in bed. She missed the sea, the way the tide rolled in and out each day, dependable and safe, the ferry she'd ridden each day to Bar Harbor, the lilt of the boat as it docked at the shore. Colin, and the memory of that magical, miserable summer, was a raw wound, one that refused to heal. And each time she caught a glimpse of a tall, fair-haired boy walking toward her on the city streets, his hands shoved in his pockets, her heart ached with loss. When she closed her eyes, his voice echoing in her thoughts, she would turn over to dismiss it, her tears coming hot and fast. It might never mend, she knew. Not all the way. She had been broken, and was now changed in that brokenness, made new. It was neither better nor worse, but simply a fact, like the depth of the haze hanging over the city.

"Well, I guess you've gone and done it now," her mother wrote in the first letter she received, the white envelope addressed to Billie Abbot, C/O Hotel Constance, and smudged with blue pen. She could feel her mother's disapproval through the words scrawled on the yellow sheet of lined paper, but there was something else, too: a kind of grudging respect. She had accomplished the impossible, done what Grace could not.

She'd gotten out.

The dishes they served at work were bland and unimaginative. Not that anyone in the well-heeled crowd noticed after a glass of champagne or a few dry martinis. *The bare minimum,* she muttered as she set out another tray of wilted cheese puffs, plates of thinly sliced smoked salmon, graying on the edges, the orange flesh strewn with dull green capers. She knew what Eunice would say, could see her lip curling in distaste at the sight of the ham-and-cheese tarts, the egg cold and congealed in the center. She could, she knew, do so much better, given half a chance. But when she'd approached Valeria, her boss, describing her warm crab dip, the lamb shanks with butternut squash puree, Valeria had just glared at her.

"All the hors d'oeuvres come frozen," she'd snapped, "from a warehouse in Queens. We just heat them up and pass along the cost. No need to fix what ain't broke, new girl."

"But if the food was . . . more interesting," Billie went on, still hoping to persuade, "we could probably double the business you're getting now."

Valeria just stared in response, her dark eyes narrowing shrewdly. A native of Puerto Rico, landing on the island of Manhattan at only twelve years old, all Valeria thought about was money—having it and flaunting it. She showed up to every event, even if only to supervise the kitchen and waitstaff, with a Louis Vuitton purse slung over her arm, her black curls pulled back in a ponytail, tied with a colorful Pucci scarf.

But Billie was determined, dogged in her pursuit. For the next nine months, she stayed the course, dropping hint after hint and wheedling her way into Valeria's good graces, staying after events to make sure the kitchen they'd used was left sparkling, taking last-minute shifts when they were offered, making herself available whenever Valeria needed her. Every night after her shift, she'd fall into bed bone tired, her muscles aching, hands still sore from the trays she'd carried, hard calluses on her palms, the tips of her fingers.

Until one evening, as she was carrying a plate of dirty glasses into the kitchen of a penthouse apartment on Fifth, Valeria turned to her from where she stood at the kitchen counter, busily counting glassware, making sure each wineglass was present and accounted for. There was nothing she hated more than taking a loss.

"All right, new girl," she said, looking Billie in the eye. "I'm giving you your shot. Friday night, we've got a private party on Park—some 'Welcome, Summer' shindig. You screw up? You're fired." She turned back to the wineglasses and champagne flutes neatly stacked in the boxes in front of her. "Save your receipts. I'll reimburse you later."

Elizabeth spent almost her entire paycheck at Balducci's, walking out of the store with three heavy shopping bags, food that she stashed in the kitchen of the hotel's restaurant, persuading the manager to let her in after hours to roll out pastry dough and blanch vegetables, stacking the trays in the wide refrigerator. She took notes in a small composition book as she worked, writing down recipes as they came to her, from what she remembered. Memory hurt, each recipe a pang of emotion, the pain running luxuriously along the length of her spine.

The day of the party, she arrived early and began working furiously in the luxurious kitchen. The copper pots set out for her on the stove, and the large bouquets of flowers throughout the massive duplex apartment brought the Archibalds' kitchen flooding back, that last day as she'd stormed out, refusing to turn back when Marcus called her name, the way the light hit the tile floors in strips of gold, how she knew, even as she moved, that she would never see him again. It was her biggest regret, not turning around to thank him, to take his hands, dotted with scars from old burns and age spots, between her own to say goodbye.

When she walked into the dining room, covering the long mahogany table with a red-and-white checkered cloth, Valeria looked over as if she'd lost her mind. "What are you doing?" she hissed, grabbing Billie's arm, her red fingernails digging into the skin. "This isn't a goddamn picnic!"

"Just wait." Billie smiled calmly as she disentangled herself, walking back into the kitchen, where the corn boiled in tall pots, the potatoes blanched and tossed with butter and rough sea salt. The clams she cooked in hunks of French butter, serving them in a cast-iron skillet. There were hand-fried potato chips in small silver bowls, next to dishes of sour cream flecked with chives, and platters of crispy fried chicken, the meat soaked in buttermilk and rolled in crushed cornflakes and flour, giving the coating an inimitable crunch. For dessert, there were slices of butternut pound cake, and a tray of tarts, key lime and lemon curd, sprigs of rosemary placed artfully across the top.

When she delivered the dishes to the table, the guests crowded around hungrily, filling their plates while Valeria looked on in astonishment. There was something exciting about watching a society maven in an evening dress wrestle with a drumstick out on the terrace, her head thrown back in laughter, her scarlet lips flaring in the light. But that was the power of good food, Billie knew. It could fill a room with jovial voices, change the course of an evening from predictable to something transcendent, a night these guests would never forget.

There was only one word for it: *magic*.

As she was clearing the last of the dessert plates, a man caught her eye. Tall and slim, he positively loomed over the dessert table, his sandy hair graying prematurely at the temples. He was dressed formally in a dark suit, and his eyes, behind his wire-rimmed spectacles, were kind as he plucked a tart from a serving tray, holding it up for inspection before taking a bite, his eyes closing in pleasure.

"Excuse me," he called out as she passed by, her arms full of plates. He smiled apologetically through a mouthful of crumbs. "Do you know who made these incredible tarts?"

"I did," she said, shifting her weight, the tray in her arms growing heavier by the second.

"You?" he asked in surprise, looking her over as if he couldn't believe his eyes.

"Yes," Billie answered. "Is that so hard to believe?"

"Frankly, yes." He laughed, a low rumble, devoid of even the slightest hint of meanness or mocking.

"I'm not sure that's a compliment," she pointed out, adjusting her grip on the tray.

"I'm Harold," he said, holding out one hand, then blushing when he realized the futility of his gesture.

"Bill—" she began, then corrected herself, her cheeks flushing. "I mean, Elizabeth," she replied, as Valeria stared at her with curiosity from the hall. "I really should get back to work."

"Wait," he said, reaching into the inside pocket of his suit jacket and retrieving his wallet, removing a white card, and placing it on the tray she held. "You're quite a talented cook, Elizabeth. I'd love to hear more some night over dinner—if you might oblige me."

"I have to go," she said hurriedly as she began walking toward the kitchen, the weight of the tray almost unbearable now.

It wasn't until later that night, after she had scrubbed the kitchen until it shone and she was standing in the elevator, her feet swollen and sore in her black flats, that she finally pulled the card from her pocket.

HAROLD NEUMEYER it read.

PUBLISHER.

Chapter Twenty-Three

The banquettes of the restaurants they frequented were covered in the softest leather, the hides as smooth as the pats of butter sizzling in the dishes of escargots, flower arrangements tingeing the air with the fleeting scent of spring, a kind of blushing, even as they moved into the hothouse of summer. Harold was all rumpled tweed, hair standing on end from constantly raking his fingers through the strands as he bent over a stack of page proofs, his voice a soft rumble in her ear. The first time he kissed her, as they strolled across the Brooklyn Bridge, the lights of the city surrounding them, something resonated deep inside her, like the soft chiming of bells from the church across the river as he bent toward her, his lips finding her own.

It was not the breathless fireworks she'd experienced with Colin, her heart racing, her footing unsteady as she swayed in the air, never sure he'd catch her if she fell. Harold was the turning of a key in a lock, a feeling of certainty she hadn't known existed. When he placed an arm around her shoulders, something quieted deep inside her. Where Colin could not choose her when it had mattered most, Harold seemed to factor her into his life from the very beginning. It was actions she needed to trust, she realized now, not words. Words, so evocative, so descriptive, filled you with their elusive, inherent promises—right before they led you down a twisting path, leaving you stranded in a dark wood.

The wound had begun, ever so slowly, to heal.

Her feelings blossomed through the meals they shared. There was the quail in rose-petal sauce at Lutèce, flutes of champagne sparkling on the white linen tablecloths, and pork and chive dumplings at the dim sum parlor she brought him to on their second date, the pungent aroma of scallion pancakes permeating the cramped space. "Incredible," he murmured after just a few bites, reaching across the table to squeeze her hand. "There's a German place on the Upper East Side I must show you," he went on, wiping his mouth on a paper napkin. "I think you'll adore it."

She nodded happily, reaching for the tall glass of beer before her, the crispness of the ale quenching the spiced heat on her lips. She could never wait until the dumplings were cool enough to eat comfortably. Instead, she popped them in her mouth the moment they arrived, knowing she'd pay the price of a scalded tongue, skin hanging in shreds from the roof of her mouth.

"What kinds of books do you publish?" she'd asked on their first date, placing a square of snowy linen across her lap as she glanced around the room nervously. Even though she was dressed in Eunice's castoffs, an ivory sundress, the delicate straps tied in ribbons that crossed her smooth shoulders, a pistachio scarf wrapped around her hair, the dining room was packed with the kind of effortlessly chic, well-heeled crowd that always made Billie feel as if her lipstick was smudged hopelessly at the corners of her mouth. But she knew how to exist in those spaces, knew how to shrug and pretend that none of it mattered. Aloofness was her greatest armor, a cocoon that hid her from prying eyes, from judgment itself.

"Cookbooks mostly," he said as the bread basket arrived, the yellow knob of butter dotted with sea salt. Harold plucked out a warm roll and broke it open, steam rising from the center. "Ever since *Mastering the Art of French Cooking*, the market has just exploded. Though I admit no one since has made the kind of impact on the masses Julia has. That woman is a force of nature," he marveled, shaking his head as if in disbelief. "Still, I think the public is hungry for the next big thing." He waved the piece of bread in the air as he spoke, almost forgetting it was in his hand before chuckling to himself and placing it back down on his plate, deftly spreading a golden slick of butter across it with a knife.

"Pun intended?" she replied, raising an eyebrow.

"Naturally," Harold answered as he picked up the roll and bit into it. "You really should meet my cousin, Margaret," he said, chewing thoughtfully. "She's been doing some catering lately. A few parties here and there. In my opinion, she's much more suited to the business side of things." He laughed. "Her food is fine, but it lacks ingenuity. Last I heard, she was looking for a chef. You two might be perfect for one another."

A week later she sat in Margaret's Upper West Side apartment, watching her flit around the room like a hummingbird, gesturing excitedly with her hands as she spoke. There were Boston ferns in the corners atop wicker stands, spider plants hanging languidly in windows, a pot of rosemary on the kitchen table with its swirled Formica top, the pattern suggesting mother of pearl, the sharp, rocky sand of the Maine coast. A large macramé weaving hung on a bare white wall in the living room, the windowsills lined with vases of blown glass in cobalt and aquamarine. The sofa was low to the floor, covered in loose beige fabric, and piled with stacks of Moroccan pillows in Nile green and indigo.

Her Creamsicle curls hung in ringlets, cascading over her white peasant blouse, the flares of her jeans swishing against scarred hardwood floors. A pair of glasses perched on the end of her bony patrician nose, her eyes the color of warm honey. Her skin was pale and dotted with small freckles, like flecks of cinnamon, her fingers weighed down with silver rings. An anklet hung with a row of tiny bells jangled as she stood at the butcher-block counter, pouring tea into tall glasses of ice.

"I've got some clients lined up," she said as she walked back over to the table holding a glass in each hand. "A few parties on the Upper East Side." She shrugged, placing the glasses on the table and sitting down across from her. "But I can't do it alone." She smiled, wrapping her hands around the glass in front of her. "The last one was a bit of a disaster. It's a lot to handle by yourself."

Elizabeth nodded. "I bet," she said. In truth, it did seem like a lot of work. At least when she was working for Valeria, the job came with its own kitchen staff. With just the two of them, there was no margin for error. And so much could go wrong, she knew from experience. If disaster struck, a burned soufflé, a broken sauce, everything would rest on their shoulders.

"Harold says you have some great ideas," Margaret said brightly. "He can't stop raving about the food you did for that party a few months ago—and you in general," she finished with a sly smile. Billie felt her cheeks flush with color. She opened her mouth to speak, maybe to protest, but before she could make a sound, Margaret went on, her words coming breathlessly. "He keeps telling me about that picnic you did for that party. He couldn't get over how you had all those Park Avenue ladies sucking chicken fat off their fingers. We could do the same menu for a Fourth of July celebration that I'm trying to book for a fashion designer who fixed up an old cottage out in the Hamptons. Seems perfect for a beach party."

Elizabeth shook her head. "No," she said firmly. "You don't want to do a picnic on the beach—people can do that all on their own. You want something a little more unexpected: new potatoes from one of the farms out there, boiled whole, sliced into chips, and fried, smashed, and mixed into blinis—one of those comically large tins of caviar. Serve it all up with big silver dishes of all the traditional garnishes, the dill and sour cream and chopped egg—but set up like it's a taco bar. A few big bottles of old vodka and some champagne too, and you're set."

Margaret's eyes widened. "Wow," she said admiringly, "I hate to admit it, but for once, Harold was right." She held out one hand across the table, and Elizabeth took it in her own, as they shook hands. "What do you think of the Pewter Spoon for a name? I think it's got a nice ring to it."

"I like it." She grinned, and in that one meeting, her life as she knew it was on the verge of transformation, altering irreparably. Years later, she'd look back at this one moment, this decision to reach out her hand, and marvel at how little she knew back then, how some meetings were so serendipitous that they had the power to change the course of one's life forever.

She gave Valeria notice almost immediately, watched her dark eyes as they glanced over her face, as if searching for clues. "You're smart," she said admiringly. "And you work hard. You'll do just fine." She reached into her purse and pulled out her wallet, extracting a handful of bills and holding them out. "Your last check," she said as Elizabeth took the cash, the bills crisp and new under her hands.

The Hamptons party was an unequivocal success, putting her name on the lips of every celebutante and society maven in the tristate area. The next year passed in a blur of weekly dinners with Harold, and the occasional tuna sandwich on the rare nights she was home. She baked and sliced and prepped so much that her hands moved restlessly in her sleep, scratching at the sheets. There was a soiree at an old, restored barn in Westchester, the rafters hung with tiny white lights, a whole pig on a spit turning slowly over a fire in the summer heat. The picnic tables set with her signature gingham tablecloths, the silverware, more elegant for its slight tarnish, the mismatched chairs bought at antique stores just outside the city.

The VIP room at Odeon, a Mad Hatter's tea party set up on long tables full of rabbit-shaped cookies, plump cream puffs, and three-tiered cakes frosted with thick pink icing. The crawfish boil out in Montauk for a debutante's wedding, the guests barefoot by the end of the evening as they tossed empty ears of corn into the sea, Billie's wrist aching and sore from doling out scoops of homemade vanilla bean ice cream drizzled with chocolate sauce and toasted hazelnuts in lieu of a wedding cake.

"We need to hire more help." Margaret sighed as they cleared the glasses from a dining table on the Lower East Side, a brunch party where the hostess, a renowned painter of abstract expressionism, had gotten so drunk that she'd fallen asleep on the terrace, sprawled on a Lucite lounge chair. The entire apartment was decorated with translucent tables and strangely shaped chairs in opaque white plastic, the carpet underfoot a thick white shag, now marred with a crimson stain from a careless guest who'd clumsily spilled an entire glass of Merlot. "I can barely keep up," she said with a long sigh, as she washed the crystal by hand in the sink.

The business was growing so quickly, Elizabeth could barely find time to eat or sleep. She found herself up past midnight every evening, it seemed, either cleaning up at an event or recounting the menu from the previous night's party in her journals, obsessively archiving recipes, noting what worked and what didn't, and detailing each success and failure so there would be a record. She knew implicitly that this time in her life would be important someday, would need to be chronicled, and as much as she tried to stay in the moment, her thoughts always drifted inexorably toward the future and what she might accomplish— anything to distract her from the memories of the past.

"I think you're ready," Harold mused one evening at his apartment, the Empire State Building in the distance, an early winter sunset framed in glass, a bloodred sky that spoke of transcendence, of warnings.

"Ready for what?" she said absentmindedly as she pulled a chicken stuffed with lemons from the oven.

"A cookbook," Harold replied, as if it were obvious. He was seated on the couch, a monstrosity in jet leather, his feet propped up on the glass coffee table.

"Right," she said as she removed the bird from the pan, placing it on the wooden cutting board to rest. "Sure. I'll get right on that," she muttered. "After I sleep for a hundred years."

"I'm serious," Harold protested, and she turned around, her hands on her hips.

"And how exactly am I going to find time for that? Please enlighten me."

"You'll figure it out," he said absentmindedly, picking up the *New York Times* spread out beside him on the couch and removing the food section. "And when you're done, I'll publish it."

She laughed aloud at the absurdity of it. "I'm a caterer," she protested, shaking her head as she turned around and began spooning roasted carrots and potatoes into serving bowls.

"The most in-demand and well-known caterer in New York City," Harold pointed out. "Who was mentioned in Page Six just last week."

"It's a gossip column," she said dismissively. "Who even reads it anyway?"

"Practically everyone, my dear." Harold chuckled. "Everyone who matters, that is."

"Even if I did have time to write one, who would even buy it?"

"Elizabeth," he began, "you have a waiting list six months long. You're on the verge of becoming a household name. You need to strike while the iron is hot, to take advantage of the fact that, like it or not, you are the culinary world's girl of the moment."

Her own cookbook. She hadn't dared dream of it, but on that first night when Harold had handed her his card, perhaps the winds of chance had been set in motion even then. Maybe that was the secret of life, she thought, as she picked up the carving knife and cut into the crisp skin of the chicken, to see opportunities shimmering in the air like brass rings, knowing that all she had to do was reach out and grab one.

∽

Three weeks later, she walked into Harold's office, an imposing glass-and-steel building in the Flatiron District, tossing a mimeographed pile of pages on his desk, the margins scribbled with notes in red pen, thoughts that had kept her up late in the night as she wrote and rewrote.

"What's this?" he asked, bemused, as he picked up the first page, glancing up at her myopically without his glasses.

"My book," she said, unable to keep the hint of pride from her voice. "The one I said I didn't have time to write."

"I'll be damned," he murmured, as he looked down at the page in his hand with a bemused expression. "How the hell did you pull this off?"

She shrugged. "I worked at night mostly. When I was too keyed up to sleep. After events. In the early mornings. Whenever I could."

"I thought your last name was Abbot," he said, looking back down at the title page. "Who is Elizabeth Stone?"

"It's something I've been thinking about for a while," she said, taking a deep breath. "Someone once told me that if I wanted to be taken seriously in life, I needed a serious name."

There was a pause, as Harold looked through the manuscript, his fingers riffling the edges. It was at that moment she felt the arc of her life rise, soaring higher, the disparate elements of it clicking firmly into place. A new world had opened up, the path before her stretching as far as the eye could see, her feet compelled to walk every inch.

"Well then, Elizabeth Stone," he said after what felt like forever, placing the pages back on the desk and getting to his feet. "I think this book might just make your name." He grinned, as he walked toward her, arms outstretched.

Chapter Twenty-Four

She arrived at Vidal Sassoon with hair the color of mouse droppings, a slight reddish tint at the ends from the summer sun, the burgundy cape the stylist draped around her shoulders leaching the color from her cheeks. But three hours later, as she stepped out onto the street, it was as if she'd emerged from a chrysalis. She walked with a new authority, her newly gilded strands glinting in the light, offsetting the tan sheath she wore, the color of coffee with rich, heavy cream, her waist cinched by a leather belt with a small gold buckle, men turning to stare as she passed.

Her cheekbones seemed higher now, her eyes wider, her face more angular. She'd become impenetrable, sleeker, polished as the hard, reflective surface of a diamond, glittering and unattainable. It was strange how the simple lightening of her hair, the strands cut bluntly to her collarbone, could change her appearance so drastically. But each time she passed a mirror, she stopped, hypnotized by her own reflection. It was as if the stylist, a tall man dressed in black from head to toe, had been a sculptor, his scissors gleaming like liquid silver as he uncovered the bones that lay beneath her skin.

It had been almost two years of photo shoots and recipe testing, interminable and exhilarating, the page proofs moving back and forth between her hands and Harold's, the pages shuffled against one another, ordered and reordered, until she thought she might go mad. In the final weeks leading up to the deadline, she had barely eaten or slept, her hair pulled into a bun, the daily ritual of showering a distant memory.

She perused the popular cookbooks of the day, absorbing the work of Elizabeth David and Richard Olney, the restaurant reviews of Craig Claiborne before tossing it all to the side and turning her gaze inward, back to the magic only she could create. And when she finally held the finished copy in her hands for the first time, turning the slick pages in wonderment, Eunice's face flashed through her mind, her eyes gleaming in triumph.

They hadn't exchanged so much as a word since that last day in Winter Harbor, but Elizabeth kept a keen eye fixed on the gossip columns, waiting for a glimpse of the Archibald name. There was a mention of the party Eunice had thrown in her Park Avenue apartment the previous winter, a charity ball she'd attended on Cape Cod, and each time the phone rang, Elizabeth held her breath, waiting to hear that familiar voice on the other end of the line, summoning her back to the past.

She thought of her own mother, a clipboard held firmly in one hand as she walked the aisles of Lambert's Grocery, her eyes sweeping the shelves for what was missing, what might be improved. They'd spoken only a handful of times since she'd left, each conversation more strained than the next, the hurt and anger in her mother's voice climbing through the wire, deserted as blueberry barrens in winter, a coppery landscape of desolation and regret.

She'd sent her mother a copy of the book, wrapping it carefully in brown paper before placing it in a plain envelope. *I did it,* she whispered quietly as she dropped the package into the mail slot at the post office. *I really did it.* She knew, as angry as she was right now, that eventually the hurt would fade and her mother would come around, grudgingly at first, and then with her hands open. Elizabeth only hoped it wouldn't take too long.

She met her own visage everywhere she turned, copies of *Entertaining with Elizabeth Stone* stacked in the windows of the midtown Barnes and Noble and Waldenbooks stores, prominently placed on endcaps at the Strand, eight miles of books, hers rising above them all. There was the book launch on Long Island, butterflies flitting across the fairy-tale garden behind the stone house, the sun setting in soft pastels as editors exclaimed over the tiny cakes and tarts, the courtyard filled with the melodious hum of excitement. There was the rave review in the *New York Times*, the profile in *Food & Wine*, and the appearance on *Good Morning America*, her knees shaking as she nodded and smiled, praying she wouldn't drop the slick brown eggs on the floor as she cracked each one into a metal bowl, whisking furiously.

Life flung itself ahead at breakneck speed as she struggled to keep up, her days an unending loop of trains, flights, cars, and hotels, the summer heat giving way to chilly nights, the autumn leaves beginning their annual descent, a Styrofoam cup of Earl Grey warming her hands as she waited at the gate for her next flight. Thirty-six cities without so much as a day off in between, an aspirational schedule for a seasoned author, much less a first book tour, but one Harold claimed was essential.

"You're not just another cookbook author," Harold said as he drove her to JFK, one hand on the wheel. "You're an icon."

"Now I've heard everything." She laughed nervously as she rolled down the passenger-side window to let in a gust of cool air, but the pang of fear in her belly, one that she felt as soon as she opened her eyes each morning, told her that he was right.

She smiled her way through Philadelphia, through Chicago, walking along the Miracle Mile, stopping to pose for photos in the street, sitting behind a card table at bookstores, the lines snaking around in a loop, out the front door of the building. Ate barbecue in Savannah and Charleston, moaning aloud when the tender meat fell off the bone, the corn sweet as granules of sugar on her tongue, her lips slick with butter and grainy with salt. She sampled corn bread and platters of fried okra, scribbling in a small notebook, jotting down ideas as quickly as they arrived. *Barbecued oysters,* she thought as she drank a glass of sweet tea in Athens, Georgia, alongside a wedge of hummingbird cake, the locals called it, sweet with bananas and spice, enveloped in mounds of cream cheese frosting. In Nashville, she walked the downtown streets lined with country bars, sat on restaurant patios, a cold glass of draft beer in one hand, the mournful pluck of guitars drifting past, her cheeks sore from grinning.

She had never felt so alive.

But it was in San Francisco where her life came full circle, the past reaching out to grab hold of her hand. At a bookstore near Fisherman's Wharf, the salt-tinged, familiar scent of the sea in the air, she sat at a long table in the back of the store, her hand cramped from signing her name in careful strokes on one flyleaf after another. The shop was crowded and warm, and she pulled her hair back in one hand, holding it at the base of her skull for a moment, just to feel the air on her bare skin before letting it drop again. Her feet ached in the pumps she wore, and hunger pangs gnawed at her belly. She wanted the quiet sanctuary of her hotel room, a hamburger waiting under a silver dome, Harold's voice on the telephone, the space between them closing like a fist.

She looked up briefly, her eyes traveling beyond the sea of people vying for her attention, and that was when she saw him. He stood at the back of the room in a denim shirt and a pair of tan chinos, his hair shorn now, skin tanned the color of good cognac. He smiled at her hopefully, the dimple in his left cheek winking in the light. In that moment time stopped, the store fell away in one dizzying rush, and it was only the two of them, the chatter in the room blotted out by the frantic beating of her heart.

She forced herself to concentrate, to focus on the crowd before her, awaiting her signature on the book they held close to their chests. This was her job, one she looked forward to after every event, but now she could barely wait for the line to evaporate, the crowd to disperse, and it took all her strength not to stand abruptly and walk to the back of the room, where he stood waiting patiently for her, leaning against the wall, his eyes following her every move.

When the last fan had walked away and she finally permitted herself to look up, the store was nearly empty, a void in the space where he'd once stood. She got to her feet, disappointment clouding her vision as much as the tears she held back as she walked out the front door. The sun was long gone, the night air cool on her heated cheeks, and she placed her bag down on the sidewalk while she shrugged herself into the wool coat draped over one arm, the light from the store casting a glow on the pavement.

"Need a hand?" a voice called out, and Colin stepped from the shadows and into the circle of light. Up close, he looked older, more grown up now, more of a man, she couldn't help but notice. There were small creases around his eyes now, his face more chiseled than she remembered, the bones prominent, as if worn down by time itself. He wore a dark peacoat, the buttons glinting like onyx.

"I'm fine," she said brusquely as she pulled the coat around her, tying the sash tightly at her waist, glad to have something to do with her hands so that she didn't have to look right at him, not yet.

"You were great in there," he said earnestly, and his voice was exactly as she remembered it, the same low, unhurried cadence.

"What are you doing here?" she asked, looking up to face him, watching with satisfaction as he recoiled slightly, taken aback by the bluntness of her tone.

"I saw you'd be here. In the paper," he said, shrugging. "I thought I'd come and say hello. It's been a long time."

"Years," she said as the anger rose inside her, filling her lungs with a plume of black smoke, so that suddenly she could barely breathe. *Years where you didn't come looking for me,* she thought as he stood there, waiting for her to speak, the fury she'd stuffed down inside her longing for its escape, to release the pressure like the shriek of steam escaping a kettle. *Years where I cried myself to sleep at night, hoping for a different ending. Where I reinvented myself out of ashes, rising from the soot like a phoenix. And now here you are.*

Ready to twist the knife again.

"I know," he said softly. "I'm sorry."

There they were. The words she had waited so long to hear, arriving too late now, when her life had finally moved on. Now that everything had changed—herself most of all.

"Good to see you, Colin," she said with a tight smile, as she brushed past him and began walking down the street, a strong gust of wind off the wharf blowing her hair back from her face.

"Billie, wait!" he called out, jogging to catch up until he was at her side once more, reaching out a hand to grab hold of her arm.

"Don't touch me," she said, pulling her arm away. It seemed that the street was tilting beneath her feet, the past rushing up to meet her as if she were falling down a long tunnel, no brightness at the end, only a darkness that threatened to swallow her whole. It was then she saw the hurt in his eyes, the bewilderment, and something inside her began ever so slightly to soften at the edges.

"Billie, I'm sorry," he began again, his eyes imploring her. "You have every right to hate me."

"No one calls me that anymore," she muttered, adjusting the leather bag hanging from one shoulder.

"What?" he asked, the confusion plain on his face. He was still so handsome that it hurt to look directly at him, a needle piercing her memory. And those memories, she saw now, were weapons. Ones that left her defenseless.

"My name is Elizabeth," she said firmly, her eyes still sparking in the dark of the street, where pedestrians moved around them as if they were an island, fixed and immovable.

"I know," he said with a sigh, running a hand through his cropped hair, still streaked with gold. "I guess you'll always be Billie to me."

She stared up at him, the years falling away in a dizzying rush. If she blinked, she'd be back in Bar Harbor, standing on that gravel drive, waiting for his hand to close around her own. A trolley clattered down the street, a bell ringing sharply. She had almost forgotten the electricity that surged between them, that charge running through her, the thread that connected them both, how he saw her so clearly without even trying, the person she hid from everyone—including herself.

"What do you want?" she asked, her voice barely a whisper.

"Just to spend time with you," he said quickly. "How long are you here?"

There was a desperation in his voice, a sound that tore at the sinew of her heart. *He is the only one,* she thought as she looked at him, *who knows the girl I once was, and the woman I'm becoming.* He was the last anchor to her past, the only tether that still held her firmly in its grasp, whether she liked it or not.

"I'm with someone now," she said, forcing herself to stay in the moment, to not look away, and the shadow of disappointment crossed his face, a dark wing unfurling.

"Just dinner," he said, holding up one hand as if to enforce the distance between them. "That's all. You have my word."

I love you, he'd said so long ago, his face contorted as he moved above her, the boat rocking in time with their movements, his hands on her waist, his thumbs imprinting themselves into her flesh. There would always be the residue of him left behind, clinging to her skin like the briny scent of the sea. *Nothing can ever change that.*

But he had let her go, tossed her aside as if she had been merely a distraction, his promises as empty as her broken heart. And now he was back from the land of the dead, the ghost of her past, standing before her as if none of it had ever happened—his cowardice, the pain that had threatened to obliterate her entirely, sucking her down into that emptiness, her despair bottomless, devoid of light. Had he grieved the loss of her, too? Stayed up nights, staring into the darkness, the bitter taste of regret on his tongue, a siren's song, the melody haunting and familiar, one he could not forget?

"C'mon." He smiled, holding out his arm, and when she linked hers through his own, she felt the crack in the world, the gaping hole of his absence, frayed and torn, become nearly whole again.

Chapter Twenty-Five

The restaurant he led her to was small, the decor soothing to the eye with its shades of linen and soot, the rough-hewed wooden furniture carefully placed. There were only a few small tables pushed close together, and an open kitchen in the back, the first she'd ever seen. The chef stood at the stove, working with a dogged concentration she recognized immediately, the same single-minded focus she felt as she toiled away in the kitchen herself, the outside world falling away.

The courses arrived as smoothly as an orchestration. Cuttlefish sautéed in butter and garlic, and string beans, deeply green, with a toothsome snap. A fennel salad and a bottle of cold white wine, the glass beaded with condensation. And finally, port in two small glasses, the rich amber of his skin. "The haricot verts are from France," Colin said as the server cleared away their empty plates, depositing a platter of cheese on the table, a rough wooden plank of Camembert and Roquefort, alongside a few roasted walnuts and a handful of wrinkled dried figs.

"We have green beans here too, you know," she heard herself say dryly, eyeing the round of Camembert.

"Just American green beans." He shrugged. "Which aren't the same thing at all. And once you have the real thing," he said, looking at her pointedly, his eyes that same distant blue green she'd once known so well, "it's hard to go back."

A surge of heat reverberated through her as an image flashed through her memory, the way he'd looked into her eyes as he slid himself inside her, his skin so young and new beneath her palms.

"Do you come here a lot?" she asked, changing the subject and leaning back in her chair, a glass of port cradled between her hands. She felt her worries begin to unfurl inside her, the stress of the tour receding into the middle distance.

"I guess you could say that," he said, reaching over to grab the bottle of wine and pouring the last dregs into his empty glass. "Since I own the place."

She looked up in surprise. "Really?"

"Really." He smiled, leaning his elbows on the table the way he always did, as if trying to bridge the distance between them. "I smuggled those damn seeds back to the States in my suitcase like they were contraband," he said, chuckling softly. He shook his head gently, as if the memory confounded him.

"How did that happen, exactly?" she asked, curious now, placing her glass of port down on the table. "Owning your own restaurant."

"Well, for starters, after you left, I enlisted in the army."

"Why on earth would you do that?" she asked incredulously.

"Because it was pretty much the worst thing I could do," he said with a shrug. "It was the opposite of everything my old man wanted for me, all his big plans. And once I enlisted, there wasn't a damn thing he could do about it. I suppose I wanted to make my own way, however I could, and this was an open door. I wound up overseas, did a tour in counterintelligence in Northern France for a year. Normandy, mostly. That was where I really fell in love with dining—but in the kitchens I worked in, not the dining rooms I'd sat in growing up. That food was technically great, but it didn't move me the same way as the family meal—the lunch the chefs cooked for the staff each day. A pot of beef bourguignon, stewing in good red wine. Duck legs grilled over an open fire, potatoes fried in the fat. That kind of thing. And when I got back to the States, I bought a beat-up VW bus and just started driving."

"Driving where?"

"Anywhere. Nowhere. I don't think I exhaled until I crossed the border from Arizona into California. Eventually, I ended up in Baja. There was a crew of chefs down there, living in an RV next to the water, cooking on a one-burner camp stove, getting their produce from street markets, grinding corn for homemade tortillas, pulling shrimp right from the nets and slapping them on the grill. I stayed down there three months, and when I got back here, I knew I wanted to open my own place."

"So, you're a chef now?" she asked, raising an eyebrow.

"Hardly." He laughed, downing the wine in his glass. "My head's always been more on the business side of things. But you can't sell something you don't understand. I come up with a concept, invest in a property and a chef. The rest seems to take care of itself. At least so far."

"Do you live in San Francisco?" she asked, picking up her glass of port again, as the server appeared at Colin's elbow, depositing a bowl of tangerines at the center of the table, the fruit still attached to the stems, green leaves against the bright orange flesh.

"I have a place here. But I move around too much to live anywhere, really," he said, reaching into the bowl for a tangerine, his thumbnail digging into the rind, separating it from the flesh. "I open a restaurant, stick around for the first few months, then I move on."

"Sounds exhausting," she muttered before she could stop herself.

"It suits me." He reached across the table, handing her the sectioned fruit. "I read that you're in New York now," he went on, his tone nonchalant. It was details, the minutiae of intimacy, but the bare facts, devoid of emotion, and for that, she was grateful.

"Yes," she answered, pulling a section apart with her fingers. "My publisher is there. And my life," she finished, knowing there was so much more she should say, but instead, she popped the fruit in her mouth. When she bit down, her mouth was flooded with the taste of bright citrus, clean and musky all at once. It was as if she'd never before eaten a tangerine, though she'd had hundreds throughout the course of her life. Her eyes widened and she stared at him, speechless.

"My idea of dessert." He grinned, clearly amused by her reaction. "I only work with specific farms. They provide us with the entire harvest exclusively. Some of it we serve like this, unadorned. Some of it goes into jams and sauces. And I always keep a few crates for myself."

"I don't blame you," she said, when she could speak once again. They smiled at one another, her mind clouded with wine, the ripeness of the fruit on her tongue, the nearness of him. She'd almost forgotten the effect he had on her, how they fell into conversations so easily, becoming immersed in them, as if they were the only two people in the world who mattered.

Harold, she told herself. *The book. Your real life.*

This needs to stop here.

"I think I've had enough," she said bluntly, pushing her chair back and standing up.

"Let me take you back to your hotel," he said, throwing his napkin on the table and getting to his feet.

"I'll be fine," she said coolly, slinging her bag over one shoulder. "I can call a taxi."

"Absolutely not," he said brusquely as they walked toward the door, pushing it open in a gust of cool night air, and she would wonder for years to come, as she looked back on it all, if that was the moment she should've protested harder, why she gave up so easily.

But of course, she knew.

∼

There was the brightly lit lobby of her hotel, the scent of carnations wafting across the room from the front desk, her cheeks burning as the night clerk watched the two of them enter the elevator, which arrived with a sharp ding as the doors slid open. The ride up to the fifth floor was silent, and Elizabeth stared straight ahead, afraid to look over at him. In the long hallway, they stood in front of her room, her key in hand. The hall was deserted, and he smiled at her, his hands in the pockets of his trousers.

"Thanks for dinner," she said, barely hearing the words she was speaking aloud. There were only his eyes, his mouth, the way he looked at her, as if he were seeing her on that very first day she walked into the front hall of the Archibald estate, their eyes meeting over his mother's slender shoulders.

"It was my pleasure," he said. "It's great to see you again. You look beautiful, by the way." He reached out to brush a strand of hair from her eyes, and this time, she let him. "The hair suits you."

She was afraid to move, to even breathe, and he leaned forward, taking her hands in his own. "I was an idiot," he said softly. "I never should have let you go."

"It's all in the past," she said weakly, pulling away and turning to slide her key in the lock. Once she was inside, she would be OK. There would be the stillness of the room, her nerves calming, the knot in her stomach unwinding, her head clearing after the wine. And Harold. Harold's voice on the phone, bringing her firmly back to the present.

"Is it?" he said, placing a hand on her shoulder until she turned around once more. "If that's true, I'll go." His eyes searched her face.

"You should go anyway," she said, her voice barely audible.

His eyes flickered with everything between them left unsaid, and then, without warning, he pulled her to him, his mouth seeking her own. There was the hard length of his body again pressing into her, time running like a river, the fortress she'd made of her heart, that cold, unhabitable steel, knocked aside with one touch of his hand.

And when they finally broke apart, she stood back and stared at him, her lips swollen and red, knowing as surely as she knew the rocky terrain of her past, that she would open the door and he would follow her inside.

Chapter Twenty-Six

JULES

New Orleans won her heart from the second they stepped out of a taxi in the Garden District, the cobblestone streets begging for flat shoes, the great mansions with their porticoes and tall white columns on every corner, the city in perpetual bloom, magenta clusters of bougainvillea clinging to stone walls, winding its way around arched doorways.

I could live here, she thought as they entered the lobby of the hotel, a former schoolhouse and rectory, history buried deep in its rough plaster walls. She could feel it in the high ceilings, the lobby with its jet marble fireplace, the stained-glass windows and ornate gold mirrors on the walls, her face reflected in the wavy glass, rippled like the surface of a pond. But being inside this languorous city of music and light was salt pressed against the open wound of her heart. No matter what beauty surrounded her, it was Mark's face she could not forget, his eyes flitting guiltily away as he'd looked over Lauren's smooth, tanned shoulder. The sounds he'd made deep in his throat before he'd noticed her there, murmurs she'd thought belonged to her alone.

The walls of her room were painted a rich burgundy, and a large soaking tub sat in the ivory bathroom, gold fixtures gleaming in the light. Gauzy curtains surrounded the queen-size bed, and french doors opened to a balcony with a bistro table and chairs. She could imagine sitting in the balmy air as she listened to the shouts of children drifting up from the street, their high, innocent voices tearing at her heart.

Elizabeth would have loved it.

"How is it possible that you've never been to New Orleans?" Noah asked as they took a seat in the bar on the ground floor of the hotel.

"Just haven't gotten around to it, I guess," she answered, perusing the drinks menu, a heavy maroon book with more pages than a novel.

"Wild," Noah said, shaking his head in disbelief. "I mean, the food alone—"

"I know, I know." Jules sighed, cutting him off. "Which of these do you think has the most alcohol?" she asked, pointing to the cocktail list.

"Getting obliterated isn't on the menu." Noah laughed as the bartender arrived, placing two glasses of water in front of them.

"This is New Orleans," Jules said, blinking at him uncomprehendingly. "You're lucky I'm not already strolling down Bourbon Street, a drink the size of the Hindenburg in my hand."

"Thank god for small favors." Noah snorted, reached into his bag, and pulled out a laptop, placing it on the bar between them. "I started writing a few nights ago, just some initial pages. Have a look," he said, as he opened it, the screen glowing a ghostly white.

Juliet Stone was always told the same story about her life, a story as evocative as one of the dishes her mother, Elizabeth, might have cooked at one of her infamous gatherings—something so classic and familiar that it felt as if you'd tasted it yourself in another life. There were her mother's years growing up on a Maine island estate, the lessons in cooking and entertaining passed down from her grandmother. Juliet knew the stories all by heart, told so often that she could recite them verbatim.

But what happens when everything you know is a lie?

"I guess there's no pretense that this is a straightforward biography anymore?" she asked as she stared at the glowing screen, rereading the words as if they would suddenly become more palatable, easier to digest, a sudden, sharp pain in her gut.

"I think that ship has sailed," Noah said dryly, reaching over to take the laptop, closing it softly before sliding it back inside his bag.

"A negroni," Jules said as the bartender walked over, hovering expectantly. She needed alcohol in her veins, something to blunt the anxious feelings churning inside her, twisting like a gathering cyclone, before they could wreak havoc.

"Same," Noah said, and the bartender nodded, walking off and filling a cocktail shaker with ice. "Why did I just do that," Noah mumbled, raking one hand through his hair. "I hate gin."

"Peer pressure?"

Noah laughed, and she liked the sound of it, gravelly and deep. So different from Mark's laugh, which came in fits and starts, as if he couldn't decide whether to give in to it entirely. "You sounded a bit . . . stressed on the phone," he said, turning to face her. "You doing all right?"

"Define *all right*," she said bitterly as the bartender slid the tangerine-colored drink in front of her in a tall glass.

"An absence of malaise?" Noah quipped, raising both eyebrows.

"I don't know anyone who has that." Jules laughed, taking a long swallow of the drink, the alcohol engulfing her chest in a sudden heat wave. Her phone buzzed in her bag insistently, as it had ever since she'd stepped off the plane. When she retrieved it and saw Mark's name, she silenced the call instantly. But she couldn't help but notice the notifications flooding the screen, a sea of green, the texts that had come through while she was still in the air, lulled to sleep in the droning quiet of the cabin.

Talk to me.

I'm so fucking sorry, Jules.

It didn't mean anything.

Please. Let me explain.

There was nothing he could say that would erase the betrayal, no words that could explain it away. She pressed the power button, turning the phone off and shoving it back into her bag, away from the light of day. Maybe if she just ignored the fact that her life was falling apart on every conceivable level, it would go away.

"But seriously," Noah said as his drink arrived. He took a sip, grimacing, and Jules couldn't help but laugh at his expression, his distaste glaringly obvious, a toddler forced to eat brussels sprouts. "How can we possibly write some regular biography now, knowing what we know? Like it or not, Jules, this is the story now."

"It's not the story Sydelle thinks she's getting."

"Sydelle's seen it," Noah said, pushing the drink away. "I've been sending her pages."

"Without discussing it with me?" Jules bristled. It was hard to not be on guard about absolutely everything now. If her husband could betray her, not to mention her own mother, the person she had trusted most in the world, then everyone else was fair game—especially a washed-up writer using her mother's story to revive his own career.

"I wasn't aware I needed your permission," Noah said evenly. "It's my job to show that we're making progress. Sending pages is routine. Sydelle's really happy with them so far."

I bet she is, she thought darkly, taking another long swallow.

~

La Bastille was tucked into a quiet corner of the Marigny, an unassuming facade among a row of pastel shops, a scarlet awning hanging across the top. Outside, Jules hesitated for a moment before pushing open the door, her hand frozen on the wood. If she didn't go in, she would never have to know. But if she never knew, then how could she ever hope to understand her mother? Or her own life, for that matter.

"Does he know we're coming?" she asked, turning to look at Noah, adrenaline humming in the synapses of her brain, jamming the circuits.

"No way." Noah laughed, placing his own hand on the door above Jules's and pushing it open. "That would ruin the surprise."

When she stepped inside, the interior was nearly empty, the restaurant still preparing for the night's service, tables half-set, the votives unlit. A woman stood behind the bar polishing glasses, her hands moving slowly but with precision. As they approached, she smiled, looking at them inquisitively.

"We're not open for another hour," she said pleasantly. "But you can put your names down and come back if you like."

"Is Colin James around?" Noah asked casually, placing his elbows on the bar and leaning on it. The bartender blushed, playing with the ends of her blonde ponytail, and Jules could not help but see Noah through her eyes, his arms, muscled and solid beneath the T-shirt he wore, his friendly, open smile.

"He's in the back," she said, turning to walk toward a door at the far end of the bar.

The minutes that followed seemed interminable. Jules looked around, taking in the tables hewn from rough wood, set with stark white china, the small vases filled with branches of bittersweet. There was one long communal table near the front window, benches flanking each side. The effect was sophisticated but comfortable, a place she could imagine seeking out on a rainy evening, tucking into one of the cozy corner tables with a book and a carafe of good red wine.

The door opened again, and a man appeared. The first thing she noticed was his silver hair, thick and luxurious, swept back from the broad planes of his face and just touching his collarbone. His skin was tanned, almost leathery, and he was dressed in a pair of beige chinos and a blue oxford that mirrored the color of his eyes. He had a presence, she noticed, one that filled the room immediately, a kind of quiet confidence. His eyes swept over her, taking her in as if she were a piece of furniture, his expression implacable.

"Can I help you?" he asked, his voice not unfriendly, but not particularly warm, either. This was a man, Jules thought as he waited for her to respond, who kept his cards close to his chest—if he revealed them at all.

"Are you Colin James?" Noah asked.

"Who's asking," he said neutrally, leaning one hand on the bar.

"I'm Noah Sharpe," Noah answered, holding out a hand in greeting. A hand Colin promptly ignored. "I'm a writer."

"And you?" Colin asked, his eyes flicking over Jules as she stood there, unsure of where to begin. "Who are you?"

"I'm Juliet Stone," she said, swallowing hard, the momentary calm she felt after downing the negroni long gone. "I think you knew my mother. A long time ago."

There was a silence, a pause where they simply looked at one another. His eyes, she could not help but notice, were the same chilly blue as her own.

"Elizabeth is dead," he said abruptly, looking away.

His tone was harsh, as if he were pushing her away with only the weight of his words, and Jules recoiled, taking a step back. She wasn't sure what she'd been expecting. But it wasn't this.

"We were hoping you might be willing to answer a few questions," Noah said quickly. "We're working on a definitive biography, and any information you could provide would be—"

"I have a business to run," Colin growled, his voice a harsh dismissal as the bartender reappeared beside him and resumed her work, her hands moving swiftly as she began polishing glasses once more.

"If you could just spare five minutes, we would be—"

Without another word, Colin turned and walked to the back of the bar, disappearing through the door he'd entered from, the blue flash of his shirt vanishing as he shut the door behind him. Jules knew without even asking that he wouldn't be coming out again.

Not until he was sure they'd gone.

~

When they stepped outside, Jules sighed heavily, looking at Noah in exasperation. "Well, that was completely unhelpful," she said, reaching into her bag and finding her phone, switching it back on. She needed to call the office, something she'd been dreading ever since she stepped onto the plane. She knew she couldn't keep disappearing like this, not while there was so much to still be sorted out.

"At least we found him." Noah shrugged. "Look, I never said this would be easy. It won't be. But I'm not giving up and neither should you."

Her phone, now powered on, began to ring, and Jules looked down at the screen in annoyance, Mark's name illuminated, the very sight of it like tearing off a fresh scab. *You want to talk?* she thought, as the pain that had been eroding her since they'd left New York spun itself into a frenzy, spilling out unchecked. *Here's your chance.*

"What?" she said in a low voice as soon as she answered, walking a few feet over to the curb and pressing the phone to her ear.

"Jules, listen," Mark said, a note of panic in his voice she hadn't heard in years, not since the early days of their courtship when he'd wanted so badly to keep her. "Just give me five minutes. Please. That's all I ask."

She bit her tongue, swallowing the words she longed to utter most—*liar, philanderer, traitor*—as an ambulance wailed its way down the street, turning sharply at the corner.

"It didn't mean anything," he began weakly, and she felt her anger rise like thick plumes of smoke.

"Well, if that's really true," Jules said, kicking one booted foot against the curb, "then it's even worse."

"We've been limping along for years," he said loudly in exasperation, and Jules held the phone away from her ear. "I kept waiting for you to come back to me, for things to be like they were, but that hasn't happened."

Mark's words stunned her into silence. Things hadn't been perfect, especially over the past year or so, but they'd stayed afloat, hadn't they? She thought back to all the nights she'd spent in bed alone while Mark worked late into the evening, the loneliness that had crept stealthily in, like the paws of a cat padding softly through the room.

"So you found someone else to give you the attention you so desperately needed?" she said when she could finally speak, her voice strained with emotion.

"It's not like that," he said after a moment, his voice clipped and tight. She could almost see him pacing the floor of their living room, late-afternoon sunlight illuminating the windows. She knew every detail of that apartment, the soapstone sink in the kitchen, the turquoise stand mixer Elizabeth had bought them for their sixth anniversary, the stainless-steel toaster. It all amounted to nothing now, the things that she'd once believed were the very fabric of her life, now reduced to a pile of meaningless stuff, one she wouldn't mind dousing in lighter fluid and setting ablaze.

"I love you," Mark went on. "It'll never happen again. If we could just—"

Jules held down the power button, switching the phone off once again as she stared out into the street, her eyes burning with tears. Even the traffic here was languid, unhurried, she thought as she took a deep breath, filling her chest with exhaust from the passing cars, the thick haze of gardenia. The hate burned like acid in her veins, obliterating the love still housed somewhere deep inside her, a shifting plain she could no longer access, and where she no longer felt safe. They'd been happy once, she'd thought. She'd believed it with every fiber of her being. But he'd sought refuge in another woman's laugh, in her hair, in between her thighs, and that she could not forget.

Or forgive.

"You OK?"

Noah's voice cut through her thoughts, startling her, and Jules turned around to face him. She tried to smile, but her mouth was set firmly in place, her eyes smarting from holding back the flood of her tears.

"I'm good," she said, swallowing hard, hoping he'd ignore the fact that she was clearly anything but, and leave it at that.

They walked a few blocks in silence, and then suddenly Noah stopped on the pavement, turning to face her. "Listen," he said, and the sky was beginning to darken, the air turning suddenly cooler, the chill mixing with the aroma of night-blooming jasmine and the oiliness of fried fish from a catfish joint on the corner, "I haven't learned much over the years, God knows, but clearly your husband is a fucking idiot."

He shoved his hands deep in his pockets, his leather jacket clinging to his torso, the animal scent of it lingering in the deep folds and creases, and it was then, when she least expected it, that Jules threw her head back and laughed, the sound rising in the night air, coloring the soft wind that blew through the coils of her hair, the trolley car clanging down the street, the sound filling her with reckless abandon.

Chapter Twenty-Seven

"The great thing about New Orleans," Noah said as he handed her a plastic cup brimming with crimson liquid, "is that you can drink practically anywhere."

They sat on a wrought iron bench in the French Quarter, the sun slipping from the sky, the sound of cicadas humming busily, the air perfumed with honeysuckle, heavy and sweet. There was a creaminess to it, Jules thought as she inhaled deeply, an opulence you could almost taste. Spanish moss draped the live oaks along the perimeter of the square, the gray tendrils drifting toward the ground in a luxurious tangle, obscuring the coarse, black bark. Jules took a sip of her drink and coughed, her eyes watering instantly.

"Strong," she managed to choke out, and Noah turned to her and smiled.

"The bartenders in this town believe in long pours," he said with a laugh, "and happy customers. You've really never had a Hurricane before?"

"Nope." She shook her head, clearing her throat. "First time."

"Well," Noah said, pushing his glasses up on the bridge of his nose, "you looked like you could use one after that conversation."

"I'm sorry," she said, her face flushing. She'd always been thin skinned and pale, and the combination of alcohol and embarrassment made her cheeks glow like a hothouse tomato.

"Please," Noah scoffed, taking a swig of his drink. "I've heard way worse. I'd ask if you're OK," he said, looking over at her, "but that would probably be among the stupider things I could say right now."

"I'm as OK as I'm going to be," she sighed, resting the cup on her knee, "considering the circumstances."

"Which are?" Noah asked, raising an eyebrow.

Jules took a deep breath. "Yesterday, I walked in on my husband fucking another woman in our apartment." She raised the plastic cup to her lips, taking a long swallow, the rum sweet and spiced on her tongue, the alcohol a slow burn, suffusing her in warmth.

"Whoa," Noah said, his face blanched in shock. She looked away, out at the traffic passing by on the road before them, the streetcars gliding smoothly down the street, as if in no hurry to reach their destination. "And that was the first time you'd talked since?"

"He's tried, but I haven't been answering," she replied, kicking one foot against the grass. "It's hard to even think of going back there." As she spoke, she wasn't sure if she meant New York or the apartment where she'd lived for more than a decade. Both felt as if they belonged to another world now, one she no longer inhabited. "I can barely look at him."

"What are you going to do?" he asked, his voice low, the timbre of it vibrating through her.

"I don't know," she said, swallowing hard. "It's strange having my life fall apart all at once. Every time I think I'm on solid ground, it crumbles beneath my feet. My mother's life, my own history—it's nothing I thought it was. And now I feel . . . unmoored."

They sat there in silence. There was a strange feeling of ease in New Orleans, as if something clenched inside her were loosening bit by bit, yielding like a plant seeking the light, green leaves unfurling, the city holding her in its grasp.

"I understand, you know," he finally said, looking out into the street. "When *Decimation* came out, I barely had time to breathe before the tour began, the interviews, the talk show circuit. It was dizzying, how fast it all happened—and dislocating. When I looked in the mirror, it was still my own reflection staring back at me. But everything else had changed. And after the tour ended, and I was back home, every time I'd sit down to write, the words just . . ." He stopped for a moment, the pain evident on his face. "Drifted away from me."

"Writer's block?" she asked, placing her cup, still half-full, down on the pavement.

"It felt like I was up against a wall of concrete," Noah said, with a short laugh. "Every idea I'd ever had suddenly seemed trite, derivative. The deadline for my second book was inching closer, and I couldn't even string two sentences together. But it was my relationship with Anya that suffered most."

"Anya?"

"My girlfriend," he said, downing the last of his drink. "At first, she was supportive. Sent me podcasts, bought books on how to reignite my creativity, signed me up for webinars. But whatever spark I'd once had on the page had vanished. I'd stare at my laptop for hours, unable to move so much as a finger." He glanced over at her before continuing, his face bleached by moonlight.

"One night, I grabbed those books and threw them in the trash. I can still see the look in her eyes," he said, shaking his head, as if in disbelief, "the hurt and disappointment. And a few nights later, after a party for some new debut author—*my replacement*, I remember thinking—I fell into bed with an editor from Random House." He smiled bitterly. "By the time I got home the next day, Anya was gone. We haven't spoken since."

"Did you love her?" Jules asked quietly, rolling the name around on her tongue. *Anya*. She pictured a Scandinavian model, tall and whip-thin, flaxen hair falling to her waist.

"I did," he said, as he set his empty cup down on the bench. "But I couldn't get back to the writer I once was, who pounded out my first novel in the dead of winter, so cold that my fingers froze on the keyboard, happier than I'd ever been in my life." His voice trailed off, and his eyes grew dim, lost in memory. "By then, my second book was years late, and my publisher was fed up. They demanded I return the advance."

"I remember that," Jules murmured.

"You and everyone else," Noah said grimly. "I stayed in my apartment for months, just feeling sorry for myself. But eventually, I pulled it together. An editor at *Vanity Fair* threw me a lifeline, asked me to write a profile of an up-and-coming starlet for the magazine, and that put me on Sydelle's radar. But I haven't written another novel since *Decimation*. Haven't even tried."

"Why not?"

"I'm not sure I can," he said simply, holding her gaze. "I don't know how to move forward . . . without going back."

"I know the feeling," she answered, looking away. The sky was dark now, a soft black, the neon city hiding the stars.

"Working on this book," Noah began, "is the first time I've felt excited about writing in a long time. I feel alive in a way I haven't in years."

"I can't really say the same," Jules deadpanned, and it was then that they looked at one another and laughed, their voices rising into the air. She laughed until her stomach cramped beneath her fingers, her jaw aching, and when she finally composed herself, she leaned over and retrieved her cup, the ice rattling like old bones. They sat side by side, as they had on the plane, and in the close confines of the rental car. But something had shifted.

"Are you going to leave him?" Noah asked after a long moment.

"I don't know," she said haltingly, pulling the weight of her hair into one hand, twisting it like a rope. "If I did, it would . . ." she continued, her eyes growing damp, "ruin everything she ever wanted for me. All her plans. I'd be letting her down."

"Who?" Noah asked.

"My mother," Jules said, as Elizabeth's face flared in her memory, how peaceful she'd looked in the early hours of that final morning, all the suffering she'd endured over the last few months of her life finally gone, while Jules's own pain was just beginning. *It was a beautiful life,* her mother had said a few days before her death, her voice fading, as if she were lost in the maze of her dreams. Jules had bent over her mother's body, tucking the sheet around Elizabeth's frail shoulders, as if to hold her in place. *Find beauty,* her mother had said inexplicably, opening her eyes wide, her fingers pulling insistently at the sleeve of Jules's sweater before sliding back into sleep.

Find it.

A group of revelers walked by, stumbling through the night, whooping loudly, and shattering the stillness. There was the sound of cicadas in the trees and woody shrubs, the cypress and oaks hanging above them with their gnarled branches, like grasping hands, the ancestral weight of the city pulling at her, drawing her back to the past, even as she fought to stay there beside Noah on that park bench, the delicate threads of her life suspended somewhere in between.

Chapter Twenty-Eight

The next morning, as Jules stepped from the shower, the scent of lemon soap in the humid air, she could still feel the silty residue of her dreams, like barnacles clinging to the underside of a rock: Mark's face, contorted in pleasure; Elizabeth's blue eyes, red-rimmed and dulled with fatigue; her mother's hand in her own. When Jules bent to kiss her forehead, just as Elizabeth had done when she was a child, her mother's skin was still faintly warm, as if death were merely a sleight of hand, a child's trick.

She shuddered, walking over to her open suitcase, rummaging through the clothes she'd hastily packed until she found a pair of wide-legged jeans and a loose black sweater, pulling the soft wool over her head. As she stepped into the jeans, she swayed slightly, grabbing on to the bed to steady herself, her temples throbbing. She'd lost count after the first three drinks slid down her throat, revelers whooping in jubilation from the balconies above on Bourbon Street, jazz pouring like honey from every open doorway in a blast of trumpets, silver sequins flashing in the light.

By the time they'd made it back to the hotel, it was well past midnight, and Noah walked her to her room, giggling as they careened down the long hall before stopping at her door, her laughter fading away as their eyes met. He was close. So close that it would've taken barely any effort to pull him to her. No effort at all. The thought was enough to shock her suddenly sober, and she turned away, grappling with her key card as she opened the door and stepped inside.

She stared at her wan face in the mirror, her lips dry and chapped, and as she twisted her curls into a bun, securing it with a clip, there was a sharp rap on the door. Her hands hovered beside her ears. She strode over to the door and yanked it open, fully expecting to see Noah standing in the hallway, yawning noisily. But it was Colin, a to-go cup in each hand, the smell of coffee hovering in the air. Despite the deep hollows beneath his eyes, he was clean shaven, hair still damp at the ends, waving against the collar of his leather bomber jacket, the color of wet earth. "I'm sorry about yesterday," he said brusquely, holding out a cup. "I was rude."

Without answering, she brought the coffee to her lips, swallowing gratefully, but instantly recoiled at the bitter taste, staring down at the cup as if it contained battery acid. "What are you trying to do," she sputtered, "poison me?"

"We make our coffee with chicory here." He smiled. "It takes some getting used to. Kind of like me, I guess."

"Is that what my mother thought?"

"No," he said, taking a deep breath. "She took to me—and chicory coffee—right away."

Jules glanced down at the cup in her hand, wondering if she could brave another swallow, if only to stop the pounding in her head. "What are you doing here?" she asked quietly.

"You caught me off guard last night. Not that it's any excuse, I know. Your friend left his card on the bar—with the name of the hotel written on the back. Probably because he knew I'd regret chasing you away without so much as a conversation."

Juliet nodded, grateful that Noah had foreseen this exact scenario, giving her and Colin a second chance to get things right. "You came here to apologize?"

"I came," he said, shifting his weight from one foot to the other, "to talk to you. Like I should've done yesterday. If that's what you still want."

She looked at him, the brusqueness gone now, as if it had been merely a facade, a prickly exterior that kept unwanted questions at bay, like cactus thorns, bright flowers among the pins and needles. But now, there was only a man standing before her, tired and unsure. A man who had known her mother as the girl she once was, known her in a way maybe no one else ever had.

Not even her own daughter.

"I'll be down in five minutes," she said, closing the door.

$\sim$

"I think you'll like these," Colin said, walking back from a take-out window holding a paper plate of beignets in his hands, the fried dough hidden under a blizzard of powdered sugar so prolific that her teeth ached just looking at it. "Your mother sure did. Once upon a time." He held the plate out for her to sample.

She took a beignet, opened her mouth, and bit down, sugar falling like new snow on her black coat, the front of her sweater. The beignet was still hot, dissolving in her mouth on contact, leaving only a hint of cinnamon.

"Oh my god," she murmured through a mouthful of pastry.

Colin grunted approvingly, taking a beignet from the overloaded plate and popping it in his mouth. "Everyone knows Café du Monde," he said after swallowing, wiping the sugar from his lips with a paper napkin. "But this place has been around just as long—a hundred and fifty years, if I'm remembering correctly—and in my opinion? It's even better."

"Kind of a locals spot?" Jules asked, stealing another beignet from the plate and biting into it.

"Definitely," he said. "If you can call me a local."

"You don't live here?" she asked, brushing powdered sugar from her fingers.

"I've always been a bit of a nomad." Colin shrugged. "I open a place, stick around for a few months, then I move on. Around ten years ago, I bought a house in the Garden District. Now it's where I spend most of my time," he said, as they began to walk down the block, a streetcar rumbling past, the exterior painted lipstick red.

They walked in easy silence down Saint Charles Avenue, past ivy-covered mansions locked behind wrought iron gates. Although it was almost winter, the sun shone down warmly, the air still almost balmy, so that Jules removed her coat, draping it over one arm, the weather a stark contrast to the chill of New York or the freezing rain of Maine. This was a city of dreams, she marveled, with something to excite the senses everywhere she turned, the massive canopy of oaks overhead, bamboo trees and glossy banana leaves, ferns hanging from balconies, horses clip-clopping down the street with their gleaming chestnut manes, the grand old mansions painted sky blue and peony pink, roses populated with the drowsy hum of bees, even at the onset of winter.

They came to a graveyard; the entrance framed by a tall iron gate. As they entered, there were roses among the mossy headstones, pops of magenta against the worn gray stone. "How did you find me?" he asked as they walked along the flagstone path leading more deeply inside the cemetery. She stumbled slightly, and Colin reached out, grabbing her arm to steady her.

"It wasn't easy," she said, regaining her footing. "You changed your name."

"That I did." Colin sighed. "That I did."

"Why?" she asked, her voice tentative, remembering his reticence just twenty-four hours ago, the hostility at the mere suggestion of being questioned about his past.

"I wanted to make it on my own," he said simply, "without the weight of my family, and all the preconceived notions and expectations that come with it. James is my middle name, so I just thought, Why not?"

"As for how we found you," she said, as they walked down the overgrown path through a long line of crypts, faded bouquets of chrysanthemums and roses placed on the headstones at their feet, moss and lichen clinging to the granite, "we went searching for my mother in Bar Harbor—and found Eunice instead."

"Well, well," Colin said after a long pause, a hint of surprise in his voice. "Good for you, Nancy Drew," he chuckled. "The old girl's not as sharp as she once was. Surprised you got anything out of her at all."

"Enough to find you." She shrugged, the trill of a bird overhead punctuating her reply. "I was hoping you might fill in the rest."

Colin stopped in front of a tomb, the statue of a young woman placed in front of the stone facade, her hair trailing over her shoulders, her head bowed, hands clasped in front of her chest. "You know," he began, the sound of bees humming among the flowers, "New Orleans is a spiritual place, more so than anywhere I've ever lived, ghosts lurking around every corner. Not just here"—he gestured to the crypts lining their path—"but in the French Quarter at dusk. On the Saint Charles streetcar. Walking among the tourists on Bourbon Street."

"Do you really believe that?" she asked. Colin's gaze remained fixed on the tomb, the maiden caught in time, forever young, her bones crumbled to dust.

"Time stopped the moment I saw her," he said softly. "That sounds like some romantic bullshit, I know, but the first time I ever laid eyes on your mother, I could barely breathe. I'd just graduated from Yale, spent most of the summer bumming around Italy until my money ran out, and I made my way back to Maine."

"To your parents' house."

"Yes," Colin said, turning away from the crypt and continuing down the path. He stopped at a bench off to the side and sat down, exhaling heavily. Jules sat beside him, angling her body slightly toward him, hoping he would keep talking. "That's where I met her. She was working in the kitchen. Helping my mother with her endless parties. You get the idea."

"What was she like back then?"

"Driven. Passionate. Reckless," he said, a faraway smile on his lips. "She loved with her whole heart, I'll tell you that much. Sometimes I think I'd risk everything now, just to feel that alive again." He looked over at her, searching her face as if he hoped to find some trace of Elizabeth there, and when they made eye contact, she saw a flicker of pain, rising to the surface. "No woman had ever looked at me the way she did, before or since. Every time she glanced my way, she'd light up like the goddamn sun. I've never felt anything like it. You know," he went on, his voice rough with emotion, "when you're young, it's easy to imagine you'll connect with so many people over the course of a lifetime. It takes years to figure out it isn't exactly true."

She nodded, remembering how, in the early days of their courtship, Mark would trace the contours of her body with his fingertips for hours, his head resting on her stomach, his lips brushing the soft skin there. They'd connected once, with such force that she'd built a world around that bond between them, bet the entirety of her life on it.

"What happened between you two?" Jules asked, as much out of curiosity as to distract herself. It was as if her mother had become a character in the book of her own life, a multiplicity of pages and plotlines, well before Jules was ever a cluster of rapidly multiplying cells, housed inside the safety and warmth of Elizabeth's body.

"I screwed it up." Colin sighed. "Royally. She never really forgave me—even all those years later. Not that I blamed her." He shook his head slowly.

"Later?" she asked, wrinkling her brow in confusion. "Later when?"

"In San Francisco," he said, turning to face her. "On her first book tour. The minute I saw her sitting in that bookstore at the marina, it was like no time had passed, no time at all. It had been years, her hair lightened, dazzling, but I would've recognized her anywhere."

"But . . ." Jules said, struggling to find words, "she was with . . . my father then, when that book was published. That was around the time they got married, wasn't it?"

Colin was silent, a struggle sweeping across his face like the tide rolling in, a helplessness he could not conceal. How was it possible, she wondered, that she knew so much about her mother's life, yet nothing at all? Her world, as she had known it, disintegrated with every secret exposed, every lie uncovered.

"Look," he said finally, his eyes meeting her own with a resignation she could almost feel, "I said I'd tell you everything—and I will. But on one condition."

"What's that?" she asked, and Colin smiled, the creases around his eyes deepening. He possessed a quiet confidence, but also a restlessness that reminded Jules of her mother, how she never could seem to sit still for any discernible length of time, flitting from one project to the next, in constant motion. It wasn't hard to imagine the two of them together, young and headstrong, the easy hope in her mother's eyes whenever he appeared, her heart leaping the way her own had pattered wildly in her chest at the sight of her husband's face.

"We do it over lunch."

Chapter Twenty-Nine
Elizabeth

"I'm glad you're home," Harold said, grinning happily as he uncorked the Dom Pérignon with a sharp pop. He poured the golden liquid into a flute and held it out to her, the deep-green bottle veiled with condensation. She smiled, her face tense as cardboard. She wanted a shower and then bed, the sheets drawn up beneath her shoulder, the sound of Harold breathing beside her, and the ticking of the clock. The minutiae of her life.

The entire ride back, she'd gazed out the oval window of the plane, contemplating the endless parade of gray skies, still feeling the weight of Colin's hands on her flesh. How the world evaporated as he took her hand, pulling her roughly to him, his lips moving across her skin, his words unintelligible, a language she did not speak anymore. There was only the space between then and now, hovering between fear and desire, already shipwrecked, sea drenched. She was a river twisting beneath him, deep and fluid, the stars buried behind clouds, rain streaking the windows, pattering against the glass.

The next morning, she'd awoken to the light touch of his fingers tracing the length of her spine, pausing carefully at the knob of each vertebra. Sunlight streaked the bed in gold bars, and she had turned toward him, lacing her arms around his neck as he kissed her, the stubble on his jaw scraping her skin. And it was then that the gravity of what she'd done struck her, the wrongness of it, the deceit of it all. She pulled away from him suddenly and sat up, twisting the sheet around her.

Your future is Harold. You love Harold.

As true as those words were (and they were undeniably true), even as she pulled on her clothes, barely glancing in the mirror, as she exited the hotel, hurrying to the front door without even a backward glance and stepping into the car that would speed her away to the airport, away from this glittering city by the bay, it was no use. No matter how many streets blurred outside the streaked, dusty window, there was still his face, older but somehow more beautiful for the years lost between them, how his hair, shorn now, had felt beneath her palms as she drew him close, the bristle of it, her heart galloping so relentlessly that she almost quit breathing entirely. She could no more have stopped it than she could have halted a flood, tearing away everything in its path, despite the procession of years that had passed and the rift that had led to their separation. He was a specter from the past, its waters murky with pain and regret.

And now, he was back, wanting what he could not have.

It will never happen again, she told herself as the flight attendant instructed the cabin for landing, waving her hands gracefully in the air. She would have the taxi ride to prepare herself, the traffic to delay the moment when she'd arrive in front of Harold's building, depositing her firmly back in her life. She stared out into the clouds as if they might offer some solace, remembering the way he'd looked into her eyes the way he'd always done, as he slid himself gently inside her. *Stop it,* she told herself as the plane began its descent, dropping incrementally through the clouds.

"The book is selling like hotcakes," Harold marveled as she took her glass into the living room, collapsing gratefully on the sofa, the leather groaning against her skin. "Stores can't keep it in stock. We really should start thinking about your follow-up. I've hired a new senior editor to work with you on it. Sydelle Hollis."

"What about you?" Elizabeth said in surprise.

"I have an entire imprint to oversee, my dear," Harold muttered, pouring himself a glass, stopping carefully a third of a way from the top so the bubbles didn't spill over.

Elizabeth closed her eyes, gritty and fatigued, the light that animated them dimmed, as if the wattage had been turned down abruptly. "Harold, I'm barely back. Can't this wait a few days?"

"Of course," he said, standing there in the living room in trousers of charcoal wool and a crisp white dress shirt, the sleeves rolled up to the elbows. He brought the champagne over to the coffee table, placing the bottle on top, the glass devoid of dust or streaks. Harold's apartment, monastic and sterile, was habitually and preternaturally clean, impervious to soot and grime, as if it repelled the dirt of the city just by its existence. "Take some time, of course . . . but not too long. Your audience is ravenous. They can't get enough of you. Not that I blame them," he said, drawing her into his arms.

The vetiver and musk of Harold's cologne enveloped her, his lips wet with champagne when he leaned over and pressed them to her own. His embrace was as warm and familiar as ever, but she was suddenly a bystander in her own life, numbed and impartial, as if watching herself from a great distance. She could still feel Colin's arms around her, the imprint of his flesh on hers, a blue haze the color of the mid-Atlantic spreading through the map of her body, staining the tattered muscle of her heart. How could she go back to her life as if nothing had happened? As if nothing had changed. *I should tell him,* she thought, bracing herself for the pain that would inevitably follow. But that was the thing about pain. To withstand it once was to know you could survive. She had remade herself from ashes before. She could do it again.

"While you were gone," Harold murmured when he pulled back, stroking her hair with one hand, "I had a lot of time to think." His expression was suddenly somber.

Tell him now, she told herself, her stomach plummeting.

Before it's too late.

Jennifer Banash

"Me too," she said. "There's something I think you should—"

"Let me go first," he interrupted, sitting up. "While you were away," he began, clearing his throat as if preparing a speech, "I missed you more than I'd anticipated. You see, I had gotten used to my bachelorhood. I never thought that would change. Until now." He smiled, and her stomach lurched dangerously once again. "You are the first person I want to see each morning, and the last person I want to talk to before I close my eyes at night. It hasn't been that long, I know, but as my father always says, when it's right, it is unmistakable. So, Elizabeth Stone," he said with a grin, taking her hand in his own, "will you do me the honor of becoming my wife?"

She felt the color drain from her face. If the proposal had come before the trip, before Colin had strolled into that bookstore and claimed her for his own once again, there would have been no hesitation, no hesitation at all. Her life with Harold was a spring rain, washing the asphalt clean. She'd earned it with every tuna fish dinner on stale saltine crackers, every bouquet of hyacinths she'd arranged in a crystal vase, each dish she'd washed in a penthouse apartment that wasn't her own, her hands red and peeling beneath endless streams of hot water. To tell the truth would derail the course of not only her life but Harold's, too. It would do nothing but bring him pain, pain he did not deserve, the very same despair she'd endured over Colin so long ago. To allow him to destroy her life once again was unthinkable. *I have earned this happiness,* she thought as her heart slowed, and she smiled, reaching out to touch Harold's cheek.

No ghost can take it from me.

Not even if the ghost was the girl she had once been, unwanted and achingly familiar, rising out of the past to find her.

"Yes," she said, as he leaned into her touch, turning his head to kiss her hand, his lips soft and smooth, pressing firmly against her skin. "I will."

Chapter Thirty

"It lacks direction," Sydelle said, standing at her desk, the pages of Elizabeth's manuscript spread out in front of her. The window was open, letting in the first sweet breeze of summer, the sheer curtains rustled by the wind. Sydelle's hands perched on her hips as she stared down at the proofs, as if their mere existence offended her. "And that certain . . . pizzazz that made your first book such an out-of-the-box hit."

Elizabeth couldn't quite put a finger on it, but something in Sydelle's demeanor reminded her of Eunice. Maybe it was the rigid inflexibility at her core, thick as a steel girder. Sydelle had a warmth that put one at ease, at least initially. But the moment she was displeased, she would stare at Elizabeth shrewdly, as if trying to figure out just what the hell to do with her.

"This is more of the same." Sydelle sighed, flipping through the pages as if she could hardly bear to touch them. She looked up, her chestnut bob swinging bluntly around her face. "A second book makes or breaks an author. We need to wow your audience, dazzle them. This feels like you're playing it safe."

Elizabeth felt the anger begin to spark somewhere deep inside. "No one," she began, standing up from her chair, "works as hard as I do."

"That may be true," Sydelle said, looking at her carefully, "but it's not coming through in these pages. The thing is," she went on, her voice carefully modulated, "you're writing about entertaining, the act of gathering friends and family together for a meal . . . but you don't have one of your own. Yet. You're getting married now." Sydelle sat back down, peering at Elizabeth intently. "Have you given any thought to children?"

"Children?" she heard herself parrot weakly. Every waking hour of her life was consumed by thoughts of pastry dough and fluted pans, writing recipes until her eyes blurred with fatigue. There were dress fittings, the flowers and place settings, the seating charts for the service, the reception. And still, even as the days flew by, one more packed than the next, none of it had blotted out the memory of Colin's mouth on hers, the way her skin came alive under his hands. At night, when she laid her head on the pillow, her eyes bloodshot and gritty, his face was the last thing she saw before she slipped into darkness. She could not imagine it, her life reduced to bottles and diapers, dragging her body, bone-weary, from her bed in the early hours of the morning, a child's cries piercing the air.

"They're saying you're not domestic enough." Sydelle rolled her eyes. "God knows I abhor these ridiculous 1950s conventions, don't get me wrong." She waved one hand in the air, her lips curving into a conspiratorial smile. "But this is business. And you're not just another cookbook author. You're a star. And we're building a legacy here, Elizabeth. Every book counts. We need to give the public what they want. And we don't necessarily have an extra nine months to devote to it."

She had lost Colin, not once but twice, and left the place of her birth, abandoning it completely, as if that land of fir and stone itself had deceived her. Her career was the one thing keeping her afloat. She couldn't lose that, too.

Not without a fight.

"What exactly," she heard herself say as she sat back down, her voice neutral and practiced, as if she were being interviewed, "did you have in mind?"

~

There were baskets of pink and white peonies, their scent filling the Plaza's gilt-edged banquet room, the tables draped in white linen and gleaming silver. And candles everywhere, the light flickering off the walls, the chandeliers laced with rows of sparkling crystal. Bouquets of white flowers sat atop round tables, snapdragons, and lilies, waxy camellias, the palest of roses.

Every week filled with planning, choosing the cake at a bakery uptown, the exquisitely rendered roses, pale peach and ivory atop tiers covered in white fondant, brought her further away from San Francisco and the hotel room on Market Street. She could almost forget his face, his hands, the way his breath felt, hot against her skin. There was blissful distraction in choosing the table linens, deliberating over the menu: *Quail eggs or quiche?* Margaret leaning over her shoulder, grabbing a pen from her hand to add to the list, or cross out an errant thought.

"You are *not* working on our wedding day!" Harold had exclaimed as she debated smoked salmon with crème fraîche on black bread or a raw bar, oysters and giant prawns heaped luxuriously on platters rimmed with shining crystals of salt and darkly verdant seaweed, and so she reluctantly handed off a set of scribbled pages to the Plaza catering staff and hoped for the best. No one, she knew, could execute those dishes the way she could. It would take all her strength not to sneak into that vast kitchen, her wedding dress pooling on the floor like sea-foam, just to dip a spoon into a pot, bringing it carefully to her lips.

She stared at the phone, willing it to ring, but it mocked her with obstinate silence. Then the snow came, blanketing the city in whiteness, the stores on Fifth Avenue draped in evergreen branches and strung with rows of sparkling lights. She awoke in the safety of Harold's arms, his limbs pressed against her own, an unbroken circle, and little by little, Colin's face began to fade from her memory again, sliding from her thoughts like the ice on the pavement beneath her feet. What had happened in the hotel stayed frozen in time, except in her dreams, the one space she could not control. And in those dreams, he waited for her, standing at the back of the bookstore, looking at her as if to devour her whole. She could feel his hands on her skin, the heat of his mouth, before he'd taken even one step toward her.

Her dress was pale ivory, the sleeves long and billowing, plunging low in the front, the back cut out but covered in lace, so that the long chain of her spine was visible through the fabric. She stood in front of the tall mirror, her hair loose to her shoulders, falling in soft waves. In lieu of a veil, she wore a crown of linden blossoms, the amber petals enveloping her in their sweet, creamy scent. Harold had suggested the haute couture of Fifth Avenue, Chanel, Dior, but Elizabeth had chosen a dress from a small shop downtown in Greenwich Village known for their understated, slightly bohemian designs. The skirt flowed out from her legs as she moved, pure milk froth, the train edged with a gentle border of lace.

The midtown cathedral where Harold had once been an altar boy, with its arching windows of stained glass, long, solemn aisles, frankincense and myrrh drifting in the air, was a blur, her nerves erasing much of the memory as she walked down the aisle alone, no father to take her hand. The reception a crush of bodies, Margaret's wide smile as she raised a glass in celebration, the room packed with Harold's friends and business associates, their voices a humming of wasps. She had managed a glass or two of champagne, a few bites of cake, the frosting shattering against her teeth as she posed for one photograph after another, the flashbulbs stunning her vision, smiling until her jaw cramped.

She'd dutifully sent her mother an invitation, the envelope thick and heavy, the paper the color of fresh straw. Every day she checked the mailbox at Harold's building, the place where they now lived together, but each time she opened the small metal box, it yawned emptily, a dark hole of lack that could never be filled. Her mother, she knew, would never forgive her. First, for leaving, and then for failing to return. It was that New England stoicism she knew so well, that innate inability to forgive.

Or ever really forget.

She dialed her mother's number, the phone ringing endlessly as she pressed the receiver to her ear. When Grace finally picked up, there was a weariness to her voice that was unfamiliar, along with a hacking cough that made her gasp for breath between her words, and Elizabeth felt a twinge of fear in her gut, suddenly on edge. "I'm fine," her mother said firmly, brushing off her daughter's concerns before they could even be raised. "Just a little bronchitis."

"You've seen the doctor?" Elizabeth asked, knowing even as she spoke that the words were futile. Her mother had always been deeply private, especially when it came to her health. Fall would deepen to winter, spring melting into summer, and somehow another year would pass without Grace ever seeing the inside of a doctor's office.

"It's my body," she would snap when questioned. "And I'll do as I please with it." No amount of cajoling or coaxing would sway her, and after a while, Elizabeth had simply given up.

"I guess you won't be able to make it," she said, the disappointment coloring her voice, no matter how she tried to stifle it. "The wedding, I mean."

"You know I'd be there if I could," her mother said softly, and Elizabeth nodded, twisting the phone cord around her hand, as if to close the space between them.

"We could wait," she said, a tinge of hope in her voice. It was the closest she could come to telling Grace she needed her there, needed to see her mother's face shining back at her from a sea of strangers, her presence the one constant in her life, unchangeable as the sun that rose each day, filling the world with benevolent light.

"When have you ever waited for me?" Grace said, her laugh interrupted by another coughing fit, longer this time. "Why start now?"

"That's not fair," she said, stifling the instinct to bite her tongue, not knowing that less than a year later, the cancer would consume her mother from the inside out, its cells replicating endlessly as tumors filled her lungs, until the morning she took her last breath in a hospital bed in Bar Harbor. Then and only then was the nurse permitted to call her, the voice on the other end of the line patiently explaining that her mother was dead.

"But why," Elizabeth heard herself stammer, a hand moving reflexively to her abdomen, her head suddenly light. "Why didn't she tell me?"

But even as the words left her lips, she already knew the answer.

"We did it," Harold said with a grin, moving toward her, pulling her in by the waist, and spinning her around so that she laughed happily, throwing her head back. The chandeliers in their suite were dimmed, the bed cool and fresh with new linen, crimson petals sprinkled across the floor, the white coverlet, a golden canopy draped over the headboard. Her flower crown crooked now, the petals wilted, she reached up and pulled it loose, hairpins hitting the carpet like rain as he took her in his arms, kissing her hungrily. His skin was smooth as abalone, and his hands roamed the contours of her skin, his breath warm on her throat, her collarbone, as they sank into the softness of the bed.

The next morning Harold slept as she made her way to the bathroom, her steps soundless on the thick carpeting. She did no more than glance at her sallow skin and bloodshot eyes in the mirror beneath the overhead light, its brutal glare. As she turned on the faucet, the water gushing into the basin, a wave of nausea gripped her, her stomach twisting in its grasp, and she held on to the marble vanity, forcing herself to breathe, concentrating on the repetition of air filling her lungs, her heart racing. But it was no use. She knelt before the toilet, her eyes watering as her shoulders heaved, and the contents of her stomach loosened, sweat breaking out on her brow and dampening the hair at her temples. Her sickness was a raft on the angry sea, and she bobbed there unmoored, the sky above her filled with thunderheads.

When she could stand again, she closed the lid of the toilet and sat down, her legs shaking, the sweat cold now, drying on her back, her forehead. There was a churning in her gut, the room at a curious tilt, as if she had stepped unaware into Alice's underground. She put one hand flat on her stomach, cradling it with her palm, the knowledge breaking over her. She tried to think back to when she had last bled and drew a blank. She'd been so busy with wedding planning, with the tour and the plans for the follow-up, that she hadn't noticed the absence of her period.

Oh no, she thought, burying her head in her hands, her limbs on fire. *This can't be happening.*

But of course it was. What did she expect, really? Until their wedding night, she and Harold had used protection almost exclusively. But with Colin, the thought hadn't so much as crossed her mind. There were only his hands, scraps of clothing floating away piece by piece, as if they were made of air. There was the hot slap of his skin against her own, her thoughts blotted out by her own need for him, that desperation that made her pull him closer, even as he slid inside her. She placed a hand over her mouth, and in that moment, there was a soft rap at the door, Harold's voice cutting through her panic.

"Everything OK in there?"

She stood up, pushing the hair from her eyes. "I'll be out in a moment," she said, her voice high and thin.

"Shall I order us some breakfast?" Harold asked, and the very thought of the plates of food that would arrive, hot and steaming, the idea of chewing and swallowing, made her grip the vanity once again, the sickness rising from the center of her being, buoyed by his words.

"Why don't you go down to the dining room?" she suggested, praying he wouldn't fight her on it, not now, not this morning. "I'll be down in a jiffy. I'm a bit of a mess," she said, doing her best to sound lighthearted. Happy. Something that had seemed well within her grasp just twenty-four hours before but now seemed as elusive as sailing the English Channel in a flimsy rowboat.

"If you insist," he said, "though I'd love to get in there and wash up. I'm a bit scruffy myself." He laughed softly.

Please go, she thought, squeezing her eyes shut, as if the act alone could make him disappear. And then there was only the happy sound of whistling as he dressed, and the rattle of keys as he made his way to the door, closing it behind him.

As soon as she was alone, another wave of sickness overtook her, and she bent over the sink, retching miserably, her body shaking with the effort. She splashed palmfuls of cold water on her face, running the tap until the basin was clean again, drying her hands on a thick white towel. The bathtub called with its gleaming porcelain, the lavender bath salts placed upon the rim, but there was no time for that now, no time at all.

She opened the door, walked back into the room, hurrying into her clothes, a pair of tan woolen trousers, a cashmere sweater the color of warm tea, her hands trembling still as she dug in her purse, clutching her wallet with trembling fingers, pulling a small scrap of paper from the billfold. *If you need anything,* he had said, pressing the paper into her palm that morning before she'd left for the airport. *Anything at all.*

She went to the phone, the dial tone throbbing in her ear, cradling the receiver between her neck and shoulder. It rang once, twice, and she closed her eyes, not knowing what she wanted more, for him to answer or for the phone to go on ringing endlessly, to be held captive in that one moment before she uttered words she couldn't take back, before it all became true. There was a click, and then his voice there on the line, that same gruffness and impatience she knew so well, and she opened her eyes, the room coming sharply into focus.

"It's me," she said, sitting down on the bed, the mattress firm and solid beneath her, the sheets still rumpled, the coverlet shoved to the floor. She could hear the surprise in his voice, the pleasure too, and before he could even begin, she cut him off, knowing that if she didn't speak the words now, she might never, the secret buried inside her, growing bigger each day.

"I'm pregnant."

Chapter Thirty-One

JULES

The restaurant was the kind of place her mother had always loved, colorful and vibrant, the mismatched tables and chairs spaced closely together, the air abuzz with chatter. The floors were wide pine planks, the bar was hung with an antique mirror of beveled glass, the dull gleam of brass sconces gracing the walls. It was a comfortable vibe, one that made its patrons want to linger, savoring the menu like a good novel, taking in all it had to offer.

The fussier and more pretentious a place was, the more her mother was sure to hate it—sometimes on sight. There was the trip to France when Jules was twelve, traveling all day by car to a Michelin-starred restaurant in Lyon, the invitation extended at the owner's request. They had barely even entered the front hall when her mother took one look at the stark, modern dining room, the black lacquer plates on the tables, the artful smears of colorful sauces rimming the plates, and promptly walked back outside. Their lunch that day was from a crêperie in town, a small shop that made the filled pancakes stuffed with ham and cheese, prosciutto and arugula to order, so airy and light they dissolved on the tongue. Artifice, of any kind, was something her mother detested above all else.

What is simple and honest, she was fond of repeating, *is always best.*

Except, it seemed, when it came to her own life.

"The chef here is from Saint Lucia," Colin said, tucking into a plate of curried goat and sweet potato gnocchi, his shirt sleeves rolled up above his elbows. Jules had ordered the snapper with hot honey and a tartar sauce made from collard greens, both surprising and whimsical, and she took a buttermilk biscuit from the basket on the table, still warm, cutting it down the center and slathering it with butter. "That's bacon honey butter," Colin pointed out, wiping his mouth with a linen napkin.

When she took the first bite, she could not help but groan with pleasure, her eyes fluttering shut. There was the creamy sweetness of the butter, the salty bacon fat singing on her tongue, the crumb of the biscuit featherlight but somehow still toothsome. Without hesitation, she dug into the plate of fish, her mouth tingling with spice. When she looked up, it seemed that hours had passed, entire days, her plate now empty. Colin leaned back in his chair, watching her in quiet amusement.

"That was the first meal I've eaten since my mother died," she muttered, looking down at her empty plate, "that I actually enjoyed."

Food was what her mother had lived for, her one great passion in life. Elizabeth had gone through her days moving from one meal to the next, planning dinner as she ate breakfast, penning shopping lists on the yellow pads she kept scattered all over the house. To eat, and to take any pleasure in the act at all, now that her mother was gone, felt like sacrilege. But now, in this place she knew Elizabeth would have loved, with a man she had known so long ago, it seemed more like an homage.

"Grief is rough," Colin said, leaning forward to pick up his glass of red wine, sipping at it thoughtfully. "It is, in its more essential terms, the loss of pleasure. The senses dulled, the world grayer. Colorless. It's the inverse of love," he went on, "that altered state of being where emotions are heightened, the world made new. But grief is the deadening of all that, the absolute loss of possibility. I find it almost impossible to explain to anyone who hasn't experienced it."

"Is that what it's like for you?" she asked, placing her knife and fork in an X at the center of the plate as her mother had taught her, so the server would know to take it away. It was a forward question, but one Jules felt strangely comfortable enough to ask. There was something about being in Colin's company that was familiar, their banter easy, as if they'd known one another for years. She remembered feeling similarly when she'd met Mark, the disparate puzzle pieces of her life falling into place the moment they'd first locked eyes on campus, her shy smile as she'd looked down and away.

"I lost her a long time ago," he said with a long sigh, the regret shimmering in the depths of his gaze. "When her death came, it was as if I'd already experienced it. Not that it made the actual event any less devastating." He looked down at the tabletop, then back up, his face suffused with sadness. "I googled you last night after I realized who you were," he began, clearing his throat as he abruptly changed gears. "The way you just showed up at the restaurant," he said, shaking his head, "it threw me. I couldn't be absolutely sure, and to tell you the truth, maybe I didn't want to know. But somehow, I ended up watching your cooking show." He pushed his plate away. There was still a gruffness to him, right below the surface, and she wondered whether he'd been different with her mother, softer, his eyes brightening at the sight of her walking toward him, the summer sun setting her hair aflame.

"You mean my mother's show," she said lightly, running a fingertip along the edge of her wineglass. *Listen, Julie.* She could still see Elizabeth's face, flushed with excitement as she licked the tip of one finger, tracing it delicately along the rim of her glass, the crystal singing out suddenly in the room, the sound ethereal and otherworldly, a chorus of angels.

"I had to sit down in a chair until the credits rolled," he went on. "The way you smiled, the lilt in your speech. Hell, the excitement in your eyes when you explained the recipe, it was almost as if she were back somehow, speaking right through you."

"I'm not my mother's doppelgänger," she said, feeling herself bristle.

"Of course not," he said quietly. "All I meant was that it threw me for a loop, that's all."

"I've heard it before." She sighed. "Not that it kept the show on the air, as it turns out."

"That's a shame," he said as the server appeared to clear the table, stacking the plates effortlessly on a round tray. There was a familiarity, a kind of echo that tugged at the very center of her being. Maybe it was the way he turned to the server, smiling decorously, or how he reached up with one hand, raking his hair back from his face, hair that waved to his collarbone, the same dense texture as her own.

Stop it, she told herself. *Stop imagining things that aren't there.*

"You said earlier that you saw my mother on her first book tour. In San Francisco?" she asked, taking a deep breath.

"I was living there at the time," he said, almost apologetically, as the server brushed the crumbs from the table with a small comb. "There was an article about her signing in the paper and I just showed up. I'm not sure what I was thinking. God knows, Billie and I didn't end on the best of terms. But you see, I never forgot her."

"I still can't believe she went by Billie," Jules muttered, as the server returned, depositing dessert menus in front of them.

"Everyone called her Billie back then—with the possible exception of my mother. Elizabeth never mentioned it?"

Jules rolled the name around her mouth, two syllables, tasting the possibility of them, strange and foreign. Over the years, there had been no mention of it, no letters perched in the mailbox bearing that moniker. "What my mother didn't tell me," she said slowly, "could fill an encyclopedia, it seems." She looked down at the menu, the type blurring before her eyes.

"I don't think it was personal."

Her head snapped up, and she stared at him in disbelief. "Not personal?" she repeated, her eyes daring him to argue with her. "I was her *daughter.*"

"I think," Colin began gently, "that what Elizabeth wanted more than anything was to leave the past behind—and everyone in it. Including herself."

The server returned, hovering expectantly, her eyes darting between the two of them, smiling brightly. It hurt to remember being that young, having that much hope. Jules looked away, out over the other diners, mostly couples talking happily, eating from shared plates. It reminded her of the early days of her courtship with Mark, how he'd reach across the table for her hand, encircling it in his own.

"Two orders of the passionfruit crème brûlée," Colin said, sweeping the menus up from the table in one hand and handing them to the server, who nodded silently before retreating.

There was a long moment when she and Colin just looked at one another before he finally broke eye contact, shaking his head from side to side, as if in disbelief. "I'm sure I'm a broken record," he said with a low laugh, almost under his breath, "but the resemblance really is uncanny."

"I've never thought my mother and I looked much alike." She shrugged. "Not really."

"It's not your looks," Colin said, reaching over for the wine bottle to refill his glass. "It's little things. The turn of your head, the look in your eyes when you think I'm full of shit. The way you hold your fork. It's like she's right here, waiting for me to disappoint her again."

It was at that moment Jules felt her defenses crumble. Whether she liked it or not, she knew that in order to have any real understanding of who her mother was, she had to get to know her, this long-gone girl, had to reach out her hand, beckoning her closer.

"What happened between you?" she asked, swallowing hard. "When you saw her again in San Francisco."

Colin sighed, drumming his fingers on the tabletop, as if to distract himself as the seconds ticked by, the wire tightening in her stomach in the silence between them.

"Time folded in on itself," he said finally, his expression almost bewildered, as if he himself didn't understand what had happened. "It was as if the years fell away the second I laid eyes on her again. We had dinner . . . and then we went back to her hotel."

Jules felt her heart pounding away in her chest, the clink of silverware and the smattering of laughter in the room fading until they vanished altogether, and all that was left was the small, circular table they sat at, a satellite the restaurant revolved around.

"You had . . . an affair . . . with my mother?" she heard herself ask, feeling as though she were watching the scene play out, as if in a movie, the same clichéd dialogue she'd heard so often on the screen.

"Yes and no," he said evasively, leaning forward in his chair.

"Either you did or you didn't," she said impatiently. "There really isn't any in between."

"Sure there is." Colin chuckled softly. "Elizabeth and I could only exist in the in-betweenness of it all, as it turns out. Hotel rooms, airport terminals. But to answer your question," he went on, "yes. We slept together that night."

Jules fell silent, sitting back in her chair as the server reappeared, placing two small white ramekins before them, the aroma of broiled sugar drifting over the table. In that one moment, her entire childhood flashed before her eyes, the house they rented on Nantucket three summers in a row, her father burying her tiny feet in the sand. The hot dogs they'd shared at Coney Island, the bun doused in ketchup, just the way she liked. Harold waving at her from the front row of every school play, his calm, reassuring smile lighting up the darkness. Her father had always been there, even when her mother could not.

"What are you saying exactly?" Jules heard herself ask, her own voice unfamiliar in her throat.

"If you're asking if we had an affair, then I guess that technically speaking, the answer is yes," he said, picking up his spoon. "Yes, we slept together that night in San Francisco," he went on, tapping the creme brûlée, cracking the top sharply, so that Jules flinched from the sound. "And yes, we saw each other over the years."

"When?" she demanded, pushing away the ramekin in front of her, her appetite vanished now.

"Whenever her schedule allowed." Colin shrugged, bringing the spoonful of custard to his lips. "We wrote letters, called when we could, which wasn't often, I'll admit. Your mother was a prolific letter writer, Jules, but I'm sure you know that."

Jules stared at him blankly. Their tryst in San Francisco had happened on her mother's first book launch—a year before Jules was born.

"You saw her on . . . her book tours?" she asked, her voice small and faraway, as if traveling over a long distance. Now it began to make sense, the urgency of those long "work trips," those days at a time when Elizabeth was unreachable, the phone ringing endlessly in Jules's ear.

Colin laid his spoon down at the side of his dish and looked up at her, his face shadowed with pain. "Mostly," he said finally. "Sometimes a stop on her tour would coincide with the launch of one of my restaurants in that city, and like some miracle, we'd find ourselves in the same place at the same time. Other meetings . . . were a bit more calculated," he admitted, and Jules felt her eyes widen in shock, her limbs numb, as if she were back at her mother's funeral, reaching out to touch her mother's long, graceful hands in the coffin, those hands that had held her, once so warm, now hard and unyielding as wood.

She thought again of her father, waiting at home all those years while Elizabeth sat in restaurants with Colin, her face shining in the candlelight. How he would perch on the end of Jules's small twin bed each night in Elizabeth's absence, her night-light, a crescent moon her mother had chosen, glowing softly in the dark. While Harold cut her toast into triangles, spreading the butter to the very edges of the bread, just the way she liked it, was her mother waking up in Colin's arms, sighing happily as she nestled closer, his lips grazing her own? The thought made the alcohol she'd drunk fade into the distance, replaced with her rage, blood hissing in her veins like steam. Her legs were trembling, as were her hands resting on the table. She pushed back her chair from the table roughly, the legs scraping on the wooden floor as conversation halted and diners turned to stare. She stood up, the white square of her napkin falling uselessly to the floor.

"Jules," he stammered, his voice filled with surprise, "if you'll just let me finish, I—"

But it was too late for that. Too late for more words, justifications she did not want to hear. She could feel the rapid pulse of her own heart, and before he could say another word, she turned and bolted from the room, slapping both hands on the wooden door of the restaurant and pushing it open. It felt good to run, her legs pumping faster, as if she were an animal, limbs unwinding as it bolted from its cage.

There was a chill in the air, a bite of wind, and Jules shivered, as much from the cold as her nerves, the high-wire act that was now her life. The French Quarter bustled with crowds, the late-afternoon sun dipping low in the sky, the air thick with fragrant spices, the scent of gumbo simmering over an open flame, and Jules hurried over the cobblestone streets, almost tripping in her haste to get back to the hotel, the stately lobby, the uniformed desk clerk nodding as she passed by on the way to the elevator. Some kind of certainty.

She ran down Saint Charles Avenue, her breath hitching in her lungs, her side aching, as if she could outrun her own muddled past, sprinting headlong into her uncertain future.

Chapter Thirty-Two

"Where the hell did you go?" Noah asked, holding the door to his room open as Jules stepped inside, still out of breath, her back damp with perspiration. He was dressed in a pair of gray sweats and a black T-shirt, his feet bare, his hair standing on end as if he'd just rolled out of bed. Clothes were strewn across the floor, and a T-shirt hung precariously from a standing lamp in the corner, the carpet sodden with wet towels. Jules navigated the mess carefully, as if the floor were made of glass, sitting down in a chair by the window.

"Don't you ever clean up?" she muttered, shaking her head in disbelief.

"I'm on vacation," Noah protested, closing the door and coming to sit on the edge of the bed. "Besides, there is such a thing as maid service."

"This isn't a vacation," Jules said, her eyes suddenly smarting with tears, the emotions she'd felt in the past few hours rising to the surface. "This is my life."

"Hey, hey," Noah said, his eyes softening, and she looked away so that she wouldn't have to meet his gaze. "What happened?" he asked gently, and she forced herself to turn and face him, the tears running down her face now. "Where were you all day?"

Jules took a deep breath, wiping the wetness from her cheeks, knowing all the while what a wreck she must look like, her eyes smeared with mascara, but she was beyond caring.

"She lied to me," she said, her voice cracking with emotion. "She lied about everything."

"Slow down," Noah said, getting up to grab his cell phone from the desk, where it had been charging. He sat back down, turning it on and placing it on the bed beside him.

"I'm not sure I want this on record," she said, eyeing the phone warily.

"That's all right," Noah said quickly, holding up a hand. "We can figure it out later, OK?"

Jules nodded. At this point, she'd lost everything: her mother, her marriage—her entire history, things she thought were irrefutable. She had to trust him now, whether it was comfortable or not.

There was no one left.

"My mother had an affair," she said, looking up at him to gauge his reaction. "With Colin."

"When?" Noah asked, leaning forward slightly.

"I guess it started on her first book tour." She took a deep breath before continuing. "But the thing is . . . she got pregnant with me around that time," she added, and Noah's eyes widened.

"Are you suggesting Colin is your father?" he asked.

"It certainly appears that way," Jules said, feigning nonchalance, while inside she was screaming. "They were in touch, they saw each other . . . for *years*. All this time we thought she was just traveling for work, and she was secretly meeting up with him, while I was left at home with my father."

"Jesus Christ," Noah breathed, reaching up and running his palm over the stubble covering his jaw, the raspy sound setting her teeth on edge. "Do you think he had any idea?"

"I'm not sure." She drew her knees up, hugging them toward her chest.

"What does your gut tell you?"

"My father trusted her implicitly. I never even saw them fight, not even once. And he was always preoccupied with work, always buried in the next project, planning a new launch."

"They say that's a red flag," Noah said, rearranging his limbs so that he was sitting cross-legged, his elbows resting on his knees.

"What is?"

"Never arguing. Supposedly it's unhealthy."

She thought back to her marriage, the few petty squabbles they'd had over the years, her tears streaking the pillow as she'd stared into darkness. How much disappointment and resentment had they both swallowed over time? Much like her father, she'd closed her eyes, and now that they were open again, nothing was what she'd believed.

"I think maybe he knew," she said hesitantly. "And he ignored it. That's the kind of guy he was, never wanting to cause conflict, bottling up his emotions like they were some kind of dangerous gas he couldn't let escape. But even if they'd talked about it, which I very much doubt, he never would've given her up in a million years, no matter what she'd done or who she'd been with. That much I'm sure of."

Jules sighed, standing up and walking over to the bed, sitting down beside him. The mattress groaned with her movement, and he turned slightly, angling his body so that they faced one another once again. "I wonder," she went on, her mood darkening, "what she must think of me now."

"Your mother?" Noah asked, his brow creased.

"I can't imagine she's not disappointed in the mess I've made. My marriage. Her business."

"I don't think that's true."

"How would you know? You don't really know me."

I don't even know myself, she thought as she glanced out the window at the darkening sky.

"From what I can see, you're doing just fine. Better than fine."

"I screwed up my mother's company," Jules said lightly. "I wouldn't call that fine, Noah."

In the quietness of the room, she could hear a phone ringing somewhere on their floor, the sound of the elevator doors opening and closing at the end of the hallway, her own heart beating steadily in her chest.

"It's funny," she went on, her voice hushed, almost as if she were talking to herself, "no matter how much we uncover, I can't seem to make it all add up—the pieces of her life. No matter how I arrange them, they just don't fit. Most of the time, I feel like I never knew her at all."

"You knew her," Noah said quietly, his green eyes gazing at her intently from behind his glasses. "You knew her as well as she'd allow. And that isn't insignificant, Jules. It's not nothing."

Jules exhaled heavily, not wanting to admit he was right. Instead, she reached up, pulling one of her curls between her fingers, twisting it tightly into rope, as she always did when she was nervous, the gesture less coy than an attempt to pull every last hair from her head. "I just wish I knew what she'd want me to do," she admitted. "God, if she could see what's happened since she's been gone, she'd die all over again—but this time of shame." She shut her eyes, and in that brief void she saw her mother's face, her lips drawn into a straight line, her blue gaze cold with anger.

"Forget your mother," Noah said sharply, and Jules opened her eyes as he leaned forward, closing the gap between them so their faces were only inches apart. "Forget what she would want. What do *you* want?"

"I'm afraid . . ." Jules answered, her voice trailing off, "to even ask anymore."

"You're not asking," he said simply, placing one hand on her leg, his touch steady and reassuring. "I am. You just have to answer."

It was then, without warning, that the sobs came from the center of her being, as though they'd been summoned, tearing themselves loose from her chest, the hard, dense ball of grief that lived inside her, the pain she hadn't allowed herself to feel or even really acknowledge since Elizabeth had died. She bowed her head, covering her face with her splayed hands, wishing she could disappear entirely. *It's like prayer,* she thought in disbelief as the tears came faster, *this kind of grief.* She was a tree bending in the wind, its leaves roughly dislodged, strewn haphazardly along the path. She wailed into the knowledge of her mother's absence, the high-pitched noise of her own grief tearing at her senses.

You only get one mother, Elizabeth had always said, usually when Jules had managed to disappoint her in some vague, amorphous way, and Jules would roll her eyes, especially during her teenage years, slamming the door of her room in protest. But now the truth of those words resounded in her gut, and despite the presence of another human being, Jules had never felt so singular, so utterly alone, in her entire life. Her mother was a cipher. Harold might not have even been her father.

She was on her own.

"Hey," she heard Noah say softly as she choked and sputtered, bending at the waist until her forehead was practically resting on the mattress. "Come here," he urged, and she sat up, blinking at him, her face slick, her eyelashes glazed with tears, and before she knew it, she was in his arms. He pulled her closer, and she could feel the insistent beating of his heart against her chest, smell the sharp sweat on his skin, the heat of him through the thin T-shirt he wore, and her mouth found his, his lips opening as the kiss deepened, his tongue in her mouth, his fingers tangled in her hair. He reached up to remove his glasses and pulled her to him, his hands firm but gentle. There was only the sound of her own ragged breathing, and she could not tell whether the cries she made were pleasure or pain as she pushed him down onto the bed.

Chapter Thirty-Three

When she woke the next morning in her hotel room, the hair sticking to the back of her neck, damp with sweat, the night before came back in a rush, and she closed her eyes with a groan. His hands on her bare skin, his mouth exploring every inch of her flesh, as if after a great drought. Sometime in the night, she'd crawled back to her own room, shoes in hand, before dawn lit up the sky.

She didn't have to wonder now how Elizabeth had felt the morning she woke in that hotel room in San Francisco, Colin stretched out beside her, fog creeping around the windowpane. She'd felt the same panic, the need to run as far as she could, away from the city and the man currently asleep next door. As if sleeping in the adjacent room could somehow make the events of the night before fade to a distant memory. *It needs to stay buried,* she thought, sitting up and throwing the covers back in a heap. Not just what had happened between her and Noah, how they'd clung to one another as if shipwrecked, but the truth about her mother's life.

Like mother like daughter, she told herself as she stood and hurried to the bathroom. In the shower, the water like needles, she turned her body so that the spray hit her from every angle, placing one hand against the tile, her mouth open in the deluge. She'd wanted to know who her mother was, had begun this journey hoping to answer that question once and for all, but she'd never expected to find out this way. No matter how many times she'd tried to walk in Elizabeth's footsteps over the years, she'd never thought her mother's story could so closely resemble her own.

By the time she'd dressed, run a comb through her wet hair, and pulled it back in a knot, glancing at her reflection coolly in the mirror, she had regained her composure. She would go home and put it behind her, forget it all, just as Elizabeth had done. She would protect her mother's legacy in a way she'd failed at until this moment. The truth would end now, with her alone. She quickly tapped out an email on her phone, replying to Sydelle's last missive about possible cover designs, a message Jules had barely skimmed. The book is off, she wrote, hitting send before she could think about what she'd done.

Her stomach turned as the elevator plummeted down, and when the silver doors opened to the lobby, Noah was there waiting, his duffel bag slung over one shoulder, eyes brightening at the sight of her, though the smile faded from his face as she looked past the hand he held out, climbing into the cab idling at the curb. The interior was stifling with the scent of the cherry air freshener, the heat blasting from the vents, and as the length of Noah's thigh pressed against her own, she moved her leg away sharply.

But even so, she could not deny the pull between them now. It made her want to put her hand on his leg, to touch the soft skin of his neck with her fingers, so that the inches between them shrank to nothingness. Instead, she turned and stared out the window, the silence growing chillier with every passing street. In the morning light, New Orleans seemed dirtier, more sordid, piles of trash heaped in the gutter, rows of colored beads swinging from streetlamps, like a burlesque dancer shedding her baubles after a long night's work.

"Are we gonna talk about last night at all?" he asked, as they sat at the gate waiting to board, a coffee from Starbucks clutched in one hand. She reached out and took it without asking, drinking the hot brew gratefully.

"There's nothing to talk about," Jules said, careful to keep her voice even.

"Isn't there?"

"I told Sydelle that I'm canceling the book," she replied, her voice even and sure, and he turned sharply to look at her. She looked away, not wanting to see the look on his face.

"You're quitting?" he said in disbelief. "Just like that?"

"Not 'just like that,'" she said, her tone incredulous. "Look, considering what we've uncovered, this is the only thing that makes sense. My mother's reputation was everything to her. I'm not going to let it be tarnished by publishing some tell-all. I owe her that much at least."

"And what about what she owed you?" he asked, an edge in his voice. "Namely, the truth?"

Jules blinked, suddenly unable to find her voice. Elizabeth had given her everything she had ever wanted. It had never occurred to Jules that she had the right to ask for anything more.

"We're doing good work, Jules," he went on, taking a deep breath. "It would be a shame to stop now, just when we're really getting started."

"Is that what this is really about for you?" she asked skeptically, regaining her footing. "Our 'good work'?"

"What the hell else would it be about?"

"Your career, maybe? Not to mention the very sizable advance Sydelle paid us for this book."

"As I said from the beginning," Noah said, his voice tight, "this is entirely your call, and I'm not going back on that now. I just think we should maybe talk about it before you make a decision you might regret."

"It's already done," she replied as she looked over at him, finally, in the chaos of the boarding gate, the announcements droning away over the loudspeakers blaring in her ears. "There's nothing to talk about anymore."

"Like hell there isn't," he said, a short laugh escaping his throat. He looked tired. His eyes, hidden away behind his glasses, were bloodshot, his jaw covered in dark stubble. She knew what it would feel like under her hands, if she would only reach out and touch him, how he'd cradle his cheek against the flat of her palm, leaning in. But it didn't matter now.

She was going home.

But as they boarded the plane, the same thought nagged at her, burrowing its way into her brain: *There's something here.* The words were insistent, even as she shuffled down the long jet bridge leading to the open mouth of the plane, the words repeating themselves as she took her place in the seat beside him amid the roaring engines and the hum of recycled air.

But it doesn't matter, she told herself, closing her eyes. *Go home,* she told herself as the plane rose higher in the air.

Forget it all.

Just as Elizabeth had done.

She had taken a deep breath as she entered the lobby of their building, her pulse skipping as she rode the elevator up to the tenth floor, her head light. There was no relief in her homecoming, no feeling of ease as she walked down the hall she knew so well, stopping in front of their apartment door, one hand trembling as she pulled out her keys. *We can fix this,* Mark had written repeatedly in his texts. And for a moment, she'd believed him.

But now, standing in front of her husband, his eyes red-rimmed, his shoulders slumped in defeat, she was as confused as ever, the clarity she'd hoped for failing to appear with every second that ticked by, the safety of home eluding her.

"You're back," Mark said, meeting her in the front hall of their apartment, her key still in the door. His face was drawn, dark circles beneath his eyes, as if he hadn't slept since she'd left. It was early afternoon, and he should've been at work, but his very presence, along with the jeans and ratty navy sweatshirt he wore, said otherwise. It was the same one he'd worn so often in their college days, the cotton now pilled. Mark had a habit of holding on to things until their usefulness was outweighed by their deterioration. For the first time, she couldn't help but see their marriage in the same light, something that should've ended long before, that had run its course years ago. Without speaking, she put her bag down, shrugging off her coat and hanging it in the hall closet before walking past him into the living room.

"Where have you been?" he asked, following her in.

"I'm surprised you're still here," she said, ignoring the question. No matter how many times she walked into the apartment, she never failed to be awestruck by its soaring ceilings, the open living area, all concrete floors, smooth marble, and fixtures of burnished gold. But the kitchen counters, she noticed, were now littered with empty take-out boxes, the sink piled with dirty dishes, as if instead of loading the dishwasher, he had simply given up.

"Where else would I be," he answered, his voice tight with emotion.

"I don't know," she answered, walking over to the kitchen and pulling a glass down from a cabinet. "Out with your girlfriend, maybe?" She moved to the sink, filled the glass with water, and drank thirstily.

"She's not my girlfriend," he said quickly. "Look, Jules," he began, taking a tentative step forward. "I made a mistake."

Mistake. Was that what had happened with her and Noah just a few hours ago? Jules wondered as she looked at her husband, the man she'd spent the better part of two decades with, who she'd thought she knew as well as her own face in the mirror. As she stood there, memories flashed through her mind: his smile on their wedding day, how, for years, he couldn't sleep unless they were curled together, his soft puffs of breath on the back of her neck. The Christmas he'd surprised her with plane tickets to Vienna, where she'd kissed him between bites of Sacher torte at the café next to their hotel, fairy lights twinkling in the snow. How in the last few years, he'd preferred to work in his study late into the night, his side of the bed cold and empty as a tomb. And even on the rare occasions he lay beside her, it was as if a chasm had sprung up between them, an invisible line running down the center of the bed.

One she hadn't wanted to see at all.

Everything in the apartment was the same, her collection of Lusterware teapots lined up on a shelf above the stove, the contours of her husband's face, as familiar as her own. But now nothing made sense. Certainly not what she'd planned the moment she'd opened her eyes that morning. And definitely not what she was about to do now. Her mother would abhor it, she knew, the silence she could no longer maintain, just to keep the peace.

I'm not my mother, she told herself as she took a deep breath.

I can choose differently.

"I think you were right," she said, and a look of confusion crossed her husband's face.

"Right about what?"

"We *have* been limping along for years, just like you said. I didn't want to deal with the distance between us, so I ignored it. The way I do with everything I don't want to face." Her thoughts flashed back to Noah, as she moved on top of him, one light burning in the room, the sweat coating his skin mixing with the brine of her own tears, how when he was inside her, it felt as if she were healing and breaking apart all at once. There was no telling where her tears ended and her need for him began.

"Forget what I said," Mark said, walking over so that they were only a few feet apart. "I did a stupid thing. A stupid, egotistical thing. But it's finished now. I already told her it's over."

"It's not about her."

"Then what?"

"It's about us. About *me.* I've been sleepwalking through most of my life, Mark. And now I think I'm finally awake."

"What does that mean exactly?"

It means I'm thirty-six years old, Jules thought, staring at her husband as if he were a stranger who had wandered into the wrong house. Or maybe she was the one who had become so strange, so unfamiliar, even to herself. *And I have no idea who I am.*

There were the pottery classes, a series she'd signed up for one fall, attending only two sessions before abandoning them completely, her only souvenir a lopsided bowl leaning listlessly to one side, as if it were disappointed in her, too. The galleries that had asked to feature her photographs, the still lifes and tablescapes she'd arranged in between the setups for the images for her mother's books, opportunities she turned down the moment they were raised. She knew what they'd all say, standing there in the gallery, a glass of wine sweating in her hand as, around her, the whispers grew. *Celebrity kids get all the breaks.* The only thing she'd ever done well, Jules realized with a sickening finality, was be Elizabeth Stone's daughter.

"I think," she said slowly, before she could find a way to stop herself, "you should move out for a while. We both need time to think."

"I don't need time," Mark said, a look of panic in his eyes. "I know where I belong. Do you really not feel the same?"

His eyes pleaded with her, and Jules opened her mouth to protest, but before she could say a word, her phone buzzed in her pocket, and she pulled it out, hoping to see Noah's name on the screen. But it was only Margaret.

Have you seen Page Six?

No, she replied. I've been out of town.

Target's pulled out of the deal. You need to come in.

"Jules, please," Mark said. "Can't we finish this?"

Wait, what's going on? Jules typed, her body turning cold, a sharp pain striking between her brows, like the brain freeze of a red, white, and blue Popsicle between her teeth. What's happening?

But there was no answer.

Who Was the Real Elizabeth Stone?

America's favorite domestic goddess was hiding a secret ingredient in her seemingly perfect life.

The late Elizabeth Stone, who died of cancer in August 2023 at the age of 64, allegedly had a long-running affair with a fellow food-world luminary. This according to leaked pages of a forthcoming biography that counter the very prim and proper image that Stone portrayed for decades in her cookbooks and TV show.

"The Elizabeth we saw on TV never had even so much as a stray hair on her head," said a publishing insider who read an excerpt of the bombshell book. "This was a woman who could throw dinner for a dozen of her closest friends at the drop of a hat, and still be able to pick up her own kid from school, too. Nothing in her life said 'messy,' and she certainly wasn't someone you'd expect to cheat."

But according to the partial manuscript, which was reviewed by Page Six, she did just that. Stone married publisher Harold Neumeyer in 1986, but according to the biography, she went back to an old flame even before the couple had exchanged their wedding vows—and kept going back in the years that followed. The identity of Stone's lover is not included in the pages, but he is described as owning several restaurants, and considering Stone's famously good tastes, they are likely to be delicious ones.

We'll have to wait for the finished book to find out the

name of Stone's lover, as well as the effect the affair had on her family life. The biography is rumored to be connected to Stone's own estate and is expected to be published this summer by Random House.

Reps did not get back to our request for comment.

Chapter Thirty-Four

Jules hurried to the subway, making her way through the crowds at the mouth of the station and down into the depths of the city. She pulled out her phone, ignoring her notifications, so many missed calls from Noah that the lock screen was full, and opening her email. Her gut sank as she saw there was still no response from Sydelle. *There are a whole group of people living in the subway tunnels,* her mother had once told her, gesturing wildly with her hands, the way she always did when she was particularly excited. *I wonder what that would be like,* Elizabeth had mused, *living so far away from society.*

From convention.

The platform reeked of urine, the stench burning her nostrils, and she leaned out compulsively, checking for the single headlight of the approaching train, the rush of wind that would accompany it. She pulled her hair down from the bun atop of her head, and it tumbled to her shoulders, ringlets of tight curls that she absentmindedly tucked behind her ears. Once it arrived, she held on to the silver pole at the center of the cramped car, swaying as they rocketed through the maze of tunnels connecting the city, remembering Noah's arms around her, his whispers in her ear.

Be with me. Be here now.

And she had. She'd let her guard down the moment she walked into his hotel room, almost without realizing it. And where had it all led?

More betrayal.

You're quitting? Just like that? She couldn't forget the disappointment in his voice—regret, she knew now, that he'd lost the opportunity to make his name anew, to rise triumphantly from the ashes of his literary career and start again, the slate wiped clean. Of course he wasn't going to let it all evaporate into thin air.

All her life she'd been making the same safe choices, hoping Elizabeth would approve, never straying even an inch from the path her mother had designed for her as carefully as she composed a cheese board or set a table. *What would Elizabeth do?* she'd asked herself again and again, especially now that her mother could no longer answer. Last night in New Orleans, she had been freed from the fixed parameters of her life, which felt suddenly as small as a fishbowl, one where she swam in endless circles, the water reflecting the same blurred view. In that moment when she'd drawn him to her, she had finally taken a risk. She had broken out.

But already that feeling was a thing of the past.

The ride up to the fourteenth floor seemed to drag on, the elevator stopping inexplicably on every floor, and when she finally reached the boardroom, still wearing the clothes she'd thrown on that morning in New Orleans, one leg of her jeans splotched with a wide brown stain from where she'd spilled her coffee on the plane, the air in the room was tense. Margaret and Peter sat huddled together at the far end of the long table, speaking softly. Margaret looked up, her face strained, and Peter raised a hand, beckoning her over almost dismissively, as if she were just another employee.

"Sit down, Jules," Peter said tersely, and the circles under his dark eyes, his collar unbuttoned, tie loosened, told Jules all she needed to know about the gravity of the situation. In all the years she'd known him, Jules had never seen Peter any less than perfectly turned out, shoes shined, shirt crisp and new, as if he bought them in bulk. Margaret was clad in a black sweater that swallowed her thin frame, a pair of gray woolen trousers, her hair twisted in a knot. Her fingernails, Jules noticed, were not only missing their signature carmine polish but were bitten down to the quick. "I take it you've seen the news?" Peter asked as she slid into a chair across from Margaret.

Jules nodded, but before she could speak, Margaret cleared her throat, a dry rasp that sounded jagged somehow, as if she'd swallowed a handful of broken glass.

"Our PR team is doing what they can to minimize the press," Margaret said evenly, folding her hands in front of her. "But it isn't good."

"How could you allow this to happen?" Peter asked, his eyes cold. "This was supposed to be a straightforward retrospective of Elizabeth's greatest hits. Not some sordid exposé."

"I didn't," she protested, knowing even as she did so that it sounded fake, as if she were making excuses. "The book isn't even finished, Peter. And to be honest, I emailed Sydelle just this morning telling her that I wanted it pulled from the schedule. Why would I turn around and leak the story anyway?"

"You canceled the book?" Margaret asked in surprise.

"I did," Jules said, exhaling heavily. "Given what we've uncovered so far, I wasn't sure I wanted the story splashed over the front page of every gossip rag in town."

"Maybe you should've thought of this before you started this little hunting expedition you seem to be on," Peter said, sitting back in his chair. "Your mother would've hated all this, you know. Having her personal life scrutinized and dissected. Picked apart. Any daughter would understand that."

"Peter," Margaret said in a low voice.

"I'm not finished," Peter went on, ignoring her. "Ever since you've stepped into a leadership role here, Juliet, this company has faltered. Since your mother passed, you've spent more time chasing ghosts than you have in this office. And now we're on the verge of collapse. Target has pulled out of the deal. Given what's come to light, they no longer want to be associated with the brand."

"That isn't my fault," she said, her voice shaking. She felt on the verge of tears, the exhaustion of the last few months arriving all at once, a blanket thrown over a birdcage, and she had to fight the urge to climb beneath the long table and lay her head down on the carpeted floor. Maybe she would wake to the sound of her mother's voice, those slightly nasal consonants that were so familiar, so much a part of Jules's history, the only lullaby she had ever known.

"None of this would've happened if I were calling the shots," Peter muttered, almost to himself, "the way your mother promised. I've been with this company for going on thirty years, Juliet. There's no one more qualified to run this operation than I am, no one who knows it better. But instead, Elizabeth let her judgment be clouded by guilt and responsibility—and appointed a dilettante as her successor."

"That's bullshit," Jules said angrily, pushing back her chair. "And you know it, Peter."

"I think the results speak for themselves," he said, looking at her archly, and she had to fight the urge to reach across the table and slap him. But she was too astonished to move, too stunned by the heat in his words. Peter had been a fixture at every birthday party Elizabeth had ever thrown for her, organizing the pony rides in the garden of her mother's estate the year she turned seven. Sat in stuffy auditoriums for both her middle and high school graduations, flying in from London just to attend her wedding. And until this moment, she'd had no idea just how deeply his resentment ran. It wasn't just that her mother was not who she'd claimed to be, Jules realized in a blinding flash; it was the unmistakable fact that no one was.

"You've screwed up basically every decision that's been put in front of you since you've taken over," he went on, his eyes narrowing. "You want to really run this company? Then find out who leaked the story. And fix it. You owe her that much, at least—"

"Peter, that's *enough*," Margaret interrupted, and when she looked up, Jules saw that behind her glasses, her amber eyes were brimming with tears.

"You're right," Jules said with a nod. "I do." She stood up, placing one hand on the table to steady herself. She walked to the door, swinging it open and closing it behind her before Peter could say another word. She looked up at the framed book covers on the wall, the glossy promotional shots of Elizabeth standing in a field of wildflowers, kneeling on the dunes of Nantucket, a straw basket looped over one arm, her rose-painted lips curved into a graceful smile.

I'm screwing it all up, she thought as she searched her mother's soft, blue gaze.

Tell me what to do.

Jules waited for the ground to shake, a gust of frigid air moving past. But there was nothing. Just the endless clicking of keyboards, and the hum of voices as Jules began walking toward the reception area. There was no hand reaching from the beyond to help her, no one to pour her a cup of tea to steady her nerves, spooning in three sugars, just the way she liked, no one to insist things would be fine in the end. She wasn't Elizabeth. She never would be. But she could be her own mother now. She could save herself.

And she knew exactly where to go. But not yet. First, she would navigate the maze of the city, board the silver subway cars, walk the familiar streets leading back to her apartment, no longer any kind of safe harbor. There would be a chill in the air, she knew, as she watched Mark pack his things, the remnants of their life together, in a few small bags. When the door closed behind him, she would sink into the couch, staring blankly into space, awaiting the tears she knew would inevitably come, a cup of tea warming her hands. *Long ago,* her mother had once told her as she stood at the stove, stirring a pot of chai, cinnamon sticks floating in a copper saucepan, the milk dotted with cloves and cardamom pods, *cloves were used for luck and protection—for courage too, Julie.*

She knew, even before she ducked down into the subway that would take her home, that to move through the next part of her life and emerge unscathed, to be reborn like the phoenix, she'd need all the strength she could muster.

Chapter Thirty-Five

"What are you doing here?"

Noah appeared on the street in front of her like an apparition, pushing open the revolving glass doors of the Midtown high-rise that housed Sydelle's office, smiling happily at the sight of her, his eyes crinkling at the corners. And in that look, she felt the pull of attraction between them once again, the same urgency she'd felt in the hotel room.

Two nights had passed since the story broke, nights where she'd paced the floors of her apartment in the dead hours until the sun rose again, appearing like a reprimand. But Noah looked as if he'd slumbered like an innocent. His hair was still damp, pushed back messily from his face, his jaw clean shaven, and he radiated the freshness of pine needles. Despite the cold, he wore his leather jacket, a white oxford beneath, a black, skinny tie knotted at his throat, coal-dark jeans shoved into boots. If she closed her eyes, she could imagine every square millimeter of his skin, could almost feel his hands against her flesh, how they'd grasped her hips so firmly as she rode him, holding her in place.

Stop it, she told herself sternly. *He sold you out. And Elizabeth, too.*

"I assume you're here because of Page Six." He reached one hand up, adjusting the strap of his messenger bag. "I've been trying to call you since the story broke."

"I'm here to see Sydelle," Jules said frostily as pedestrians wove around them. They were breaking a cardinal rule, Jules thought as a man pushed past, muttering his distaste under his breath, standing in the middle of the street like tourists.

"Me too." Noah grinned. "We just finished. She's all yours, as they say."

"Is she now," she said lightly, and he looked at her curiously, as if unsure what to say next.

"What's going on, Jules?" he asked. "Am I missing something here?"

"Apparently not," she snapped. "You don't miss a thing, do you?"

"What do you mean?" he replied, the smile draining from his face. "Look, I've only tried calling you about a hundred times—don't you ever check your phone? But since you're here I can tell you now in person: I had nothing to do with it."

"Really," Jules said flatly.

"You actually think I'd lie to you?" Noah asked, his frustration evident in his tone, the way he took a step toward her, looking into her eyes as though to convince her otherwise. "I guess you don't think much of me. Despite . . . what happened between us."

Jules tried not to think about the way he'd held her in his arms, his hands sliding between her thighs, the feel of his skin, so new under her fingertips, the taste of him in her mouth, honeycomb and cinnamon.

"They're *your* pages," she pointed out, regaining her composure. "You're the only one who knows the whole story."

"Jules, I told you—I've been sending Sydelle pages for weeks. So let me ask you something," he said, looking at her sharply. "Why are you here, anyway?"

"Don't change the subject."

"Just answer the question."

"I already told you. To see Sydelle." She pushed the weight of her hair back with one hand. "She isn't answering my emails."

"Maybe you should think," Noah said, staring at her intently, "about why that might be."

A police car wailed down Sixth Avenue, lights flashing, passersby muttering in exasperation as they moved past, the beat of the city thrumming all around her in time with the rapid beating of her heart.

"You've got to be kidding," she said slowly. "I've known Sydelle since I was a child. She was one of my mother's closest friends." *But does that mean anything anymore,* a voice inside her pointed out, *considering how your mother lied for years on end?*

To you. To everyone.

"I guess at the end of the day, that doesn't mean as much as one might hope," Noah said grimly. A woman jostled Jules from behind, bumping into her rudely, and she was propelled forward, Noah grabbing her arm to steady her.

"Or maybe," Jules said, wrenching her arm away, "you're just some washed-up hack who doesn't know what he's talking about."

The city seemed to stop as they stared at one another, the impudence in her gaze almost daring him to fight back, to lash out as she had done, drawing blood, the wound deep beneath the surface.

"Wow," he said, dropping his eyes and looking down at the pavement. A long moment passed, the wind blowing through the coat she wore, so sharp and frigid that she thought she might freeze to death where she stood, consigned to a land of snow and ice like a maiden in a fairy tale, her skin a cyanotic blue.

"Sunglasses! Scarves!" a vendor called out from his post on the corner, a table set up before him piled with colorful wool. Noah looked up, and the indifference she saw reflected there made her want to reach out a hand, gather the words from the air, swallow them down like bitter poison.

"I think we're done here," he said, looking up at her as he brushed past and walked down the street, the first flakes of snow falling from the sky, dusting the shoulders of his leather jacket, the flakes landing solidly in his dark hair.

~

Nothing about Sydelle's office reminded Jules of her mother, and for that she was grateful. It seemed that anyone who spent any length of time around Elizabeth Stone inevitably picked up her preferences, her mannerisms, her aesthetic. But there was no sign of her mother's careful hand here, no artfully placed throws or pillows to cushion a seat, no luxurious fabrics. Jules looked around at the relentlessly beige decor, the nondescript blond wood furniture, the framed book covers gracing the walls. The atmosphere was curiously sterile. There were no family photos or mementos gracing Sydelle's desk, no ephemera marking the passage of time. Just a neatly stacked manuscript on the clean blotter before her, a red pen lying off to one side.

"What a lovely surprise," Sydelle said as she sat down behind the desk, smiling broadly. "But the timing is unfortunate as I'm on deadline for a project." She raised a hand, gesturing at the pile of papers.

"We have to talk, Sydelle," Jules said. "I'm pulling the book. I assume you got my email?"

As always, Sydelle was impeccably turned out in a camel-colored sheath, a black cardigan thrown over her shoulders. Her silver bob shone beneath the harsh overhead lights, her only adornment a slim gold band on her left hand. It occurred to Jules that in all the years Sydelle had been her mother's editor, shaping one book after another, Jules had never once met the woman's husband. What else had been hidden away in plain sight, Jules wondered, as Sydelle looked at her, the smile sliding from her face.

"As I've said," she began, "your timing is quite unfortunate, Jules. We've already put a substantial deposit on reams and reams of paper that is presently sitting in a warehouse in China, waiting to be printed, not to mention the exorbitant amount we have earmarked in next year's budget for a big PR push leading up to publication. And of course, there's also the sizable advance we've paid out to both you and Noah."

"I'll return my half," Jules said quickly. "I don't need the money."

"That isn't the point. We've signed a contract. I'm afraid pulling the book isn't an option. The ball is rolling. I can't stop it now."

"Can't or won't?" Jules asked, and Sydelle just stared at her, eyes cold as glaciers.

"In light of what's been uncovered," Sydelle answered, "it would be financially disadvantageous to do so. And I have a responsibility to this company."

"You have a responsibility to my mother," Jules pointed out. "To her legacy. And to me. But I guess you weren't thinking about that when you called the *Post*."

Sydelle sighed, pushing her chair back, standing up. She walked over to the window, peering out at the slice of sky. "This is about the story, Jules," she said carefully. "Your mother's story. It's bigger than you. But now that bits and pieces are already out there, the rest is going to come out—one way or another. I highly suggest that you be the one to tell it."

"It's my story, too," Jules said, her voice wavering with anger.

"That may be so. But no one's interested in your story, Jules. This is about Elizabeth, which should be nothing new for you," she said with a shrug.

"What exactly do you mean?" Jules said, feeling herself bristling.

Sydelle turned to face her, crossing her arms over her chest, her hands resting gently along her biceps. "You've only ever been in service of your mother's story, Juliet. Furthering her narrative. Which is exactly why I encouraged Elizabeth to have you in the first place."

"Excuse me?" Jules heard herself say, her words tinny and distant, as if traveling over time and space. The room was the same as when Jules had entered it. Sydelle's face as familiar as ever. But it was as if Jules were in a simulacrum, an alternate universe where the story could change at any second.

"It widened her demographic substantially," Sydelle said with a tight smile. "Gave her respectability. More important, it gave her an endlessly generative vein to tap into. Why, your birthday parties alone were the genus for *Elizabeth Stone Occasions*, which as I'm sure you know, sold over a million copies in its first printing."

"That's . . . impossible," Jules went on, a strange feeling creeping over her, pieces falling into place like fall leaves covering the pavement. And still, she felt the need to refute it all, to turn away from it entirely before the idea could take hold.

"You see, Jules, she was building her brand as a domestic goddess," she went on. "How could she *not* have her own child?"

Jules sat there, as if lost in the banks of a great fog. Although Juliet Neumeyer-Stone was the name printed on her birth certificate, she had always been referred to as Juliet Stone, both in her daily life and the pages of her mother's books. *It just sounds cleaner,* her mother had always said with a wave of her fingers. Jules had never questioned it, never thought she had a reason to until this very moment. Had she always been window dressing? Just another extension of the brand?

I hope you don't hate me someday, her mother had said a few days before she'd slipped away, the light in her eyes dimmed to a flicker as they settled on Jules's face, a look of peace washing over her features. *My favorite view,* she had always insisted, reaching one hand out to smooth Jules's hair back from her face. Elizabeth could have told her then, in that very moment when they'd locked eyes, a deathbed confession while there was still time. But her mother had chosen to say nothing, nothing at all. She'd left without so much as an explanation, letting Jules believe Harold was her father, even when she knew there was the distinct possibility it might be otherwise.

And now, Elizabeth is dead and buried, she told herself, as if she needed the reminder. *Where you cannot ask her anything anymore.*

Sydelle turned to glance out the window once again, the snow coming down thicker now, covering the city in a haze of whiteness. "At least she had the same degree of discretion about this ridiculous affair as she did about you."

"You didn't know?" Jules heard herself ask.

"My dear." Sydelle laughed softly. "Your mother had the innate ability to make everyone she crossed paths with feel intimately close to her. I always knew that sense of familiarity was an illusion—especially with her fans. But it turned out to be the same with me, too. I knew no more than you, or anyone else, for that matter. I saw what Elizabeth wanted me to see. No more, no less."

Jules sat there, the enormity of all she'd heard slowly sinking in. Despite the long talks, her mother's insistence that they share everything, clothes, shoes, even the morsels of food on her plate, at the end of the day, it seemed their relationship had been little more than a meticulously constructed ruse. Elizabeth Stone was a persona, a carefully curated image. But what was far, far worse was the fact that Jules had never had the opportunity to know herself, either—not even on the basest of levels, her identity, the very reason she was born hidden away, as if it were yet another distasteful fact Elizabeth had glossed over, making it prettier, shinier, more digestible.

"I'll give you and Noah an extra six weeks to deliver the manuscript," Sydelle said, turning around to face her. "But that's it."

Nothing felt real, the room she stood in, the woman in front of her, the blunt cut of her silver bob swinging like a knife—not even her own skin. She was a blank page, the narrative she knew by heart now deleted, a landscape of desolate whiteness glaring back at her, waiting for her to pick up a pen and begin.

Chapter Thirty-Six

ELIZABETH

When the blood came, arriving precisely at the twelve-week mark, Elizabeth stared at her underwear in disbelief, a mass of toilet paper still scrunched in one hand. The bathroom tile was cold against her bare toes, the nails painted the pink of pointe shoes. There was a dull throb in her lower belly, a slow, deliberate ache that spread from the front of her pelvis, creeping around to the small of her back, like the tightening of a fist.

In the taxi on the way to Mount Sinai, she bent at the waist, the pain sweeping through her now, her abdomen hot and swollen. She could feel a stream of blood trickling past her thigh, slowly making its way down her calf to pool in one shoe. *This can't be happening,* she told herself, closing her eyes as the driver lurched around stalled traffic, the car swerving violently. She thought of the christening dress she'd bought at a shop on Madison just the day before, a row of tiny stitches in the hem, satin ribbon along the neckline, the feel of it candy-slick. How she'd carried that scrap of fabric to the register, as light and insubstantial as a broken promise.

"I've read that spotting at this juncture is fairly normal," Harold said reassuringly, squeezing her hand, but when she opened her eyes and looked over, the fear written so plainly on his face said otherwise.

In the ultrasound room, the technician, so warm and effusive only moments before, fell abruptly silent as she moved the wand around Elizabeth's abdomen, the gel cold and sticky on her skin. "I'll get the doctor," she said quietly, and it was only when she left the room that Elizabeth allowed the tears to come, sobs that racked her small frame, as if her body were trying to rid itself of her own pain, along with the child who could not stay.

"What do you want me to do?" Colin had asked on the phone, as she'd stood there in the hotel suite at the Plaza, the pear-shaped diamond twinkling on her left hand. "I'll do anything," he'd said hurriedly. "I can get on a plane today."

Elizabeth had sat down on the bed, the telephone cord curling around her fingers.

"It's too late," she said, the tears falling, though she brushed them away as quickly as they arrived.

"It's never too late."

"In this case," she said with a dry laugh, another wave of nausea causing her to clench the receiver tightly in her fist, "it is. I'm married."

"But you're pregnant," he pointed out. "With my child."

"We don't know that," she said, practicality taking over. "There is the possibility that it's Harold's. You know that."

He fell silent, and in that void, she cursed all they could not say across that wire, the impossibility of it all, the things she did not dare utter, words she knew would take hold, leaving her hopelessly mired in the past.

I love you. Come get me.

"Are you going to tell him?" he asked, but in his lack of affect, she could hear the resignation creeping in already. He had always given up too soon where she was concerned, relented far too quickly.

"There isn't any point," she'd said, her words as hard as sheets of peanut brittle.

"The point is that I love you," he said quickly. "Are you really telling me this is where it ends?"

She'd hesitated for a moment, barely a fraction of a second, and then hung up, placing the phone gently back in its cradle with a faint chime that reverberated in the stillness of the room. There had been letters in the weeks that followed, missives she was careful to intercept before Harold got home from work, plain white envelopes she pushed beneath a stack of her neatly folded sweaters in the bedroom closet, Colin's words, his cramped writing still that of a schoolboy, making her breath lurch in her throat.

And in the small hours of the night, when the apartment was quiet but for the traffic gliding by on the street outside, she found herself at the kitchen table, pen in hand, words flowing effortlessly in the starkness of jet ink, as they seldom did in life, her script filling page after page until the light appeared slowly in the sky, bringing with it the hope of a new day. *I want to stop thinking of you,* she wrote, afraid of her own words as they bled onto the page. *Writing to you. Dreaming of you.*

Why are we doing this to each other?

When she returned from surgery, she lay in the hospital bed, one hand over her belly, as if to protect the child, long gone, from its own inevitable demise, her womb scraped clean as the empty shell of a mollusk. She had never felt so empty, so devoid of life. "We'll try again," Harold had said, reaching out to cover her hand with his own.

Elizabeth had just nodded, turning over to face the wall.

Chapter Thirty-Seven

JULES

The first thing Jules did when she got home was rearrange the furniture. She donned her oldest clothes, a T-shirt washed so often it was threadbare and a pair of boxers Mark had left behind, as she dragged the sofa from the center of the living room, exposing a litter of gray dust bunnies that Colbie pounced on immediately, batting at them with her soft paws as Jules slid the couch under the long row of windows. With a single call to Goodwill, she disposed of the chrome lamps and understated wool rugs Elizabeth had chosen, the decor swaddled in Bubble Wrap before two burly men hauled it all away.

After they left, she stood in the near-empty space, the sofa and a lone chair left over from her college days the only remaining decor, the seat a moth-eaten purple velvet that her mother had always despised, her wedding photos packed away in boxes, pushed to the back of the guest room closet. The lights of the city twinkled outside the curtainless windows, and as she turned to survey the bare floors, her footsteps echoing off the empty walls, she felt the darkness that had clung to her since the day they'd put her mother in the ground lifting slightly, like a plane tentatively departing from the flat confines of a runway.

She carefully removed the prints from her old portfolio, filling the dusty rectangles on the empty walls with images she'd taken over the years, skaters in Tompkins Square Park, the glittering silhouette of the Brooklyn Bridge against a moonlit sky. A bodega cat hissing at her approach, its tail a curl of jet smoke. A little girl at a water fountain, her rosebud mouth dripping as she looked up, startled. She pulled her mother's books from the shelves, where they were lined up chronologically by age, ripping out the pages with one hand, throwing the pages into the hearth, the flames licking at her own face smiling up at her, the paper curling into the blue flames until all that remained was ashes.

In the weeks that followed, she spoke to no one. She kept her phone on silent, and when it died, she walked right past the charger as if it were invisible. Spent nights curled on the couch, a glass of bourbon in one hand, Colbie purring beside her, the past replaying itself like stark images from a film she was forced to repeat. *Why didn't you tell me?* she wondered endlessly.

But she knew the answer now, her asking only performative, much like her mother's fabricated life. Somehow, despite all that had been purposefully hidden from her, she understood Elizabeth better than ever now. Her mother had lived a lie—and had been rewarded for it. Why shouldn't her only daughter follow suit?

She forced herself to leave the house, impulsively signing up for a membership at a yoga studio a few blocks away, a small, tidy space full of hanging green plants, the air smelling of frankincense. As she sat cross-legged, her eyes closed, head bowed, a sense of calm washed over her, so new and unfamiliar that she quickly placed one hand on her heart, just to make sure it was still beating. And when the woman beside her, corn silk hair pulled back in a ponytail, struck up a conversation, Jules turned to her, smiling tentatively as she offered up her name.

When she finally plugged her phone back in, she braced herself as the screen glowed whitely, the apple signaling her return to civilization. It took the better part of fifteen minutes to scroll through the sea of notifications, so many calls and texts from Mark that Jules immediately lost count, emails from Margaret, voicemails from reporters asking her to comment on the Page Six story, and among them, a single text from Noah.

Eunice is in the hospital, it read. At Mount Sinai. Thought you'd want to know.

"Hey," she said when he picked up the phone. "Is she OK?"

"I don't have details, beyond what's in the papers, but she seems to be stable." There was no warmth or familiarity in his voice, and she remembered their last encounter, how she'd stood there in the street, hurling words like daggers.

"I'm really sorry about what I said," she began, walking over to the window, the sky outside gray and forbidding, the clouds heavy with snow. "I shouldn't have lashed out like that."

"It's OK," he replied in that same neutral tone, as if they were discussing paint colors. "You've had a lot on your mind."

"Mark moved out," she said, moving over to the sofa and sinking into the cushions, drawing her feet up beneath her.

"Wow," he said, and she could picture him raising an eyebrow in surprise. "How do you feel about that?"

"It's weird," she said, glancing over at the wall that had once held their wedding photos. "One minute I'm grateful to be alone . . . the next I'm sobbing uncontrollably. But . . . it's not all just about my marriage."

"What, then?"

"That day I went to see Sydelle," Jules began, "she told me . . . she said Elizabeth had me for the sole purpose of furthering her career. It was all part of the facade, apparently. The Elizabeth Stone brand."

"She *what*?"

"Noah," she said, swallowing hard, "nothing is what I thought it was. Not my marriage. Not my relationship with my mother. And definitely not my life. I feel like I'm starting from scratch."

She paused, and in that silence, she could almost feel him nodding. "There's a kind of freedom in that," he said, when he finally spoke again. "Starting over. You can rewrite the story any way you want. It's powerful stuff, Jules."

"I don't know," she mumbled, blinking away the tears that had sprung up alongside that admission, the pain a white-hot ember in her chest, the room as blurred and unfocused as her life. "It's hard to see what power lies in that."

"And you believe her?"

"I don't know what to believe anymore," she admitted, closing her eyes.

Do you know how much I love you? her mother had crooned from the time Jules could walk. *My darling*, she would say, picking her up and nestling her close. Nothing had made her feel safer than being in Elizabeth's orbit. Her mother was the sun, her hair resplendent with fractured, golden light, and Jules the pale glimmer of the moon, circling around her. *You only get one person in this life*, Elizabeth would whisper, and Jules would close her eyes, drinking in her mother's perfume, a clutch of white roses, hummingbirds flitting among the petals. A kind of whirring.

And you're mine.

Hers to lie to, Jules thought angrily. *Hers to shape.*

Hers to control.

"Look, I know this isn't the best time to talk about this . . ." Noah said gingerly, his voice trailing off. "But actually? Scrap that. Maybe it's *exactly* the right time. Listen, after we left New Orleans, I spoke to Colin. He told me that he and your mother saw each other over the years when she traveled for work—"

"Yes, I'm well aware of that," she interrupted, slightly annoyed now.

"But he said it was always platonic," Colin finished. "That after that night in San Francisco, he and Elizabeth never slept together again."

Jules exhaled, running one hand through her tangled hair. Whether or not the affair had continued over the years seemed inconsequential now, given the very real possibility that Colin was her father.

"Why didn't you tell me this before?" she demanded.

"You didn't really give me the chance," Noah pointed out. "The thing is, Jules . . . this changes the entire scope of the book. This isn't just a story about your mother anymore. It's about *you*."

"No one cares about me. Or my story." The words caught in her throat like the slender barbs of fishhooks, the metal piercing her flesh, silencing her. *Dilettante,* Peter had called her—someone who dabbled in everything, committing to nothing at all.

An amateur.

"Your story is *the* story now, Jules," Noah said impatiently. "Without you, it's just another book of recipes with some gossip thrown in. Look, I know you don't want to think about any of this, much less write it all down, and I'm telling you this as your friend, not necessarily your cowriter, but I think seeing this through could be good for you, cathartic even. I've thought that from the first day we met—even more so now, given what we've learned."

"There's no way I'm baring my soul for that woman," Jules said darkly, remembering Sydelle's careful tone, so removed that she could almost feel a stark chill creeping over the office. "And she made it very clear that we have to deliver. She's extended the deadline by six weeks."

"Well, what if we just didn't? What if we took the idea somewhere else?"

"Could we do that?" she asked, wrinkling her brow. "From what she said, it didn't seem possible."

"We're contracted to write a biography," Noah said matter-of-factly. "A retrospective of your mother's career. It's become much more than that—it's another story entirely now. You could sell it to another publisher as a memoir, and Sydelle couldn't do a damn thing about it."

"Just not turn in the book? Return the advance? That's no problem for me, but . . . you'd have to give back your half, too. I couldn't ask you to do that," Jules said, shaking her head.

"It wouldn't be the first time." He laughed softly, the sound sending a shiver through her. "But now that the story broke, Jules," he went on, "every publisher in town will be circling like sharks once they hear you've left Sydelle."

"I don't know." She sighed. "It feels overwhelming. Starting all over again."

"You're doing that anyway," Noah pointed out, "whether you write it down or not. And don't worry about me. There are always other projects. Hell, maybe I'll write a novel based on Colin's life—he's certainly interesting enough."

Jules sat there, the thoughts swirling in her head like snow. Maybe Noah was right. If she dragged out the skeletons of the past, shining light on every secret, the elaborate scaffolding surrounding Elizabeth's kingdom would fall. But when the smoke finally cleared, it just might make room for something more honest.

Something real.

"If I do this," she said slowly, "I need to do it my way."

"I think," Noah said, chortling softly, "that's what I've been suggesting all along."

~

Just standing in a hospital was enough to give Jules déjà vu. The antiseptic smell of the hallways, the dingy paint on the walls, an institutional green, the sounds of endlessly beeping machines transported her right back to her mother's final days, Elizabeth's bones jutting through the cotton nightgown she wore, the flowers on the bedside table wilting on their stems, as if they preferred to die right along with her. The food her mother had refused, turning away from every dish as if eating now brought her no joy at all.

When Jules entered the room, Eunice lay motionless in bed, a monitor chronicling every beat of her heart. Slight to begin with, she'd shrunk considerably in the past weeks, her bones now as frail as matchsticks and nearly buried beneath a pile of sheets, a cashmere blanket, cloud gray, resting on top. But her hands, mottled with age spots and threaded with veins, still flashed with diamond rings. Her eyes were closed, and her chest rose and fell with every labored breath. She looked, Jules thought as she stood at the bedside, as if she'd become a child once again, the metal bars reminiscent of a crib. Just then Eunice opened her eyes, peering curiously up at her, her initial surprise slowly giving way to recognition.

"Well, if it isn't Juliet Stone." She smiled. "Come to pay me a visit."

"How are you feeling?" Jules asked, reaching over to take Eunice's hand in her own, brittle as kindling, her jewels scraping against Jules's palm.

"At this age, who can tell?" Eunice looked up at her impishly. "They say I've had a 'minor cardiac event.' All I know is that I'm finally being called home." Her eyes clouded, drifting past Jules and out the open door. "He's driving me batty with that incessant pacing," she muttered in exasperation.

"Who is?" Jules asked, turning to glance at the empty doorway.

"The admiral." Eunice snorted. "He thinks he can hurry things along by annoying me as much as humanly possible. He forgets that I survived thirty years of marriage," she said, looking over at Jules, her blue eyes crystalline once again, "so I know a thing or two about patience."

"You know a lot of things," Jules said as Eunice closed her fingers around her hand more tightly. "Things my mother never told me. I don't know how to make peace with it all," she went on. "I don't know if I can."

Eunice nodded tersely, the lines around her eyes and mouth deeply carved, as if in clay. "Your mother was a complicated woman. God knows, they've said the same about me." She sighed. "The path she walked wasn't easy, Juliet. But the rewards . . . well, they were immeasurable. Why, look what she made," she said, reaching up with the other hand to stroke Jules's cheek for a brief instant, her fingers gnarled but her touch as light as wings.

"Yes, to help her career," Jules said, choking on the words, her throat tight.

There it was again, that feeling of vertigo sweeping through her, the world as she knew it falling away, her steps skirting the edge of a cliff, the void of the water below, dark wreckage just beneath the surface. Eunice let go of her hand, looking up at her sharply.

"She made you in every way that counts," she said, her voice indignant. "Surely you see that."

"I need to ask you something," Jules began, "and I want you to tell me the truth."

Eunice nodded, her eyes fluttering softly, as if it were difficult to not close them entirely.

"Is Colin my father?" she asked, flinching slightly, as if bracing herself for impact.

There was only the beeping of the heart monitor as Jules waited for an answer, the sound an insistent refusal.

"No," Eunice said, her voice firm and unwavering. "He is not. Though I will admit I often entertain the fantasy that you are my granddaughter. It is a way, I suppose, of keeping Elizabeth with me all these years. But the truth is that your mother had a miscarriage, Juliet, and rather a bad one at that. Common enough in those days, and certainly now as well. Why, I had two myself before Colin was born . . . a nasty business, it was . . ." Her voice trailed off, and she sighed again, the sound like the echo of waves against the shoreline.

In that moment, Jules felt the weight of all she'd been carrying over the past few months slip from her shoulders in a flood of relief. *At least there is one thing, in my life that is irrefutable, beyond reproach,* she told herself. But even with that certainty, she knew that fact alone would not fix her the way she'd hoped. It could not even begin to make up for all her mother had secreted away over the years, all she'd kept hidden.

"That may be so," Jules said when she had finally gathered her thoughts. "But I still don't know how to forgive her. I don't know if I can."

"Well," Eunice said, closing her eyes, as if exhaustion had overtaken her, "it is often the bitterest pill we swallow, this thing called forgiveness. And yet, it is essential, Juliet. Essential. Without it, there is no growth, no understanding. Without it, we are stuck in the muddled labyrinth of our pride." She shook her head, as if the thought had agitated her. "If you can understand your mother," she said, opening her eyes once more, "you can forgive her. Perhaps that is what you must undertake in writing this book, Juliet—understanding." Her voice grew weaker with every syllable. "Forgiveness will arrive on its own. It will appear with no fanfare, no blaring of trumpets. Like death itself."

"What if it doesn't?"

"That is the risk you must take." Eunice smiled. "A life's work, some might say. But I know you are up to the task. You are your mother's daughter, after all."

Jules nodded, biting her lip to keep the tears from falling. She knew implicitly that Eunice would not have tolerated it. And for the first time, those words held no rancor, no mistrust. They were finally simply the truth.

She was Juliet Neumeyer-Stone, daughter of Elizabeth and Harold.

"The Degas," Eunice said with a smile, "is yours, of course. I had my lawyers draw up the papers just last week."

"That is . . ." Jules began when she could find the words, "beyond generous. I can't possibly—"

"You can and you will," Eunice said, glancing over at her sharply. "I won't hear another word on the subject." She sighed, releasing Jules's hand and patting it once, as though it were Jules who needed comforting. "It is a curious thing, this tiredness," she mused. "I feel as though I've been run ragged . . . Colin is on his way from New Orleans, and I intend to hang on long enough for him to make an appearance. That boy never did have any knack for timing." She chortled softly, closing her eyes again.

"Rest easy," Jules said as she leaned down to kiss Eunice's dry cheek. As she drew closer, she saw that Eunice's lips, chapped and papery, were moistened with ointment, the same lemon-scented swabs Jules had dabbed on the corners of Elizabeth's mouth in the hours before her death. As Jules bent down, Eunice's eyes fluttered open briefly, staring at her unknowingly, her pale lashes beating against her cheeks before her lids slipped closed once again.

Chapter Thirty-Eight

After she left Mount Sinai, Jules did what she always did when she needed to think: she rode the subway. She knew that most would've sought solace in nature, walking the snowy paths in Central Park, the boat pond glazed over, lily pads trapped under ice like high art, crowds of skaters spinning by on Wollman Rink, their shrieks filling the air. But, like her mother, Jules had always preferred the anonymity of crowds. Descending into the underworld of the city, watching the stations flash by, hearing the garbled voice of the conductor announcing each stop, had always quieted her mind, putting her instantly at ease. There was something womb-like about being underground, the dark tunnel enveloping her, the repetition of one stop following the next, the metal doors lulling her into a stupor as they opened and closed.

Passengers entered the car and exited in an endless, undulating wave, the tide advancing and withdrawing, the train humid with bodily heat, the salt and grease of fried food. A child, maybe all of three, twirled around the metal pole, singing nonsensically, and across from her, a man ate from a Styrofoam container, holding a drumstick delicately in one hand, chewing thoughtfully.

If you can understand your mother, you can forgive her.

She turned Eunice's words this way and that, trying to absorb them, as if by osmosis. She understood her mother better than ever now. But still, forgiveness remained stubbornly out of reach, an abstract concept, one that refused closure, no matter how much she longed for it. It was the heat of her anger that kept it at bay, a feeling she could not seem to shake, no matter how hard she tried to snuff it out, to bury it as she had buried Elizabeth, the fury and indignation exhausting her until all she wanted was to somehow be free.

But still, the fire burned on.

By the time she arrived home, the sky was dark, and the snowfall had ceased, the streets an unblemished white, marred by only the footprints she left in her wake. Before heading into her building, Jules looked around, marveling at the sight of the city, so still and silent, her breath hovering in the air. Elizabeth had always said the first snowfall of the year was the real magic of the season, the streets transformed by a dusting of white powder, icicles sparkling off the awnings, heralding Christmas, the holiday Jules had always loved most but one she couldn't imagine celebrating this year, the first she'd spend without the stockings her mother had made hung on the mantel, her eyes brightening as Jules walked through the door.

Maybe I should just get out of town, she thought glumly, as she pushed through the revolving door and stepped into the lobby. Christmas in Mexico City, pigeon in mole sauce instead of turkey with oyster stuffing, didn't sound so bad. Jules knew that anything would be better than sitting alone in her near-empty apartment, staring at the walls.

Manuel, the doorman, stood behind the desk, waving a hand in greeting as she approached, his cap slipping over his forehead. When Elizabeth had died, he'd removed his hat to expose his carefully trimmed silver hair, holding the cap over his heart as if in tribute. "A great lady," he'd murmured, and Jules had nodded in response, her eyes nearly swollen shut from the constant assault of her tears.

"Package for you," he said, pulling a box, rectangular in shape and covered in brown paper, from behind the counter. There was no address label, just her name written across the top in black ink. The box, when Jules reached out to grab it, was surprisingly light, and she clutched it in her arms as she traversed the lobby, the elevator whisking her upstairs.

Inside the apartment, all was as she'd left it, as if time had failed to pass. It had been weeks, but Mark's absence still startled her, the silence she was expected to fill with her presence alone. She hung up her coat, then moved into the kitchen, putting the copper kettle on for tea as Colbie slunk into the kitchen, yawning widely. While she waited for the water to boil, she took a knife from the drawer and slit open the box. Inside, a card rested on top, the kind of stationery her mother had always preferred, the stock thick and heavy to the touch. She removed it from the box, one hip leaning against the counter, and began to read.

> Juliet—
> I checked in with Sydelle about the book, and she filled me in on your meeting. Your mother entrusted these letters to me when her illness took a turn for the worse. Her wish was that they be kept secret, but it sounds like with all the headway you've made, none of the broad strokes you'll find here will take you by surprise. But I think that reading them might help you a great deal. And I know if Elizabeth were still here, she would very much agree. In any case, they are yours now—to do with as you will.
> Love,
> Margaret

The kettle whistled, long and shrill, a plume of steam escaping into the air, and Jules looked up, startled. She placed the card on the counter and switched off the gas on the burner, the tea forgotten now. Jules turned back to the box, reaching inside to retrieve a stack of envelopes tied with a red ribbon, the color more rust than rose. Some were addressed to Elizabeth, others to Colin, years of correspondence. She opened the envelope on top, the paper soft and creased from the passage of time, her eyes scanning her mother's careful script, the curling letters she knew as well as her own handwriting.

Dear Colin,

She's perfect. So tiny and new, the soles of her feet like velvet. When they put her in my arms for the first time, she was perfectly quiet, just staring up at me with those big blue orbs that looked as though they'd visited this planet more times than I could say. An old soul, my mother would've called her. The moment our eyes met, I knew her instantly, her fingers gripping on to my own for dear life. I wish my own mother were here to meet her. I see so much of her in Juliet. A trio of nesting dolls, the three of us: Grace, me, and now my daughter. I understand, far too late it seems, why my mother hid her illness when it would have been so easy to confide in me before it was too late. She was shielding me from the ugliness of it all, Colin, in the only way left to her. There is nothing, I tell you, nothing I would not do to protect this tiny being from heartache. It seems so odd that they allow you to take a baby home with no license, no training whatsoever. But it doesn't matter. I have never been so ready for a challenge in all my life, despite a complete lack of preparedness. The thing is, and I feel foolish saying it, or, I suppose, writing it down, but when I look at her, I know the reason I exist.

Jules brought one hand to her mouth, holding it there as she read. *Oh, Mommy,* she thought instantly. As far back as she could remember, her mother had always been Mom or Elizabeth—maybe Mama early on, before memory had taken hold—but now, reading her mother's words, so full of wonderment, there was no other name that made sense to her, none at all. Transfixed, she gathered up the box and sank down on the floor where she stood, opening each envelope, one after another, years of conversation preserved in amber, Colin's slanted, messy scrawl filling the page.

> Billie,
>
> Our time in Dallas was far too brief, as always, but that you made time at all is always a thrill. The new restaurant is going well, sort of a ribs and corn bread style joint. Very down home. I think you would approve. Though I must confess that each time you leave, it is getting harder to let you go. I know it is madness to ask you to reconsider, to even suggest it, given your happiness at home, and often I feel as if I am intruding into that place of calm contentment you have built for yourself.
>
> You ask if I have been "dating," and by that, I assume you'd like to know if there is anyone to rival your charms. I can honestly report that the answer is no. I won't lie; there have been dalliances. But I think I may be destined to remain an eternal bachelor, grizzled and bearded, growing increasingly more cantankerous with every passing year.

Jules paused for a moment, reaching up to wipe away her tears, which had been falling steadily ever since she'd opened the first letter and begun to read. She took a deep breath and opened the next envelope, cutting the pad of one finger with the knife-edge of the paper, and she reached up and put it in her mouth, tasting salt and iron.

> Dear Colin,
>
> The launch went well, though to say I am exhausted would fail to properly convey my present state of inertia. I have interviews tomorrow on Good Morning America and CBS, and all I want to do is melt into a

lawn chair in the summer heat and watch Juliet splash around in the pool. She's getting so big, Colin, you wouldn't believe it. Where does the time go? She looks up at me, and I see her whole life reflected in the clarity of her gaze. No man has ever looked at me the way she does, as if my very presence could stop time. She happily sits for hours while I pose her, giggling as the camera clicks, the stylists fussing over her, arranging the frosted cakes and petits fours as if she were royalty. I cannot believe this is my life, singular and wildly beautiful, that I get to have this wild proliferation of happiness.

Still. I dream of your face.

Jules felt a sharp pain, as if her heart had been pierced by the silver thread of a needle. She clasped the letter to her chest, taking one breath after another before laying it down, smoothing the creased page with her palm. No matter how hard she'd tried to make her mother happy, she'd never been able to shake the nagging suspicion that no matter what she did or how hard she tried, she was always somehow coming up short. There was an unruliness in her, a stubbornness that Elizabeth longed to assuage, her cool, practiced hands shaping Jules like a ball of wet clay. But as she continued to read, she could hear the astonishment in her mother's voice, the love shining through her words clear and unmistakable as a bell chiming softly at dawn.

My dearest Billie,
You looked so lovely at our luncheon that you almost took my breath away. France suits you. You relax into things, become the softest version of yourself, like a kitten curled up at a warm hearth. I confess that when you spoke, I tuned out much of the time, imagining the luxury of coming home to you each evening, how

lucky Harold must be to be greeted by your smiling face. Even across the table, I could feel the pull between us, and though we talked of asparagus and tart crust, my new home in New Orleans, a city you have grown to love as I do, all the while I was drinking you in, savoring these small moments together, squirreling them away in my memory to keep me company in your absence. These stolen hours, delicious as they are, hardly sustain me. But I will try my best to be content.

But it was the next letter that stole the breath from her lungs, her anger evaporating in a rush of sadness, the rage that had consumed her for weeks finally extinguished, a waning bonfire in a sudden downpour.

Colin,
I have started this letter no less than four times, crumpling it up and beginning again. What you ask isn't simple, and I think you know that. You are right in many ways. I could leave Harold. I could live with you in your house in New Orleans, that grand, decrepit manor you bought on a whim, having fallen in love with it as I did, and I could bring it back to life, make it beautiful again. About all that, you aren't wrong.

But would we be happy?

I can't be sure, as every road not taken is always an eternal question mark, but something tells me that I'm right about what I'm about to say: I don't think we're built for that. Not with each other. I know this admission will hurt you, and the thought of causing you pain makes me want to escape my own skin, which is why I've put off answering at all. But I can't lie, either. There is also the fact that I could no more upend Juliet's life or pull her away from her father than I could end my own. I could not live with the guilt, Colin. And I know you wouldn't want me to. It's too large a price for everyone to pay, all around.

But there is also Harold. And the fact that I love him, and the life we've built with one another. I know you wish this weren't so, and maybe you imagine I stay out of obligation or convenience. But to say so would be a lie. I fear you and I will always be stuck somewhere in between, not willing to fully let go, but unwilling to take that final step toward one another. And maybe that's how it is meant to be—at least in this lifetime. And who am I to argue with fate? I hope you will someday settle down, create some stability in your life, all I cannot offer you. I will hate every minute of it, but it will quiet something in me, too. And I hope it will for you as well.

But know that even as I write this, I will look for you in every port, in the crowds of each cluttered bookstore, and on the waves of every ocean I cross, searching for the curve of your smile.

The sheet of paper slipped from her hands, drifting down to the floor to join the pile of others, and Jules pulled her knees to her chest, hugging them fiercely. There were more envelopes to be opened, more letters, and in time she would read them all, speaking the words aloud like an incantation, committing them to memory as if in prayer, words that had the power to revise the past and shift the trajectory of the future. She held the raw materials of her mother's complicated story in her two hands, the rubble from which she'd carve out her own bright future.

Chapter Thirty-Nine

ELIZABETH

Mornings were the time she loved best. Aurora, the clarity of a new day, the simplicity of the light, so clean and new, the birds warbling gently in the garden, flitting from bud to blossom. Harold in the bathroom, humming as he shaved, the sound of water splashing in the basin of the sink. That cadence of her life had a texture, a taste, crystallized as dark honey. If she failed to wake with the sun, there were Juliet's small hands gently patting her face, those somber blue eyes gazing down at her, her daughter's sweet voice filling her ears.

Mama, it's time to get up now.

There were pancakes in the kitchen, a puddle of melting golden butter in the cast-iron pan, and Juliet at her feet, a bowl between her small knees as she turned the wooden spoon, flour spilling on the oak floors Elizabeth had refinished herself, a dusting of it in her daughter's hair, a smudge decorating one pink cheek. After the last crumb was gone, the dishes piled in the sink, the plates smeared with Vermont maple syrup, Juliet sat in her high chair, sticky and spattered with milk, her sippy cup overturned in a puddle. It was as far away from an "Elizabeth Stone" kitchen as one could imagine, a scene that would've horrified her readers, but none of that mattered on these perfectly imperfect mornings.

Not a fig, her mother would've said, and in those moments she wished more than anything that Grace had lived long enough to meet her only granddaughter. That the rift between them had not been fully mended before her mother had slipped away was Elizabeth's greatest regret. But she also knew it was what Grace had wanted, and once her mother had made up her mind about something, she was as immovable as steel.

She plucked Juliet from her high chair, happily waving her syrupy hands in the air, one curl stuck to her cheek, and drew her daughter's body close, holding the soft weight of her against one hip. Juliet held her hands out in front of her face, and Elizabeth took the small fingers in her mouth one by one, sucking them clean. "Mmmmm," she said happily, making the excited cooing sounds she knew would make Juliet erupt in glee. "Delicious! My favorite recipe!"

Juliet giggled maniacally, and Elizabeth walked with her over to look out the kitchen window, her daughter clinging to her neck, her smooth skin fragrant with milk and sugar. There were no shoots today, no strategy meetings, no trips that would take her far from where she belonged. Just her daughter's face, lovely and constant as the North Star. Beyond the glass, the garden erupted in the heat of high summer, the tomato plants standing tall on their wooden stakes, her heart full, the dahlias turning their faces upward, in search of morning light, excellent and fair.

Chapter Forty

JULES

The room was so crowded that Jules could barely move, a rainbow of books lining the walls, her own among them, piles of hardbacks on display tables scattered around the shop, the title running up the length of the spine in curving script: *Finding Elizabeth Stone: A Daughter's Journey in Search of Her Mother—and Herself.* The store was nestled among a row of quaint shops lining the cobblestone streets of South Street Seaport, and Jules felt almost as if she were back in Maine, the scent of brine in the air, the ozonic tinge of the sea. But in the city, that aquatic freshness was muddied with the plumes of exhaust from passing cars, the rankness of an overflowing dumpster. And inside the bookstore, myriad perfumes mingled in the heat, the windows opaque with condensation, a crush of bodies that jostled and pushed against one another.

She clutched a glass of tepid white wine in one hand, leaning forward to better hear the woman in front of her, dark hair pulled back in a neat bun. "It's so universal," the woman said excitedly, "your story. Something we all can relate to. Not that mine is as dramatic, of course." She laughed, and Jules smiled politely, glancing over at Noah, who stood near the front of the room, talking animatedly with Margaret, clad in a crimson sheath, apricot curls piled atop her head. It had been almost a year since they'd last seen each other, and as he looked up and their eyes met, he raised his glass in her direction. His hair was longer but still swept back from his face. He wore a black blazer and a pair of jeans, the heavy, dark frames of his glasses shielding his green eyes, and at the sight of him, her pulse skipped a few beats.

After Jules returned not only her half of the advance but Noah's too, the book sold at auction to a new publisher, but as a memoir, and for far more money than before. When it was time to start writing, she spent a weekend at her mother's house, and never left, settling in for the long road ahead. She'd set up her workspace not in Elizabeth's tastefully wainscoted office, with her French country desk carved from white oak, but in the kitchen, the heart of the house. She perched on a stool at the marble counter, a pot of chili bubbling away on the stove, winter giving way to spring, the crocuses in her mother's garden pushing their heads up through the wet soil, searching for the light. She spent months reading the correspondence between her mother and Colin, committing their words to the labyrinth of memory, immortalizing them on the page.

But one evening, as she rummaged in Elizabeth's desk drawers in search of a pencil, the sky lavender in the twilight, her hands brushed across another stack of correspondence, this time between Harold and Elizabeth, birthday cards they'd exchanged over the years, postcards from her mother's book tours, love notes her father would leave scattered around the house for her mother to find. She read them as the stars appeared one by one in the darkened sky above, and through those worn pages, she began for the first time to know her mother as a friend might—and the way a daughter never could.

As she worked, she started to see that Elizabeth's story had never been black-and-white, never easy to unravel or contain. Her mother was a woman torn, in love with a man she could neither relinquish nor forget, but also with her husband, devoted to the family she had nurtured with her own two hands, the tendrils of it surrounding them like wisteria framing a doorway. She'd posed them in fields of wildflowers, on beaches, the white sand like sugar beneath their feet, a picnic spread out before them, loaves of rough bread, olives in a mason jar, chunks of feta in brine, Harold's arm around her shoulder, the child perched in her lap. It was good for the brand, yes. But it was a good life, too.

One her mother knew was irreplaceable.

During those long months, Noah would check in from time to time, texting late at night, her phone lighting up at her desk like a beacon, guiding her home. *How's it going?* he'd ask, and Jules would answer briefly, keeping her replies short, even when his questions inevitably strayed into deeper, more personal territory. *How are you? How are you really?* Her cheeks would flush, remembering the night in the hotel, how she'd felt in his arms afterward, something inside her quieted at last. She was consumed by the book, the retelling of the trajectory of her entire life, but there was also the fact that she did not know where Noah fit into that story, or if she even wanted him to. *Maybe too much has happened,* she thought in the moments she allowed herself to think of it at all.

Or maybe not enough.

A few days after she moved into her mother's house, she met Mark in the city, at a coffee shop near his hotel. The smooth, mocha-colored interior was as nondescript and bland as the coffee itself, but a place she knew would be seared into her memory for the rest of her life. When she'd asked for the divorce, her hands folded calmly on the table, a white circle on the finger where her wedding band once lay, he'd begun to argue, laying out point after point as if from a numbered list.

We can do this, Jules, he kept repeating, as if trying to convince not only her but himself. But he could see by the look on her face that it was no use—she was already gone. And in the long nights that followed, she found herself weeping as she wrote, her hands moving across the keyboard as if on autopilot, her face slick with tears. She remembered how young she'd been when they'd first met, the terra-cotta hue of the leaves, the hope in her eyes as she looked up at him, a man who only a few years later would become her husband. And the very act of that remembering wounded her in a way she hadn't anticipated.

Months passed as she cobbled together a first draft and was thrown right back into edits, the book fast-tracked, the publication schedule moving at a fevered pace. There was no time to take so much as a breath, much less think of anything else. She wrote and revised late into the night, her confidence growing with every line, her thoughts spilling out onto the page, as if she could not get them down fast enough. And as the word count rose, she began to see herself in those pages, her image shimmering just below the surface, suspended in the wreckage of her mother's story.

She spent hours poring over old photo albums, the images mottled with age, her mother's face staring up at her, so young and full of hope. She realized, far too late, that the voice she'd been hearing in her head for as long as she could remember was never Elizabeth's, but her own. *I'm just trying to help,* her mother had always said, a nervous smile on her lips. But it was only after reading her mother's letters that Jules realized the truth: Elizabeth had never wanted her to struggle. So she'd created a perfect life for her only daughter: the handsome husband, the elaborate stage set of an apartment. She may have been overbearing, but Jules could hardly rest the blame for that solely on her mother's shoulders. Jules had tolerated it for all these years, never protesting, never saying a single word.

Even in her marriage, she'd thrown blinders on, smiling until her jaw ached. *Don't ruin it,* she told herself as she stared at her image trapped in the pages of her mother's books, her wedding dress the perfect flat shade of ivory, the diaphanous veil Elizabeth had picked out drifting to the ground. But as she read her mother's letters, Jules felt as if she were seeing her for the first time in those soft, worn pages, her flaws as well as her brilliance. The spell was finally broken. Whether the book was a success did not matter now.

Out of her mother's rocky past, Juliet Stone had found her future.

"You did it, kid," Peter had admitted grudgingly when they'd gone over the sales numbers for the past month. Somehow, the book and all the buzz around it, the television appearances Jules had done prior to publication, had put Elizabeth Stone back on top. There was the book, set to debut at the number one spot on the *New York Times* bestseller list, the film rights snapped up and casting already underway, and a full line of Elizabeth Stone products finally about to hit Target shelves. Most surprisingly, the Travel Channel had reached out, wondering whether Jules might be interested in her own series, visiting the kitchens of mothers and daughters across the globe, cooking family recipes from old index cards and books, worn slips of paper passed down through generations of women.

After her long, self-imposed solitude, she was suddenly busier than ever. There was the impending tour, twenty-five cities, countless airports, the pieces of her life whirling around her like brightly colored confetti. But first, her book party. Finally, the dark-haired woman ceased talking as Noah walked toward her, and Jules smiled, unable to contain her own happiness at the sight of him.

"Great turnout," he said as he stopped in front of her, leaning forward to kiss her on the cheek. "I thought my first book party was a big deal, but it could've fit in the bathroom of this one." He chuckled.

"Believe me, I'm as surprised as anyone," Jules said. "If you'd told me this would happen six months ago, I never would've believed it."

"You deserve every bit of it," Noah said firmly, raising his glass to his lips. "You've more than earned your success." He swallowed the remainder of the wine, placing the empty cup on a nearby table, her book stacked on top. *Her book.* She still couldn't quite believe it.

"So you read it then, I take it?"

"Cover to cover." Noah smiled. "You really did it, Jules. You're a writer now. No one could've told this story but you."

"I heard about your new novel," Jules said, suppressing a rush of happiness at the word *writer.* "How does Colin feel about it? Have you talked to him?"

"It is fiction, so it's only really the three of us who know"—Noah laughed—"but he's been a surprisingly good sport. I have to admit, Jules, seeing those pages stacked up felt pretty good, like I was my old self again. I have you to thank for that."

"You're back in the game." She nodded slowly.

"In terms of my career, yes," he said. "The jury's still out on everything else."

For a moment they just looked at one another, and Jules felt her cheeks grow warm, as much from the heat of the room as the nearness of him. "Do you want to talk outside?" she asked, looking away. "I could use some air."

"Sure," he said with a nod as she glanced back over at him. Why was it so hard to look at him, now that so much time had passed, she wondered, as she followed him through the crush of the crowd and to the front of the store, grabbing her coat nestled behind the register on the way, the bell over the door ringing as they stepped out into the night, the wind off the water whipping her hair back from her face, the air tinged with salt.

Jules shivered as she put her coat on, tying the sash firmly at her waist, as if to arm herself for the conversation that was about to take place. "Wow," Noah began, gesturing with one hand at her coat, the sleek black dress she'd worn hidden beneath. She'd dressed carefully, leaning into the mirror, her hair in wild tendrils around her face, her lips rose red.

"You don't look so bad yourself," she said lightly, returning the compliment. In truth, it was hard to be this close without reaching out and closing the space between them with the touch of her hand.

"How's the divorce going? I wanted to ask before now, but I didn't want to pry."

"Final next week," she said, not wanting to ruin the moment by mentioning the endless negotiations with Mark's legal team, the tense phone calls, their fifteen-year history slowly erased with every document signed, every clause underlined in red.

"How does it feel?"

"Like . . . a whole new life." She smiled. "One that's finally all mine."

"I'm glad," he said. "I guess you've had some time to work through things since we last saw each other."

"Not enough," she said quickly, and the minute the words left her lips, as much as she wanted to snatch them back or claim otherwise, she knew they were the truth. "I've always been somebody's wife or someone's daughter. This is the first time I've belonged just to myself. I don't want to lose that feeling, Noah. Not when it's so new."

"I guess a drink is out of the question, then?" He grinned, and she couldn't help but smile back, even though what she wanted most was to lean forward, pulling him close.

"For now," she said, knowing by the way he looked at her that they had time, all the time in the world, if she wanted it. "For the first time in my life, I know I'm on the right path. I just need to walk it on my own a little longer."

"You know where to find me," he said softly, and she nodded, reaching out to grab hold of his hand, grasping it firmly for a long moment, his warm fingers encircling her own, before releasing him once again.

And after the signings, after the smiling and handshaking, after the store had shut, the books sighing on their shelves, still and patient, she entered the night, the lights of the city sparkling around her, the fabric of it like rough satin, holding her in its embrace. It was at that moment she knew she had arrived home for the very first time, the cells of her being rearranged and reordered, the future rising up to greet her, like the arms of a mother, opening wide.

Thank You

Joelle Hobeika, Viana Siniscalchi, Josh Bank, and the entire team at Alloy Entertainment. My editor, Alicia Clancy, and everyone at Lake Union who helped bring Elizabeth Stone to life. My incredible agent, Kelly Van Sant. My neighborhood haunt, Rita & Maria Café, for letting me sit undisturbed for hours while I worked through endless revisions of this book. Gina Frangello, sister of my heart—twenty more years of friendship wouldn't be nearly enough—and my family: Kay Dichter, Jonathan Dichter, Alex Dichter, Willy Blackmore, Lee Anne Blackmore, Martha Blackmore, and Bill Blackmore.

And last, but never ever least, my daughter, Story.
I love you, forever and always.

About the Author

Jennifer Banash is the author of *The Rise and Fall of Ava Arcana*; *Silent Alarm*, which was a finalist for the American Library Association's Best Fiction for Young Adults; *White Lines*; *Simply Irresistible*; *In Too Deep*; and *The Elite*. A former professor of English and creative writing, she is also the former cofounder and editor of Impetus Press, an independent publishing house that championed works of literary fiction with a pop edge. For more information, visit https://jennifer-banash.com.